Love and Smoke

ALSO BY JENNIFER BLAKE

Love's Wild Desire
Tender Betrayal
The Storm and the Splendor
Golden Fancy
Embrace and Conquer
Royal Seduction
Surrender in Moonlight
Midnight Waltz
Fierce Eden
Royal Passion
Prisoner of Desire
Southern Rapture
Louisiana Dawn
Perfume of Paradise

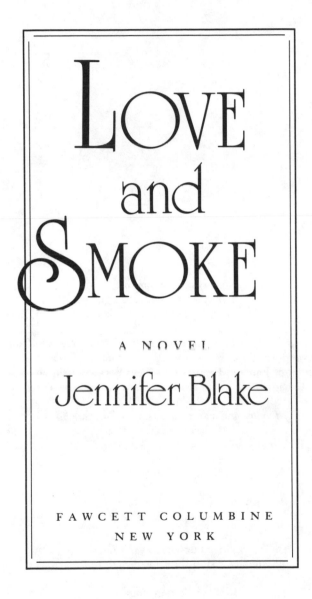

LOVE
and
SMOKE

A NOVEL

Jennifer Blake

FAWCETT COLUMBINE
NEW YORK

A Fawcett Columbine Book
Published by Ballantine Books
Copyright © 1989 by Patricia Maxwell

Library of Congress Cataloging-in-Publication Data
Blake, Jennifer, 1942–
Love and smoke : a novel / by Jennifer Blake. — 1st ed.
p.   cm.
ISBN 0-449-90430-X
I.   Title.
PS3563.A923L6   1989   88-92422
813'.54—dc19

Text design by Ann Gold
Manufactured in the United States of America

First Edition: June 1989

10   9   8   7   6   5   4   3   2   1

L'amour et la fumme ne se cachent pas.

Love and smoke cannot be hidden.

Old Louisiana Creole proverb
Louisiana Keepsake, 1988
Lillie Petit Gallagher

Love and Smoke

1

She could destroy him.

The knowledge of her power was like white heat in Riva Staulet's brain as she sat watching the man on the speaker's platform. There was pleasure in it, and triumph. There was no man she despised as much as Edison Gallant, the newly announced Democratic candidate for governor of Louisiana, and none who had hurt her more. At the same time, the consciousness of her will to use that power made her uneasy. She was not vindictive by nature, and the satisfaction she felt at having the means to stop Edison seemed wrong. Not that she meant to allow such scruples to stand in her way. The consequences of failure were too great.

Nothing of the turmoil Riva felt was apparent. She sat with her hands loosely clasped in her lap and an expression of polite interest on her clear-featured face. She was still beautiful at forty, a woman of elegance and grace dressed in monochromatic perfection in cream linen with the lustrous double strands of the famous Staulet pearls about her neck. Her hair was glossy with health and without a sign of gray in the golden brown, classic chin-length style. Her oval face had a serious cast, in part the effect of her dark, straight brows. A wide-brimmed hat of cream Italian straw shaded green eyes that had a warm gold rim around the iris, and cast lacy shadows across her high cheekbones. It was a practical hat against the hot Louisiana sun that beat down on those gathered for this "old time" political rally, but at the same time it added an air of mystery. She looked like a lady, cool and self-possessed, but one who kept her secrets.

Riva knew exactly what she looked like, and why. If she had

learned anything in the twenty-five years since she had last seen Edison Gallant, it was control of her emotions.

He had changed. He was heavier, his voice was richer and deeper, and there was silver shining in his perfectly cut blond hair. There was about him the burnished appearance that actors and professional politicians take on. Regardless, his eyes were still piercingly blue, and there was something about him that made every woman in the audience sit up a little straighter and smile when he looked her way.

Every woman except Riva Staulet. She met his gaze as it moved over her without a flicker of response. Her stillness, the impassive watchfulness of her, caught his attention, for he paused in his sweep of the audience. Uncertainty flickered across his face and was gone. He gave the smallest possible nod in her direction before he continued with his speech.

Edison didn't know her. He thought he did, no doubt, thought he recognized the widow of the well-known businessman Cosmo Staulet, the woman who was now co-owner, with her stepson Noel Staulet, of Staulet Corporation, a multinational company with interests as diverse as sugar and oil, marine insurance and microprocessors. It was not surprising that he should think so. Her face often graced the business and social pages of newspapers all over the state, particularly those of the New Orleans dailies during the Mardi Gras season, and was not unknown in the tabloids of the larger cities on the Eastern Seaboard and in Europe. She had been cited for her efforts toward historic preservation and restoration, both in general and on her own antebellum plantation known as Bonne Vie. Her decorating skills as shown in her "cabin" in Colorado and her villa in the islands had appeared in *Architectural Digest* and *Modern Home*, and she had been approached more than once by those behind the television program "Lifestyles of the Rich and Famous," though she had refused the opportunity to be featured. She was a woman of high visibility but one selective about where she chose to appear. However, it was not who she was that was important at this moment, but who she had been.

She would swear that Edison did not recognize her at all. She did not know whether to be pleased or angry, complimented or saddened.

Riva had known of Edison's political maneuvering for some time, for years, in fact. She could have put a stop to it long ago, and perhaps she should have. It was Cosmo who had counseled restraint. Mere revenge was beneath her dignity, he had said. Let the past remain in the past. Everyone knew what happened when you touched pitch.

Cosmo had been fond of maxims. He had also been wise. It didn't matter. He was gone, had been dead these six long months, and things had changed. She would have to touch pitch. The only question was how dirty she would get.

The people on the platform behind Edison looked hot. The two other candidates for office who had already spoken and Edison's campaign chairman, the organizer of this south Louisiana political rally, sat squinting while perspiration trickled down their faces. Edison's wife, in navy silk, fanned herself with her handkerchief, and his sandy-haired son twitched his broad football player's shoulders and tugged at his shirt collar.

The smell of the jambalaya, rich with ham and shrimp, that was waiting to be served wafted over the gathering. Mingling with it was the alcoholic yeastiness of the chilled kegs of beer that had already been broached and the hay scent of the park's freshly mown grass. A soft breeze brushed over the crowd, alleviating the heat for an instant and stirring the leaves of the live oaks that were dotted about the grass to a cool-sounding whisper. The instant the wind died, the hot and humid air closed in again.

Beside Riva, the man who was her escort for the occasion shifted in his chair, then lifted a fist to stifle a yawn. She gave him a swift smile of apology. Listening to political speeches, she knew, was not Dante Romoli's idea of a fun way to spend a Saturday afternoon. Dante only shook his head with its close-cropped brown curls, his dark gaze wry but patient. He was with Riva, and that was what mattered.

There came the clatter of applause. Edison Gallant, with a last two-handed wave, stepped away from the microphone. His campaign manager made an announcement about the gumbo and the jambalaya that had been waiting as long and was as spicy-hot as the audience was overheated. People began to rise from their folding chairs, chatting among themselves, moving to seek the shade of the oaks or the food tents set up in a row.

"Aunt Riva! Over here!"

Riva turned at the hail. Bearing down upon her was a young woman so vividly attractive that heads swung around as she passed. Her hair was golden blond and curled abundantly about her shoulders, and her eyes were clear and sparkling green. She moved with a model's long, confident stride and such total disregard for how she looked that it was disarming. Riva's face lighted at the sight of her niece, her sister's daughter, and she braced herself for Erin's exuberant hug.

Erin greeted Dante, then turned back at once to speak to Riva. "If I had known you were coming, I'd have saved you a seat in the shade. Why didn't you tell me?"

"It was a last-minute impulse."

"There must be a lot of that going around. I met Noel just now. Seems one of his old college buddies is in charge of this get-together and persuaded him to come."

Riva looked past her niece and nodded to the tall, dark man who sauntered in the girl's wake. Her greeting was as stilted as the one she received in return from Noel Staulet, her dead husband's son by his first marriage. Since she had seen Noel scant hours before at the breakfast table, there was no call for transports, but the reserve between them suddenly struck her as absurd, as absurd as the familiar pain it gave her. They were two adults, and it was more than twenty years since the afternoon Cosmo Staulet had sent his only son away for her sake. Noel had not been a displaced child at the time, but a young man fully five years older than she had been herself. She recognized that Noel had valid reason to resent her and tried to make allowances. The relationship between them had been less than cordial since his return from near exile in France just before Cosmo's death, but surely it would do him no permanent injury to be pleasant in public.

Her niece Erin was rattling on, claiming her attention. "I know what it is, though, Aunt Riva, you can't fool me. You wanted a look at Josh, that's what. Wasn't it sweet of him to sit up there sweltering just to support his dad? And isn't he a certified hunk? Come on, I'll introduce you. You can meet the next governor, too!"

Riva permitted herself to be pulled forward. Perhaps it was better this way, more natural. She glanced over her shoulder at Dante, who had fallen into step beside Noel as they trailed after Erin and herself. Dante's presence at this meeting would be comforting, but it was unplanned. If it turned out to be a mistake, it could not be helped.

Edison was holding court under the gnarled branches of a grand old live oak. There were members of the press gathered three-deep around him, something Riva might have expected if she had taken the time to think about it. She hung back, unwilling to interrupt what was apparently an impromptu news conference. Erin veered to one side, waving to Edison's son.

A grin split Josh Gallant's square face as he saw Erin. He lifted a hand, waded out of the congestion around his father. As the introductions were made, Riva gave the young man her hand. There was something about his confident blue gaze, the curve of his mouth, the lift of his chin that made her throat close for a stifling instant.

"Mrs. Staulet," he said, "I've heard so much about you from Erin that it seems I know you already."

She summoned a smile. "Yes, I . . . have to say I feel the same."

The young man shook hands with Noel and Dante, then glanced over his shoulder. "I think the press hounds have had about enough. I know Mom and Dad will want to meet you."

A moment later, Riva was standing before Edison Gallant and his wife. A nervous tremor moved down her spine, then faded away. She held her head high, drawing on years of poise gained in rarefied social circles and buttressed by old money and new accomplishments. She was no longer a barefoot country girl in a faded gingham dress. There was no reason to be intimidated.

"Erin's aunt? I would have said her sister," Edison said with practiced charm as the formalities were completed. "It's a great honor and a pleasure to have you here. My wife and I appreciate you taking the time from your busy schedule."

On cue, Anne Gallant murmured, "Yes, indeed." She stood a little stiffly, as if self-conscious in her role as political wife. She was perfect for the part, very much the Junior League matron with a white Peter Pan collar on her dress, navy and white spectator pumps, and no jewelry. Regardless, there was an odd mixture of boredom and apprehension in her hazel eyes. As she glanced toward her son Josh, who had an arm around Erin, the fixed smile on her face grew warmer and more animated.

"The pleasure is mine," Riva said, and was proud of the even, composed sound of her voice. She dismissed Edison's comment as obvious flattery. However, the light of appreciation in his eyes was unsettling. She preferred this contact between them to be imper-sonal, and over with as quickly as possible.

One of the photographers with the news crew that was moving off looked back. When he saw Riva and her niece, he swung around to return, taking the lens cover off his camera once more. Whether he recognized her or was only attracted by the picture she and Erin made with the new candidate and his wife and son was hard to tell, but his attention appeared to be fixed on Erin. The dark-haired and lanky young man grinned at the girl before he lifted his camera and began to focus.

Riva was used to being in front of the camera, but this wasn't a meeting she cared to have recorded. She lifted her hand in a gesture of denial. It was never finished, however, for Edison was already flashing his quick smile, already putting his arm around Erin. The five of them froze in place as the camera clicked and whirred.

The photographer called his thanks, walking backward with his gaze still on Erin, before he finally swung around and broke into a trot to catch up with the other newspeople. Riva wished she knew what paper the young man was with so that she could kill the picture. Failing that, she could only hope that with so many others taken today, this particular one would hold little interest.

Edison turned back to Riva. "We were speaking of Erin, weren't we? She's really been a fantastic help at campaign headquarters. More than that, she does wonders for the looks of the place."

"I'm sure the experience has been valuable for her." Riva's voice was clipped. Erin was a law student at Tulane, so she was hardly the giddy volunteer he made her sound.

I hope so," he answered easily. "She's certainly valuable to us."

Noel Staulet and Dante Romoli were introduced to the others as they joined the group. For a moment they all stood exchanging pleasantries, discussing Edison's speech, commenting on the large turnout of people. Then Josh left with Erin on the pretext of searching among the food tents for something to eat.

There was a lull in the conversation. Edison Gallant glanced around, as if in search of other worthy citizens whom he should greet. Riva felt Dante's hand on her elbow, saw him ready to excuse himself and her with him, and she took a steadying breath.

"I wonder, Mr. Gallant," she said, "if I might have a word with you?"

His attention instantly returned, his blue eyes holding speculation. "By all means. I'll have my secretary set up an appointment. Perhaps lunch on Monday?"

"Now, if you please. I'll only keep you a moment, and I believe you'll find it beneficial."

Riva was aware of Dante's concerned gaze upon her and Noel's quick and narrowed glance. She ignored them as she waited for Edison's reply

His gaze moved swiftly, though with discretion, down the curves of her body before returning to her face. He smiled with a brief movement of smoothly molded lips. "As you like. Shall we walk over there under the trees?"

He neither excused himself nor apologized to his wife and the others, but turned at once in the direction he indicated. Riva touched Dante's arm, said she would meet him at the food tents in a few minutes, then moved to join Edison. It was Noel's stare she felt on her back, however, as she and the candidate for governor walked away.

Her mind felt numb. She could not quite believe that she was calmly strolling over the grass with the man she had detested for so long. To give herself time to decide how to say what she must, she talked inanely about the organization of the rally, which men's clubs had cooked the jambalaya and the gumbo, which business in town had contributed the tents, and how such things indicated support for his campaign. At last they came to a spot in the deep shade of a live oak that was far enough away not to be overheard, yet near enough so that the presence of possible observers would prevent any unpleasantness.

Riva removed her hat and ran her fingers through her hair to loosen it. She met the eyes of the man beside her and lifted her chin. "I'm afraid I may have misled you. The matter I would like to discuss isn't political."

"That's too bad." His tone was noncommittal, though his smile was warm and his blue gaze bright. "I was beginning to look forward to a close association with Staulet Corporation. And with you."

For an instant, Riva was reminded of what she had once seen in this man, once felt for him. There was genuine charm buried under the layers of self-interest. It had not always been buried so deep.

"The problem," she said, her voice hardening, "is that our association is entirely too close already."

His brows snapped together in a frown. "I don't understand."

"I'm speaking of my niece and your son Josh."

"Josh? What has he done?"

"Done? He hasn't done anything. It's who he is."

He stared at her for a long moment. Finally he said, "You'll have to forgive me, Mrs. Staulet, but I haven't the vaguest idea what you're talking about."

"I don't want your son seeing my niece. I want you to put a stop to it."

A laugh that held both surprise and annoyance broke from him. "Josh is over twenty-one; they both are. What do you expect me to do?"

She had anticipated his attitude and his question. "You can send Josh to your campaign headquarters in north Louisiana, to Shreveport."

"And I should do that on your whim?"

"It would be advisable."

"Your advice, of course."

He was losing his caution as his temper rose. No doubt he had accepted that he wasn't going to get a donation from her.

Gently she said, "It's something more than that."

"Are you threatening me?"

"How can you suggest such a thing?" Her words carried a faint edge of mockery. How good it was to have the upper hand after all these years.

"I think you had better tell me exactly what you're getting at, lady."

"I've told you. I don't want my niece having anything more than she already has to do with any member of your family, and it's to your advantage to see that I get what I want."

"If I don't?"

"Then the press will learn that twenty-five years ago you committed bigamy."

Bigamy. The word hung between them in the hot stillness. From far away came the sound of voices and laughter and the music of Cajun fiddles now ringing out from the raised platform where Edison had spoken. Overhead the leaves of the live oak rustled for an instant in a breath of a breeze, then fell silent.

Edison's eyes slowly widened. The color left his face. His gaze flickered over her features, testing them one by one. He moistened his lips.

"It can't be."

"Oh, yes, it can."

"You? Little Rebecca Benson? No . . ." His voice trailed away. He looked away from her clear gaze, staring out blindly at the crowd before turning his attention back to her face as if drawn.

Riva could almost see him weighing the situation, trying to find a way out, trying to think how damaging the charge might be to him. The consequences could be great. The current political climate did not allow public figures much in the way of moral lapses.

She said, "I assure you, I *am* Rebecca."

"I would never have dreamed it, not after seeing your pictures in the papers all these years. I really can't make myself believe it. But it has to be. No one else—"

"No one knows except me, and I would like to keep it that way."

"Proof," he said, his voice stronger now that his shock was wearing off. "You have no proof."

"I have a copy of the marriage certificate recorded in Arkansas."

She had been married to this man, or so she had thought. For four weeks she had slept with him, made love with him, cooked and cleaned for him, and tried to make a home for them both in a roach-infested apartment of crumbling grandeur on a New Orleans back street that always smelled of frying onions and garlic and cats. Then one day Edison Gallant had said they were not married at all, that it had been a trick. He already had a wife; therefore, the vows they had exchanged together had no meaning, were legally invalid. He had walked out and not come back.

"God, but you've changed," he said abruptly.

"That should be no surprise. I was only fifteen." The words were acerbic.

"Old enough."

Old enough for a night of hasty fumbling in the backseat of a '60 Chevrolet convertible, for games on grimy sheets, for loss and humiliation.

"Never mind," she said tightly. "I think you will agree that it's best that Erin and Josh don't see each other."

"God, when I think about—"

"Don't! All I want from you is your promise to send your son away."

He gave a slow shake of his head. "Why should I do anything with my son? Why can't you tell your niece not to see him?"

"I prefer it this way."

"What is it? Am I a pariah? Is this some weird case of the sins of the fathers?"

She sent him a hard look, suspecting some undercurrent of meaning. But there was nothing in his face to indicate it. The surface reasons were enough, for now. She gave a small shrug. "As you say. You must understand that I don't want the slightest risk of ever having to acknowledge you as a family connection. At the moment, Erin and Josh are just friends. I would prefer not to turn it into some Romeo and Juliet affair by my opposition."

"I agree they're friends. I also think you're blowing this up way out of proportion. Josh is a good boy, as fine a boy as any girl could expect."

There was fatherly pride in his voice. It gave her a better opinion of him than anything she had yet seen. Her gaze level, she said, "He must take after his mother, not that it matters. I've told you how I feel. And I've told you what I want done about it."

His face hardened and he pursed his lips. "People who want something should be prepared to offer a return."

"What do you mean?" The timbre of his voice made her nerves contract.

"That I think we should talk, say, over that lunch I mentioned earlier."

"There's nothing to talk about!"

His gaze held hers, and a corner of his mouth lifted. "I say there is. You're trying to blackmail me, and I don't like it."

"This isn't a question of blackmail." There was a suffocating feeling growing in her chest. She should have known it would not be easy.

"What else would you call it?" He put his hand on her arm. "I think, though, that I can persuade you to forget the whole thing."

She shook off his hand. "You must be insane!"

"Am I? How is it going to look, the lovely and rich Mrs. Cosmo Staulet mixed up in a sordid little affair years ago, letting herself be gulled into a false marriage? You can't expose me without exposing yourself, can you? Your friends will laugh you out of town. Who will trust the head of a corporation who has so little judgment?"

"That may be," she said, "but what you don't understand is that it may be worth the trouble to me to stay free of you and yours."

"Is it worth your place on the board of Staulet Corporation or the risk of devaluing the company's stock? I doubt the other members would think so, particularly Noel Staulet. In fact, Staulet would probably be glad of an excuse to force you out. If you're bound to give him the opportunity, there's nothing I can do."

He was sharp, she had to give him that. She had not realized her difficulties with Noel were such common knowledge, and she had certainly not expected Edison to fasten at once on her weakest point.

"Why are you being so obstructive? What I'm asking is no great thing."

"It's the way you asked, lady. I don't care to be treated lightly, and I don't like being threatened."

Quietly she said, "It's more a promise."

"Is it? That's something we still have to thrash out, as well as just what you're going to do for me if I should, by some stretch of the imagination, decide to agree. Now about that lunch date—unless you would prefer dinner?"

The hint of menace in his invitation made her temper rise even as it rang a warning in her mind. There was nothing she could say to convince him at this moment. He was too set on opposing her, on besting her since she had dared to challenge him. It was possible that she might think of some way to bring him to reason in the time between now and a luncheon engagement, but meeting him again anywhere, at any time, was the last thing she wanted to do.

Beside her, Edison stiffened. Riva turned her head to see Noel coming toward them. Cosmo's son moved without haste, with one hand swinging free and his suit coat slung over one shoulder with a finger hooked under the collar. As he neared, his manner was casual but there was nothing relaxed about the way he watched them.

Edison spoke softly so as not to be heard by the approaching man. "The Royal Orleans Hotel, Monday at one. We'll have room service. My secretary will call with the room number."

"Thank you, no," she said with an edge of contempt for so obvious a ploy, then countered with the most patronized restaurant she could call to mind on such short notice. "Commander's Palace. My secretary will reserve a table. In my name."

Before Edison could answer, Noel reached them. His voice was calm and easy as he spoke. "Erin sent me to tell you she is perishing with the heat and has invited a bunch of friends from Tulane back to Bonne Vie for a swim. She has gone on ahead to be sure everything is ready."

"That's fine," Riva answered, though she gave a him a searching look. It was not Noel's habit to run Erin's errands, or anyone else's for that matter. However, his arrival gave her a chance to make her departure. "It's really too hot to think of eating just now. I believe I'm ready to go home myself."

"Sounds good to me." Noel turned away with no more than a nod to Edison.

Riva gave Edison the polite farewell she reserved for virtual strangers, then walked away with Noel. She did not look back.

She and Noel moved in the general direction of the food tents and the speaker's platform and the parking lot, which lay beyond them. Their route took them through patches of blinding white-hot sunlight to pools of dappled shade that were cool by contrast, from areas of feet-scuffed dirt to stretches of St. Augustine grass like jewel-green cut-pile velvet.

Riva was grateful for her rescue from a situation that had been getting out of control, though she absolved Noel of any intention of playing the knight errant. She sent a swift glance up at his face. Leafy shadows flickered over his features as he moved, heightening his pensive, withdrawn expression. His appearance, the shape of his head, the set of his wide shoulders, brought a fleeting memory.

This was the way Cosmo had been when she and her husband had first met. He had been forty-six to her sixteen, just as Noel must now be nearing forty-five or six. Noel had his father's air of distinction, that indefinable impression of the aristocrat made up of good bone structure, impeccable taste in clothing, and the confidence that comes from having ancestral portraits in the attic that let you know exactly who and what you are. His black hair had touches of silver at the temples, and his face was brown from the sun. His brows were dark and thick over deepset gray eyes, and his firm chin was finely stippled by the dark beard under the skin. There were laugh lines slashed in his cheeks beneath the high facial bones, and a hint of sensitivity in the chiseled shape of his mouth, though these last two aspects of his personality were not ones he showed to Riva. Not now, not for years.

As if attracted by her scrutiny, Noel turned his head to look at her, saying, "Gallant isn't strong on concrete plans or facts and figures in his speeches, but it seems that what he lacks in substance he makes up for in charisma."

"I suppose he has time to improve before the election."

"Four months isn't that long, not when there are eight other Democrats in the field, not to mention the three Republicans."

"The summer will take its toll, as always."

Noel nodded. "I don't remember my father ever mentioning that he knew Gallant or supported him."

"My father." Noel always gave Cosmo that formal title. There was a time, Riva remembered, when he had called him Dad or Pop, but that was long ago. "I don't believe Cosmo ever met him."

"The two of you seem on friendly terms."

"Not at all."

Noel turned toward her, his gaze direct. "If your association with Gallant is a business matter, maybe I should know about it."

There was logic in that assumption, since anything she did that affected the Staulet Corporation was also his concern. She suspected, however, that it was no more than an excuse to find out what her purpose was in speaking to Edison. "It has nothing to do with Staulet. As a matter of fact, it concerns Erin."

"Speaking to him about Erin is supposed to be to his benefit?" His tone was dry as he watched her.

She forced a smile. "Allow me a little latitude, if you please, as a fond aunt."

"I suppose you were trying to convince him to pay her for her hard work."

It wasn't a bad suggestion, one that might serve as an excuse. She fanned herself with the straw hat she still carried, suddenly feeling overheated. "Erin has spent hours at his headquarters in New Orleans. Don't you think she deserves to be paid?"

"I think she's having fun being involved in the campaign and going around with Josh Gallant. Erin's not the kind to become an earnest, slogan-spouting drudge for a political machine."

Erin and Noel had become close since his return. Riva's niece had been in and out of Bonne Vie for five years, beginning with the day she started at Tulane. Though she lived on campus, the plantation house was her home away from home. Her parents,

Riva's sister Margaret and her husband, lived in the northern part of the state. They could not afford to send their daughter to college, particularly such a fine one, so Riva had stepped in to provide both education and a getaway place from academic stress for Erin. It had been a pleasure and a joy, until the girl met Josh Gallant.

"I'm glad you appreciate Erin's finer points." Riva was a little testy on the subject of Erin's future just now, though she trusted it wasn't too obvious.

"Who wouldn't? It's not often you find such a combination of beauty and brains."

Brainy and beautiful, and older by more than seven years now than Riva was herself when Cosmo had married her. Riva felt a twinge of something that might have been envy or even jealousy, if that had not been so ridiculous. She had no interest whatever in being appreciated by Noel Staulet. Anyway, she had at least managed to deflect his attention from Edison.

Or so she thought. She should have remembered Noel's habit in business affairs of subtle moves followed by sudden attacks.

"I would be careful about getting entangled with Gallant if I were you," Noel said. "He has a reputation as a man who likes women, in great variety and often."

Riva sent him a sharp glance. "There's no need to worry. I have no intention of getting entangled."

"I wasn't worried, just thought you should know."

"You will excuse me if I find your concern a bit puzzling." It had been more than twenty years since he had shown this much interest in her personal life, since he had looked at her or addressed her as anything more than a fixture in his father's home or a business associate. It often seemed, in fact, on his rare visits over the years, and even during his stay at Bonne Vie since Cosmo's death, that he avoided seeing her or speaking to her at all unless it was absolutely necessary.

A muscle flexed in his jaw and he turned his dark gaze on her. "There was a time when sarcasm didn't suit you."

"Meaning that now it does?"

"I don't know. Maybe I'm wrong, maybe it always did."

Riva opened her mouth to speak, but nothing came out. She was stunned by the dark reflection of pain she thought she saw in his eyes. A hard knot gathered, aching, in her throat.

An instant later, the moment was gone, and all that was left was embarrassment. Riva looked away. They were nearing the tents. For something to say to break the tense silence, she asked, "I don't suppose you know which way Dante went?"

"No." The answer was not cordial.

"I'll have to find him since I came with him."

He gave a curt nod. "I'll see you back at the house, then."

As he strode away, Riva stood watching the stretch of his long legs and the dynamic way he carried himself, as if there were reserves of strength inside him that were seldom called upon, strength unneeded in the business world in which he moved. He was an intensely private man, one difficult to know, though he was acknowledged by many as a strong ally. It was a pity he could not be hers.

Old lovers, like old friends, made dangerous enemies.

2

There were no gates closing off the drive at Bonne Vie, no guardhouse, no security guard on duty. The only sentinels, in fact, were the oaks, the row of huge live oaks so ancient some had branches the size of tree trunks trailing heavily to the ground, acting as supports. The stately trees marched in a straight line toward the house, their inner limbs arching over the gravel drive with the loftiness of a cathedral roof so that the fine old house appeared like an altar at the end. The historic structure was protected by its isolation and possibly by the awe it inspired. Bonne Vie was one of the most famous antebellum plantation homes in the South, its setting and beautifully proportioned façade instantly recognizable from a thousand book covers and picture-postcard views.

Cosmo would never hear of fortifying the place against theft and vandalism or even the curiosity seekers who sometimes came up the drive. Bonne Vie, he had said, was neither an armed camp nor a prison; it was his home, no more and no less. Riva had done nothing to change matters since his death. It helped, of course, that there was a small army of yard boys, houseboys, maids, a cook, and a chauffeur always about, each with a traditional attachment to the place and the Staulet family. No intrusion went unseen or uninvestigated. There had never been any trouble.

Dante Romoli swung his Alfa Romeo in on the drive and sent it purring toward the front of the house. Twenty yeards from the front steps, he steered to the left into the parking area on that side and drew up beside the three or four other vehicles already there. He climbed out and moved around to the door on Riva's side.

The powerful sports car had made short work of the fifty or so miles between the town where the rally had been held and Bonne Vie, but still Riva was stiff, probably from sheer tension, as she allowed Dante to draw her to her feet. She gave him a smile that held both thanks and apology. She had not been good company on the drive; her thoughts had been too busy elsewhere.

"You'll stay, won't you?" she asked. "I can offer you a late lunch to make up for the one you missed. With Erin's crowd entrenched, it might be nice if there's someone else around who's over thirty."

Dante did not hesitate. "You know me, I try never to miss a meal."

It was a joke of sorts between them, one of many. They went back a long way together, to the sixties and a greasy kitchen behind a famous French Quarter restaurant and also to a sleazy topless bar on Bourbon Street, to a time when they had both been on their own, both down but not out.

Dante's preoccupation with food had begun then. Given his continued closeness to it, to its preparation, to its taste and the infinite variety of its possible flavor combinations, he should have been as big as a whale. He did worry at times about his love handles, but he was trim enough, even with the compact build of his Cajun-French and Italian heritage. He pretended to fight a hard battle to stay in shape, with racquetball and tennis and a two-mile run every morning, but the truth was that he had a metabolism and business schedule that allowed him to eat as he pleased without gaining more than the odd pound or two.

There was good reason for his fascination with food. He was now the owner of Lecompte's Restaurant, an establishment fully as well-known and respected for its fine cuisine as Commander's Palace and one with even deeper roots in New Orleans history. It had been a going concern since 1843, the scene of many a famous dinner and infamous scandal in the rich period before the Civil War when cotton was king and afterward during the Gay Nineties. The original owners had sold it in the midtwentieth century and it had passed from hand to hand until Dante, who had worked there as a busboy, had bought it ten years before.

Owning Lecompte's had been the culmination of a dream. He had restored the place with love and meticulous care, returning the decor to its original look of a Paris bistro. He had then hired a renowned chef and set about making the place pay. Money was important to Dante, though it was more the making of it than having it. It was his heavy investment in a chain of spicy fried-chicken eateries, one known for the quality of its product, that had given him the chance to own Lecompte's. He never forgot it was fried chicken that had made him a restaurateur, and certainly never apologized for it.

Nor was Dante content with having reached his main goal. He had recently opened a new restaurant and nightspot out on Lake Pontchartrain where the younger crowd was being drawn as much by the finely prepared seafood as by the high-decibel rock music and innovative lighting.

Bonne Vie, as always, seemed to welcome Riva home. There was something about it that fostered comfort and contentment, like a gracious friend who makes no judgments, no demands. It was neoclassical in style, with plastered walls painted a soft peach-pink. Massive in appearance, it measured seventy feet square, with two and a half stories plus a belvedere and upper and lower galleries, or balconies, on all four sides. It was supported by a total of twenty-eight Doric columns reaching from the ground to the roof line. However, to Riva, its size was not intimidating but protecting.

The rooms inside were spacious, with high ceilings edged with lacelike crown moldings and furnishings that were a mixture of Staulet antiques and modern overstuffed pieces to soften the formality. Regardless of its scale, there were only eight main rooms, four upstairs and four downstairs, along with a few smaller ones that had been turned into dressing rooms and baths. A wide hallway bisected the house on both floors. Downstairs, the hall swept in wide-open and commodious welcome to the French doors at the rear. The curved stairway with its mahogany railing rose from the back of the hallway on the right, while through the French doors was the brick-floored lower back gallery. This porchlike area was furnished with pastel-cushioned chairs of wrought iron placed around glass-topped tables and great urns holding arching ferns or pink geraniums underplanted with variegated ivy. A pair of wide brick steps descended to the brick terrace, which, in turn, stretched to the swimming pool. Beyond the pool were the spreading grounds set with trees like an English park, grounds that sloped down to the ornamental pond that was centered with a small island holding a folly, or oversized gazebo, built like a small Roman temple.

The white marble–lined pool with its standing rank of columns at the far end always reminded Riva of the Roman pool in the movie set of *The Great Gatsby*. It was not quite so large and there were clumps of palms here and there adding a tropical note; still, the effect was of slightly pretentious classical splendor. Nonetheless, if you had to have a pool attached to an antebellum mansion, a better style would be difficult to find. Cosmo, who had built the pool for Riva when he learned how much she enjoyed swimming, had only followed the neoclassical tastes of the nineteenth-century planters.

The sound of raised voices and the splash of water drew Riva and Dante through the house and out toward the pool. The college-age bunch was in possession, diving and splashing in the deep end and toasting themselves on towels spread out around the edges. The smells of chlorine and coconut-pineapple-scented suntan oil hung in the air, along with the aroma of food. There was a buffet table to one side on which were set platters of thinly sliced roast beef and ham, a huge pot of gumbo, and bowls of potato salad, macaroni salad, green salad, and assorted fruit. To accompany this were three kinds of homemade bread and four kinds of pie and cake. Cold drinks, wine coolers, wine, and beer were embedded in crushed ice in a copper barrel to one side.

Erin, with the help of the kitchen staff, had made good use of her headstart in reaching the house. In the time she had spent at Bonne Vie, she had grown accustomed to the style of living it represented. Riva could not help but be glad, even as she prayed she wasn't spoiling her niece.

Catching sight of Erin across the pool, sitting on the edge, Riva waved a greeting.

Erin called out, "Where are your swimsuits? Aren't you two coming in?"

"Maybe later," Riva replied. "First we need sustenance."

"Noel wouldn't come in, either. He had to leave as soon as he got here, something to do with a call from the airport."

"The airport?"

Erin shrugged with insouciance as she adjusted the bright pink bikini that just covered her generous curves. "That's all he said."

Riva nodded, then handed a plate to Dante before taking one herself and pointing out what she wanted from the buffet to the maid who stood behind it. Noel, her erstwhile stepson, came and went as he pleased with little explanation; they could count themselves lucky to have been told as much as they had this time. If he missed his lunch, it was no concern of hers.

It was as she took a seat at one of the gallery tables that Riva noticed the young man who surged with strong strokes through the glinting aquamarine water of the pool. He made for Erin and pulled himself up on the marble edge to sit beside her. He raked his fingers through his hair, slicking the water off his sandy-blond head as he laughed down at Riva's niece.

Riva went still in the act of unfolding her napkin. The young man was Josh Gallant.

She should have known. He and Erin had been together at the rally. Even if Erin had not wanted Josh at Bonne Vie, she was too well schooled in manners to have left him out of her invitation. The smile Riva's niece gave him, however, made it plain that he was more than just welcome.

Something really must be done. It must.

"Anything wrong?" Dante asked as he dropped into a chair beside Riva.

She gave him a distracted smile. "No, nothing. Did you try the raspberries? They were delicious at breakfast."

He answered her question with a nod. "I've been experimenting with this Hungarian dessert made with sponge cake soaked in rum and then covered with layers of vanilla custard, raspberries, and cream sprinkled with almonds. You don't see raspberries that much here, but they're cheap and plentiful along the Washington coast this time of year. And this torte, you should taste it, *chère!*"

He went on, speaking of other Hungarian tortes rich with chocolate and hazelnuts or walnuts and cream that the chef at Lecompte's had been trying. Tortes, Dante said, were going to be the next dessert fad. Riva let his words wash over her as she returned her attention to her niece and Edison's son in the pool. They were swimming now, circling each other so that their bodies glided together in the shifting, sparkling water. It reminded her, achingly, of another pool, another summer.

"Which one of you is the little air force wife, all deserted and lonesome?"

Those had been Edison's first words that day at the pool.

The water hole they called a pool was actually a wooded pond, spring-fed and overhung with maples, beeches, and pin oaks. It was located behind the Benson house where Riva, known then as Rebecca, lived with her widowed mother and her sisters Margaret and Beth, though it belonged to their next-door neighbor. It was a favorite hangout that hot summer of '63, mainly because the town swimming pool was closed.

Civil rights was a sore issue that year, with marches and demonstrations on Main Street and before the local school-board office. There was a strong push for integration of all public facilities, from the schools and the local buses to the public restrooms at the courthouse and the municipal pool. People were particularly at odds about the pool. There was a much newer and nicer one in the black section of town. Why, in the name of heaven, the blacks wanted to come over to the white pool where the cracks were patched with tar and the foot bath looked like a locker-room toilet was something the whites could not understand.

The reasons were there, of course, but they didn't seem to matter in the heat of the conflict. There were agitators in the black section of town, known as the Quarters. Northern liberals full of idealism and liberal ideas were fomenting changes they didn't understand and whose consequences they were going to leave in the laps of white Southerners. Feelings were running so high, especially between the redneck boys who felt they had been pushed around enough and the militant blacks who were tired of backing down, that the town fathers had decided it was better to close the white pool rather than risk a drowning when some fool tried to integrate it.

The upshot was that during the torrid days of that summer the white kids could run the no less dangerous risk of integrating the blacks' pool, or chance drowning in the local creeks and ponds. So they congregated at the pond behind the Benson place, two miles south of town.

It was mostly boys of high-school age and those a little older who were allowed to go swimming. Creek and pond water was always murky from stirred mud and the dark sap of trees; there were underwater snags, sudden drop-offs in the mud bottom, and no lifeguards. You had to be a decent swimmer to survive the hazards, one of the main ones being the unsupervised horseplay. Younger boys were too inexperienced to go alone, and older ones were, for the most part, hard at work. As for the girls, the pond was isolated, which allowed opportunities for all sorts of improper behavior that had nothing to do with horseplay. Most mothers refused to permit their daughters to go.

The Benson girls' mother, however, could usually be talked into anything. Mrs. Benson had little strength to argue. The reason was her heart, which had been weak for years. Most of her days were spent lying on the couch watching the one television station that serviced their area while swatting at flies and trying to breathe the hot air that the attic fan pulled through the half-opened windows. Her three daughters did all the cooking and cleaning, washing and ironing. They bought the groceries, paid the bills, and saw that their mother took her medicine. They felt they were able to take care of themselves and entitled to any diversion that was offered after their hard work.

Beth, the oldest, was their leader. She was a married woman of nineteen, therefore experienced with men, or at least one man. Her young husband Jimmy was in the air force, some kind of specialist in electronics, and he had been stationed in the Philippines for over a year. Beth wrote to him on Mondays and Thursdays and seldom thought of him during the rest of the week. She had a lush shape and a wicked twinkle in her brown eyes. She liked to have fun, to go places with music and laughter, and she liked to swim.

The boys at the pond whistled and yelled as the three sisters came down the hill that June day. The girls made quite a picture with their sun-streaked blond hair, long tanned legs, and brief swimsuits worn under their dead father's old shirts. None of them were underdeveloped. Though far from looking like triplets—Beth was tallest, Margaret more stocky and plagued with the Benson hips that broadened at the top, while Rebecca had smaller bones that gave her a svelte, streamlined look—they were still amazingly alike in face shape, coloring, and movements.

Their reactions to the blatant appreciation of their audience were different. Beth laughed, calling a happy greeting. Margaret, two years younger than her older sister and never comfortable with her body, blushed tomato-red. Rebecca, just fifteen, managed an uneasy grin as she stood straighter.

They hung their shirts and the towels they carried on a tree limb and waded into the water. It was like a tepid bath, with cooler currents washing about their thighs as they moved in deeper. They paddled about, trying not to stir the mud any more than was necessary, giggling a little among themselves, and flinching away from the delicate, tickling nibble of fish.

They pretended not to be aware of the boys, though they missed nothing of the fancy swimming strokes, the diving from the crude wooden platform built on a tree, and all the rest of the general showing-off for their benefit. Nor were they surprised when a couple of boys approached a few minutes later.

Edison had asked his question about the deserted air force wife as he raked his fingers through his hair to slick it back, spraying water droplets onto his broad shoulders that glistened in the sunlight falling through the trees. He stood before them with water lapping about his chest, a young man exuding confidence and bold appeal, one more than just handsome and well aware of it. At his elbow was Boots Green, a slow-moving, slow-talking boy with the coppery coloring of his ancient Indian heritage, one known for his solid dependability and his nickname, which came from his clod-hopper footwear.

"That would be me," Beth answered Edison. She looked him over as frankly as he looked at her, then slowly licked the water from her lips.

Edison's grin was brash. "Then your lonesome days are over."

"You think so?"

"I know it."

The three girls knew who the newcomer was, just as they had known he was at the pond. Everybody in town, certainly every girl of marriageable age, knew that the Bensons' next-door neighbor, old man Gallant, had his nephew staying with him. The nephew was a college man no less, studying law at Tulane. He lived in south Louisiana and drove a sharp white Chevy convertible. It was the same convertible that the Benson sisters had seen from their kitchen window as it bumped along the log road behind their frame house, the road that led down to the pond. He was the main reason they were there.

Beth wasn't a pushover. She tossed her head and swam away, calling something over her shoulder to Boots so that the other boy followed her. Instead of going after her also, Edison Gallant stayed where he was, talking to Margaret and Rebecca. The three of them exchanged names and told where they lived and what they had been doing that summer as if they didn't already know all about each other.

As he talked, Edison's gaze strayed back and forth over the soft globes of the girls' breasts under their suits. Finally he gestured toward the top of Margaret's ruffled two-piece. "Are the two sweet things you have under there real, or are they just falsies?"

Margaret gasped and looked wide-eyed at Rebecca. Nobody had ever dared to come right out with such a thing before. If this was south Louisiana manners, they weren't sure they liked them.

"Come on," he insisted, "a guy likes to know where he stands."

Margaret ducked her head in acute embarrassment, stammering her denial of wearing falsies. Rebecca's own embarrassment made her angry. She scowled at Edison before she spoke. "I'll tell you where you stand. We stand over here and you stand way over there, that's where!"

"Oh, a little spitfire. I like that," he said, and moved toward her in the water. Rebecca felt his hand graze her waist and his leg slide along hers. Before she could move, he was behind her, his arms encircling her and coming up under her breasts so that their pale and tender swells were pressed above the neckline of her suit. "Nice, little spitfire, both are very nice, indeed."

Warmth flowed through Rebecca as she felt him behind her, surrounding her. His audacity took her breath away, but even more shocking was her own tingling reaction to his nearness. This new sensation inside her clashed with her outrage. It was purest instinct that made her drive her elbow backward toward his rib cage. The blow did little damage, for he was already releasing her and gliding toward her sister. Rebecca staggered in the water, off balance. Margaret gave a muffled scream as Edison swam past her with his hand reaching out under the rippling surface toward the tops of her legs.

"Hey!"

It was Boots who called out as he waded toward them with Beth right behind him. He was bigger than Edison, and his face was set in a heavy frown. He considered Margaret his girl, even if she didn't always choose to recognize it. Then Beth dove forward, big sister to the rescue, flailing past Boots, shoving Edison, and splashing water in his face.

Edison retreated, backstroking, spluttering. "What do you think you're doing!"

"You know what, you big joker! Go pick on somebody in your own league." She surged upright with her hands on her hips. Water poured down her magnificent Amazonian shape, and anger blazed in her eyes.

Edison gave her a cocky smile. "Like you, maybe?"

"I'm a match for you any day."

"Think so?"

"I know so," she said, and tossed her head with its mane of hair as she stared him straight in the eye.

"A spitfire, a prude, and a wonder woman. What a choice!"

"You sound like some bad movie," Beth said, her tone scathing as she turned back to Margaret, who seemed on the verge of humiliated tears. Boots was already there, however, encircling the sniffling girl with a protective arm.

Beth's quip surprised Rebecca into a chuckle. "He does sound like a movie, a gangster movie."

The insult had gone home, for a flush crept under Edison's skin. "Do I, now? Maybe you'd like to see what gangsters do to smart-mouthed girls?"

"Back off," Boots said, a low warning.

Edison looked at the other young man, his gaze moving over Boots's deep-chested form. Edison's belligerent stance eased a little. "Come on, coz, I was just having a little fun."

"The wrong kind."

"Is that so? Will it make it all right if I get down on my knees and say I'm sorry?"

"You don't sound sorry to me."

There was a dogged note in the bigger boy's voice. They all knew Boots; he was peaceable, never started a fight, but he usually finished the ones he took on. That Edison called him coz was a reminder that the two were related in some distant fashion, third or fourth cousins. It was no great matter. Most people in the town, which was once an isolated farming community, could scratch up a kinship with each other if they tried hard enough, went back far enough.

"Never mind, Boots," Beth said. "I think we'd better be going."

"Don't let me run you off," Edison said in swift protest. "We were just getting to know each other."

"I'm not sure we want to know you," Beth told him. Margaret and Rebecca swiftly agreed.

"Don't you?" Edison said softly. "Don't you, now?"

They left the pond without answering and returned to their house.

Not much was seen of Edison Gallant for a time. The summer grew hotter and the civil rights situation more tense. Beth began to write to her husband once a week instead of twice. Other nights she mooned around on the front-porch swing in the dark, or else sneaked out of the house in the late-night hours, driving off in their mother's old orange and white Mercury. She never said where she went except "just driving to get cool."

One Saturday night, however, Rebecca and Margaret rode into town with friends to a movie. The story was sappy, but at least the movie house was air-conditioned. Afterward, not quite ready to go home, they walked around the courthouse square.

There had been a demonstration that day with blacks carrying signs and marching in the streets. Several arrests had been made on the charge of disturbing the peace. Most of the demonstrators would be held overnight and then released; their arrests were as much to avoid trouble between them and the irate crowds that had gathered to watch the marching as from any wrongdoing. The jail on the top floor of the courthouse had neither fans nor air-conditioning and the windows were open. Through them could be heard the voices of the demonstrators shouting slogans and singing "We Shall Overcome."

The slow, sad sound sent a shiver along Rebecca's spine. She understood the anger of her neighbors at having integration forced down their throats; she herself could become indignant at the failure of Washington and the liberal press to show any understanding of the money needed to make changes or the emotional problems involved. On the other hand, what the blacks were asking did not seem out of reason. They were citizens and fellow human beings, and deserved the dignity of being treated fairly, equally.

There was one singer's voice that rose above all the others, a strident soprano. Everyone knew about the woman who was singing; she was a tough-looking white female with cropped hair who wore army-surplus fatigues and T-shirts without a bra. She was living in the Quarters with a black family. She had been thrown out of one house, however, after being threatened with a razor by the wife who thought the civil rights worker was getting too cozy with her man. The civil rights worker had sworn it wasn't so, but no one believed her.

The squeal of tires caught Rebecca's and Margaret's attention. The sound came from a Chevy convertible taking the corner in front of the courthouse too fast. Music blared from the car's radio and the reflection of the street lights gleamed along its shining white paint. At the wheel was Edison Gallant, laughing and shouting something to the girl at his side. The girl was Beth.

Margaret gasped as she turned to look at Rebecca. Her face was pale with shock and wrath. "How could she? It's a sin, the sin of adultery, that's what it is. Just wait till she gets home."

Rebecca, staring after the couple, was dismayed. At the same time, there was something about the shiny white car, the wild ride in the warm night air with the music on the wind, the young man leaning so close, laughing, that affected her with helpless longing.

Beth was late that night. Margaret met her at the front door. There were a great many things the middle Benson sister was embarrassed to talk about, but moral misconduct was not one of them.

"Have you gone stark raving crazy?" she demanded in an outraged whisper, keeping her voice low so as not to wake their mother. "What do you mean riding around town with Edison Gallant where everybody can see you?"

Beth gave the other girl a hard stare, then reached into her purse, took out a cigarette, and lit it. She took a deep pull, then blew out the smoke, obviously not inhaling but just as obviously enjoying the act. "What's bothering you, sis? Is it really that I was out with Edison or just the fact that we were seen?"

Rebecca watched the other two from where she lay sprawled on the living-room couch. She knew what Beth was doing was wrong, but she still had to admire her nerve. She would be glad when she was old enough to take the hurtful things Margaret sometimes said as Beth did, without caring.

"You have a husband!" Margaret cried, her eyes wide and accusing. "What about him?"

"He's not here, and where he is, he's having his fun. Over there on that island the streets are crawling with women who'll do anything for a dollar. He wrote to tell me he has some things to show me. Well, I may show him a thing or two."

"Oh, Beth," Rebecca said in sympathy. She could hear the pain behind her sister's words, even if Margaret could not.

"That's disgusting'!" Margaret cried.

"Think so? You should try it." Beth puffed on her cigarette again.

"When did you pick up that filthy habit?"

"Edison smokes."

"You'll catch what-for if Mama finds out."

"She won't."

"She just might!"

"You always were a tattletale."

"I am not!"

"Anyway, Mama will just sigh and say that if I want to ruin my life, that's my lookout."

"That's just what you're doing, running around with that smart-alecky Edison Gallant! What you see in him, I don't know. I thought you hated him."

"He didn't do anything to me. And he apologized for playing games with you and Rebecca. Anyway, he isn't nearly as bad as he makes out; it's just an act. The girls he dates in New Orleans expect it, so he obliges."

"Oh, sure," Margaret sneered. "It sounds like an act, him teaching you all those dirty things."

"The dirt's in your imagination, little sister."

"Is that so? Boots told me the only reason Edison's here is because of some trouble with a girl."

Beth's eyes narrowed. "What kind of trouble?"

"He didn't say, but you can't be too careful."

"You be careful, and I'll do what I want."

"If you think he means anything, that he's thinking of anything permanent, you're sadly mistaken!" Margaret's lips twisted as she spoke.

Beth shook her hair back from her face. "Edison has money to spend and he likes to spend it on me, which is more than you can say for most of the men in this town. What makes you think I want anything permanent?"

"If you don't, you're nothing but a whore!"

"Poor Margaret. If you understood yourself as well as you think you do everybody else, you'd be a hell of a lot better off."

"What's that supposed to mean? If you think I like Edison—"

"Did I say that?" The words were too innocent.

Margaret seemed to swell with her outrage. "What you're doing is trashy, you hear, trashy. Keep on, and you're going to get your-self in trouble. Then see if I help you!"

Beth ground out her cigarette on the bottom of her shoe before she gave Margaret a crooked smile. "If your help comes with an-other bawling-out, I guess I'll pass."

Beth pushed by Margaret, then went through the living room and into the hall bathroom.

Rebecca sat up. She chewed on the inside of her mouth as she watched Margaret, studying her red face, her heaving chest, and her clenched hands.

Finally she asked, "Do you?"

"Do I what?"

"Like Edison, the way Beth thinks?"

"No, I do not!"

"Don't bite my head off, I just wondered. You don't seem much in love with Boots."

"Boots is . . . Boots. He may not be too exciting, but he's safe, and he would do anything for me."

"You think Edison's exciting?"

Margaret gave her an exasperated look. "Don't talk about things you're too young to know about!"

Rebecca's head came up. "I'm only two years younger than you, and I know as much as you do! You mean sexy, that's what!"

"It's still an idiotic question." Margaret sat down on the couch, pulling her skirt down over her knees. "Oh, Edison's good-looking, but he's the worst kind of flirt, all smiles and soft words until he gets what he wants. Why, do you know what he said to me last week? He said he bet I kissed better than any other girl in town just because I kept my mouth puckered up like a prune all the time."

"I didn't know he had said anything to you, didn't know you had seen him."

"Well, I did, outside the grocery store. He kissed me, too, before I could stop him!"

"He did?" Rebecca's eyes widened. "Did you like it?"

Margaret shuddered and gave an exaggerated shake of her head. "What's more, he said you were the sweetest little thing he'd ever seen and that he'd like to gobble you up in one mouthful like a piece of soft candy."

"He didn't!"

"He meant something dirty, I could tell."

"How?"

"I just could, that's all. Maybe it was the look in those big blue eyes of his, like he was laughing at us, at me and you and Beth."

A frown drew Rebecca's brows together and her soft young lips thinned. "I'll make him laugh."

"You stay away from him, you hear? Stay away."

It wasn't easy. Edison began to drop in at the Benson house three or four times a week on one pretext or another. He was politeness itself to Mrs. Benson, talking to her as if she were an older sister, making such a charming impression that the older woman encouraged him to come as often and to stay as long as he liked. He soon caught on to the fact that Margaret and Rebecca were not going to make a scene that might disturb their mother. He took shameless advantage of that circumstance, flirting with them, teasing them, and gradually ingratiating himself.

The truth was that he was not as wild as he pretended, that he could laugh, talk, stir fudge, and shake popcorn kernels over a stove burner just like any country boyfriend. Whole hours could pass without him making an off-color remark or trying to steal a kiss in a corner. He seemed to enjoy being part of the family. It was a rare experience, he said; his own parents had been in their late thirties when he was born. He had never really been a child. His mother had always called him her little man and made him sit and make conversation with her friends when they came to call. His father had been a judge who seemed to mete out restrictions and punishments to his son with no more feeling than he did the most hardened felon who appeared before him. Their deaths within a year of each other had meant freedom to Edison. He was still enjoying the release.

June eased into July, and July melted into August. September loomed. As the opening of school drew nearer, the civil rights violence that had faded somewhat during the worst of the heat began to pick up again. The marches increased in number. There was a sit-in at the local drugstore. A few crosses were burned in people's yards in the Quarters or in front of businesses that were too co-operative with blacks. There was excitement one weekend as TV cameras from a national network were seen about town. However, nothing ever appeared on television. Rumors circulated about the possibility of federal officers, or maybe it was federal marshals, being on hand to see integration enforced on the first day of school.

The thing that the Benson girls paid most heed to was Edison's trouble with his car. The convertible developed a knock and had to be put into the shop. It was important that it be fixed; Edison would be going home in a few days since classes would be starting again at Tulane. When he came by that last Saturday evening, he was driving his uncle's old gray sedan.

He didn't stay long. Mrs. Benson was extra tired with the hot spell that wouldn't let up. Beth wasn't feeling well, a touch of a twenty-four-hour stomach virus, something that had been going around the past week. Margaret had weathered it the day before and was still pale. When Rebecca pointed out to Edison that he might get the stomach bug, too, he soon found an excuse to move on.

It was a sultry night, with heat lightning flashing in the south-west and crickets and peeper frogs calling for rain. The air seemed thick, laden with the smell of dust. The unremitting hot weather of the past few weeks had everyone's nerves on edge. It left them wanting something, waiting for something, without knowing what it was.

They went to bed early at the Benson house, as if turning off the lights and lying down would make the air being pulled through the screened windows cooler. It didn't help. Rebecca turned on her narrow bed, lying across the mattress so that her head was prac-tically on the windowsill; still, perspiration gathered under her neck and trickled into her hair.

Once she thought she heard a sound like a muffled groan. She sat up, but it didn't come again. She glanced over at Margaret, who shared the other twin bed in the room. She had not stirred. The noise must have been one of the prowling dogs that were always hanging around since Mama sometimes threw table scraps out in the backyard for them to find. Rebecca lay back down again.

The next time the moaning came, it was more audible. The sound came from the back bedroom beside the kitchen, Beth's room. Rebecca sat up and slid from the bed. Beth's stomach ailment must be worse. There was some medicine in the refrigerator.

Rebecca padded into the kitchen without turning on the light. Finding her way in the dark had always been like a game, and besides, sudden bright light hurt her eyes. The dim light in the refrigerator was no problem, however, and she quickly found the bottle of thick pink liquid on the door shelf.

She had shut the door and was turning away, heading for the kitchen drawer for a spoon, when the glare of headlights lit up the room and flashed around the walls. She swung to stare out the back window. There was a car hurtling along the log road leading down to the pond. It bounced and swayed with its speed, for the headlights made wild zigzag sweeps among the trees. She could hear the whining roar of its engine. It rounded a curve, heading downhill, and everything grew dark again. A moment later, the noise of the car died abruptly as the motor was turned off.

Some couple was certainly in a hurry to go parking, Rebecca thought. Other than deer-spotting, the illegal hunting of deer by spotlight, parking was about the only reason anybody ever went down the log road at night.

At the sound of another moan, she swung away, moving toward her sister's bedroom.

"Beth?"

She pushed open the bedroom door a crack but could see nothing in the darkness. When there was no answer, she took a step inside, then another.

"Bethie?"

The only sound was labored breathing, and it seemed to be coming from the floor just in front of her. Frowning, she went toward it.

Her bare foot touched something wet and warm on the floor. A shiver moved through her. There was something wrong, something terribly wrong. Holding her hands out in front of her to feel her way, Rebecca moved around to the bedside table and switched on the small lamp. She looked down and a strangled gasp caught in her throat.

Beth lay in a pool of blood. Her cotton nightgown was soaked from the waist down, and her hands were stained. She was drawn up into a fetal position, her eyes closed, her blue lips parted with her shallow breathing. Just in front of her, as if it had fallen from her fingers, was an old-fashioned fountain pen sticky with blood.

The next twenty-four hours were a confusion of flashing lights and hospital smells, grave voices and screams. Beth died from the loss of blood at four in the morning. Their mother immediately collapsed and had to be admitted to the hospital under sedation and with careful monitoring of her heart. Margaret went to pieces, overcome with guilt for all the things she had said to her older sister, afraid that if she had not said them, Beth might have tried to get help in time. The tranquilizers their family doctor prescribed turned her into a zombie barely able to function, much less make decisions.

It was Rebecca who planned the funeral and chose the casket, the dress Beth would wear, and the family spray of pink roses and carnations. It was she who called relatives and spoke to the pastor of their church about the service and the music. Torn between staying with her mother at the hospital and sitting at the funeral home as the representative of Beth's family while relatives and friends filed in to pay their respects, she shuttled back and forth between the two until she was exhausted.

It was also Rebecca who talked to the two FBI men when they came to the hospital.

They showed her their identification, apologized for the intrusion on her grief, and asked politely if she would answer a few questions. Had she and the other members of her family been out of the house the night before? Wasn't it unusual for them all to be home on a Saturday night? What time did they ordinarily go to bed? What time had they retired the night before? Had they seen or heard anything unusual?

It was a good thing, Rebecca thought, that she was so tired, so drained of emotion; otherwise she would have been too nervous to talk. As it was, her replies were brief and matter-of-fact. It occurred to her to ask what it was all about, but she wasn't sure if people being questioned by the FBI were allowed to put questions to them in return or if the solemn men in their dark suits would bother to answer a fifteen-year-old girl.

In any case, she had nothing to tell them. There had been that car on the log road, but no one could say it was unusual, exactly, to see one there. More than that, she could not go into how and why she had seen it without explaining how she had found Beth and why her sister had died. That last information was being carefully suppressed. Their family doctor, the man who had treated their mother for years, had, in a protective gesture, put down the cause of Beth's death as massive hemorrhaging from a perforated bowel. For their mother's sake, nothing must jeopardize that story. Mrs. Benson did not know of the botched, self-administered abortion, had not seen Beth's condition. Rebecca and Margaret had removed the bloodstained pen and thrown a quilt over their sister before calling their mother that night. Anyway, the car at the pond could hardly matter. What was important was that Beth, beautiful, fun-loving Beth, was dead, and their mother could be dying.

It was not until later that evening at the funeral home that she learned of the death of that other young woman, the brassy and militant civil rights worker. She had been killed when the truck in which she was riding with a pair of black men was fired on by a bunch of white hoodlums in a dark-colored, late-model car. The white men had sped away, leading the town police on a high-speed chase before losing them somewhere out in the country south of town.

Beth and the civil rights worker lay in state in adjoining rooms at the funeral home, two young women tragically dead. Beth would be buried the next morning; the other girl's parents, in town overnight, would be taking her back that same day to Massachusetts for burial.

There was a constant stream of visitors. Most of them moved from one viewing room to the other in morbid, shifting curiosity. Hour after hour Rebecca endured the smell of the funeral flowers, the platitudes and attempts at comfort, and the inquiries about her mother's condition. Margaret sat for a while, then let dear, dependable Boots take her away. She couldn't stand it, she said. She just couldn't.

It was late when Edison came. He walked into the viewing room and stood staring down at Beth in her casket. He was still for so long, and there were so many muttered comments and remnants of gossip running around the room, so many stares, that finally Rebecca rose to her feet and walked to stand beside him as a gesture of support.

He turned his head to look at her, and tears glistened in his eyes. His voice was soft and tight when he spoke.

"I didn't mean to kill her," he said.

3

Noel Staulet came to a halt just before he reached the French doors that led out onto the back gallery. Through the rectangular glass panes he could see Riva and Dante Romoli seated at one of the glass-topped tables. The hat Riva had been wearing had been tossed aside on the seat of a chair. The reflection of the afternoon sun on the bricks of the terrace gave a delicate sheen to one side of her face. She had kicked off her cream-colored shoes and sat with one leg curled under her. She and Romoli were sharing a newspaper while drinking their after-luncheon coffee from eggshell-thin china cups.

The cups they were using were from the set Noel's great-grandmother had bought in France on her honeymoon tour. Still, it was not that solecism that made him frown and slowly clench his hands into fists. It was the ease between the two of them, the ease of a couple who knew each other so well that neither appearances nor silences mattered.

Never in all the years Noel had known Riva had she ever been so relaxed with him. Never had he seen her stretch with so much disregard for the way her dress clung to her slender shape or smother a yawn with such unconcern for how she looked with her soft lips parted and her eyelids heavy and half-closed. With him, she was always on guard, always controlled.

He could hardly complain; he was the same with her. He kept a tight rein on every word, gesture, and glance when he was with her. It was a habit stretching back more years than he cared to consider, one so stringent he wasn't sure he could break it if he tried. It had been hard won, that control, manufactured from sleepless nights, gut-straining effort, and iron will. It had been brought into being almost twenty-five years ago to cover a multitude of emotions he had no business feeling: rage that his father had so quickly replaced his dead mother, shame that he had chosen a girl young enough to be his daughter, and pity for the girl so obviously out of her depth. There had also been rampant curiosity about the nature of the physical relationship between her and his father, plus envy for the right the older man had to take Riva into his bed and Noel's own sheerest lust for her beautiful body. The last was most important, or had been until he had crowned his postadolescent stupidity by adding love to the list.

He had been in love with his stepmother. God, the guilt of it, and the burning, secret joy. It could not last, of course. It had almost been a relief when his father had put an end to it. Still, there had been nothing like it since. Nothing.

A musical yet strident ringing broke the quiet as the old-fashioned bell was twisted at the front door, which was down the hall behind him. Noel had already alerted Abraham, Bonne Vie's butler of forty years standing, that there would be guests. The elderly man moved with stately calm to answer the summons that meant Constance and the children had arrived. Noel had meant to warn Riva as well. Now it was too late.

Noel turned to watch through the open doorway as his ex-wife directed the pair of houseboys who were bringing in the luggage, pointing out the pieces she wanted from the mountain of matched Vuitton being unloaded from Noel's Mercedes, which was parked before the door. He should, he thought, have taken the plantation van to the airport. That was the only vehicle on the place roomy enough to hold the belongings Constance felt necessary for her comfort on even the shortest visit.

She had allowed him to transport most of the Vuittons, but not the children. There had been room for Pietro at least after everything was loaded, but she had refused to let the boy leave her side, insisting that both he and Coralie ride in the taxi with her. Apparently, Noel thought, he was a father who could not be trusted with his own children, though Constance was supposed to be bringing them to visit so they would not forget him. His anger over her unreasonableness pleased her immensely. She was Italian, and more than that, of Sicilian noble family, the former Lady Constance di Lampadusa. She did not have to be logical, nor did she see anything wrong with petty revenge.

The children, with nine-year old Coralie in the lead, were climbing out of the taxi and stumbling up the steps. Noel went to meet them. As he passed Abraham, Noel nodded toward the back gallery. The old man inclined his head in grave assent before moving off down the hall to inform the mistress of the house that she had company.

Pietro, not quite seven, was tired and out of sorts with jet lag and inclined to whine. He missed his nurse, who at the last minute had not been able to bring herself to get on a plane going over the ocean. Constance was unused to coping with the children by herself. In an effort to keep her young son quiet, she had plied him with chocolate, the evidence of which was still smeared on his face. With his mop of black curls, huge black eyes, and woebegone expression, he looked like a poster child for Save the Children.

Coralie, in contrast, was silent, staring around her with wide-eyed self-possession. The dress she wore was from Milan's most famous children's designer, her shoes were handmade from a last that was changed every three months, and the doll case she carried was of glove leather lined with silk and engraved with her initials in gold. She looked like a misplaced princess but was too pale and withdrawn to be healthy.

Noel walked out the front door. He knelt to hug his daughter, then reached to pull his six-year-old son against him. He felt chocolate rub off on his shirt collar, but he didn't care. His children's bodies against him were warm and welcome, bringing a tightness to his throat. It had been a long time.

"Welcome to Bonne Vie," he said, his voice soft. Then he picked up Pietro and took his daughter's hand. He stood back to allow his ex-wife to precede him, then moved with the two children into the house.

He stopped inside the door. Riva was approaching from the direction of the back gallery. She had retrieved her shoes and reapplied her makeup and was once more serenely composed. Dante lagged half a step behind her. The look in the Cajun's dark eyes was wary, as if he expected trouble.

"Constance, what a nice surprise," Riva said, extending her hand.

Constance barely touched the other woman's fingers. "I am sure it is more of a shock than a surprise. You must forgive me for not warning you. I was afraid Noel would say I should not come."

The words were correct, but the manner was proud, just short of offensiveness. It was one of the things that had first attracted Noel to the woman who had become his wife, that magnificent disdain for what other people thought.

There was also her looks, of course. She had been so different from Riva, with an attraction that had a medieval quality like some dark, subtly erotic portrait from the time of the Borgias. Her gray eyes tilted up at the corners and her nose was straight and aquiline. Her bottom lip was full and curving, though the top one had a willful thinness. She wore her long hair parted in the center and drawn back into a thick ballet dancer's knot on the nape of her neck. Constance was often exasperated with her body, saying she looked like an earth mother, too fecund for high fashion. She affected instead a look both barbarian and bohemian, the last a deliberate concession to her chosen career as a designer of jewelry that was more artwork than ornament. For the plane trip she had worn a dress of natural wool and linen with a fringed hem, along with crude gold jewelry with an Etruscan look and an accent scarf thrown over one shoulder. She was a woman with the kind of bodily opulence and fiery temperament that most men seemed to enjoy. Noel had once thought he might become lost in it. It was not her fault that he had not.

Riva had introduced Dante and was offering to show Constance to her room, suggesting a bath and a rest, perhaps a drink or a meal on a tray. It might have been an effort to dispose of the other woman long enough to adjust to her presence. Constance seemed to think so.

"There is no need whatever for you to exert yourself for me," the Sicilian woman said. "I'm sure Noel will show me where I am to sleep."

The sultry tone of her voice made the words suggestive. Catching the quick glance Riva sent him, Noel felt the heat of a flush and swore under his breath. He should have known Constance would not be able to resist making trouble. Pietro, sensitive to the undercurrents in the air, began to whine again, rubbing one eye with his fist.

Constance went on. "But if you would be helpful, Madame Staulet, perhaps someone could be found to look after Coralie and Pietro. Travel is so difficult for children—the waiting, the sitting still so long. They have had a hard day."

Dante Romoli spoke up, his face alight. "I volunteer. They might like a swim to work out the fidgets. I promise to watch them like a hawk."

The children's mother frowned doubtfully. "I had a nursemaid in mind."

"I make an excellent nursemaid. At least temporarily."

Riva intervened with a smile. "It's perfectly true; he does. Dante has at least twenty honorary nieces and nephews, the children of friends, who adore him. Your son and daughter will be quite safe."

Constance pursed her lips, her gaze measuring as she looked at Dante. Finally she said, "I suppose it will be all right."

"Good," Riva said. "While Dante is watching them, I'll see if a woman can be found to take charge during your stay."

"I'll try to find their swimsuits, then. If Noel will take me to their rooms . . . ?" Constance looked at her former husband from under her lashes.

The impulse to refuse was strong inside Noel; still, it would be best to set things straight between Constance and himself as soon as possible. He gave his son to Dante and let Riva take Coralie's hand, then turned toward the stairs rising at the back of the long hall. "This way."

They mounted the curving treads with the Oriental runner in silence. He showed Constance to one of the bedrooms at the front of the house for the children and indicated that her own would be across the hall.

"Where do you sleep?" she asked, her lips curved in a provocative smile.

"Downstairs. My father's old room off the library."

"You mean you displaced your stepmother? What terrible manners."

His face tightened. "Her room is up here next to yours, as a matter of fact."

"She and your father had separate bedrooms, then? How civilized, though I'm sure I can't blame her. How many years' difference was there between them?"

She was baiting him and he knew it. "Thirty. Why?"

"She's such a very young widow. How is it that you haven't told her you're madly in love with her and swept her to the altar?"

"Is that what you've been expecting?"

"For these six months and more."

"Sorry to disappoint you." His voice was dry.

"What can be holding you back? Surely it cannot be respect? I thought mourning was out of fashion, that grief was in bad taste."

"You thought wrong."

"Did I? The lovely Riva is certainly not wearing black."

"We won't talk about Riva."

She stared at him with a twisted smile. "You never did, did you, my love? The woman ruined my marriage, but I was never allowed to discuss her, and I still must never cast the least little slur on her name."

"There is no slur possible. She had nothing to do with the break between us."

"Oh, please! You may play the fool, but I am not one." She swung away from him with her silk scarf swirling around her and went to stand at the window.

He frowned. Sympathy for an ex-wife was an inconvenient emotion. Constance had never been able to accept the fact that he cared more for his freedom than for her title or access to her body. She could only explain it to herself by making some big dramatic triangle out of it.

"No act or deed of Riva's persuaded me to leave you," he said. "She learned about it only when it was over."

"Tell me you didn't leave because of what you felt—still feel—for her."

"That," he said quietly, "is none of your business."

"How can you say this thing?" she cried as she swung around. "It was always there between us, this unnatural fixation of yours for that woman. I hate it! I hate her!"

The only way to prevent a screaming fight, he had learned long ago, was to distract her. "And you came all this way to tell me that. Funny, I thought it was me you hated."

"Never. I never hated you, this I swear." She gave him a strange look compounded of disappointment, passion, and speculation before she went on. "I came because I wanted to know why you have not announced your engagement to Riva Staulet. I think now I know."

"Do you? I hope you don't mean to keep it a secret."

"You have a rival."

His lips twitched in a smile as he repeated, "A rival."

"That is the right word, yes? I mean there is another man, this Dante Romoli. He stands in your way."

"You always did have an active imagination."

"Yes," she agreed without umbrage, keeping her sights on her main interest. "He's very attractive. And good with children; that's important in a man."

Noel was aware of a certain tightness in his chest, but he refused to acknowledge it. "Maybe you should go after him yourself, if you think he's so great."

"Maybe I will. It would be a fine revenge, would it not? To take her man as she took mine?"

"Don't be ridiculous. They've known each other for years. Whatever is between them, there's nothing you can do to change it."

He expected her to flare up again. Instead, she went still, staring at him. Finally she said, "You don't know what is between them? You don't know whether they are lovers or only friends, whether they have ever been lovers?"

"I've never asked."

"Because," she said with narrowed eyes, "you don't want to know. Maybe you would like it if I did take this Dante from her. Maybe you would be . . . grateful."

As she spoke the last word, she moved toward him and reached up to smooth her fingers along the line of his jaw. He caught her wrist and brought it down. "Not that grateful."

She cursed him, snatching her wrist from his grasp and whirling away. "You are an imbecile! And I was crazy to come, crazy to think you might have recovered your senses, might want me and your children back again!"

"Yes, you were. Though if you would care to give me full custody of Coralie and Pietro, that's another matter."

"I'm sure! Never mind. I believe I will stay for a nice long visit. And when it is over, we will see who is crazy."

"I should point out that I have not invited you, and this is my home."

"Yours with your stepmother!"

"No, mine alone. She has an interest only in the holdings acquired by and with my father since their marriage. That is Louisiana law."

"I spit on your laws. What her interest in this house might be, I neither know nor care, but I feel sure she will be interested in hearing how you feel about her."

Not a muscle moved in Noel's face as he absorbed the threat. "What makes you think she doesn't know?"

Constance laughed. "She looks at you with the eyes of a woman who sees a danger instead of a promise of loving, an enemy rather than a lover. She doesn't know."

"Tell her," he said softly, "and she won't be the only one who sees an enemy."

The amusement faded from her face. "It may be I'd rather have you as that than as nothing at all."

*   *

Riva changed her linen dress for a caftan of open-weave cream cotton worn over a cream and coral maillot before she went back out to the pool. She wore no shoes. She loved going barefoot and never missed an excuse. She always felt freer that way, more herself.

For Riva, clothes were a deliberate form of disguise. She used them to present the image she wanted, one of cool, aristocratic elegance. Sometimes she was able to feel that she and the image merged, but not often. In the beginning, it had been Cosmo's taste and direction that had created the façade. However, she had quickly discovered its usefulness and made it her own. If behind it she was still a country girl, always a little intimidated, a little out of her depth, few were privileged to know it.

Dante Romoli was one of the few. He grinned at her when he saw her bare feet and the way she kept to the shady areas on the terrace to avoid the sun-heated bricks. He had changed also, using one of the swimsuits kept ready in the cabana behind the pool's Roman columns.

He was standing in the shallow end of the pool, which was nearest to the house. Coralie and Pietro were both wading after a big blue ball that he had thrown. The indifference of the two children was gone, replaced by wary pleasure.

Riva lowered herself onto the edge of the pool. She stripped off her caftan, then dangled her feet in the water. She was ready to play if Noel's son and daughter looked inclined to accept her, but did not intend to force the issue. As for the exertion of swimming, it just wasn't in her at the moment. Early-morning laps were her favored form of exercise, but she was no sun worshiper. A deep rich tan might be a sign of affluence in some parts of the country, but in Louisiana it showed either youthful carelessness or idiocy. Not only was sunbathing in the muggy heat torture, it was downright dangerous. Moreover, in that part of the country skin the color and softness of a magnolia petal had never quite gone out of style.

Erin's college friends were playing a game of water tag. Since Erin was "out," she swam toward Riva, then stood up in the shallow water and waded to take a seat beside her aunt. As she dragged her long hair over one shoulder to squeeze the water from it, she nodded at the two children. "I can't believe Noel's wife is here. I thought she despised him."

"I suppose he has some sort of visiting rights."

"She has her nerve, coming without so much as a postcard."

Riva lifted a shoulder. "That's the aristocracy for you."

"The kids are cute, though kind of quiet. What's she like?"

"I forgot you've never met her. She's nice enough."

Erin lifted a brow, her gaze sparkling. "Do I detect a lack of warmth there?"

"I hardly know her, really," Riva protested. "I've only seen her a few times myself, once here just after the marriage and maybe twice in Paris."

"I never understood what happened to cause them to divorce. There they were living in France and having children, and the next thing I knew she was carving metal with a blowtorch for jewelry in some garret and Noel was single again."

"Hardly a garret," Riva said with a crooked smile. "In fact, it was a garden apartment that just happened to be located down the street from the old haunt of the Duchess of Windsor. Other than that, you know as much as I do. If you want more, you'll have to ask Noel."

"No, thank you! I like my head, I'll have you know."

"I don't blame you." Noel was not the most approachable of men on many subjects; on personal matters he was impossible. He had always been that way.

They were silent a few minutes, watching Dante with the children. He had discovered that they swam like dolphins and moved with them into deeper water. Coralie was clinging to his back with her arms around his neck while Pietro stood on Dante's bent knees and leaned back, holding his hands for support. Dante turned slowly like a lopsided and wobbly human merry-go-round so that the water swirled around the three of them. The children, shouting shrilly in glee, were to all appearances doing their best to drown him.

Erin nodded her head at Dante. "He should have kids of his own."

"It generally takes a mother."

"I know that, smarty!"

"I was wondering if your education had been that neglected." Riva gave the girl a droll look.

"Sure you were. Don't try to change the subject. What about you?"

"I'm too old."

"No, you aren't. A lot of women have babies after forty. You just have to be careful."

"Thank you, doctor," Riva said.

"It's no use, Erin!" Dante called. "Your aunt is being discreet. No talk of marriage, much less babies, for at least six more months."

Riva frowned. She should have remembered how well voices carried over the water. "I never said that."

"Didn't you?" he asked, all innocence. "I could have sworn you did."

Dante's black gaze gleamed with something like a promise, but an instant later Coralie managed to get a stranglehold on his neck, diverting his attention once more. Regardless, Riva could feel Erin's gaze on her own face. She could imagine what the girl was thinking, what she was wondering. Riva had known for a long time that everyone suspected her of having an affair with Dante. Everyone, including Noel. This affair was supposedly of ancient standing, so ancient it had a quasi respectability. The truth was complicated, and known only to her and Dante. It suited them to keep it that way.

A wolf whistle, low and reverent, echoed over the water. It came from one of the college men in the pool. His gaze was trained on the back gallery, and he stopped swimming so suddenly that he sank and came up sputtering.

Stepping from the evening shadows gathering under the gallery, moving across the terrace, was a woman. She moved without haste, in superb unconcern for the fact that she was within an inch, or two at the most, of being naked. Her swimsuit consisted of three small triangles of sea-blue silk threaded with silver that were held in place by tiny, braided silver ropes. From her shoulder hung three panels of silver cloth so light they wafted around her with her every movement. Her dark hair hung in a thick, shining braid over one shoulder, and her voluptuous body was evenly, richly tan.

For an instant, Riva wished she had not been so sensible about the sun. Then rising to her feet, she made Constance welcome.

The woman greeted her children's cries with a wave, acknowledged Erin's friends with a nod, then removed her panels of silver cloth and let them fall to the bricks. Lifting herself on her toes, she dived into the pool. She swam to the end and back, ignoring the young college men who moved out of her way as if they weren't there. Constance approached Dante and came to a halt in front of him, treading water.

"It was kind of you to look after Pietro and Coralie," she said, her voice husky. "I did not thank you adequately before and would like to do so now. I am in your debt."

There was admiration in Dante's face as he looked at her, but behind it was wariness. "By no means," he said. "It's my pleasure."

"It's unlike them to warm to strangers so quickly. You must be a most unusual man."

"I just offered them a chance to scream and yell and commit mayhem, since transatlantic flights give me that urge."

Constance smiled as if uncertain whether to believe him. "Do they?"

"Every time." Dante fended off an attack from young Pietro by swinging him up and onto his shoulder, then tipping him into the water.

The Sicilian woman turned her head away from the splash, then moved around Dante to where the water was shallow enough so that she could settle onto her feet. Her eyes narrowed in appraisal, she said, "You have a most interesting face, like an old coin."

Dante grimaced. "I know. Mine is what's called a noble nose."

"Distinctive rather, I would say, and faces happen to be a hobby of mine."

"At least it serves its purpose."

Riva, watching the pair in the water with the children cavorting around them, recognized Dante's evasive tactics. Privately she thought that if Constance meant to interest him, as it seemed she did, she would do better to use less blatant means. In spite of his free-wheeling life-style, Dante was the most conservative of men.

There was a scraping sound from the terrace. Noel had come outside and was taking a chair. He had removed his tie and opened his shirt collar and was rolling the sleeves of his shirt to his elbows. A maid, following him, placed a tall and frosted glass garnished with a sprig of mint on the table before him. He spoke a soft word of thanks, then picked up the glass and drank, his gaze on his former wife in the water. His expression was carefully blank.

Riva picked up her caftan and pulled it on over her head, then got to her feet and walked to where Noel sat. He rose to pull out a chair for her, and she dropped into it.

"Would you like a drink?" he asked.

She shook her head. He resumed his seat and reached for his glass to take another swallow. She watched the smooth glide of his brown throat as it worked. Finally she said, "Will Constance and the children be with us long?"

"A month or two."

"How very . . . nice for you."

He gave her a straight look. "I'm sorry for the inconvenience."

"It doesn't matter. This is your house."

"You run it."

That much was true. "With a great deal of help. Your guests are no problem."

"I never thought they would be. You're always prepared, aren't you?"

There was a trace of irony in his words, as if he resented her efficiency. Since it was unlikely he would give her any satisfaction if questioned about it, she ignored it. "Your father taught me to be."

"Of course. You were well trained, the chatelaine of Bonne Vie."

"A competent hostess, I hope."

"Oh, I'll give you that."

She felt a sudden revulsion for the barren politeness of their words. It was a form of warfare. It might be better to have everything out in the open so that, like the children in the pool, they could scream and yell and commit mayhem. Then again, there were some things best covered by reticence.

"Now that you mention it," she said, rising to her feet, "perhaps I should go and see about dinner."

Noel did not speak as she walked away. But he watched her go, watched until the pale color of her caftan was only a dim glimmer in the hall.

"Papa! Papa, did you see me swim?"

It was Pietro, calling out as he clambered from the pool. He ran toward Noel, leaving wet footprints on the terrace with every step. A smile curved the lines in Noel's lean face, and he felt his heart swell inside him as he reached to catch the small, damp body of his son and swing him into his lap. He had been afraid Pietro had grown away from him in the time they had been apart. Both children looked a great deal better for their water play; the boredom and fatigue that had made them so listless had been banished.

"Yes, indeed, I saw you," Noel answered, his voice warm and deep. "You did fine."

"I remembered what you said. I remembered everything you showed me when you lived with us."

"I see that, and I'm proud of you."

"I wish you'd come home. I miss you, Papa."

Coralie, following her brother more slowly came to lean against her father's shoulder. She dragged free her hair that was plastered with water to her neck and tucked it behind her ear with a curiously adult air. Still, her voice was thin and childish as she asked, "Can't you come back home with us, to Paris?"

Noel put his arm around his daughter, gently smoothing her fine-boned, sun-warmed shoulder, while at the same time holding Pietro closer and brushing the boy's fine, tangled curls with his lips. "I miss you, too, both of you, more than I can say, but I can't go with you."

"Why?" Coralie demanded.

Noel's gaze above his son's head strayed once more to the hall of the great house where Riva had disappeared. "I belong here."

"What about us?"

"I wish you could belong here, too."

"So do I," Pietro said, then squirmed in Noel's arms. "Don't, Papa, you're squeezing too tight!"

"Sorry," Noel said softly. "I'm sorry."

4

Edison Gallant waited inside the limousine for the hotel doorman to open the car door. The man was hired to play the servant; let him do it. Besides, Edison enjoyed watching through the long car's dark glass as the tourists gawked and particularly relished the moment when he stepped out onto the sidewalk and they began to mutter his name out of the sides of their mouths. Limos were a part of the big-shot image, even if they were hired. People expected it, and he meant to give them what they expected. Anne considered the big car an affectation, but he didn't see her refusing to ride in it with him.

It was Anne who had chosen the hotel down in the French Quarter. He would have preferred the Sheraton or the Marriott on Canal, away from the congestion of the narrow streets, but she had gone on and on about the Royal Orleans and its ambience and the fact that there had been a hotel on the spot for more than a hundred and fifty years. He had finally agreed to stay there just to shut her up. She was nuts about anything old.

The place wasn't old, really, just made to look that way, with rows of arched windows and wrought-iron gas lamps. The service was good, and he was willing to admit the address had a certain style. It was just a step to eating places like K-Paul's, Brennan's, and Antoine's; no need to call the limo, so you saved that cost. But there was no getting away from the row of tourist buggies across the street, with their moth-eaten mules picturesque as all get-out in straw hats with their ears sticking through. Those he could have done without. He wasn't thrilled by the smell of mule shit.

While the doorman in fancy livery handed his wife out of the limo, Edison gave the chauffeur his instructions for the next morning. Then he followed Anne through the heavy brass-and-glass doors being held open for them. Inside, they mounted the marble steps to the long, chandelier-hung lobby where they waded through the luggage of conventioneers checking in, then turned toward the elevators.

They had the elevator car to themselves, a small miracle. As it began to rise, Anne turned her head to look at him. "You were quiet driving back. Is something wrong?"

It was a trick of his wife's, waiting until they were alone but not quite private to spring questions on him. She knew it annoyed him; sometimes he thought that was why she did it. She also knew he would give her an answer without what she liked to call his vulgarisms in case someone overheard. The damned image required it. Most of the time.

"Shove it," he said.

The quiet in their suite was as deep and cool and luxurious as the cut-velvet pile carpet. Edison flung himself into a chair and demanded a bourbon on the rocks. Anne moved to the credenza to pour the drink from the set-up tray, taking ice from the bucket left ready. She handed it to him in silence, then moved into the bedroom. He heard her in there, moving around, going into the bathroom.

Edison took a deep swallow of his drink, then set the glass on a side table and stripped off his jacket. He threw it on the floor and loosened his tie. God, he needed a shower. After standing around in the heat all afternoon, he smelled like a boar hog.

He wanted to relax, but that was something that was getting harder and harder to do these days. It was a crock of shit that he had to give up smoking for the image. Maybe he'd take a pill after a while. He got to his feet, picked up his drink, and walked to the window. The view was of a courtyard of sorts on the roof of a lower floor, a small area with potted trees and chairs in groups on a floor of aggregated rock. Boring as all hell. He shoved the drapes aside and propped himself against the wall, staring down.

Rebecca Benson. Riva Staulet. He still felt as if somebody had kicked him in the stomach. Or, more likely, the balls. He thought he had forgotten. He had sure as hell tried hard enough.

God, but she had been sweet, the tenderest little piece of tail he had ever had. That had been some summer, his last as a free man. He had thought he was such hot shit with his Chevy convertible and his line of baloney for the girls, but he hadn't known the half of it.

That day down at the pond . . . Old Boots had been so afraid he was going to shock the Benson sisters. Guess he had, at that, but they were so ripe and ready for it that it had been irresistible. It had gone all over him when they laughed at him. He had sworn to himself that he would have all three of them before the summer was over. He'd never told anybody that, not even Boots. He would never have understood. Edison did, though. He had had something to prove to himself. He had needed to prove he could win to make himself feel good, to prove he could get past people's defenses and make them like him enough to give him what he wanted in spite of themselves. He had to make them love him. At least for a while. After he had what he wanted of them, it didn't make any difference how they felt.

Beth had been easy. Hell, she had used him as much as he had used her. She had been ready to get her own back against her husband overseas, ready for a little excitement and some of the rolling around in the hay she had gotten used to as a new wife. The other one—what was her name? Mary? Martha? No, Margaret, that was it—had been the pious type. Everybody knew that that kind was sometimes the hottest. She had been all giggles and coy smiles, pretending to be outraged when he had kissed her though she had liked it fine and given him all sorts of encouragement. He'd have gotten into her panties, too, all right, if there had been time.

There hadn't been.

He still broke out into a cold sweat every time he thought of the night that summer had ended for him. His convertible had been in the shop, so he had borrowed his uncle's car. He'd been riding around, drinking beer and trying to keep cool, him and Boots and two or three others. They had found the sawed-off shotgun under the car seat where his uncle kept it, what with things being so unsettled with the civil rights mess. It was Boots and one of the other idiots who had started playing around with it, yelling about going down in the woods to spotlight rabbits and deer.

When the truckload of blacks had overtaken and then passed them, they had all thought it was a big laugh to wave the gun at them and give chase. It hadn't seemed such a bad idea to Edison, either. The driver of the truck had been that brassy Yankee bitch. He had put a move on her one night at the movies, and she had called him a white-assed mama's boy and told him to run along home. It had felt fine to put a scare into her, to show her he wasn't as wet behind the ears as she thought.

They had gone after the truck, and the bitch at the wheel had tried to lose them by flooring the accelerator. They had chased the truck up hills and around curves on two wheels, down back roads, and up and down the streets of the residential section on the edge of town. Then the Yankee woman had gotten tired of running. She had brought the truck to a squealing halt, backed it up, swung it around in a tight turn, and headed it toward his uncle's car. She had damn near run them off the road, sitting behind the wheel grinning fit to kill. The boys in the car had cussed and yelled, and he had turned around in a cloud of dust in somebody's front yard, then given chase again. Once more, the bitch had turned the truck around, coming toward them.

Somebody had yelled, "Shoot at 'em! Make 'em duck! That'll make 'em grin out of the other sides of their faces!"

The shotgun had been shoved into Edison's hand since he would have the best shot at the driver. He had held the thing awkwardly in one hand, steering with the other, as he waited for the truck to come closer. He had seen the brassy civil-rights bitch's face in the glare of his headlights as she laughed at him. He had raised the barrel of the gun and pulled the trigger.

He had meant to shake her up. That was all, as God was his witness. He hadn't even aimed at her, not really. But the oncoming truck's windshield had exploded into a thousand pieces and the woman's face had sprayed blood. The truck had veered off the road and across a lawn before slamming into the side of a house.

Edison had stomped down on the accelerator and gotten out of there, gotten clean out of town and into the country. The boys in the car had cussed and screamed at each other. It had been Boots who had directed Edison down past the Benson house and onto the old logging road that led to the pond. Most of the boys, including Boots, had gotten out there and walked home.

Edison had just sat there in the car for a long time, until his hands stopped shaking. Finally he had driven back to his uncle's house and parked the sedan in the garage. He had taken the shotgun and cleaned it carefully, then put it back where he had found it. When that was done, he had let himself into the house, fallen into bed, and dropped instantly into a soundless sleep.

Beth's death, on top of the other one, had torn him up as nothing had before or since. He had looked at her, lying so waxen and lifeless in her coffin and, knowing his child had died with her, been wrenched by guilt. He had thought he was drowning in pain, more pain than he ever wanted to feel again, more than he would ever allow himself to feel again. It was little Rebecca—Riva—who had taken him out of it.

He had driven her home from the funeral home that night, and they had sat out in front of the house in his car for some time. They had talked of Beth and how she had been, how much she had enjoyed living, how terrible it was that she was gone. They had both cried a little and comforted each other until Edison had nearly convinced himself that he had loved Beth a little and was devastated at her loss, just as he told Rebecca. They had rambled on in that vein until he had gotten a hold of himself, until he had noticed the way Beth's little sister's breasts lifted under her blouse and caught the fragrance of her hair. He had become so engrossed then in the way she looked and how much he wanted to reach out and grab her that he had ceased to pay any attention to what she was saying.

Then he heard.

"What?" he said, and the word sounded stupefied to his own ears.

"I said," she repeated, "do you think I was right not to tell the federal men about the car I saw going down to the pond? Do you think I'll get in trouble for keeping quiet?"

Christ. He had to think. He sat up straighter. "Who—who else have you told?"

"Nobody. At first I didn't think too much about it. Since then, there hasn't been time, what with Mama in the hospital and Bethie—well, there just hasn't been time."

"What about Margaret?"

"She wasn't there. I got up to see about Beth by myself. But I know the car had something to do with that woman being shot, now that I think about it. Whoever was in it was in too big of a hurry, and they're saying it was last seen heading south, toward our place. I'd hate to think there was something I could do to help catch the ones who killed her but just stood by and did nothing."

"You don't really know that there was a connection between the car and the—the killing. It was probably a couple out looking for a place to park."

"That's what I thought at first, but something about the way that car took off down into the woods bothers me."

He made an airy gesture in the darkness. "Forget it. Ten to one, the whole thing will blow over. It's best not to get too involved with the government."

"You really think so? That's your—your legal opinion?"

His legal opinion. God, wasn't that sweet? She already thought of him as a lawyer. "That's it," he said, and sat up in the seat, stretching so that when he relaxed again his arm lay along the seat behind her. He couldn't depend on her to accept what he said without question, so it would be just as well if she had other things to think about.

He leaned toward her, inhaling the warm sweetness of her that was made up of sunshine and starched clothes, a trace of apple-blossom cologne, and the headiness of young female. She turned her head to look at him in the darkness. The light gleaming from the bare bulb in the porch ceiling of the house caught in her wide eyes. For an instant, Edison felt a shaft of purest terror. Her look was so full of sorrow and innocent wisdom that it was as if she could see right through him.

He had to close those eyes. He pressed his mouth to the fresh curves of her lips, which were as gentle and moist as a child's. He put his hand on her breast, squeezing the soft yet firm flesh under the cloth; there welled up in him the hot urge to take her quickly, roughly, on the car seat.

He didn't do it. He didn't because she pushed away from him.

"I—I thought you loved Beth."

"I do, I did. But you're so much like her it's almost like having her back again. Except that you're something more, something so sweet and precious that I know you could make me forget."

"Forget Beth?"

Her tone held horror. He had to say something quick. "No, no, never that, but you could help me bear the pain and the shame."

He leaned his forehead against hers with a sigh that was not entirely faked. When she did not draw away, he kissed her again, slowly, thoroughly.

This time she was less abrupt. Still, she dragged her lips from his and eased away from him, then got out of the car. He opened the door on his side and stepped out to join her, walking her to the front door. There was plenty of time, he told himself.

There had been. He had gone with her to the funeral, standing with his head bowed, penitent, in the sun. He had driven with her to bring her mother home from the hospital and stayed to entertain the older woman and help Rebecca and Margaret cook supper. He had stayed in town, in fact, until it was past time for his classes to begin at Tulane, and still he could not bring himself to go.

He had been afraid.

He had been afraid of what Rebecca knew and of what she could see inside him when she looked into his eyes. He had been afraid of what she might say if he wasn't around to stop her, afraid of what she might tell her mother or her sister that would set the police on his trail and take away his future. And he had wanted her as he had never wanted anything in his life. He had wanted her not only because she was something sweet and somehow special, but because if she gave herself to him it would show she trusted him, liked him, did not think him too terrible to love.

One night he had been so terrified that, instead of taking her home after they had been to the Dairy Queen for an ice cream sundae, he had turned the car down the logging road and parked beside the pond. Turning to her, he had said the words that had been hovering on the end of his tongue for days.

"Marry me."

"Oh, Edison, you don't mean it. You have years more of college, and I—"

"What about you?"

"I'm only fifteen."

"Old enough," he said, and kissed her, tasting her lips as if they were candy with a soft center hidden inside her mouth.

"Mama will never sign the papers," she murmured when she could speak.

"We can go across the state line. There's no waiting period in Arkansas; they don't even ask for birth certificates."

"But Mama would be so hurt, so surprised. It might kill her."

"She'll be a little hurt at first, but you know she likes me, and she'll be glad to think you're settled with a lawyer for a husband."

"Margaret would have to take care of her alone."

"Margaret's a born martyr; she'll love it. Besides, she's going to marry Boots any day now, and they can live with your mother." He punctuated his arguments with kisses and caresses. He could feel the swift beat of her heart in her chest like the struggles of a small, trapped animal. Under his hand the nipple of her breast was firmly budded. He could sense the curiosity under her confusion. Girls were always curious.

He whispered love words without knowing what he said, distracted by the urgent throbbing of the member between his legs. With one hand, he unbuttoned his shirt, then took her hand and pressed it to his hairy chest, smoothing her palm over it until she began to explore on her own.

How small her waist was, yet how full and soft her breasts. Though there was wiry strength in her, she seemed so slim in his arms that he had the feeling he could take her without too much effort. Regardless, he was afraid to frighten her, did not, in truth, want to frighten her. Sweet, sweet, she was the sweetest little cherry he had ever tasted.

As he opened her blouse, her breasts made him catch his breath, they were so pink and blue-white and perfect. He ached with appreciation as he took the nipples into his mouth one after the other. The soft little sounds she made maddened him so that he sucked too hard and made her cry out, then had to soothe the pain.

The skin of her thighs was so silky on the inside. She was so small, yet so warmly moist under her panties. There were some soft protests that had to be overcome at that intimate touch, but he knew how, knew where to rub, gently, gently.

Tight, she was so tight, so perfect. He felt inflamed, his brain on fire. And the steering wheel was gouging his back. Catching his breath, he pulled her up from where she was lying half under him on the seat. He opened the door on his side and helped her out, then leaned the seat forward and urged her into the backseat of the car.

"Edison, no," she whispered, trying to turn away. "I . . . don't want to do this. Take me home. Please."

He knew just how much attention to pay to such last-minute objections. He pushed her inside. She stumbled, then fell across the seat. He slid in beside her, slamming the door after him. Then he reached for her and fastened his mouth on hers while searching for the open front of her blouse. He cupped her breast, then bent his head to suckle at the nipple.

Her breathless protest destroyed his control. He thrust her back, fumbling under her skirt and pushing it up with his arm even as he dragged her panties down her legs. With his knee across hers, he unfastened his own zipper and pushed down his pants and briefs. Then he was upon her, nudging his knee between her legs, spreading her, positioning himself at that small, diamond-shaped opening. With a hard thrust, he pushed inside. He heard her cry out, felt her arch under him trying to shudder away. He paid no attention, intent only on the hard throb of his blood and the tight, engulfing heat of her. He shoved deeper, twisting his hips, shivering with pleasure. Unable to stop himself, he bucked and rammed then, thrusting, pushing her legs wider, her knees higher, until with a harsh, rasping grunt he buried himself in her depths.

It was moments later before he realized she was shaking as if with a chill, her chest heaving with suppressed tears. For a fleeting instant, he felt like a bastard, then it was gone. He petted her and gave her his handkerchief and whispered apologies and all the other words he knew she wanted and needed to hear. He helped her straighten her clothes and her hair, when all he really wanted to do was snatch up her skirt and have her again. Finally he held her arm while she climbed back into the front seat, then took his place beside her and revved the engine. He turned the car around, heading out away from the pond. Reaching out, he put his arm around her, held her close against him on the seat. At the main road, he turned in the direction of Arkansas. There was no more argument.

Edison Gallant, standing in a hotel suite in New Orleans, took another long drink of his bourbon. He had taken care of the danger Rebecca, dear Riva, had posed to him once, and he could do it again. It would tickle the hell out of him, in fact, to go about it in the same way. The high-and-mighty Mrs. Staulet would learn the mistake she had made in trying to jack him around. Just thinking about it gave him a hard-on.

Behind him, Anne emerged from the bedroom. She had taken a bath and put on a rose silk robe with matching slippers. She was flushed and carried the scent of the Chloé bath powder she used. She did not look at him but kept her lashes lowered and her face expressionless.

Edison's mouth hardened. He hated that withdrawn act, and Anne knew he hated it. It reminded him of his mother, who always used to retreat into coldness when she was annoyed with him. His wife ought to have known better than to ask stupid questions. If she didn't like the answers she got, it was her own fault.

He drained the glass in his hand and moved to the credenza to replenish it. He looked over his shoulder at Anne, who had picked up a magazine. His voice neutral, he said, "Riva Staulet is a stunning woman, don't you think?"

"I suppose." The answer was cool.

"She has it all; looks, a first-class business head from all accounts, high social standing, and now money since old Staulet packed it in."

"Indeed."

Anne's voice was sharp and her grip on the magazine had tightened. Edison noted both reactions with satisfaction. She knew what was coming. He said with deliberation, "I'd like to have a piece of her beautiful, rich ass."

Anne looked at him with revulsion and pain in her face. Her voice was steady, however, almost dispassionate, when she spoke. "I'm sure you would, since you seem to have that ambition toward most women. I have to say, however, that I think it's doubtful Riva Staulet will allow you the pleasure."

"Oh, you think so?"

Anne nodded a judicious assent. "She appeared to me to be a woman of taste."

He grunted. It was a hit. It would cost her. He put down his glass and moved toward her. "And what about you?"

She tossed the magazine aside and got to her feet, heading toward the bedroom. "I," she said distinctly, "am not in the mood for games."

"Too bad. I am."

He moved swiftly to cut her off, catching her shoulder and spinning her around to face him. He jerked the belt at her waist free and snatched the robe from her shoulders. She was naked under it as he knew she would be. His prim and proper wife had a sensuous streak that sometimes amazed him. Not that she ever got off on sex; it was just that she had ways that made it seem she should have been good at it.

She pushed at him, and he grabbed her wrist, pulling her against him. He put his hand on her buttock, squeezing, pumping the hard lump at his groin against her.

"Leave me alone," she cried. "You stink of sweat!"

"And you like it, don't you?" He released her wrist and sank his fingers into her hair, then covered her mouth with his, pointing his tongue and pushing it deep. He moved his other hand over her backside, spanning the crevice. She went rigid.

He laughed deep in his chest, then backed her into the bedroom, continuing until he fell with her across the bed. Stripping off his clothes, he rolled over onto her and dragged her into position. He pushed into her and felt her accommodate him to prevent her own discomfort. He surged back and forth in frenzied effort, while in his mind he was back in his Chevy and the woman under him was tight and hot little Rebecca. He groaned in disappointment as well as in pleasure when he came too soon. He wished it could have lasted longer, not for Anne's sake but for his own.

Anne Gallant lay unmoving for long moments after her husband had finished and flopped away from her. She felt numb, her legs leaden weights hanging over the edge of the bed. At the same time, her brain was on fire and tears ached in her throat.

She refused to cry. Moving carefully, as if her body were too taut and full for true balance, she got up from the bed and made her way into the bathroom. She leaned for a moment against the vanity table, staring at herself in the mirror. Her face looked swollen and there were circles under her eyes. Her breasts were sore and the lower part of her body seemed engorged. Sickness rose inside her but she swallowed it down.

She had been used. She knew it and despised herself for permitting it. It was always that way, would always be that way. She had learned to remedy the physical problems; she knew how to find her own release, and she would, in a moment, while she bathed again. She just wished that it wasn't necessary.

She was frigid. The reason wasn't hard to find. She had read enough to know the cause was lack of stimulation, to understand that it wasn't her fault. Probably. Yet there had been a few times when Edison had tried to help her. The trouble was, she had known he was trying for his own pleasure instead of hers or else to prove something to himself. She had also known that his impatience could surface at any moment, and most likely would surface long before she was ready.

The trouble was, it made her feel less than a woman not to be able to come with her husband. The trouble was, it hurt to be used without that ultimate benefit.

She had asked herself a million times over why she stayed with Edison. The truth was, she had been in love with him since they were children in dance class together. Their courtship had had the approval of both his parents and her own; their marriage had been accepted as a given, planned by the older people, if not arranged. When they were first married, his masterful ways in the bedroom had been rather exciting, though she had felt there must be something more. Later, when she had discovered what was missing, she had thought it was male ignorance at fault and had sought, delicately, to rectify matters. It hadn't worked. Edison had resented any attempt to improve his technique. He had failed to see anything wrong with it since he claimed to have satisfied other women with it, and he himself was more than satisfied.

It had been years before she could bring herself to recognize that the problem was he cared for no one's feelings except his own, that he had closed off all consideration for others, that he loved no one so much as himself. By then he had been deeply involved in politics, and her leaving would have been a severe blow to his career. Men who could not manage their marriages were at a disadvantage when their ability to manage a political office was called into question. That fact had become a weapon to use to modify his public behavior toward her. It was still a factor in the silent warfare she carried on against him. He did not always have things his own way. He paid, insofar as she could manage, for every slight, every bruise. When all else failed, she spent his money on things that gave her the pleasure he did not, would not, give her.

Still, there were times, such as now, when she could hardly bear to stay.

But where else could she go? She had a liberal arts degree, but no real job training. Worse than that, she had no ambition. She had never wanted a career, never wanted anything except to be a wife and a mother. She enjoyed volunteer work with her charities, particularly those having to do with children or the preservation of old historic homes and landmarks—that much she had in common with Riva Staulet. In addition, she was vain enough to think she had some talent as a political hostess. None of these things seemed likely to produce the money for the life-style in which she had always been maintained.

That was it. She hated the thought of reducing her standard of living. There were certain things she had been used to all her life: a comfortable and even luxurious home, household help, good food, the company of the best people. And she didn't think she would be any good at doing without them. If that made her a snob, well, then, she was a snob. The only problem was that she sometimes suspected it made her a fool.

There were also times when she wondered, furtively, what it would be like to make love to another man. Often, when Edison flew himself in his plane, she daydreamed about what it would be like if he should crash. She chose what she would wear to the funeral, how she would act, what she would say, where and how she would live afterward. And she played with the idea of being free to find someone else, another man, when a decent length of time had passed.

Sometimes at boring luncheons she amused herself by imagining having a torrid relationship with the speaker or some other nice-looking man on the dais. Other times, she would mentally undress them. She found herself, in the past few years, watching the backsides of football players or staring at the crotches of men in bathing suits. She felt so frustrated and depraved at times that she had an almost uncontrollable urge to walk down the street with her blouse unbuttoned or to pick up the phone and dial some strange man and say—she didn't know what she wanted to say. Such impulses troubled and humiliated her, but they were only in her mind. And there they would stay.

She hoped they would stay there.

Riva did not like the cellular phone in her limousine. She had agreed to it mainly because she had wanted to be instantly available during the time when Cosmo had been so ill, but also because Erin had suggested it, and it seemed to Riva that she would be falling behind the times in her niece's eyes if she didn't have one. But having it in place meant she was subject to interruption even while riding in her car and that she hated.

The early-morning trip into New Orleans was one of Riva's favorite times for getting things done. She had a built-in lap desk fitted with a small, voice-activated dictaphone, a notebook of camel leather with pocket divisions and a slim gold pen clipped inside, a miniature printing calculator, and a gold-topped stapler. With this portable office, she could get through as much work in the hour of travel time as she could accomplish in an entire morning once she arrived at the Staulet Building. The difference was the constant demands on her time and attention at the office.

When Noel had first come home and begun to take his father's place, she had felt obligated to suggest that he ride into the city with her each morning, though she had hedged the invitation about with all sorts of possible reasons why he might find it inconvenient. His refusal had relieved her beyond measure. She could think of nothing less conducive to work than having him sitting silent and disapproving beside her. Cosmo's presence had never bothered her. He had read his *Wall Street Journal*, *Barron's*, and *Forbes* in companionable silence. Actually, she thought it had amused him to see the way she made her time count.

The shrilling of the phone, intruding on her concentration, always startled her, just as it did this morning. She looked up to watch her driver George, who was married to Bonne Vie's cook Liz, hold the stretch Lincoln steady at seventy miles an hour with one hand, turn down the Mozart tape that was playing, then reach to answer the summons.

"It's Miss Margaret," he said, passing the receiver back.

The voice of Riva's sister came loud and harsh into Riva's ear. "I don't know why I have to go through a half-dozen people every time I want to talk to you. I guess it adds to your sense of self-importance to have someone else answer every phone you own."

"What it adds to is my time and privacy, Margaret. How are you?"

"I'm well enough, for someone who has been having heart palpitations since I saw the paper this morning! It's a nightmare coming true. You must have been out of your mind!"

"Possibly," Riva answered with irony. "What are you talking about?"

"That horrible picture, that's what! Don't tell me you haven't seen it?"

"No, I haven't," Riva began, then stopped.

She knew with abrupt, bitter certainty which picture Margaret was talking about. It was in the nature of things that the shot of her and Erin with Edison and his wife and son taken by that young photographer would be splashed over half the newspapers in the state. If she had wanted it publicized, it would, of course, have disappeared into some dead file somewhere and never been seen again.

"How could you allow it, Riva?" her sister demanded. "You, of all people? It's disgusting. It makes me sick to my stomach. Something has to be done!"

"I'm doing my best, Margaret."

"Well, it apparently isn't good enough! If you can't fix things, I'll have to come down there and take care of it myself."

"By all means. How?"

"I don't know! Can't you talk to Edison, make him see reason?"

"That's what I was trying to do when that picture was taken. He wasn't particularly cooperative."

"If worse comes to worst, you can always tell him—"

"No," Riva said, her voice hard.

"Don't bite my head off. You know you can't just let this thing go on!"

"I have no intention of it. I'm supposed to see Edison at lunch today. We'll come to an understanding or else."

"Oh, really, Riva, this is no time to be trying to throw your weight around. You're going about it all wrong, I just know it. Remember, you catch more flies with honey than with vinegar."

"Thank you very much for those words of wisdom. Unfortunately, honey is likely to attract rats, too."

"What do you mean?" Margaret's voice was sharp.

"I mean, Edison hasn't changed. His help may have a price."

"What can you possibly do for him? Oh, I suppose you mean a campaign contribution."

"I believe he has a more personal service in mind."

Her sister's scandalized breath was perfectly audible. "You're not suggesting that he wants to go to bed with you after all these years. You must be imagining things!"

"Thank you, dear. How good you are for my ego."

"Your ego has nothing to do with it. This is a serious matter."

"I, more than anyone else," Riva said with quiet emphasis, "am aware of that."

"Yes, well, I suppose you are," came the grudging answer. "But I'm so worried I can't think straight. Whatever it is Edison wants— a contribution, support, introductions to your high-powered friends, whatever—you'll just have to give it to him. That's all there is to it."

Margaret didn't know what she was saying. Riva had to assume that that was it, anyway. Her sister really wasn't rational where Erin was concerned. "I have no intention of giving Edison anything; he's had enough from me. His worry should be what I can take from him."

"Dearest heavenly Father, Riva! You'll ruin everything. Edison won't stand still for being threatened."

"We'll see."

"Oh, my heart! I can feel it beating a mile a minute. I can't stand this, Riva, I can't. To think things should turn out this way. I can't believe it's happening."

"Go take your medicine and lie down," Riva said, her voice soothing. Margaret was certain she had their mother's weak heart, though all the doctors could find were nervous palpitations. "Everything will be fine."

"I hope you're right, oh, I hope you're right. But you'll call me after your lunch with Edison, won't you? I can't stand not knowing what's going on."

"Yes, I'll call you. Don't worry."

After a few more reassurances, Margaret hung up. Riva handed the receiver back to George, then sat back on the seat, watching the flow of interstate traffic around the limousine and the passing buildings without seeing them. It would be nice, she thought, if she could reassure herself.

5

The first thing Riva did when she reached the Staulet Building was to have her secretary call for a reservation at Commander's, as the city's premier restaurant was affectionately known.

She wished for the thousandth time that she had never agreed to the meeting with Edison. She should not have entered into any discussion with him on Saturday but only told him what she wanted and left him to do it or accept the consequences. That had been her plan, and it disturbed her to have it changed. However, there was no point in fretting over what could not be helped at this moment. She pushed all thought of it from her mind, concentrating on the problems at hand.

Staulet Corporation was an old company. It had had its beginnings just before the Civil War when Cosmo's great-grandfather had loaned money to a friend who was a cotton broker. The man had been a poor manager, and Staulet, though he came from a line of Creole aristocrats who scorned trade as a demeaning occupation, had taken an interest in the brokerage in order to protect his investment. He had discovered that he liked buying and selling, particularly when it came to parcels of land. It was he who had built Bonne Vie and also the folly in the middle of the pond. Though he had given his share of gold to the Confederate lost cause, being an astute man he had also shipped a considerable amount to England just before the blockade closed around the South. That money had enabled him and his son to prosper during Reconstruction, adding more land to their holdings.

By the time his grandson, Cosmo's father, had come of age, the company had owned vast amounts of acreage in sugarcane and rice. It had also acquired enormous holdings of Louisiana swampland, much to the amusement of its competitors. It was this Staulet who had conceived a passion for travel by ship and also for commercial shipping, the last due mostly to his interest in bringing home the treasures he had collected in the Orient. He had sold his ships when the airlines began to cut into his profits, but by then he had amassed the collection of Chinese porcelain he donated to the state museum on his death. Among his other acquisitions were the fine jade collection that was a feature of the Staulet Building's ground-floor entrance area and the great bronze Buddha that graced the folly at Bonne Vie.

It was Cosmo, however, who in the early fifties began to dabble in oil leases, turning the swamp muck the corporation had held so long into liquid gold.

Oil had played such an important part in Cosmo's fortunes that it had been hard for him to accept that it could decline. Riva was the one who had convinced him that the flush times of the oil embargo could not last, that he was dangerously overextended in that area. She took no credit for projecting the decline that followed, nor for recognizing that microprocessors were going to fuel the surge that would carry them upward to the next level of prosperity. She had discovered this last from listening to Noel. But by then, Cosmo had been in no mood to see or hear his son, much less heed his advice. Her contribution was that she had encouraged Cosmo to allow Noel to go ahead in France with the development of this technology and actively supported the use of the Asian connections Noel had made that allowed the electronic components to be built so cheaply. In this at least she could feel she had held father and son together instead of driving them apart. It helped.

The morning went by much too fast. It seemed to Riva that she had just gotten started when her secretary tapped on the door and put her head inside to tell her the limousine was waiting downstairs to take her to the restaurant.

Riva closed the file she had been working on and capped her pen. Putting both aside, she took her purse from the bottom drawer of her mahogany desk and checked her makeup. She was just standing up, brushing the paper residue, an inescapable part of paper-work, from the skirt of her coral suit, when the door opened once more.

It was Noel who stepped inside. He paused when he saw her standing, then closed the door behind him and walked into the room.

"On your way to lunch with Gallant?"

"As it happens, yes."

"I don't suppose you need reinforcements?"

She stared at him in surprise for an instant. If she hadn't known better, she would have thought he was offering her the protection of his presence. That was, of course, foolish. "I told you this has nothing to do with the corporation."

"So I understood."

"But you doubt it?"

"Did I say that?" His tone was irritable.

"No, of course not, that isn't your way. In fact, you say very little, so I am left to guess at what you mean. I assume you are afraid I will embarrass the Staulet Corporation by becoming too friendly with the man who will probably be our next governor, and maybe getting involved in the kind of private, under-the-table arrangements that lead to public indictments. I can tell you that is the furthest thing from my mind."

"And from Gallant's, I would imagine. I expect his interest lies more under the covers."

She hadn't blushed in years. Embarrassment for doing so now brought a snap to her voice. "Since mine doesn't, there's no cause for concern."

"There would be even less if this appointment was turned into a business luncheon."

"Are you so curious that you're inviting yourself to join us?" Saying such a thing was a calculated risk. She had to see Edison alone.

"I am trying, without apparent success, to put you on your guard."

"Save your breath. I'm always on my guard."

His face hardened. "Very true," he said, "I should have remembered."

He stepped past her desk to stand at the floor-to-ceiling picture window that flooded her office with light. Pushing one hand into his pocket, he stared out over the view of rooftops and isolated spots of greenery in French Quarter courtyards toward the great crescent bend of the Mississippi River. Beyond him through the glass, Riva could see a freighter easing along on the wide, muddy waterway, a container ship with its boxlike truck trailers loaded with goods for Africa or South America or some other exotic place. Coming from the other direction was one of the excursion boats built to look like an old-fashioned steamboat with red and white paint, double smokestacks, and a rear paddle wheel. Watching the two meet in the bend was like seeing the past and the present converge, then go opposite ways.

The day was bright and hot beyond the window, Noel was silhouetted against the sun-proof glass. His stance was relaxed, his shoulders under the excellent tailoring of his suit broad and square. Still, tension vibrated in the air between them, making Riva restless. It was not a new sensation; she should be used to it by now. She wondered sometimes if Noel felt it when they were together. He never seemed to, appearing instead so remote and self-contained that she longed to hit him, shock him, anything to break through the barrier he had erected between them.

She took a calming breath before she spoke. "I promise you I will do nothing to jeopardize the corporation. Now are you satisfied?"

"Do you think that's all I care about?" He asked it without turning.

"Not at all. I should have said that I will also do nothing to injure the Staulet name."

He gave a hollow laugh. "Oh, yes, the family name."

"Your father thought it important."

"I don't doubt it. I'm not my father, nor am I remotely like him."

"He . . . was a fine man."

"I don't need you to tell me that."

This was skirting too close to the pain of recent loss and also to old heartache. She glanced at her watch, deliberately making her tone dismissive. "I'm sure you don't. I had better go or I'll be late."

He turned to face her, an oddly intent expression in his dark eyes. "You're afraid of me, aren't you?"

"Don't be absurd! Why should I be afraid of you?"

The words were firm enough, but there was a panicky feeling in Riva's chest. Noel had always been sensitive to the emotional undercurrents that swirled beneath most conversations, most relationships. There had been times in the past when he had understood her fears and insecurities much too well. Such empathy now was something she could do without. She took a tighter grip on her purse and measured the distance to the door with her eyes, wondering if he would try to stop her if she started to leave.

"I don't know why, but you are. You can't bear to be in my company for more than a few minutes at a time. You speak to me as little as possible. You sit as far from me as you can at any table. If I enter a room, you make an excuse to leave it. You concoct elaborate plans so you won't have to ride in the same car. What is the matter?"

"Nothing is the matter. You're imagining things."

"Oh, sure. Tell me you aren't wondering this minute how you can get out of this room."

"I have an appointment!"

"You can't think I'm going to attack you, make violent love to you on your office floor?"

Startled, she met his gaze. The only answer that came to mind was the bald truth. "No. Never."

A soft sound left him, almost like the ghost of a laugh. His dark gray eyes lighted with a flicker of something that was gone so quickly that she could not be sure whether it was pain or passion or a combination of both.

She moistened her lips. "You . . . I have to admit you have ample cause to resent me. If it wasn't for me, everything would be yours—the corporation, the house, everything."

"You lived with my father for twenty-odd years. I, of all people, should know how hard you worked for what you gained."

There was a sting in that remark, and she felt it. Her tone acid, she said, "There was no question of work."

"I don't doubt it. I know my father would have given you anything you wanted, no matter what you did. The fact is, you became his right hand, someone he could not do without."

She lifted her chin. "Well, I didn't want or expect to be made co-owner of everything with you."

"You wanted it all?"

"I'm not so stupid. I know that was impossible under Louisiana law."

"Otherwise, you might—"

"No! No, I didn't mean that. I would have been perfectly happy with a reasonable income."

"Reasonable to you," he said softly, "being riches itself to anyone else."

It was useless to explain or to expect him to understand. She should have known it. She lifted a shoulder in a careless gesture. "Naturally, I didn't expect to live in a housing project and shop at garage sales."

"Instead, you are president and CEO of the corporation you helped build to its present position. What could be more natural, and right?"

"If you really thought that," she said as she watched his face for every changing nuance of expression, "you would have no reason to try to force me out."

"Exactly."

"Then what are you trying to do?" The question was abrupt, dictated by suspicion.

He rubbed a hand over his hair, then cupped the back of his neck. "What I started out to do was to clear the air between us. We have to learn to work together, you and I, somehow, some way. We can't do that without trust."

"I thought we had been doing it for six months."

"Does what we have been doing bear any resemblance to the relationship you had with my father as chairman of the board? Is there discussion between us, give and take, complete understanding throughout the decision-making process?"

She shook her head with slow reluctance. "Hardly."

"Then we haven't been working together."

"You realize that what you describe may be impossible for us?"

"I do," he answered, his tone carrying a hint of steel. "And if it is, one of us will have to go."

"Which one?" she asked, because she could not help it.

He walked to the door and held it open. His gaze was measuring and somber with regret as he looked back at her. "That's up to you."

He left her then. Riva stood for a long moment staring at the door he had closed behind him. Her hands were shaking; she noticed that fact without surprise. No one had ever been able to upset her carefully maintained equilibrium like Noel. Had the things he said been a plea or a warning? She could not make up her mind. Nor could she decide which possibility disturbed her the most.

It had grown hot with the advance of noon. The air was saturated with moisture so that breathing was difficult and clothing clung to the skin. On the ride to the restaurant, the acrid and oily exhaust of cars and buses crept into the car, and the glare of the sun off windshields and chrome trim was like facing a battery of spotlights. Stepping inside the door of Commander's, then, was like entering a cool shrine, one dedicated to quiet and luxurious ease and the pleasures of the palate.

The ritual of being shown to her table, of having the menu placed before her and her napkin shaken out and draped gracefully over her lap, was soothing. She approved of her location, a corner table in an upstairs room overlooking the courtyard. As pleasant as the tables in the court below might appear, with their wrought-iron and glass tops dappled by the shade of a huge and ancient live oak, it was much too hot outside for comfort. On the second floor she could have the coolness of air-conditioning as well as the illusion of being among the upper branches of the great oak, almost as if in a tree house. The dark green of the oak's foliage was repeated in the interior decor, adding to the effect.

Edison had not yet arrived. Riva was glad in a way, since she was late due to Noel's intervention. She disliked not being on time; to her mind, it indicated a lack of organization. That Edison had not put in an appearance did nothing to improve her opinion of him on that account, but she also suspected that his lateness came from a form of power play that she despised.

Her impression was confirmed when he arrived. Edison took charge at once, asking for the sommelier and ordering a bottle of Pouilly-Fuisse with a great deal of discussion about vintages and vintners. He declared himself starved and, after barely tasting his wine, opened the menu and summoned the waiter. Without consulting Riva, he began to outline a meal of five courses, including lobster for two. Riva tried to protest, but she was ignored.

"Excuse me?" she said in a louder tone, directing a firm gaze at the waiter.

The man turned to her with deference and a shadow of relief. "Yes, Madame Staulet?"

"My guest will have what he pleases, of course, but I would like the house salad, a crabmeat soufflé, and fresh blueberries."

The look Edison gave her held equal parts of astonishment and anger. Unruffled, she picked up her wineglass and sipped. He completed his order in brusque tones, then sat back in his chair while the waiter gathered up the menus and went away.

Edison continued to stare at her and then the anger died out of his eyes to be replaced by bemusement. He laced his fingers together on the table's edge and gave a shake of his head as he said, "I can't get over it."

"Yes?"

"I can't get over how much you've changed. I'm dumbfounded."

"No one stays the same."

"Oh, sure, but it's as if you wiped the slate clean and started over."

She should have remembered, Riva thought, that it was part of a politician's bag of tricks to be able to size up people. She smiled. "Are you suggesting that I've successfully obliterated my lower-class past?"

He shrugged. "Something like that."

"If so, it wasn't deliberate. I suppose I'm what's known as a 'tweener,' someone who no longer fits in his or her old life but isn't really comfortable in the upper echelons, someone not quite one thing or the other."

"You certainly look as if you belong in the higher reaches."

"I expect you mean that as a compliment, so I'll thank you."

"But still, I can't help remembering—"

The nature of his memories was plain from the leer in his blue eyes. She said coolly, "I never look back. It isn't profitable."

"Never?" he asked, his voice soft.

"Not if I can help it." She held his gaze, unflinching, for a moment, then deliberately changed the subject. "Where is Anne today? I suppose she's out campaigning for you?"

"She has a talk this evening at some ladies' club, but I left her on Royal Street, wandering in and out of the antique shops."

"She'll find better bargains out on Magazine."

"Bargains are the last thing she needs. We have enough old junk already."

"I happen to like old junk, as you call it."

He grunted. "Then that's the only thing you two have in common."

His attention had strayed. He was gazing about the rest of the restaurant, checking faces. A woman at a table close by smiled at him, and he automatically nodded in return, at the same time reaching to touch the knot in his tie and smooth his hair.

"A modern man, I see."

If he caught her dry tone, he failed to acknowledge it. "I grew up with old furniture, old dishes. I like things brand spanking new, with clean lines and no clutter and curlicues to catch dust."

"That's fallacy, you know. Dust shows up much worse on clear, flat surfaces."

"Since I don't do the dusting, it makes no difference to me."

"Exactly so," Riva said, and smiled as she watched him take her point.

"Are you baiting me?" he asked, scowling.

She lifted a brow, her green gaze as clear as mineral water. "How can you think that?"

"You always were bright. But we aren't here to talk about that, or even about Anne or antiques or dust. I want to know what you meant by threatening me."

"I thought I had made that perfectly plain. This meeting was not my idea, you know. I said all I intended to on Saturday."

"Did you now? I thought I answered you, too, but that's not the end of it by a long shot."

"Hardly. You must decide whether you will cooperate with me or risk the storm caused by the information I can give to the press."

His lips curved in a smile without humor. "The risk, as I pointed out before, isn't all mine. You won't go to the press."

"I've changed more than you know, believe me."

"And even if you did, it won't get you what you want, which, as I understand it, is to separate Josh and Erin."

"No," she said pleasantly, "but it will give me a great deal of satisfaction."

"I could give you satisfaction." His voice deepened suggestively. "If you play your cards right, I might even see my way to sending Josh out of town for a month or so."

The arrival of the waiter with their salads prevented the necessity of a reply. Riva sat back with her lashes lowered, striving for control. She dared not pick up her wineglass, for her hands were shaking again. She hated confrontation, hated the emotional upheaval of the past few days. What had happened to her staid, even life?

She wondered if it would not have been better to ignore the relationship between her niece and Edison's son. Maybe she was overreacting; maybe it would come to nothing. She might even be making matters worse with her protectiveness. Certainly she was making things worse for herself.

Nevertheless, she could not stop. Having gone this far, she would see it through. She was also going to make a few things clear to Edison Gallant.

When the waiter had gone, she leaned forward. "Listen to me very carefully," she said, "because I'm not going to say it again. I will not, repeat, not, go to bed with you."

"Oh, I think you will," he said, and spearing a forkful of salad, he thrust it into his mouth and crunched down on it. He chewed steadily, then smiled at her.

She picked up her own salad fork, prodding a piece of crisp spinach for which she had no appetite. "Has it occurred to you," she mused, "that there is another—shall we say scandal for want of a better word?—that I could mention if I chose. All I need to do is drop the merest hint. Members of the press are the best detectives in the world, with the best sources. I would not have to be directly involved at all."

He swallowed hard, the color receding under his tan. "What do you mean?"

"I believe you know."

"You bitch."

The virulence of that hissed term startled her. She met his gaze across the table and saw terror and murderous rage reflected there. A chill moved through her. On its heels came puzzlement. She had been thinking of Beth and of Edison's part in her death. The incident could be damaging to him, but not nearly so much so as his bigamous marriage to her. After all, there was no proof. An instant later, she was assailed by the conviction that Edison was not thinking about Beth at all.

Her eyes narrowing, she said, "There are a great many things I could call you also, none complimentary."

He was not to be goaded into further indiscretions. His features smoothed into a meaningless smile as he sat back in his chair. He watched her for a long moment before he said, "I underestimated you."

"An error, I hope, you will not make again?"

"It's unlikely. How much do you know? Exactly how much?"

She had the feeling she knew nothing at all, though she didn't intend to say so. "Enough."

"Knowledge can sometimes be dangerous."

The words were quiet. That was what made them suddenly frightening. "Often," she said.

"You should know that I intend to be governor, no matter what I have to do, no matter who gets hurt."

She lifted her chin. "Can it be that you are now threatening me?"

"Only trying to come to an understanding."

It was a moment before she spoke, then she said, "Isn't this all getting a little out of hand? What I asked of you is such a simple thing."

He gave a slow shake of his head. "You're interfering in my life."

"You interfered in mine long ago, or this would not be necessary."

"That's something I don't understand. Just why is all this so necessary to you?"

"I told you. I don't want you for my niece's father-in-law."

"Mighty concerned, aren't you?"

"I have to be. Margaret is no match for you, and you are unlikely to listen to Boots." She held his gaze, refusing to give an inch.

"Yeah, Boots. We have family connections already, you and I. That makes Erin and Josh what? Fifth, sixth cousins? There's no harm in that."

"It's too close for my liking. Anything is too close."

He leaned toward her. "Well, get this straight. I'm not doing a damn thing to break up whatever fun Josh may be having with his little cousin. If he's giving it to her, fine, more power to him. It proves he's my son. And I don't give a shit how big you think you are or how much weight you think you swing. If you value your sweet ass, you'll be mighty careful what you say about me and who you say it to. Play games with me, lady, and you'll get hurt. Or dead."

Riva stood up with grace and dropped her napkin onto the table. "What a way you have with words," she said with cool irony as she turned from him, "and with women. Oh, yes, you're a real lady-killer."

"Riva," Edison said in strangled tones. "Riva!"

She did not look back as she walked away. He sounded furious or frightened. She heard the clatter of silverware as he pushed violently from the table, getting to his feet. He was coming after her.

That he would actually pursue her through a public restaurant was unbelievable. She increased her speed just short of breaking into a run and wove among the tables. She heard Edison's footfalls, his muttered apologies as if he had stumbled against a diner. Ahead of her were the stairs. She hurried down them and emerged in the lower room filled with people enjoying sumptuous lunches. There were probably friends and acquaintances among them, but she did not pause to look as she made her way toward the entrance door.

The maître d' was at the reservations desk. Riva signaled to him in breathless haste. "I'm sorry, but I have to go, a small emergency. Mr. Gallant will take care of the check."

The man nodded with aplomb, as if it was quite usual for a woman of Riva's standing to run pell-mell from the establishment. Then he moved to intercept Edison.

Riva pushed through the heavy front door and out onto the side-walk. Her driver, George, did not fail her. He was waiting in the limousine at the curb on the cross street opposite the restaurant. When he saw her emerge, he put the limousine in gear and swept toward her through the intersection, swinging to a halt with a flour-ish. She opened the door and stepped inside. The limousine pulled away, away from Edison standing under the marquee of Com-mander's with his napkin still in his hand and the maître d' holding one arm.

Her escape, leaving the leading Democratic candidate for gov-ernor behind her looking foolish, should have been a triumph. In-stead it felt like a mistake.

6

To all appearances, Anne Gallant was shopping for antiques. She wandered in and out of the shops along Royal Street, crossed over to Chartres, then doubled back and came up Royal once more. She picked up pieces of porcelain and silver and put them down again, trailed her fingers over satinwood and ebony tabletops, and listened with a smile of bemused appreciation to the mellow chime of a clock that had kept the hours in the private rooms of Louis Quinze. She wasn't looking for anything in particular, unless it was a piece of jewelry, traditional sop to the feelings of injured wives. What she was doing was waiting for adventure.

It was a game she played with a "what if" scenario. What if she should be kidnapped and put on a ship making for some foreign port? What if a mafia don should come along and scoop her up in his black limousine? What if a door in a wall should open and a handsome man in the costume of a hundred and fifty years ago pulled her into one of those hidden courtyards and into the past?

It was purest fantasy, of course. She didn't expect anything to happen to her. Why should it? It never had. And even if it did, she knew very well she was too uptight, too much aware of the consequences, to enjoy it.

Regardless, there was nowhere quite so satisfactory for her private game as the New Orleans French Quarter. So much that was dangerous and mysterious had happened in this place once known as Sin City, also the Town Care Forgot, and lately, the Big Easy. "Let the good times roll" was as much a philosophy as a slogan in New Orleans. It seemed that anything was possible there.

Edison didn't approve of her explorations alone, though she thought it was less concern for her safety than for what unsavory situation she might get herself mixed up in. She thought that he did not actually forbid the outings because he was sometimes just as happy to get her out of the way.

New Orleans did have a reputation for seaminess, particularly the French Quarter. There were side streets she avoided in daylight and would not have ventured down at night for the world. The fact was that she liked the faint feeling of risk. Not that she ever felt it on the main streets such as Chartres, Royal, and Bourbon; there were too many tourists and police patrols for that.

She loved the Quarter: the smells of cooking seafood and caramelizing sugar from its many restaurants; the sour tang of mustard from the carts of hot-dog vendors; the whiff of greenery and flowers from hidden courtyards; and the scents of old books, antiques, potpourri, incense, and love oil from the varied shops. And always the smell of the river, that gentle overlay of damp and mud. The contrasts of the Quarter were fascinating: the fern-hung balconies railed with lacelike wrought iron crowded against run-down joints where practically nude men and women danced on the tables; the luxury hotels standing beside dim and dingy bars dedicated to the preservation of jazz; the pristine walls of an old convent or cathedral not so far away from a neon decorated hole-in-the-wall selling sex toys.

New Orleans, it seemed to Anne, was alive in a way so few places dared to be. It was like an elderly woman who has lived not too wisely but well enough to have interesting memories; who sometimes dressed herself up for company, but if everything was not quite perfect, if her lace was a little torn or her shoes grubby, she gave it not a thought. She took her pleasures as they came, saw they came often, and expected others to do the same. She was as she was. People could like her or leave her alone. It was, perhaps more than anything else, that lack of self-consciousness that brought Anne back again and again. She had so little of it herself that it was limitlessly seductive.

In her ramblings, she passed by the old beveled-glass and mahogany doors of Lecompte's, Dante Romoli's restaurant. She and

Edison had eaten there before on their trips to the city, and it had always been an occasion to remember. The restaurants of New Orleans, of course, were second only to those of Paris in that combination of zestful appreciation for food and the consummate formal service that is gratifying to some but intimidating to many. Lecompte's was among the best of them.

Anne saw Dante on the sidewalk across the street a few minutes later. He was just going into what appeared to be a television station, as unlikely as such a place seemed there among the tourist shops and historical-research collections. She was proud that she had recognized him after only being introduced once. She had always been terrible at putting names and faces together, a bad trait in a politician's wife. Her success now was most likely because she had been thinking about him.

A display of antique jewelry in the window of a shop across the street caught her eye. She waited on the curb for a bus and a tourist buggy to pass, then walked over to inspect it. There were some interesting pieces in the window, but most were of the Art Nouveau period, and her special interest was Victorian garnets and jet.

She had started to turn away when, just down from where she stood, Dante Romoli emerged. Someone inside the television building was still shouting after him. He turned back to answer with his hand on the open door.

"I still say you'd be a natural," the man inside called. "Nobody in New Orleans knows as much as you do about food."

Dante shook his head. "My Cajun accent can't hold a candle to Justin Wilson's, and Paul Prudhomme has me beat hands-down for size. Besides, I'm a restaurateur, not a chef!"

"With your looks, you could put 'em both off the air with sheer sex appeal. And I know you can cook because I've heard about the fancy omelets you whip up for the sweet young things who stay for breakfast. You could always do one of those."

"Sure I could, if you bring your cameras to my apartment," Dante bantered.

"You mean it? We can come and film?"

"The devil, no! I don't go in for that kinky stuff."

There was the sound of a curse without heat. Dante grinned as he let the door close and swung away.

Anne saw that he was going to come toward her. With a moment to collect herself, she summoned her most gracious smile. She meant to nod in greeting and pass on by, as with any chance encounter. Instead, she met his dark eyes, alight with laughter and friendliness, and came to an abrupt halt.

"Mrs. Gallant," he said as he neared, "good morning."

"How are you?" She offered her hand since there seemed nothing else to do. She thought for a moment he was going to lift it to his lips and was aware of a slight disappointment when he merely tipped his head in a Gallic gesture nicely combining respect and appreciation.

"How did you manage to escape?" he asked when they had exchanged the usual courtesies. "I thought your whole time campaigning was spent speaking at club luncheons and shaking hands outside mills and plants."

"Somebody made a terrible mistake, I'm sure, but I had a free morning." Her smile was warmer than it might have been. His ready understanding of her feelings gave her a distinct and unusual feeling of rapport. There was also the unwavering intensity of his dark gaze, which made her feel that she had his whole attention.

"Are you just strolling?" he asked. "Or were you going somewhere in particular?"

"Oh, I was just looking, mostly at antiques. There are so many lovely old things along here." Anne made a vague gesture up and down the street.

"I'd be glad to help you find anything, if I can. I have a fair knowledge of who carries what in the shops."

"I was looking at jewelry," she said, then, compelled by a need to seem more serious in her pursuit of antiquities, added, "also a chair, maybe a rocker in wicker."

Dante frowned. "The jewelry is easy, but the chair may be a problem. Wicker rockers weren't known for lasting. But I know this little place over on Magazine that might have one."

"Really?" She had no thought of going, but having introduced the rocker, she had to sound interested.

"My car's just around the corner. I'll run you over there."

"Oh, I couldn't let you go to the trouble, Mr. Romoli, though it was kind of you to offer. If you'll just give me directions—"

"Call me Dante. And it's no trouble, *chère*. No trouble at all."

Before she knew it, Anne was being handed into a low-slung red Alfa Romeo. It crossed her mind as they pulled out into the street from the parking garage that she was being criminally stupid, getting into a car with a strange man. She could just imagine what Edison would have to say about it. She wasn't sure how it had come about, really, but she wasn't afraid. Dante Romoli inspired confidence with his easygoing manners and courtesy. That it might be an act was possible, but she didn't think so. Anyway, he was a friend of Riva Staulet's, wasn't he? He had to be respectable.

She could not be sure, however, that he was being so helpful without a purpose. She had developed an instinct over the years about people who wanted something. She didn't like to think that Dante was trying to use her to get to her husband; still, she knew it was possible. But that was all right. Now that she was with him, there was something she wanted from him, too. Perhaps it had been there, at the back of her mind, from the moment she saw him.

She wished she was dressed a little nicer. Her blue denim skirt worn with a red tank top under a chambray shirt was fine for the warm day, but even the red-banded straw hat she wore with the outfit failed to make it dressy enough to match Dante's white silk shirt and perfectly cut gray slacks. His tie and suit jacket lay on the backseat of the car and his shirtsleeves were rolled to the elbows; still, his appearance had the daunting elegance lent by European tailoring.

It was silly to be worrying about such things, of course. In a moment Dante Romoli would drop her off in front of an antique store, then go about his business. Since it was unlikely anyone would see them together, it made no difference how she looked.

It was as much to fill the silence between them as to take advantage of the opportunity that had been presented to her that Anne spoke. "Riva Staulet is an unusual woman. Have you known her long?"

Dante sent her a glance edged with speculation. "Quite a while, but not as long as your husband, I think."

"Oh, you're wrong. Edison only met her this weekend."

"Sorry, my mistake."

There was something in his voice that disturbed her. Anne said, "It seems odd that our path has never crossed hers. I mean, we must have attended some of the same events, such as charity balls, parties in Baton Rouge, inaugural balls at the governor's mansion, and so on."

"That's the way things happen," Dante said with wry acceptance. "From now on, you won't be able to move for tripping over each other. Or me, for that matter."

"That will be nice."

He sent her a look bright with amusement. "Spoken like the polite candidate's wife."

"No, no, I mean it," Anne protested, then, as he laughed out loud, realized she was being teased. It was a novel sensation. It had been a long time since anyone, other than her son Josh, of course, had been interested enough in what she thought and felt to tease her.

"Seriously," Dante said, "it will be a pleasure to see more of you and your husband, though I doubt campaigning will leave much time for socializing." As she smiled in agreement, he went on, "Your husband's chances of winning seem good."

"Yes."

"Contributions are critical up to the last minute, I know, but I expect his campaign chest is in good shape, considering the number of his supporters."

"I suppose so, though there's always room for more."

"I can't think what he could do for a company like Staulet Corporation in return, though."

"Nor can I," Anne answered in firm tones. "Or what Staulet Corporation can expect."

They had stopped for a red light. They looked at each other across the width of the car. A smile started in Dante's eyes, and Anne felt one slowly curving her own mouth. They laughed at exactly the same time.

The light turned green, and Dante set the Alfa Romeo in motion again. "All right. I won't pump you about your husband if you won't pump me about Riva."

"I can assure you it would do no good. I don't know anything. I must say that I admire your loyalty to Mrs. Staulet."

"You stonewalled pretty well yourself."

"I'm sorry; it becomes second nature."

"No need to apologize, *chère*. It's really no business of mine what took place between the two of them."

"Mrs. Staulet didn't—"

"No, she didn't say, beyond the fact that they would be having lunch today, and I suppose she would have if she had wanted me to know. It's just that—well, I was there at the rally, and I'm as curious as the next person."

"I know what you mean. Edison didn't care to discuss it, either." Unconsciously, Anne massaged her left wrist and the bruise that marred the pale skin there. Dante followed that gesture for a brief instant before he looked away.

"I'm sure it's just business," he said, his voice carefully neutral.

"No doubt," she agreed, also without inflection, then changed the subject.

They spoke of the state economy, the hotel where she and Edison were staying, conventions, and the world's fair held in the city a few years back. They were still talking when they reached the shop on Magazine, so Dante parked his car and went inside with her. They wrangled in a friendly fashion over the merits of the Victorian furniture she liked—which she called solid and beautifully carved and he labeled overweight and overornamented—and the early French Louisiana country pieces he preferred—which he said had elegant simplicity and she insisted were too plain.

Anne watched the man with her. She watched the way he touched the woods and the velvet and silk coverings of the pieces of furniture they passed, as if they were alive. When he turned his head, she stared at the way his hair lay in thick crisp waves against his scalp and the neat, flat shape of his ears. She studied the openness of his face and looked for the sudden leap of laughter in his eyes. It was addictive, she discovered. She could not stop looking at him.

They found a wicker rocker, but, thankfully, it needed too much repair for Anne to consider buying it. In the search, however, she came across a bronze cherub with vine leaves in his hair and his arms full of grapes, like a young bacchanal. It was a lifesize garden statue from some old garden and only semirestored so that much of the verdigris remained. She loved the little bronze boy on sight.

It was Dante who bargained with the store owner for a considerable discount, then carried the paper-wrapped statue out to the car and laid it with care on the backseat. Naturally it was impossible, after that, to refuse his invitation to lunch.

Since Anne vetoed anywhere fancy, they went back to the Quarter to Ralph and Kacoo's, where they ordered plates of crawfish, which was in season.

And they talked some more, covering every subject under the sun. The crawfish set Dante off about his Cajun heritage. With a little prodding, he told her about what it was like to grow up in the midst of dozens of uncles, aunts, and cousins and among the rivers, canals, and lakes; about fishing, hunting, and trapping when he could find the time; about dancing at weddings on Saturday nights and going to mass on Sunday mornings. His mother, he said, had not been able to speak English until she started going to school, and it always deserted her when she was angry. When she had died, his father, an Italian with ties to the vegetable stalls in the French Market, had moved back to New Orleans. It was at the French Market, where the great chefs came personally to pick out the freshest fruits and vegetables for their menus, that Dante had begun to be interested in food. That, and working as a busboy at the old Lecompte's after his father was killed in a brawl.

For the most part, however, it was Dante who asked the questions, about Josh and his ambitions, about her duties as a political hostess, about how she liked them and why she didn't. When he had teased her about a half-dozen things, from her refusal to take off her hat and show her flattened hair to her finicky method of eating crawfish, she retaliated by ribbing him about being a TV chef, admitting she had overheard the offer and his reply. She didn't mention the pretty young things for whom he made breakfast omelets, however; that was getting a bit too personal.

They had finished eating and were sipping the last of their vin ordinaire, when he suddenly set his glass down and reached out to take her left hand. In a smooth motion, he turned it over, exposing her bruised wrist.

"What happened, *chère?*" he asked.

Anne felt the rush of color to her face. She tried to draw her hand away, but could not. "It's nothing, really."

"I suppose," he said with irony, "that you hit it on the door."

"Something like that." She could not meet his eyes as she agreed. She should be annoyed at his prying, she knew, but somehow, without her quite noticing how, they had gone beyond that. Besides, there had not been so much warmth and concern in her life that she could rebuff it easily.

"You don't like giving speeches, you don't like being a political hostess, and you live with a man who apparently mistreats you. The obvious question is, why do you stay?"

"Well, there's always been Josh. A boy needs a father when he's growing up, and Edison is not really so bad at that."

"Josh is grown now."

"Too, it would do so much damage to Edison's career. I would hate to be responsible for ending his chance to be governor."

"I can see that as a reason for him to treat you gently, not for you to take abuse."

"Maybe. Then there's how Edison would take my leaving to consider. He wouldn't accept it without a fight, and I'm afraid it could get . . . ugly. Besides, most of the lawyers I know are his friends and colleagues or else his political connections. It would be hard to find someone I could trust to protect my interests, someone I could be sure that Edison would not get to and influence in some way."

"I see that you've at least thought about ending the marriage."

"Oh, yes, I've thought about it." She met his gaze then, and her own was pensive. "But I was brought up Catholic, and though I've strayed from it, since Edison has always insisted that I go to his Protestant church with him, it's hard to get away from the lessons on the sacred nature of the marriage vows that I learned as a child. Besides that, marriages are peculiar things. They begin with love of one sort or another, and whether it lasts or it doesn't, they take on a life of their own. Tearing one apart is a little like killing something. I've just never quite been able to bring myself to start the process."

He brushed his thumb over the bruise with a feather-light touch. "You have to do what you think best, I guess. I'm sorry if I seemed to be prying into what doesn't concern me."

"No, no," she murmured, nearly incoherent. His concern and understanding were like balm to a wound she had not, until that moment, admitted to herself that she had.

"If there's ever anything I can do, *chère*, I hope you will let me know."

Tears pressed with a bitter ache behind her eyes. She might have allowed them to fall from sheer weakness brought on by sympathy if she had not been distracted by the electric warmth of his fingers on her skin. Somewhere inside her she felt a strange giving sensation, as if some portion of her being had shifted. It was a disturbing feeling, one she was not sure she liked.

"You're a phenomenon in your own right," she said without looking up from their linked hands, "a truly kind man."

He released her. "No, I'm not. If you listen to Riva, I have a colossal ego, the kind that makes me think I have to help everybody who comes along."

"I don't believe that."

He gave a slight shrug. "It may be true, I don't know. I just like people and hate to see them hurting."

"There must be plenty who take advantage of you."

"Sometimes, though I'm no sucker. At least, I don't think I am. I know what some people are like; I also know that some just need a chance. I expect the best, and usually that's what I get."

Anne had heard Edison say that last line before, though he had been speaking of things rather than people. They were entirely different, Edison and this man. Edison was so fair and Dante so dark. Edison dominated her with his superior height, while Dante was only three or four inches taller and spoke to her as an equal.

Edison talked of himself, whereas Dante's interest was in his companion. Edison looked for people's weaknesses; Dante for their strengths.

But Edison was her husband, and the morning had somehow slipped into the afternoon.

"I had better go," she said.

"Yes, of course," Dante said, and signaled for the waiter. "I'll run you over to your hotel."

"There's no need," she protested. "I can walk."

"You could, yes, but don't you think that chunk of bronze you bought might get a bit heavy?"

"That isn't a chunk of bronze, I'll have you know, but a valuable work of art!" She followed his lead back to their bantering with gratitude for his sensitivity.

"In that case," he said promptly, "you don't want to risk it by dragging it about the streets, now, do you, *chère*? I'll take you to the hotel doors and consign your statue to the care of a hefty bellman. He'll only drop it once or twice, I'm sure."

She was relieved to know that he didn't intend to go with her into the hotel. Meeting his steady gaze a moment later, however, she realized he knew that, and she was ashamed.

Dante paid their check. As they left the restaurant, he said, "I never did ask you what you mean to do with your little bronze man."

"Cherub," she corrected. "I have a garden room at home. There's a place for him under a palm tree, one of those Victorian parlor palms. But I wish I had a courtyard for him like some of those tucked away here in the Quarter. They've always fascinated me."

"Have they?"

There was a thoughtful inflection in his voice as he unlocked the car door and held it for her to enter. In reply to it, she said, "They're so hidden away, like private pleasures."

"Now that," he said when he had walked around and settled into the driver's seat, "is a provocative statement if ever I've heard one."

Heat flooded her face. "I didn't mean—"

A grin tugged the corner of his mouth as he cut her short. "I know, *chère*. Have you ever been in one—courtyard, I mean?"

She refused to rise to his baiting. "Only those that are part of restaurants, such as Brennan's or the Court of Two Sisters."

"Then you're in for a treat. My apartment has one."

He sat waiting with his hand on the key in the ignition. Anne stared at him, meeting the liquid blackness of his gaze with suspicion burgeoning inside her. She wished she knew what was in his mind instead of having to guess, wished that she had not been quite so sheltered during her married life so that she would know how to handle situations like this.

She checked such thoughts with an effort of will. There was nothing in Dante's face to cause them, nothing at all. If he could accept that she had meant nothing salacious by her remark, then she could extend the same courtesy to him.

She tested a smile. "I would love to see your courtyard."

It was located behind a house on one of the quiet back streets of the Quarter that Anne had always avoided. Dante called the place to which it was attached his apartment because he lived in the upstairs portion and used the lower floor as an office, but it was actually a house. It had a balcony skirted with black-painted wrought iron, pedimented doorways, thick wooden shutters that actually opened and closed, and a bronze plaque attesting to its historical past and, therefore, its present value. To reach the courtyard, it was necessary to go through a tall and solid door set into a brick wall, then down a narrow flagstone passageway edged with ferns and impatiens.

Dante left Anne in the courtyard while he went to ask his housekeeper to make coffee for them. She watched him disappear under the upper gallery that ran around the building and ascend the steps leading up to that railed overlook. After a moment, she heard the voice of the black woman who took care of him raised in cheerful compliance.

She gave a slight shake of her head. Not only was there a housekeeper present, but in the ultimate gesture toward honorable conduct, Anne was not, apparently, to be invited into the house. She had to smile at her suspicions.

It was warm in the court with the sun pouring down into it, heating the moss-edged bricks and slanting across the rosy brick walls. The heat was tempered somewhat, however, by the spreading shade of a pin oak and a golden rain tree and the quiet trickling of a tiered wrought-iron fountain. The green and white leaves of caladiums and the soft gray of dusty miller made cool patches here and there, while color was added by the crisp pink of begonias and more impatiens. Circling the tree trunks were dense stands of dark green aspidistra, while sheltering under the oak was a wooden perch holding a brilliant green parrot with a yellow head and touches of salmon-red and dark blue on its wings.

Anne walked over to the bird. Softly she said, "Hello there."

The bird sidled closer, cocked its head, and gave a wolf whistle of piercing clarity. "Hello, pretty girl," it said.

Anne laughed, enchanted. She reached to touch the parrot, but it sidestepped away, pausing just out of reach to eye her with orange-rimmed black pupils that contracted and expanded in some odd parrot rhythm. She talked to the bird for a few minutes more, then turned away.

There was a pair of chairs webbed with narrow white plastic and a marble-topped white metal table near the perch. Anne moved to one of the chairs and sat down, gazing around her. Somewhere nearby could be heard the sound of traffic, but it was only a distant murmur, no more disturbing than the soft breeze that rustled the treetops. A cardinal flitted to the fountain and took a drink. The wafting breeze brought a breath of gardenia fragrance from an eight-foot-high shrub at one end of the house. Anne leaned back in her chair. The parrot made a small clicking noise with its tongue and ruffled its feathers while fussing quietly to itself. With the gentle tinkling of the fountain, it was an oddly slumberous sound. She closed her eyes, breathing deeply.

She must have dozed, for when Dante spoke beside her she started, disoriented, as she opened her eyes.

"It is peaceful here, isn't it?" he said.

"Very. And lovely. Thank you for inviting me."

He had brought the coffee tray himself. It held a small-scaled silver coffee service, a napkin-covered cake stand of old gold-rimmed china with a pattern of pink roses, Waterford glasses with iced mineral water, and a Waterford bud vase holding a single pink rose. As he set the tray on the table beside her, he said simply, "My pleasure."

She sat up straighter in her chair. "I like your parrot. It's almost as charming as its master."

"He must have whistled at you. He likes the ladies."

"Also like his master?"

Dante shook his head with a grin. "Actually, it's because it happens to be my housekeeper who feeds him and cleans his cage and sees to him when I'm away. Me, he tolerates for the sake of the unsuitable things I feed him, such as these tea cakes." Dante removed the napkin from the cake plate to reveal the soft cookies. "He'll be joining us any minute for his share."

It was true. Using beak and claw, the shining green bird was climbing down from his perch. He arrived at Dante's chair in time to clamber up his pants leg and perch on his knee. As Dante handed the parrot a piece of tea cake, the bird stood on one leg and held the cake in the other claw while he nibbled at its edges in a shower of crumbs.

"Can he fly?" Anne asked.

"Oh, yes, usually. His wings are clipped for the summer, so he can stay outside now and then without venturing too far."

"What's his name?" As she spoke, Anne gestured toward the coffeepot to ask if she should pour.

"Please," Dante answered, then went on. "He's called Cracker Jack, after his favorite food. He has a sweet tooth that won't wait."

She filled the coffee cups with care and added milk. The byplay with the bird had eased any awkwardness there might have been between them. Also, there was a soothing normality in what she was doing, as if she had done it a hundred times before. She had, of course, but not for this man.

"I really do love your courtyard," she said, "and I especially like your house."

"I thought you might appreciate it. I'm attached to the place myself, been here for years. I used to rent a room in it, ages ago. When the widow who was my landlady died, I bought the place from her heirs. Riva helped me restore it."

"I might have guessed."

His dark brows drew together slightly. "Guessed what?"

"That it was Mrs. Staulet who helped instead of a girlfriend or a wife. Have you never been married?"

He gave a small shake of his head. "No time, I suppose, and too little opportunity."

"That can't be right," she said in disbelief.

"What do you think then, that I'm gay?"

She looked up at him, her eyes widening. "It never occurred to me. Are you?"

"No," he said, his face lighting as he laughed at her reaction, "though I'm sure there are those who think it's possible."

"Yes, well, there are some who apparently know otherwise."

He stared at her for a moment, then shook his head with an injured air. "If you are referring to what Miles from the TV station said, I deny it categorically. He makes me sound like a damned playboy! What I meant was that I've been so involved with the restaurant."

"Except for when you are taking Riva Staulet around."

"Yes." The word was flat. He looked away.

There it was again, the refusal to be drawn about that woman. Anne wondered what Riva Staulet had done to be worthy of such protective loyalty. In an odd way, she envied her for it.

"Forget I mentioned it," she said in subdued tones.

He lifted a brow as he turned back to her. "What? When you're showing such a flattering interest in my love life? To tell you the truth, I spent so much time working in the early days that women were an afterthought. Lately they all seem either too young and thoughtless or else so jaded by the ripe old age of twenty-five that they make me feel like a schoolboy."

"An altar boy, rather," she murmured.

"What!"

She gave him a delighted smile, one as near to an outright grin as it was possible for her to come. "I thought you would appreciate that."

He looked across the table at her for a long moment, then gave a pensive nod of his head. "I do, you know, in a way."

The understanding between them seemed, for that brief instant, deep and immutable. Then he shifted his attention to the pink rosebud that sat on the tray. He reached for it, dried the stem on a linen napkin, and began to remove the thorns one by one. When it was safe for her to hold, he presented it to her.

"For you."

Anne took the flower and lifted it to her face to inhale its sweet scent. It came to her as she breathed deep that everything Dante Romoli had done that day had been directed toward giving her pleasure. The shopping, the humor, the food, the hidden courtyard, his pet, the coffee and cakes, and now the rose, each was a small gift, a generous sharing of himself.

Slowly, almost against her will, the thought drifted into her mind that he would be no different in bed. He would tend to his lover's needs and wishes with perfect care and infinite concern. Never would he willingly cause pain or take his satisfaction at another's expense. The pleasure of his love would be his pleasure.

Shock at the trend of her reasoning rippled along her nerves. She set down the coffee cup she was holding so quickly that it rattled in the saucer. "Now it's really time for me to go," she said.

Dante did not argue with her but put the parrot back on its perch, then escorted Anne to his car and drove her to the Royal Orleans. Their good-byes were said on the sidewalk. They were somewhat strained since Anne kept looking over her shoulder, afraid that Edison would be returning at any moment. She did not forget to thank Dante for the lovely day, however, or to give him her hand a final time.

She had wished him quickly gone, but the moment his red car pulled away from the curb, she thought of a dozen more things she could have said, wished she could say. At the same time, she was exhausted and wanted nothing more than to lie down.

Edison was nowhere in sight. The hotel lobby was quiet, nearly deserted at this hour of the evening, since it was past the hour for most check-ins, not quite time for the cocktail crowd. Anne followed the bellman bearing her statue around to the elevators. Together they stepped inside. The doors closed, and she gave a sigh of relief.

The bellman looked at her, saying, "It's been a hot one today."

She agreed, though privately she wondered if she looked as overheated as she felt.

"Tomorrow'll be the same."

She nodded. Yes, it would, and all the tomorrows after that. But there would never be another day like the one just past. Never.

It followed, then, that there was no reason to tell Edison about it. Still, she had never kept anything from him before. One reason had been that she was always so afraid he would find out, anyway, and the consequences would be twice as bad. Another was that she had little she wanted to keep secret.

She wanted this day. She wanted it as it had been, clean and free and filled with laughter, instead of having it besmirched, turned into something that she must think back on with shame.

It was hers. She would keep it.

7

The young man came from nowhere. One moment Riva was leaving the Staulet Building on her way home, letting the heavy glass-and-polished-steel doors swing shut behind her as she moved toward where her car waited; the next he was blocking her way.

Riva stepped back, bringing her briefcase up as a shield. George, already getting out of the limousine to open the door for her, broke into a run toward her.

"Excuse me, Mrs. Staulet," the young man said quickly, "I didn't mean to startle you. But could I speak to you a minute?"

It was still a second before Riva recognized him: the young photographer from the political rally. She held up her hand to bring George to a halt. Her chauffeur backed off but did not return to the car, instead taking a stance with his hands clasped behind his back.

"What do you want?" Riva asked.

Her tone was not friendly and the look in her eyes something even less than that. While she waited for an answer, she surveyed the photographer from the top of his head with its straight black hair to the toes of his scuffed suede walking shoes. He had the kind of lanky build usually given to people who can and do eat anything they want, though his shoulders were square. His fair skin and blue eyes, with his dark hair, hinted at a touch of black Irish in his blood. The daring of the Irish was also in his makeup somewhere, for he was unintimidated by her appraisal.

"I tried to make an appointment through your secretary, but

apparently she has orders to discourage all press members. Using the name of the paper to get to people can backfire sometimes. Actually, my business was unofficial. It concerns your niece."

"I don't understand."

A rueful smile flickered across his face. "Neither do I, exactly. She's not the kind of girl I spend time with as a usual thing. But I've been looking at that picture I took Saturday and I can't get her out of my head. I would just like a chance to get to know her."

"Why come to me?" There was no relenting in Riva's manner. This was the person responsible for calling public attention to her meeting with Edison. He might really be interested in Erin; then again, he might not.

"Meeting your niece is beginning to look like one of those impossible-quest games. I found out that she's at Tulane, but if she has a phone number, it isn't listed. Your staff at home and here at work won't give it out, and they won't say where she lives. Her mother, when I called there, jumped down my throat, accusing me of being either a paparazzo or a pervert, or both. My last hope is to throw myself on your mercy."

"What makes you think I'll help you?"

"I don't know. I guess because you seem like a reasonable lady. Besides, you might think it's better to humor me than to leave me wondering why everybody's so protective of your niece."

He was intelligent, she had to give him that. Also nervy. She could hardly fault him for the last; it was a quality she admired, in moderation. "Erin," Riva said slowly, "is very open and trusting. She doesn't quite realize that the world is full of people who are users."

"And you think I'm one?"

"There's that possibility."

He nodded. "There is, at that. I can tell you I'm not, but I don't know that there's any way to prove it."

She had expected anger, belligerence, an attempt to persuade her. She was disarmed by his agreement and impressed against her will. On closer acquaintance, he was an attractive young man—a bit unformed yet, but attractive. A young woman might find his combination of rough-edged looks and confident manner compelling, if she happened to like the dark, intense type.

Abruptly she said, "On the other hand, Erin is certainly old enough that she doesn't need anyone to screen her dates. I won't give you her number, but I'll take yours. If she's curious enough, she can call you."

"If that's the best you can do—"

"It is."

He began to dig in his pockets for a pen. "I'll take it."

Inside the limousine moments later, Riva sat staring down at the card on which Doug Gorsline had written his name. Should she give it to Erin or not? She could not quite think why she had said she would, except that it had seemed like a good idea to widen her niece's circle of friends, especially her men friends. It might well be, of course, that the cure she was inviting would be worse than the complaint.

If that were possible.

With sudden decision, she tucked the card into her handbag. Then leaning her head back against the soft plush seat, she closed her eyes.

It sometimes seemed that she was always tired. The cause wasn't hard to find. For years she had juggled her position at the company, her duties as Cosmo's wife and caretaker of Bonne Vie as well as their other properties, and her social obligations. There was someone to help her at every turn, someone to cook and clean, make phone calls, place orders for repairs and refurbishments, and do the physical upkeep, but in the end the responsibility was hers. That had been true even before Cosmo became ill, and it was certainly true now. She enjoyed the life she led for the most part, but there were times when the houses and cars, the antiques and fine furnishings, the domestic staff, the secretaries, and especially the vast structure of the corporation seemed intolerable burdens.

She dreamed of being free. The urge just to get into her car and drive away was sometimes so strong that her hands itched to feel the steering wheel. She thought of going to Mexico and buying a house in some small village where she would be known as that crazy American woman who went barefooted and kept chickens like a peasant. She pictured a rough thatched hut on a beach on some Pacific island where she would lie in a hammock until the sun went down, then walk along the shore, barefoot in the sand. Crazy dreams.

A part of the problem was Cosmo's death. She was not over it, not really. The strain of that time, the sleepless nights, and the days of helpless watching as he slowly got on with the business of dying had taken more of a toll than she had realized at the time.

There were many who thought she must be relieved by Cosmo's death. They didn't understand. It was as if some support she had not known she was using had been taken away. More than that, there were many kinds of love, and losing any form of it was cause for grief.

Now there was this thing with Edison. The strain of it was beginning to show. She could see it and feel it.

Riva thought George had looked at her once or twice in his rearview mirror. He was like a watchdog, endlessly alert to her moods, her needs, her safety. Often she took him for granted, but not always.

When she felt his gaze on her once more as they turned in at the drive to Bonne Vie, she spoke without opening her eyes. "What is it, George?"

He spoke in a low baritone. "I hate to bother you, but my old lady called earlier. She says would you have time to talk to her for a few minutes when you get home? Miss Constance has given her a whole list of things she wants cooked for her two kids, things Liz never heard of in her life. She's willing to try most anything, but she has to have something to go by."

Constance. Riva had almost forgotten she was at the house. Perhaps it had been inhospitable, not to mention cowardly, to leave her alone for the day. Still, the woman was Noel's guest. Since he had not hesitated about going into the city to work, Riva had seen no reason why she should stay at home.

Meeting George's anxious gaze in the rearview mirror, she said, "I'll run down to the kitchen as soon as I change."

"Liz can go upstairs."

"That's all right. I know she'll be busy with dinner."

There had been a time when Riva had worried about the proper behavior toward servants, what they expected of her as a mistress, how she must conduct herself in order to retain the respect accorded to her initially as Cosmo's wife. Discovering that she had no aptitude for standing on ceremony, she had decided just to be herself. To her surprise, it had served her well.

In spite of the problems in the kitchen, dinner was superb. It was a light and simple meal, the kind Cosmo had liked in the heat of summer. There were chicken breasts baked with garlic and a medley of garden-fresh vegetables in salads and side dishes, plus Liz's famous quarter-sized biscuits.

"Where," Constance asked halfway through the meal, "is the chicken à la d'Albufera I ordered for the children?"

"There was some problem with a recipe," Riva answered. "If you can furnish the cook with one, she'll be happy to try it tomorrow."

"Otherwise not?"

"So it seems."

Constance lifted a brow. "What kind of cook do you have?"

"A very good one," Riva said pleasantly, "but American and Southern and New Orleanian."

It was possible, perhaps, that people did not often have the last word around Constance. There was surprise in the glance her son Pietro, who was seated on Riva's right, gave Riva from under his incredibly long lashes. She smiled at him, and a flicker of a grin quirked his mouth before he returned his attention to his food.

For an instant there was a compressed sensation in Riva's chest. She glanced toward where Noel sat, preoccupied, at the head of the table, though he spared a smile for his son. Noel's son. Cosmo's grandson. She would have to be careful or she would find herself growing attached to Pietro. That would not be wise.

Constance reclaimed Riva's attention. "Where is your friend Dante? I expected him to join us this evening."

There was something in the other woman's voice that made Riva look at her more closely. Constance was wearing a dress of flowing red silk with a surplice bodice that revealed a great deal of her warm Mediterranean tan and made a setting for her barbaric gold necklace. Her makeup could not be called ostentatious, but it was perhaps a little too much for a family dinner.

"You will see him tomorrow night, I expect. There is to be a benefit gala that I hope you will attend as my guest, and I'm sure Dante will be on hand. But most evenings he prefers to keep an eye on things at his restaurants."

"Restaurants?"

Riva explained about Lecompte's and Dante's other establishment on the lake.

"How fascinating, particularly this one of the more informal atmosphere. Perhaps I will visit it while I'm here, to be able to say what it's like when I return to Paris."

There was more than a hint of patronization in the other woman's tone, but Riva ignored it. "I'm not sure you'll care for it. It's directed toward a different crowd from what you must be used to, the college crowd. The food is excellent, but the music is on the loud side."

"I adore loud music."

"You must do as you like, then. You're welcome to take one of the cars, or George can drive you."

"What? Do you not wish to go? I would never leave so attractive a man to fend for himself night after night, particularly among beautiful and well-dressed women."

Riva shrugged. "Dante can take care of himself. Besides, most of those beautifully dressed women you mentioned have a man with them to fend off Dante."

"He's a ladies' man, then? He plays the field?"

"You might say so, when he has the time."

"And you don't mind?"

"It's no concern of mine."

Constance stared at her with a frown between her brows. Riva glanced from the woman to Noel, attracted by the abrupt movement he made as he reached for his water glass. He looked at her over the rim and in his face was both concentrated interest and irony.

Riva turned to Pietro, asking what he and his sister had done that day. She was regaled with the tale of a squirrel they had chased up and down the front lawn and of the ices flavored with strawberries that Liz had made for them and they had eaten in the kitchen. Tomorrow they were to go to the zoo; Papa had promised.

Riva looked down the table at Noel once more. A smile hovered at one corner of his mouth as he watched his children, but he made no comment. His amusement faded as he caught her glance.

"What about you?" he said. "How did your meeting go?"

He was speaking of her luncheon with Edison. She wondered if he had already heard of how she had fled from Commander's Palace with Edison on her heels. It wouldn't surprise her; New Orleans was, in some ways, a provincial town. In the business community everyone of importance knew almost everyone else, and the unusual attracted talk as surely as sugar water drew hummingbirds.

"It was . . . instructive," she answered finally.

"I take it you discovered that your interests and Gallant's didn't coincide."

He did know. And if the hard light in his gray eyes was anything to go by, she was going to have to find some explanation for him. Constance was interested also, for she had straightened in her seat and was looking from her former husband to Riva with her head tilted to one side.

Before Riva could frame an answer, however, the doorbell rang. The sound was grating, strident, as if the old-fashioned mechanism had been given an impatient twist.

The door was opened by a maid since Abraham was serving at the table. They heard the murmur of her greeting. Then a higher-pitched, demanding voice could be heard.

"Where is my sister? I have to see her at once. At once, do you hear!"

It was Margaret. Riva got to her feet, dropping her napkin on the table. By the time she reached the dining-room door, Margaret was halfway down the hall. Behind her was Boots, bulking large and red-faced in the dimness and carrying a suitcase.

"Riva, there you are," her older sister began at once. "I had to come. I swear, my heart hasn't stopped throbbing from the moment that man called. The very idea! I gave him a piece of my mind, then when Boots came home from work I met him at the door with my bag all packed. I've got to go down there, I told him. That's all there is to it, I've got to go."

"What man is this?"

"That photographer, the worm who dared to put that vile picture in the paper!"

"Oh, I see." Riva put her arm around Margaret, half in a hug of greeting and half to keep her from barging into the dining room. "Hello, Boots. Have you two eaten?"

Margaret gave a harsh laugh. "Eaten? How can I eat when my child's welfare is at stake? We didn't stop for anything, not even to use the restroom!"

"Then why don't you come upstairs now? We can talk, and a place can be set at the table for Boots. I'm sure he's hungry, even if you're not."

"He's always hungry," Margaret said with a shade of bitterness. "I'm not made that way. Things upset me so I can't eat a bite."

"Maybe you would like a cup of coffee?" Riva directed the other woman toward the stairs. Her sister's face was pale, making the fine lines of age stand out in stark relief. Her hair, cut short and tightly curled as if to hide the liberal streaking of gray, looked as if she had not combed it since she got up that morning. Her casual cotton pants and shirt were the same kinds of things she wore around the house, which was odd. Margaret usually made an effort to dress well when she came to Bonne Vie. It appeared that, for all the melodrama of her entrance, she was genuinely distraught.

"No coffee, not with my nerves in this state. But a glass of tea would be nice. With lemon and lots of ice."

Riva had tried before to point out that tea had the same effect as coffee, but Margaret could never be brought to believe it. They mounted the stairs with Boots panting along behind them. The maid had offered to take the suitcase Margaret's husband carried, but he had refused. When they reached the bedroom he and Margaret always used on their visits, he dumped his burden on a rack with petit-point holding straps. Muttering something about unloading the rest of their things from the car, he left the room.

"Oh, Riva," Margaret said, walking to the bed and dropping down to sit on its side. "I couldn't believe it when I saw that picture.

I had heard Erin talk about this Josh, but until I saw him with his arm around her, it never dawned on me . . . I was shocked, that's what I was, shocked! I've been trying to keep up my spirits, but my heart has been misgiving me all day. It's God's punishment, that's what it is. It's His punishment for what we did all those years ago!"

Riva stared at her sister. Punishment. The word echoed in her mind. That night, all those years ago, the night she had eloped with Edison, she had been afraid of God's wrath. Then, all those years ago, it had been a very real fear.

What she had done with Edison in the backseat of his car was wicked, or so the preacher had said in church. It was fornication, carnal knowledge, the forbidden fruit discovered by Adam and Eve. Rebecca, huddling against Edison's side, was fairly sure she knew why it was forbidden. Anything so powerful must be a great distraction from godliness, though most preachers, so far as she could see, were against it on general principle.

The exact degree of wickedness was confusing. Since there was no commandment against it, it must not be a sin exactly. Still, the preacher had said it would be punished and he must know. The only way to make things right was to marry Edison. But if she ran away with him, the shock when her mother heard of it might kill her. Edison could say what he wanted, but she knew her mother wouldn't be happy. If anything happened it would be her fault, and that would be a terrible punishment, indeed.

Why had she done it? Why had she let Edison make love to her? She hadn't intended to at all. She had just felt so sorry for him, and she had been taught to help those who were in pain. He was young and handsome and experienced in a way that made her vaguely uncomfortable. It had been exhilarating to have someone so sophisticated paying attention to her. Somewhere in the midst of her compassion, her own lack of experience and her new, surprising reactions had betrayed her. It had seemed impossible to draw back, and then it was too late.

She had expected the pain, she had read enough confession magazines to know about that. Still, somehow she had expected there to be more to it. There had been the faintest intimation of pleasure, a hint of relief, and then it was over. Edison had enjoyed it, or so he had said, though he had had all the labor and had groaned more as if he were in agony. She was left feeling messy and sticky and on edge. And afraid.

The ride to the Arkansas line took no more than a couple of hours. They stopped in some small town just over the border. Edison had the name of a man who would perform the ceremony, though Rebecca could not get it straight whether he was a preacher or a justice of the peace. They stopped at a service station to ask directions to the man's house. When they found it, they were met by a pack of hounds that sniffed around the car and lifted their legs at the tires. Edison would not get out but sat and blew the horn.

Considering that he was awakened from a sound sleep, the man was cordial enough. He looked hard at Rebecca's pale face but asked no questions after Edison handed him his fee in advance, a folded wad of cash. When the short ceremony was over, the man stood over them while they signed the marriage certificate. Afterward, his wife offered glasses of Kool-Aid and slices of pound cake. Edison refused, saying they had a long way to go before morning.

On the return trip, Rebecca sat staring at the trees along the road slipping past in the dark. It was over. She was married. There was nothing to be done about it now. She felt drained and cold in spite of the warm night. Finally she slept.

When she woke, dawn was graying the sky. The land was flat and filled with high waving grass as far as the eye could see on either side of the road. It was a moment before Rebecca could think what the grass was; then she knew. Sugarcane.

She sat up with a gasp. "Where are we?"

"Nearly home."

"What do you mean? This isn't the road home!"

Edison turned his head, and the grin he gave her was odd-looking in the greenish glow of the dash lights. "I did some thinking while you were asleep. I didn't want to listen to my uncle rant and rave about us getting married or have your mother crying all over us. It's too late to go back to Tulane this semester, and I've always wanted to live in New Orleans. We'll go down to the French Quarter, take an apartment, have us some fun. What do you say?"

"I want to go home!"

He scowled. "Your home is with me now."

"But I have to talk to Mama. She'll think something awful has happened to me. Margaret will know I didn't come home last night. She may have called the police already!"

His face changed, she saw that before he covered it up, though she wasn't sure what it meant. After a moment, he said, "I hadn't thought about that. You can call them from the next town."

"I don't have anything to wear. You don't, either."

"I can have some of my stuff packed up and sent. As for you, most of what you owned wasn't fit to wear, anyway. I'll buy you a new dress or two."

"Not fit to wear! It's as good as anybody else's." She jerked around in the seat to stare straight ahead.

"Not anybody who matters."

"Well, of all the things to say! I suppose you think my family doesn't matter."

"Not much."

There was a horrible feeling inside her as she turned her head to stare at the man behind the wheel. She didn't know him, she realized. She didn't know him at all. Tears rose behind her eyes, but she refused to let them fall. The hum of the car engine was loud in the quiet.

Edison flicked a glance in her direction, his gaze lingering on her breasts under the cheap cotton dress as they rose and fell with her rapid breathing. He reached out to squeeze one of the soft globes, and a lascivious sheen appeared in his light blue eyes. "Never mind. I have a feeling you won't be needing many clothes for a while, anyway."

He had been right.

They found an apartment on a French Quarter back street. It had not been quite as Edison promised, since rent was higher than he had expected. It was, in fact, one half of the upper floor of what had once been a fine old house before it was divided for rental. The windows shook in their frames, the paint was cracked, and the wallpaper was peeling in places; still, Rebecca rather liked it. By her standards, the rooms were large and airy and the back courtyard, even with its broken bricks and dry and rusty fountain, had charm.

The other tenants were a curious assortment. Next door was the elderly woman who owned the house, a widow who always dressed in black, kept cats, and was only seen after dark when she put out her meager garbage. Downstairs was a mulatto woman who had two alternating visitors, a white man at night and a black man during the day. Across from her on the lower level was a young man who was seldom seen since he slept all day and worked the night shift at one of the Quarter restaurants.

Edison made no effort to work at all. He spent his night hours prowling in and out of the bars of the Quarter and his days sleeping, dragging Rebecca into bed, or yelling into the phone at his lawyers. His uncle, it seemed, objected to footing the bill for the New Orleans escapade and was so furious over his nephew's failure to continue his education that he wouldn't even speak to him. Since his uncle was also the major trustee of his estate, Edison's allowance was cut in half. It would be reinstated in full when he registered at Tulane again. There was only enough money, so Edison said, for a change or two of cheap underwear and a couple of cotton shifts for Rebecca.

She intended to ask Margaret to send her a few things but was given no opportunity. When she called, Margaret screamed at her over the phone.

"You think you're smart, don't you, running off like that! You think you're in high cotton, strutting around like Mrs. Astor in diamonds and furs while I'm stuck back here with Boots! And Mama! I guess you know it nearly killed her when she found out you were gone?"

"I can see why, if you were yelling like you're doing now."

"Don't tell me how to handle Mama, Miss Priss!"

"No, but is she all right? Is she really bad?"

"I thought I was going to have to call the ambulance, I really did. Her lips were so blue they were nearly purple, and I expected every breath to be her last."

Rebecca bit her own bottom lip. "Let me talk to her."

"I don't think that's a good idea. It might upset her again, and she just this minute dropped off for a nap."

"I won't say anything to disturb her. You know she would want to talk to me."

If Margaret heard the pleading note in her voice, she was able to ignore it. "I really don't think it's a good idea. I have to take care of Mama now, you know. You might show a little concern for her health, too, instead of thinking of yourself and what you want."

"I suppose. I—I'll call again later, to see how she's doing."

"You do that," Margaret answered. She hung up without even asking where Rebecca and Edison were going or how they were going to live.

Somehow, Margaret seemed to think that Rebecca was settling into a life of wealth and ease. She could not have been more wrong. The apartment had a small table fan but no attic fan to alleviate the daytime buildup of the stifling heat of that interminable summer, and certainly not the air-conditioning unit Edison seemed to think necessary. Rebecca's habit of going out in the cool of twilight to sit on the back stairs leading up to their rooms, he found common.

Edison, who had never had to worry about buying food, begrudged every cent spent at the grocery store. At the same time, he sneered at Rebecca's pitiful efforts to feed them both for a week on two pounds of fatty hamburger and a couple of packages of noodles. He often flung his full plate into the sink, calling the food garbage, then slammed out of the apartment to eat elsewhere. Since he seldom returned before dawn, however, Rebecca could sit outside as long as she pleased. She at least gained a nodding acquaintance with her neighbors that way. Sometimes they even spoke, especially the widow.

The apartment, which had seemed so full of light when they first took it, had several dark corners in the kitchen and bath that were havens for dampness and insects. The widow next door gave Rebecca a kitten, which she said would help the problem as cats loved to catch roaches. Edison came home to find the kitten curled up on his pillow. Over Rebecca's tearful protests, he kicked it out the back door.

It rained every afternoon. Rebecca came to dread the rain, for the thunder would wake Edison finally, and he always wanted her then. It didn't matter that he stank of stale sweat and tasted of stale whiskey. Her protests irritated him, the least show of reluctance enraged him so that she was left with bruises more than once as he forced himself on her. When he bothered to think about her needs at all, he seemed to consider that the harder and faster he rubbed between her thighs, the more likely she was to catch fire. All she did was become so numb and raw that in desperation she urged him to get it over with quickly. That part, at least, was never a problem.

A week faded into two, then three. It was an afternoon in the middle of the fourth when Rebecca heard the cat. It was mewing in plaintive distress. The sound came from the back of the house from the old courtyard that was overlooked by the bedroom windows. Edison lay sprawled in sleep in the bedroom. The droning of the fan he lay under helped to mask the cat's cries; still, Rebecca grew anxious that the extra noise would wake him.

She let herself out the back door and hurried down the stairs. The mewing was louder outside. It was coming from the pin oak tree that grew in one corner of the courtyard. Rebecca walked under its spreading branches, then looked up.

The cat was on one of the upper limbs. It was the half-grown kitten the widow had given Rebecca. It clung in terror to its perch, too inexperienced and disoriented to find its way down.

The limbs of the old pin oak drooped low over the courtyard, but its trunk was slick and tall, without any low branches. Rebecca looked around for a ladder, a bench, anything to give her a boost up, but there was nothing. She tried talking to the cat, coaxing it to come to her, but its fear was too great for it to listen. Helpless and hating the feeling, she stood staring up at the trapped animal.

Somewhere in the south, thunder rumbled. A stray gust of wind swayed the pin oak, setting its heat-drooped leaves to clattering. The cat clawed its perch, howling.

Thunder, and soon it would rain again. Rebecca, standing there with her anxious gaze on the young cat, felt a suffocating tightness in her chest. It grew, pressing upward until it burned against the back of her nose in acid tears. She ached with it, and with the realization that she was as trapped as the cat and no more able to help herself than she was to help it.

"She's got herself in a fix, hasn't she?"

Rebecca whipped around at that half-humorous, half-sympathetic comment behind her. She faced a young man with wildly curling brown hair, olive skin, and the kindest eyes she had ever seen. He wore only a pair of cut-off jeans, and his eyelids were heavy, as if he had been asleep. It gave him a gentle look, yet there was strength in his features and in the well-defined muscles of his square shoulders. Her vision blurred as she stared at him. Concern rose in his face, and he reached out to touch her arm.

"Hey," he said, his voice soft, "nothing's that bad, *chère*."

Rebecca took a deep breath and brushed a hand over her eyes, forcing a smile. "No, it's just this stupid cat."

He lowered his hand. "For smart animals, they can be dumb sometimes. I told her not to climb up there when I let her out."

It was their downstairs neighbor, the young man who worked nights. She had seen him now and then in the evening as he went off to work and on Sunday going to or returning from mass. He always spoke a quiet and friendly greeting, and he always smiled.

"She's yours?" Rebecca asked. She almost added "now."

"I suppose. I found her prowling around my door a while back and made the mistake of feeding her. Now she thinks she belongs or, more likely, that I belong to her."

As thunder rumbled again, rolling closer, Rebecca turned to glance back up into the tree. "I wish there was some way to get her down."

Surprise flashed across his face. "Nothing to it. That's what I came out for."

He stepped to the tree trunk and put his arms around it, then swarmed up it with the agility of well-worn habit. In a moment he was lying across a thick limb and reaching down to pluck the cat from her perch. He swore under his breath as the cat turned and clawed up his arm and shoulder to his head, where she clung for dear life. Then wearing the cat like a hat, he swung down from limb to limb, hung for an instant from the lowest one by his hands, then dropped to the ground. He firmly detached the cat's claws from his scalp and cradled her to his chest, stroking her with soft murmurs.

Rebecca reached out to brush her fingers over the cat also. Her hand touched that of the young man, and she looked up. As she met his eyes, her lips curved in a smile of relief.

His gaze held hers for a long moment and a hint of color rose in his face. He swallowed. "My name's Dante. Dante Romoli."

The cat in his arms began to purr and rub her chin into the soft-looking curls of his chest hair. A laugh took Rebecca by surprise. She drew her hand back without haste as she gave Dante her own name.

A drop of rain fell on his shoulder. It was followed by another and another, which made fat, wet splotches on the old bricks under their feet. Then abruptly it was pouring down, a warm torrent. They broke and ran, separating as they neared the back stairs. At his own door, Dante halted, watching her. She stopped at the foot of the stairs to flash him a last smile.

"Thanks," she said, then whirled around and ran up the stairs, back to her apartment.

Edison was awake. "What," he said as she came through the door, "were you doing down there with that dago?"

Rebecca felt her heart contract in her chest. Edison stood naked in the middle of the floor with his hands on his hips and ice in his blue eyes. "The cat our landlady gave me was up in the tree and couldn't get down. Dante went up—"

"Oh, so you're on a first-name basis with him. What else have you two been doing while I was gone nights?"

"Nothing! This was the first time I ever said more than two words to him, honest. It was the cat that—"

"Don't give me that crap! I saw you pawing him. You're just like your sister, can't keep your hands off men."

"Beth?" she said in shock. "How can you say such a thing when she's—"

"Her being dead doesn't make her less of a whore."

"She wasn't like that, she wasn't! You ought to know, you're the only man she ever went around with besides her husband!"

"Poor jerk overseas, expecting to come back to an innocent bride, and what happens? She gets herself knocked up."

"By you!"

"It was a trick to get me to marry her, the stupid bitch. She practically threw herself at me."

Rebecca looked at him, at the defensive belligerence of his stance, the patchy redness of his face, the selfish light in his eyes. Inside her, the fluttery fear died. "You don't really believe that," she said. "You're just saying it to make yourself look better, to make yourself feel better because you know it's your fault she's dead."

He reached her in two strides. The blow caught her on the jaw, sending her reeling backward. She struck the wall, and a cry was jarred out of her. He was upon her then, dragging her up with a hand clamped on the front of her blouse. He shook her viciously, holding her against the wall.

"Don't ever say that again!" he said, his face twisting in rage. "Never!"

She could taste blood in her mouth. Her breasts ached from the tightness of his grasp on her blouse. But there was a white heat in her brain. From it she cried, "I won't, because I won't be here!"

It was almost ludicrous, the change in his face, as if it had never occurred to him that there might be consequences for the things he had said and done to her. Then he laughed. "Oh, sure, go running back home like a baby."

"It's better than being here with you."

Anger leaped into his eyes, then congealed there. He released his hold with a sudden open-handed gesture. "Go ahead, then. Nobody will listen to a word you say. Nobody is going to believe it's anything except the ravings of a little bitch who got her cherry stolen and didn't get the payoff she expected."

"Believe what?" Her knees were trembling. She pressed her hands flat against the wall for support.

"Oh, don't play games with me. I know that you know; I can see it in your eyes when you look at me. Why the hell else are we down here?"

What was she supposed to know? There was only one thing she

could think of. "I know you feel guilty about Beth, no matter what you say."

He was still, his gaze riveted on her blank face. After an instant, he said, "Yeah, that's it. I'm the one who told her she should get rid of the brat. I even told her how I had read this book that said how to do it. I as good as killed her and the baby."

"There was no need to run away, no reason to come down here. Nobody's going to put you in jail for it, though they should."

His eyes narrowed again. "Nobody's going to blame me, period, or have the chance to cut off the rest of my allowance over it. You're the only one who knows, and nobody's going to believe a word you say about anything."

"Because I ran off with you and got married?"

The sound that came from his throat was coarse, and his mouth twisted in a sneer. "That's just it, baby. You didn't."

Her head began to throb with a dull ache. Through her mind ran a sense of disaster so strong that she shuddered. Her voice a thread of sound, she said, "What?"

"We're not married. How does that grab you?"

"But the ceremony, the paper we signed—"

"They don't matter. I wasn't a free man. I married the youngest daughter of my dear mother's best friend last May. We didn't get along too well. She went back home to Mama and I went to visit my uncle, a temporary arrangement. That means that the ceremony I went through with you is invalid. Null and void. It doesn't count."

"You knew that all along."

He gave a careless shrug. "Of course I did. I'm going to be a lawyer."

"Why?" she cried. "Why did you do this to me?"

"I couldn't let you go around telling everything you know."

"I wouldn't have, ever. For Beth's sake."

"I couldn't count on that. Besides, I had a yen for you, a yen a taste or two wouldn't fix. You should be proud. It's not often I come back for seconds, much less thirds or more."

He was talking too much. There was something he was con-cealing behind his swagger and loud words; she could feel it. Still, the insight was pushed aside by the questions crowding in upon her.

"All this time," she said, "all this time, and we haven't been married at all."

"Living in sin. Hasn't it been fun?"

Sickness moved through her. "That was why you didn't want to take me home with you."

"How bright you are."

"I thought it was because you were ashamed."

"Of my hick country bride? Well, yes, it might have been a bit embarrassing."

It was the tone of his voice, superior and patronizing, that struck deep inside her. She covered it with a spurt of anger. "That would have been too bad."

"I never let it worry me." He turned on his heel and walked away into the bedroom.

He hadn't worried because there was no need. He never intended to take her home with him. She heard him moving around, dressing. Slowly, she allowed her legs to give way so that she slid down the wall to sit on the floor. She put her hand to her bruised cheek. It felt hot, already sore. Inside her was a solid ache too big, too deep for tears.

Edison came out of the bedroom a few minutes later with his extra clothes wadded under his arm. He stood over her, staring down. "The rent is paid for another month; the old witch next door made me give her two months in advance plus a deposit. You might want to think about staying. From what I've seen of Margaret, she's not going to want you bringing your troubles back home and upsetting darling Mama."

It was not concern that prompted the suggestion, she knew, but the desire to keep her from going back. Nevertheless, there was enough truth to it that it was a moment before she could speak. "Margaret's my sister. She won't turn me away."

He snorted. "You'll grow up one of these days."

She raised her head. Her voice weary, she said, "Just get out if you're going."

"Oh, I'm going, all right. But I could use a little piece first and I'm wondering if it's worth the trouble."

She stared up at him while deadly opposition rose inside. Something of it must have shown on her face, for he shifted, then answered himself.

"Probably not." He backed away a step, then turned and walked out the door.

She sat where she was as his footsteps faded away down the stairs and the Chevy ground to life and was driven away. Still, she did not move, but stared straight ahead, doing her best to think of nothing. Finally, there came creeping in upon her the thought of Beth dying in a pool of blood, laughing, caring, bursting-with-life Beth. And all for Edison Gallant, the man who had just left.

It was then the tears began, a flood of warm grief as relentless as the subtropical rain that drenched the courtyard outside.

8

"Mama's in the hospital."

"Oh, Margaret, is she bad?" Rebecca could feel the fear, like poison, running with the blood through her veins. Her clasp on the telephone receiver was so tight that the ends of her fingers were numb.

"She had another spell. Her heart just runs away with her. She hasn't been the same since Beth died and you ran off."

"I want to talk to her. I have to talk to her, Margaret."

"I don't think that's a good idea, not after what you just told me. She thinks you're married to a rich man who's going to take care of you for life. She's kind of got over you taking off and convinced herself it's a good thing that she doesn't have to worry about you anymore. You can't tell her different, not now."

"You mean you convinced her."

"What if I did?" Margaret demanded, her voice strident. "She needed something to ease her mind."

"Well, she has to know sometime it didn't work out. I have to come home."

"You can't do that!"

"What do you mean, Margaret? There's nothing else I can do! Don't you understand? Edison is gone."

"What did you do to make him go?"

"I didn't do anything. I told you, he tricked me!"

"I can't believe it, I really can't. Just think what people will say!" Margaret moaned. "They're going to believe there was never a marriage at all."

• 123

Rebecca took a deep breath and let it out. "I guess they will, but I can't help it. Edison's gone and he isn't coming back. The rent's paid for another month, but I don't have any money to eat, to pay bills. I have to come home!"

"I don't suppose you have the bus fare, either?"

"No. Oh, Margaret—"

"Just a minute, let me think."

The silence on the other end of the telephone line seemed to stretch forever. Rebecca expected any minute to hear the operator come back on and ask for more money. There was no phone in the apartment, of course. She had had to go to the pay phone at the grocery store down the street. Across from the store, two tough and grubby-looking guys with hair down to their shoulders were watching her. She lifted her hand to cover the bruise on her face and turned away from them.

"You could get a job," Margaret said finally.

"Doing what? And what am I supposed to eat while I do it?"

There was another silence. Margaret sighed. "All right. I'll send enough money for you to live on for a couple of weeks. Maybe Mama will be stronger then and you can come home."

"Wouldn't a bus ticket be cheaper? I know the last round of hospital bills took about all the extra money."

"I'll get it from Boots."

"You can't do that. It wouldn't be right."

"I don't see why not; he's my husband."

It was a moment before Rebecca could speak. "You and Boots got married?"

"Why not?"

"And you didn't let me know so I could come to the wedding?" Pain was thick in Rebecca's voice. She felt as if she were being cut off, shut away from her family.

"I don't remember getting an invitation to yours!" her sister snapped. "Besides, if you're as bad off as you say, you couldn't have made it up here for it."

"I might have, before Edison took off."

"It doesn't matter now. We have to do what's best for Mama."

With an effort of will, Rebecca pushed her own problems aside as she tried to look at things from Margaret's point of view. She said, "Mama always did like Boots."

"Yes, he's a great comfort to her, and to me, of course. I think it helps her to know he will be around after she's gone."

"Margaret!"

"I know. I know it's terrible to think things like that, much less say them, but it's something we have to face. We have to. Oh, Rebecca, I'm so afraid!"

That cry from her sister remained with Rebecca long after she hung up the phone. It helped her to think that Margaret wasn't just being mean and spiteful, that she really was concerned for their mother. It had hurt to think, even for a moment, that Edison might be right about her sister.

All the same, Rebecca was more alone than she had ever been in her life, and more lonely. The city that had at first seemed wonderfully easygoing and accepting of all comers began to feel merely uncaring, as if human pain and death might be accepted as easily as everything else.

The money Margaret had promised arrived. There was not much of it, but it was enough if Rebecca ate mostly macaroni and cheap tuna. There was one good thing, she discovered, about Edison being gone; she could share her fish with the cat. The animal came mewling around the morning after he left, as if she knew it was safe.

Rebecca had been on her own for a week when one evening she heard footsteps mounting the outside stairs. Her stomach muscles tightened as she turned toward the doorway. It stood open, except for the wire mesh of the screen door. She had forgotten to flip the lock into place on that flimsy barrier, and there was no time to do it now.

The footsteps drew nearer, then slowed to a halt. A man's form appeared against the screen. He raised one hand that was balled into a fist.

It was Dante Romoli who rapped lightly on the door frame with his knuckles. Rebecca let out her pent-up breath and crossed the room to open the screen.

"I've come about the cat," Dante said. His dark gaze lingered on the shadowed coloration on her cheek before he looked away, scanning the room behind her.

"Oh, did you want her back? I didn't mean to take her away from you."

"It's not that. I just thought—well, it seemed she was more welcome up here lately. And I never hear anyone moving about except you. I wondered . . . Is everything all right?"

Rebecca was warmed by his concern. "Yes and no. I'm all right, if that's what you mean."

"That's good." He relaxed a fraction. "But what about your husband? I couldn't help but notice—that is, I haven't seen his car when I leave in the evening or when I come back in the morning."

"No, he . . . he left."

"For a trip or something?"

"For good." Her voice was husky as she made the answer.

He nodded as if he had expected nothing else. A moment later, he smiled. "Have you eaten?"

She shook her head. It was often late before she ate, if she ate at all. She didn't have much appetite. Anyway, once she had eaten, there was nothing else to do except go to bed.

"You know, *chère*, I was telling the chef down at the restaurant about my grandmama's crawfish étouffée yesterday. He made up a batch, trying out the recipe, then gave me what was left. It's a whole big pot. I could use some help eating it."

"Don't you have to go to work?"

"It's my day off. Will you come?"

It required more persuasion, but she agreed in the end. Before the pot of étouffée was gone, she had told him everything. Somewhere in the midst of it, she began to cry again. She flinched when he put his arms around her, but there was nothing in his hold except sympathy and human warmth. He held her for a long time, murmuring soothing nonsense that she recognized as French without having the least idea what he was saying. It didn't matter. When she finally sat up, wiped her eyes, and sniffled one last time, she felt better.

She saw a great deal of Dante after that. She accused him of taking her in like he had the homeless cat, though he only laughed and said she was better company. It was Dante who got her the job washing dishes. It was he who showed her how to keep up with the endless piles of china and silver that appeared at her elbow, how to keep from scalding herself with the near-boiling water, how to grease her hands to prevent them from becoming raw and swollen.

And it was Dante who, after watching her fight nausea for the third night in a row as she scraped plates free of their cold food congealed in greasy sauce, asked if she was pregnant and so forced her to face her condition.

She stared at him, her face pale and her eyes dark green with distress as she pressed her fingers to her lips. "Oh, Dante, what am I going to do?"

"Marry me," he said.

She loved him in that moment, because it was said without hesitation, without so much as a shadow of doubt on his face.

"Thank you," she said, going on tiptoe to kiss his cheek, "but I can't."

He was frowning when she backed away again. "Why not?"

"This isn't your problem. You've done enough for me, and I can't let you do any more."

"Did you ever stop to think I might be doing it for me?"

Rebecca shook her head. "You want to own your own restaurant, to make something out of yourself. You don't need a wife and another man's baby."

"It's because I'm Cajun and just a busboy."

"That has nothing to do with it!"

She knew he was touchy about his birth. The Cajuns, descendants of the Acadians of Nova Scotia who were expelled by the British during the wars between France and England in the mid-eighteenth century, were people of the bayous and backwaters of Louisiana. They were God-fearing without being puritanical; given to large families; fond of dancing, drinking, and gambling; and blessed with a fine capacity for being content with their lot. Because of these traits they were looked down on by some as lacking in the drive and ambition for success. They were also people of touchy pride, if Dante was any example. They made no apologies for their way of life and were quick to resent any slur on it, quick also to resent any personal slur. Dante felt no shame himself for being a busboy, but was irritated by those who thought it was all he could do, all he would ever be.

Now he nodded. All around them was the bustle and shouting, the steam and rich smells of the kitchen. As one of the chefs walked by and frowned at them, Dante picked up a plate and began to scrape it. "But I would like to take care of you, *chère*."

"You do that, every day." Her nausea was under control for the moment. She reached for a plate and began to scrape also.

"You know what I mean."

"Yes, I know, and it's sweet of you," she said with a tremulous smile, "but I—I really have to go home. That's where I belong, not here."

"You miss it, your home." It was a statement.

"I dream about it sometimes, the way it used to be before Beth died."

"Why are you still here, then? Why not just go?"

"I can't. What if Mama got too upset over what happened to me, so upset about me being pregnant and not married, that she died?"

He turned his head to give her a serious look. "I think you are afraid, *chère*, afraid of what will happen to your mother, yes, but also of what your sister will say. And, most of all, afraid of loving."

He was right. For a short time she had thought she loved Edison, thought he loved her. She had been wrong. What she had felt was a potent mixture of compassion and the first stirrings of physical desire. What Edison had felt other than lust, she had no idea. Now all she wanted was for everything to be as it was before, with her safely back home with her family. The last thing she had any use for was another husband, another man to cook and clean for and answer to for her comings and goings, another man to share her bed and take her body as if it was his right.

"I just don't know," she answered finally.

"I could love you, you know." He watched her, waiting for her reply.

"Could you?" she asked.

"It would be easy."

"You're an unusual man, Dante."

"And good-looking, too. Plus I love children and will make a terrific papa."

She shook her head, smiling at his enthusiasm. "I don't doubt it, when you find the right person."

"You could be the right one, if you would."

"Then what would I do for a friend?"

He looked away for a long moment. Slowly he breathed in and out. He squared his shoulders. When he turned back again, his face was clear. "All right, but what will you do?"

"I'll have to talk to Margaret. Then I'll know."

Margaret, when Rebecca called once more, was horrified. She couldn't believe it, she said over and over again. The pregnancy was a judgment upon Rebecca for what she had done. Their mother had been disturbed about Rebecca and asked after her, so Rebecca could talk to her, but on no account must she mention this latest tragedy. If she did, Margaret refused to be responsible.

It seemed impossible, once her mother was on the phone, to be anything other than cheerful. She was fine, Rebecca told her mother. Edison was fine, New Orleans was fine, everything was fine. The relief in her mother's voice was her reward.

"I've been so worried about you down there, Becky," her mother said, using her childhood name, her voice soft and warm and faintly sad. "Margaret couldn't tell me much about you when you called and seemed to have no idea how to reach you on short notice. Have you been having fun?"

Fun.

"Oh, yes, Mama. It's just that . . . everything takes a little getting used to."

"I understand, but you mustn't forget us."

"No, no, I won't, Mama."

"Well, I'll go then. I'm getting a little tired, and it's time I went to lie down for my nap. You'll remember what I always told you, won't you, now that you're going among all those fine folks?"

Rebecca tried to think, though all she could really concentrate on was the breathless sound of her mother's voice. "I don't—"

"If you can't be a lady, at least act like one. That's what my mama told me and I found it a help. Now you take care, Becky, and let us hear from you."

"Yes, ma'am."

When Margaret came back on the line seconds later, there was excitement in her voice. "I have an idea," she said. "I know just what we're going to do. It'll work, I know it will."

The peculiar thing was that it did.

Margaret sent Rebecca more money with instructions to go to a good gynecologist, one who could help her determine exactly how far along she was. When Rebecca could say with some certainty that she was three months pregnant, Margaret announced her own three-month pregnancy and began immediately to wear maternity clothes and to collect a layette. When Rebecca was eight months into her pregnancy, Margaret suddenly developed complications that required her to visit a specialist in New Orleans, then remain nearby until her confinement.

She visited no specialist, however, despite the story given out to neighbors, nor were there complications of her nonexistent pregnancy. She merely moved in with Rebecca and set herself to wait.

Her vigil did not require a month. Whether because of miscalculation, Rebecca's youth and small size, or the exacerbation of Margaret's presence, Rebecca went into labor a week later.

Margaret would not at first believe that the baby was really coming, that Rebecca could know what was happening to her. When she was convinced, she turned hysterical and rushed around the apartment in her nightgown wringing her hands and looking for a telephone that wasn't there. Rebecca had to tell her four times that she must get dressed and go down to the grocery store to call the doctor. Margaret balked then at going out into the street at night and in the chill rain of the New Orleans winter.

The pains were coming fast and hard. Rebecca had gotten dressed but had little strength to talk. There was something wrong. She had read the books about childbirth that Dante had brought her from the library, and she didn't think matters should be proceeding so violently so soon. When her water broke on a grinding pain, she gasped out, "Dante, go get Dante."

"What do you want with him?"

Margaret had no use for Dante. The two of them had disliked each other on sight, perhaps because Dante was Rebecca's champion in all things and did not trouble to hide the fact that he considered Margaret a busybody and an interloper.

"I need him."

"But he has nothing to do with this. Or does he?"

Rebecca, standing with her body swollen and drawn with pain and her shoes full of warm, blood-stained water, glared at her sister in sudden, consuming rage. She screamed, "Get Dante!"

Silenced, Margaret ducked out into the wet night. In a moment she could be heard downstairs pounding on his door.

It was Dante who delivered Rebecca's child. The baby, a girl, cried with her face screwed up and red so that she looked furious with the world. Her cries were strong, however, in spite of her premature birth. Dante gave her to Margaret while he tended to Rebecca. Her sister bathed the baby with awkward and gingerly care, dressed her and wrapped her in a blanket, and brought her back into the room just as Rebecca was settling back in the bed in her nightgown.

Rebecca lay with the baby in the crook of her arm and her hair, glinting in the glow of the overhead light, spread around her on the pillow. She touched the delicate skin of her child's face, spread the tiny hands, and marveled at the long fingers; she felt the delicate and rapid beating of the tiny heart in that small, warm body. She looked up with shining eyes at Dante, who sat beside her on the bed. His thick curls were standing on end, there were shadows of weariness under his eyes, and blood—her blood—smeared the T-shirt he wore. Still, there was satisfaction and even bright exultation on his face.

A smile of clear beauty curved her mouth, and she held out her left hand to him. "Thank you," she said simply.

He stared at her, and tears rose in his eyes. His voice husky with reverence, he said, "Ah, *chère*, you look like a young madonna."

Margaret, standing at the bed's foot, cleared her throat. "What a sweet thing to say, Dante. I don't know how you knew what to do, but you've got my thanks, too."

He did not look away from Rebecca as he answered. "It was

nothing. I used to help my grandpapa who had a little piece of farmland on the river road. He showed me what to do for the cows at calving time."

"Ugh!" Margaret exclaimed. "It can't be the same."

Dante merely lifted a shoulder, as if the comment was unworthy of a reply.

Margaret went on. "Anyway, it's a good thing. Now we won't have to go to the hospital."

"What are you saying?" Dante released Rebecca's hand and came slowly to his feet to face Margaret. "We should call an ambulance right now. Both your sister and the baby should be checked. I'm not a doctor. What if something isn't right?"

"She looks fine to me. They both do."

"But you don't know that!"

"If we don't go to the hospital, we won't have to register the baby for her birth certificate here in New Orleans. I can arrange everything later, with Mama's doctor. He'll do it for us, when I explain. Anything that makes this baby more mine has to be good."

"Yours?" he said slowly. "You're going to take Rebecca's baby?"

Hot color rushed into Margaret's face. She put her hands on her plump hips. "I'm not taking it! She's giving the baby to me!"

Dante turned to Rebecca. "Is this true?"

Rebecca swallowed on the ache in her throat. "It's the best thing to do. Don't you see?"

"No." The word was hard, uncompromising.

"She'll have a normal home with two parents and lots of love, the love of three people instead of one. And I can see her whenever I want, as long as I want. This way no one will be hurt, not my mama and not the baby. It's the best for everybody."

"Who says so?"

"Well, Margaret, but—"

"What about you?"

Rebecca looked away with her teeth set in her bottom lip. Her voice wobbled as she answered, "It's best for me, too. I'd have to take care of her and earn enough to keep us both. It's just—just too much."

"You aren't going home, then?"

Margaret broke in, her hands gripping the foot rail of the cheap iron bed. "She can't, not now! It would be too obvious. She would be bound to be silly over the baby, besides being weak and all that. People might get suspicious, start to talk. Mama would surely know something was wrong."

Dante turned back to Rebecca with pain and compassion in his face. "Oh, *chère*."

Tears gathered in Rebecca's eyes, spilling down her cheeks in warm, wet paths. Her voice thick, she repeated, "I have to think of what's best, for everybody."

Dante didn't answer. He clenched his hands, then let them relax, falling open at his sides. Turning, he walked out of the room. The door of the apartment closed quietly behind him.

In the bedroom at Bonne Vie, Margaret's iced tea arrived. She drank down half of it before the maid who had brought it had left the room. Refilling her glass from the pitcher on the silver tray, she paced up and down beside the bed.

"What about this photographer, Gorsline?" she asked. "What does he want? Why is he hounding us?"

Riva spoke from where she stood at the window. "The idea seems to be that he's interested in Erin."

"Baloney. There's more to it than that, there has to be. Don't you have any idea what it could be?"

"None." Riva could have told her sister about seeing the young man earlier that afternoon. She did not. It was unlikely that Margaret would understand the impulse that had made her take Doug Gorsline's number to give to Erin, and she was in no mood to listen to certain condemnation for it.

"You saw him at the rally," Margaret said, a line between her brows as she frowned. "Do you think he could be bought off?"

"Oh, please, Margaret, this isn't a soap opera! Nothing so melodramatic as bribery is necessary. And even if the situation were different, I think it would be unwise to offer money. If he's really after something, it would be like giving a hound a scent of blood."

The other woman drank from her glass of tea, then wiped her mouth with her fingers. "You may be right. But I still wish I had some idea what he wanted. Do you think he's heard something about Erin?"

"What do you mean?"

"You know very well what I mean! About you and Erin."

Riva knew, of course. She acted obtuse in an effort to make Margaret speak plainly, to identify Erin correctly as hers, Riva's own daughter. Her sister would never speak the words, had never referred to Erin as other than Riva's niece from the moment she had left the New Orleans apartment with the baby when she was a week old. Even making her find other words to say the same thing always gave Riva a perverse kind of satisfaction. Margaret, however, never seemed to notice. Riva could not help wondering if it was because her sister lacked the imagination to understand how Riva still felt about the loss of her child, or if it was just that by some peculiar logic Margaret managed most of the time to convince herself that Erin really was her own daughter.

Returning to the problem at hand, Riva said, "It seems more likely it's Edison that Gorsline is after. Edison's the one who's running for office, after all."

"Pray God you're right! The thought of this photographer with Erin makes me sick!"

"It would be preferable to Erin with Josh, don't you think?"

Margaret moaned and stumbled to a chair of tufted velvet. "Oh, God, don't mention it. Why? Why, of all the young men she might have met, did she have to fall in love with that one?"

Riva lifted a hand, rubbing it tiredly across her eyes. "Sheer bad luck or coincidence, or maybe even the genes, since they met in political science class. It was Josh, of course, who found the position for Erin at his father's headquarters. But, anyway, there's nothing to say they're in love."

"And nothing to say they're not!" Margaret snapped back, then slumped with her head against the high back of the chair and her tea glass tipped at a precarious angle. "Why, in heaven's name, couldn't Edison agree to separate them? Why?"

"Because," Riva explained evenly, "he doesn't like to be told what to do, especially by a woman."

"I knew it. You approached him all wrong."

"If you think you can do better, you're welcome to try."

"I couldn't do any worse," Margaret said, sitting erect again and draining her glass before setting it on the tray beside the chair with a rattling crash. "Though, really, I don't understand why he's being obstructive. He's the one with the most to lose."

"He doesn't think so. In fact, he's so arrogant he thinks he's safe, that I will do nothing no matter what I may say."

"Why shouldn't he think so? That's exactly what you did years ago. Nothing."

"There was nothing to be done."

Margaret gave her an incredulous look. "But there was! He could have been made to pay support for Erin. You were entitled to that much, and I'm sure a good lawyer could have gotten it for you."

"I didn't know that then. In any case, I didn't want it."

"Well, some people are not so picky about money!" her sister said in great dudgeon. "In fact, he should still be made to pay."

"Impossible, since Erin's of age. Anyway, I couldn't ask for anything without telling him Erin is his daughter, and I will never do that. Never."

"It might be for the best to tell him. Have you thought of that? He could hardly refuse to separate Josh from her then."

"You don't know him if you think so."

Margaret stared at her, her eyes wide, almost calculating. "No, I don't, not like you do. What's he like now? Is he still as handsome as ever?"

"I suppose." The answer was offhand since Riva's thoughts were still busy with Margaret's suggestion.

"You suppose? Don't you know? Didn't you look at him?"

There was a thread of anger under the curiosity in Margaret's voice, as well as a thread of envy. Riva looked at her closely. "What difference does it make?"

"Good gracious, Riva! Edison Gallant was the best-looking boy ever to set foot in our town. He used to come to our house and eat at our table, and now he's going to be governor. You'll probably be invited to the governor's mansion for the inaugural ball. Why, Boots and I might even be invited, as Erin's parents. Just think of it! Doesn't it mean anything to you?"

Riva moved to stand over her sister. Her voice even, carefully controlled, she said, "Edison Gallant is not to be trusted. If he learns about Erin, he will use it as a weapon."

"For what? What possible use could he make of it?"

"He could use it as a means of getting to me."

Margaret gave a scornful laugh and waved a hand around at the expensive room. "Oh, come on, Riva. How?"

"By threatening to tell Erin. I know you don't want that."

Margaret paled until the tracery of red veins in her cheeks stood out under the skin. "Oh, God, no. He wouldn't do that."

"He would, in a minute, if I didn't do what he wanted."

"He wants something concrete from you?" Margaret's gaze narrowed. "You know what it is now?"

"I tried to tell you before. He has an itch to get me back in his bed." The words were spoken ironically in an effort to make light of them.

"Oh, that," her sister said with a dismissive gesture. "How do you know he really has any such idea?"

"He made it very plain when I asked him to send Josh away."

"You mean, he might really do what you want, separate Erin from his son and keep them apart, all for the chance to get into your pants?"

Riva grimaced at the expression. "You could put it that way."

"Well, for crying out loud," Margaret said with a laugh that had a razor edge of scorn. "It isn't as if it's any great sacrifice for you, Riva. What are you waiting for? If that's all he wants, let him have it!"

9

Riva had almost forgotten the charity benefit ball. It was Margaret, rifling through the contents of the antique silver letter holder on Riva's secretary-desk in her bedroom the following morning, who found the tickets. Riva had paid for more than she needed with her customary generosity toward causes that gained her approval; there were an even dozen to this gala in support of Louisiana's valuable wetlands. The ball would take place at the old mint building at the edge of the French Quarter that evening. Margaret, with the extra tickets clutched in her hand, became pink with excitement. If Riva was going, there was no reason she and Boots could not go with her.

Riva, getting dressed, glanced doubtfully at her sister. "I suppose I should go since I promised my support and the wetlands are one of Noel's special interests, but are you sure you want to? It will be black tie, and since you won't know anyone, no end of boring."

"Of course I want to go," Margaret cried. "I can run downtown with you in the car and rent a tux for Boots. As for me, I'm sure you have something I can wear."

Riva's sister walked to the doors of the closet that lined one wall of the cream and old-rose bedroom and flung them open. She stared for a bemused moment at the neat rows of color-coordinated dresses and suits, evening gowns and furs, each with their matching shoes and handbags placed beneath them. Then taking a deep, ecstatic breath, she began to pull evening gowns from the array.

Riva watched Margaret without a word. As girls growing up, she and Margaret and Beth had always worn each other's clothes.

That Margaret should make herself free with Riva's closet, taking whatever caught her fancy from it as if it were a clothing store, was nothing unusual; she had been doing it for years. It was not just a holdover from the past, however; it was almost as if Riva's sister felt entitled to share whatever Riva owned.

"I do think you could increase the allowance you give me, Riva," Margaret said. "Lord knows you can afford it, considering what you must spend on clothes."

"I don't know what my clothes have to do with it," Riva answered. "The money is supposed to be for Erin's expenses."

"I can take care of her myself, thank you. Besides, a girl her age doesn't need that much money for clothes and such; it'll give her ideas above herself. But I think you should have enough consideration for your own sister to want her to look nice without having to resort to hand-me-downs."

"You don't have to accept the clothes I give you."

Give was not quite the word, but it didn't matter. In a way it was true, Riva thought. She could buy what she wanted, replace anything she particularly liked that Margaret took from her closet. That their lives had turned out so differently, hers and Margaret's, wasn't Margaret's fault. The fact that it was not hers, either, crossed her mind, but was quickly dismissed.

"Oh, I don't mind," Margaret said in haste. "At least my friends have never seen you wear them."

Riva gave a silent sigh, then reached for her checkbook. "How much of an increase would you like?"

Margaret had put on weight in the last few years, a few pounds here, a few there. Her tendency toward broad hips had been accentuated. She didn't let that stop her from wearing Riva's clothes. She sucked in her breath to fasten reluctant zippers, hooks, and snaps and postured in front of the mirror as if she could not see that the skirts were too tight, that delicate fabrics were stretched out of shape or lines ruined because of bulges they were never meant to cover.

Riva's one consolation was that Margaret was usually attracted to her younger sister's errors of judgment, to the clothes whose colors and fabrics Riva had discovered did not suit her. This time was the same. Margaret's attention settled on a gown of iridescent glass beads and sequins on gold chiffon that Riva had worn once during the Mardi Gras season just past, then decided was too flashy for anything else. As little as she cared about it, however, she hated to see Margaret wear something so unsuitable for her shape and pinkish-red complexion or so heavy for the hot weather.

"Don't you think that's a bit much for summer?" she asked. "There's an Italian silk, an Armani, over there. I had intended to wear it, but it would suit you very well since it has a full skirt."

"Are you suggesting I need a fuller skirt?" Margaret demanded.

"I'm just saying it would look good on you."

"I bet you really wanted to wear this glitzy number yourself. You were spectacular in it in all the papers."

"I showed you the one I'm going to wear."

Margaret gave the dress Riva indicated a scathing glance. "You can have those wimpy colors. I like something with a little more life to it." She took the heavy, close-fitting beaded dress from its padded hanger and began to wriggle into it.

By the time they were all ready to leave for the gala, Margaret had also appropriated a pair of Riva's evening shoes, her beaded bag that matched the dress, the services of her hairdresser, and several generous splashes of Riva's special perfume, one of ancient vintage but delectable scent called Paradise that was made exclusively by the Bourbon French Perfume Company on St. Ann Street in the Quarter. She swept into the limousine as if it belonged to her, pushing ahead of Constance as well as Riva and taking the center of the front-facing seat.

Constance, elegant and cool in black and white voile, raised a brow. As she seated herself, she drawled, "How very like your sister you are, Mrs. Green. I had not realized until this moment."

The double disparagement—of Margaret for dressing in Riva's finery, as all the household knew, and of Riva for being as mannerless as Margaret had just shown herself—was lost on Margaret. She smiled with satisfaction. "People have always said so."

"I should imagine they would."

The chill tone of the other woman's voice wiped the smile from Margaret's face. Before she could speak, however, Noel stepped into the car behind Boots and spoke to George, and they moved away down the drive.

The old United States Mint, a building of Victorian solidity painted rust-brown, had been the site of the manufacture of United States coins from the late 1830s to the first decade of the twentieth century except for a brief hiatus during the Civil War. Afterward, it had served as a federal prison and a Coast Guard office, though in recent years it had been completely renovated and dedicated as a branch of the state museum. It was fitting that the building was sometimes available as the scene for spectacular parties and balls. In the 1840s, the mint's superintendent had held a fancy-dress ball for his daughter's debut there, the only social event ever to take place in a United States Mint building. It was, to Riva, a typical example of New Orleans irreverence for bureaucracy.

The interior was spacious and airy, with a grand staircase in the center tying together the three floors of exhibits. As with much else in the city, it was a curious and oddly complementary mixture of the new and the old, of bright lights and shining surfaces combined with fine, refinished old woods and excellent workmanship. Behind the building, enclosed by a stone fence, was a courtyard lighted by fairy lights strung through sheltering trees.

For the gala, formal wear for men was much in evidence. There had been a time, during the sixties and early seventies, when a tuxedo was seldom seen in the city, but in the last few years they had become necessary apparel in men's closets again.

Perhaps as a result, or perhaps simply because this was New Orleans, the bars set up here and there were much patronized. Courtesy champagne also flowed freely. Silver chafing dishes rendered up hors d'oeuvres of shrimp and crabmeat in crisp pastry shells, crawfish, and small hot sausages in barbecue sauce, plus stuffed mushrooms and other such delicacies. There were desserts served in fluted glasses and made with chocolate and fresh strawberries and cream custard. Set among the food were ice sculptures of the wild ducks, geese, egrets, pelicans, and cranes whose migratory habitat in the marshlands of the state the gala was supposedly helping to preserve.

Music for dancing was plentiful. There was a string quartet on the third floor playing waltzes for the older or more romantic guests, a Cajun band making foot-tapping, two-stepping rhythms on the second floor, and a jazz ensemble swinging and winging it in the jazz-preservation room. One of most popular places, however, was the courtyard where the lighting was dim, the night breeze pleasant, and a modern combo played effortless cocktail music that was suitable for dancing yet did not present an insurmountable obstacle to conversation.

The group from Bonne Vie stayed together for a short while, long enough to exchange a few dances. Dante, Riva's escort, as usual, led her out onto the floor first. They moved together easily and comfortably, if without verve; for Dante, the exercise was only an excuse for his quick, humorous comments on everything and everybody. Boots, on the other hand, didn't have much to say, but was a surprisingly accomplished dancer for so large a man, his movements smooth and in perfect step. There was something about the way Riva's body fit Noel's, however, as if the two of them were designed to move in harmony, that made dancing even duty dances with him different from anyone else. More than that was the way he responded to the music, as if he had an affinity with it above the average and used it to express all the things he ordinarily kept locked inside. It was not a new discovery; she had noticed it before years ago when they had first danced together. Regardless, she had the feeling that he was unaware of the extent to which he allowed the music to become a part of him.

The Bonne Vie party separated finally. Riva strolled here and there with Dante until he was snared by a matron wanting to discuss a wedding-rehearsal party to be held in one of Lecompte's private rooms. After being hailed by an acquaintance, Riva wandered away on her own. She carried a glass of champagne around with her, though when it was gone she replaced it with mineral water. The food laid out in such bounty enticed her, and she accepted a few samples. Often in her ramblings she paused to exchange greetings with friends and those not so friendly, and also to pose with some of the organizers of the evening for the society-page photographers from *New Orleans* magazine and the *Times-Picayune*.

After a time, she was attracted by the rich sounds and the clatter of applause coming from the jazz room. She moved in that direction. Finding a crowd congregated around the doorway, she edged her way through expertly, then worked forward to a place on one side of the gathering. From that vantage point, she had a fine view of the combo that was the main attraction.

The ensemble consisted of a trumpet and clarinet, along with piano, bass fiddle, and drums. The tune they played was a strong, sad, and brassy rendition of a jazz favorite straight from old Basin Street. The earthy, funky beat of it surrounded Riva, catching at her heart, curling in her stomach, and tingling in her feet so that she was forced to move with it.

The black trumpeter was great and the clarinetist fine, but it was the drummer who brought life to the piece. The rhythm he coaxed from the drum skins was complicated and sensuous, a double heartbeat pounding out in steady and perfect sync that increased in speed and swelled in volume by almost imperceptible degrees. With every repeat of the basic few measures of the song, the beat grew stronger, though it slipped at intervals into an oddly spaced trip-hammer stutter that added excitement. The message in the rhythm was primitive but effective, a paean to the love that is celebrated in the dark as bodies move in unrestrained pleasure toward an instant of suspended time.

The drummer was Noel.

There was concentration in his face and close accord between him and the other players. But there was also bright laughter in his gray eyes, the measure of his pure enjoyment for the free-flowing release of the music. Riva, watching in amazement, felt his reckless joy. It was in the intense vibration of the sound, in the quickening tempo and the precision of his movements that stemmed from sheer creative instinct, but most of all it was in the fact that, for this moment, he was totally unconscious of who and where he was.

She had no idea how Noel had come to be part of the entertainment or how long it had been going on. She was bemused by this side of him that she had thought dead since a stormy afternoon on an island. Still, there arose in her as she watched the fear that her presence would destroy the joy for Noel. Why should it not? Hadn't it always done so before?

With slow care, she faded back into the crowd, retreating, threading her way toward the door. She kept her gaze on Noel as she went, but he did not look up. She was glad when she could no longer see him for the press of bodies, for it meant that he could no longer catch sight of her.

She was back out in the central hall when the jazz piece rose toward a throbbing crescendo. The sound followed her, rich and turbulent with trumpet notes of mind-stopping, nerve-stretching purity supported by the rising and defiantly blending strength of the other instruments. And then suddenly, in a triumphant burst of strident melody and a thunderous drumbeat of finality, the music ended. The last note was, for some reason Riva could not quite explain, a relief.

The mint's courtyard offered coolness and relative quiet. Riva began to make her way there. Dante caught up with her near the outside door and, discovering where she was headed, promised to join her there in a few minutes with fresh glasses of champagne.

Outside, Riva found a seat on the low retaining wall that bounded one side of the flagged area and sat watching the dancers. There were other people nearby, but not so close that she felt compelled to talk. It was good to have a moment's respite.

She could see Margaret and Boots among the couples swaying under the trees. They looked good together, her sister and her husband, even a bit sophisticated, with Boots in his black tuxedo and the multicolored beads on the dress Margaret wore glittering as they caught the light from the tiny bulbs strung overhead.

The music ended and the band called a five-minute break. Margaret and Boots left the floor. Margaret said something to her husband, and he nodded and left, most likely in search of the bar. Riva's sister stood alone in the shadows to one side of the fountain, her back to Riva.

Riva saw a man detach himself from a group near the door and circle around the fairy-lighted trees and chattering groups of people. It was Edison, and for a moment she thought he had seen her there in the night dimness. It was Margaret, however, who was his goal. He approached her from behind. As he drew near, he reached out his hand and cupped one cheek of her buttocks in a quick, thrusting grasp.

Margaret gave a small scream. She spun around, stumbling backward. Edison looked stunned for a moment when he saw her face. Nevertheless, he recovered in an instant, apologizing.

"I'm sorry. It was a mistake. That dress—I thought . . . that is, I didn't mean anything. I just stumbled, nearly fell."

Margaret blinked and glanced around her. When she saw no one paying any attention to the small incident, she relaxed, moving closer. "Edison," she said, "Edison Gallant. Don't you know me?"

It was Edison's turn to glance around. Looking back again, he said, "Should I?"

"I'm Margaret, Riva's sister. You thought I was her, didn't you, because she was in all the papers in this dress last Mardi Gras."

"Not at all."

"Oh, no, you thought it was your wife." The words were archly playful.

"I told you, I stumbled," Edison muttered, his voice barely audible.

Margaret laughed with a high-pitched, breathless sound. "Riva's here somewhere, if you want to talk to her."

"Why should I want to do that?"

"I thought there was something you wanted from her."

Edison looked at Margaret, letting his gaze travel slowly over her body until a flush appeared on her cheeks. "Maybe," he said in a low, suggestive tone as his gaze returned to hers, "I should take it up with you."

Margaret's eyes widened as she gasped. An intrigued look crossed her face. It was easy to see that she was tempted, yet held in check by fear and prudence. Her gaze moved beyond Edison's shoulder and she saw Riva. "I—I don't think so. My sister is over there, behind you."

Edison turned to look over his shoulder. With no more than a nod, he moved away from Margaret, walking toward where Riva sat. He was scowling as he came to a halt. "I suppose you saw that?"

"I suppose I did."

"I hope you had a good laugh."

"It had its amusing moments."

"Shit," he said under his breath. He stared past her into the darkness.

It was interesting that it mattered so much to him that he had looked foolish. It was a sign of the size of his ego, of course, but it also made him more human.

He cocked his head as he slowly swung back to her. "You haven't run away yet. I'm surprised."

"I wasn't running away from you yesterday, just leaving an unpleasant situation." Riva kept her voice even and coolly neutral.

"Whatever it was, I'm glad you're still here. We need to talk."

"I thought we made our positions clear enough."

"There are a few details that escape me. Could we go somewhere?"

She gave him an ironic glance. "If you mean leave the mint, no."

"You don't leave a man much room to maneuver, do you? Funny, I don't remember you being that way."

"Don't you?"

"As a matter of fact," he answered, his voice dropping lower, "I don't remember the two of us having problems at all. You were always ready to do whatever I wanted."

"The way I remember it, you were too wrapped up in what you wanted to care whether I was ready or not."

"God, you were sweet, the most delectable little piece of—"

"Do continue," she invited with a bright smile. "I'm sure your constituents attending this gala will be most entertained."

"You know, I like feisty women. They turn me on."

"Need I say that was not my intention?"

He ignored her comment. "Women who just cry or sulk are a bore. You excite me."

He was, she noticed, keeping his voice down. She looked over his shoulder, scanning the crowd. In a deliberate change of subject, she said, "I wonder where Dante can have gotten to. He has been gone long enough to bring champagne from Paris."

"The friend you were with at the rally? I saw him with a hot-looking foreign number when I was making the rounds just now. He was teaching her how to do the Cajun waltz."

"Was he? That was nice of him." Dante must have come across Constance. Since Noel's wife knew so few people, he would have felt obligated to spend a few minutes with her.

"Jealous?" he asked.

Riva merely smiled.

"I'd offer to bring you a drink, but I'm afraid you would disappear. Though if you'd like to go in search of the bar, and incidentally see what your friend is up to, I'll be glad to go with you."

It would be better than sitting there with Edison standing over her. Besides, since the music had stopped out here, the crowd was beginning to thin out, gravitating toward the tuneful whine of the Cajun fiddles inside. Margaret had gone with them. It seemed a bit too much like being deserted for comfort.

"All right," Riva said.

As she started to rise, Edison extended his hand. To accept his offer of help was natural, no matter how little she needed it. His fingers closed on hers, then tightened, dragging her upward. The sudden surge was unexpected. Off balance, Riva fell against him. He caught her to his chest with one hand on her breast and the other clamped around her waist.

"There now, that's where you belong," he said in satisfied tones.

"Let me go!" Riva spoke through set teeth as she braced her hands against his chest. She was aware of a curious glance or two cast in their direction but thought the light was too dim for anyone to know who they were. To struggle would be the surest way to draw attention.

Edison sighed, then released his hold. As she stepped back, he tilted his head, giving her a rueful grin. "I did it again, didn't I? Everything I do around you seems wrong. I guess I'm just nervous. Finding you again has thrown me for a loop."

She didn't trust his smile or his humble words. It was galling that he could think she would. "You might try treating me as you would any other business acquaintance. That's all we are."

"But not all I'd like to be, baby."

146 •

"Don't call me baby. I'm nobody's baby, particularly yours, and haven't been for a long time."

He reached to take her hand. "Look, I made a mistake yesterday. What you said was so unexpected that I didn't know how to answer, didn't think about what I was saying. Please don't hold it against me. Let's start over, have a nice long talk somewhere about old times. I'm sure we can work this problem out."

His voice was deep and sincere, honeyed with charm. She had to admire his acting ability and even to wonder if it was really all acting. She tried to ease her hand free, but he would not release it. "There's nothing to talk about, nothing to work out. I've told you what I want. I can't—I won't—settle for anything less."

"Don't be so unreasonable. My son is important to my image as a family man. I need him to stay close."

She pulled her fingers from his clasp with a quick jerk. "Then go campaign somewhere else besides the New Orleans area."

"There's a big block of voters here—the biggest in the state—besides which you're here."

"My being here has nothing to do with it," she said in sharp tones. "As a matter of fact, I think it's the height of stupidity for you to be talking to me here in this place. Aren't you afraid some photographer will come along and take a picture or that people will talk?"

"My wife's here somewhere, she'll cover for me. Besides, I can always claim we were discussing contributions."

The way he said the last word was infinitely suggestive. Riva's lips tightened. "If you won't consider your best interests, then I will have to consider mine."

She swung away from him. He caught her arm, then let go abruptly as he looked beyond her. Riva turned her head. Noel was approaching across the flagstones, ducking under a tree limb gilded with lights, which made silver-blue gleams in the dark waves of his hair. In his hand was a glass of champagne.

"I hate to interrupt your discussion," Noel said as he drew near, "but Romoli sent this with his apologies." He handed Riva the drink, scanning her face at the same time. He glanced at Edison with a short nod of greeting before turning back to Riva.

She accepted the glass of wine he offered with an automatic murmur of thanks. Noel's assessing glance made her feel oddly shaken. Somehow she had never noticed how dynamic he was, not just physically but inside himself. That strength was armored in politeness, but it was unquestionably there. It could be that the characteristic was pointed up by the contrast to Edison, but it was still a revelation. It was apparently a night for revelations.

Noel went on. "I'm also to tell you that we are going on to Romoli's place out on the lake. Constance, it seems, is hungry for something more than nibbles, and nowhere else will do."

Riva, hearing his dry tone, wondered if he resented his former wife's interest in Dante's restaurant or if he suspected it was in Dante himself. The last idea drew her brows together in a frown.

Edison shifted restively. "I expect I had better find my wife. It's about time we left, too."

He waited a moment, as if he half expected an invitation to join the party from Bonne Vie. When none was forthcoming, he walked away with stiff strides.

Noel went on as if no one had spoken. "If you don't care to go with the others, I'll be glad to ride back home with you after we drop them off."

"No," Riva said quickly, too quickly, "I always enjoy going out to the lake." To be alone in the limousine with Noel for that long, dark ride was not a prospect she cared to face just now.

His face tightened, but he only said, "Romoli suggested that we go on ahead since he'll be bringing Constance in his car. Shall we?"

At his brief gesture that indicated that she should precede him, Riva moved toward the entrance door leading from the courtyard back into the building. It was necessary to make her farewells and to speak to those who called out to her in her progress through the crowded rooms. Finally they were out the front door and moving down the walk toward the wrought-iron gates.

The limousine was parked at the curb along with two or three others like it and a long line of other luxury cars, among them Dante's Alfa Romeo since he had met them at the mint. Riva and Noel walked toward the limousine. As they drew closer, however, they could see that the long car was dark and deserted.

"Where is everyone?" she said in surprise.

"George is probably in the nearest bar. I doubt he expected us to leave so soon. Hold on."

Noel swung away from her and walked back to the gates, where he spoke to the man on guard there. He returned in a moment. "Someone will call to let him know we're ready."

"That doesn't explain where the others are," Riva pointed out.

Noel shrugged. "They'll be along. Margaret had to wait for Boots. I believe he had gone to the restroom."

"We might as well go back inside," Riva said. Standing around on the sidewalk in the dark was awkward, especially with Noel. He was being polite, but there was an edge to his voice that made her nervous.

"We can wait in the car."

"It's locked." She tried the handle to prove it.

He pushed his hand into the pants pocket of his tailored evening suit. "I have an extra key."

"How convenient." The words were sharp.

He refused to rise to the provocation. "Just a habit, being prepared for any possibility."

There was nothing to be done except to climb into the long vehicle when he opened the door and held it for her. She settled onto the rear seat and he slid in beside her. He closed the door after them and the interior lights went off, leaving them in darkness.

Neither spoke for long moments. They watched a couple leave the mint and walk arm in arm along the sidewalk toward their parked car. Somewhere a police siren sounded, growing louder then fading away.

The topic Riva chose to fill the silence was dictated by her own curiosity, though she selected her words with care. "I believe someone said you sat in with the jazz group tonight. I didn't know you were a musician."

"I'm not," he answered shortly.

"Groups as good as that one don't let just anyone play with them in public."

"The man on the trumpet is a friend from Paris, though he was born in New Orleans. Jazz is big over there, has been since the twenties, and he had a gig at one of the clubs in the Pigalle district a couple of years back. I used to go to see him and his boys, and they let me play around with the drums. We expatriate Louisianians got into the habit of after-hours jam sessions."

"Consoling yourselves with music from home?" she suggested, disturbed by the image his words evoked.

"You might say that."

There was no encouragement in his reply to enlarge on the subject. Riva fell silent.

"Don't you think," Noel said, turning toward her, "that having an affair with Edison Gallant so soon after my father's death is a little tasteless?"

His attack was disconcerting. "I'm not—" she began, at a loss, then stopped, took a deep breath, and started again. "There is no affair."

"Oh, yes, you were in his arms because you were dancing."

"What were you doing, spying on me?" Counterattack, she had discovered, was often the best way to answer unreasonable charges.

"The scene was rather public, not that that seemed to bother you. Funny, I thought that was the one thing we had in common, respect for my father's memory."

The words were hurtful. Her voice was stifled as she said, "So it is."

He turned toward her, bracing his arm on the seat back as he hovered over her. "Then what in God's name is going on with you and Gallant? Why won't you tell me?"

"It's my business, mine alone!"

"Your affair, you mean," he said in bitter contempt. "If you're so hard up for affection, why go to strangers? We've always kept it in the family before, haven't we?"

"Noel!" she cried, her eyes widening in disbelief.

Before the word had left her mouth he caught her shoulders to draw her to him. His lips, firm, slanting, came down on hers. The touch burned, flaring in moist heat along the curves of her mouth, spreading over the surface of her skin in ripples of sensual delight. Her muscles trembled with the effort of resistance and the equally urgent need to abandon it. Some instinct of self-preservation held her back; still, she could not prevent her hand from straying to his shoulder. She smoothed her palm upward, tangling her fingers in the thick and silky waves of hair at the base of his neck.

He traced the line of her parted lips with his tongue, touched the pearl glaze of her teeth, and tasted the sweet and fragile inner surface of her mouth. She met his tongue with her own, twining, drinking the flavor of champagne and his own sweetness.

He smoothed his hand over her hair and down the tapering line of her back, drawing her nearer. He inhaled her perfume, that heady blending of roses and gardenias and jasmine and other more exotic scents that was so much a part of her, holding it inside him as if he would hold her essence.

He went still. His muscles hardened, and a tremor ran through him. He thrust her away from him, releasing her and propelling himself away until he came up against the far door with his shoulder. One hand was pressed down on the seat, the other clenched in a fist on his thigh. He stared out the window, his face shadowed and unreadable in the dim light of the street lamps and the exterior lighting of the restaurant across the road.

"What is it?" she asked in a ragged whisper.

He breathed deeply, once, twice. When he answered, his voice was remote, stringently contained. "I'm sorry, I shouldn't have done that."

"No. Why did you?"

"It won't happen again."

She sank back, leaning her head against the seat and closing her eyes. There was a stinging sensation under her lashes, and she blinked it away. "I don't belong to the Staulets or anyone else. I belong to me."

"Yes, I know."

She opened her eyes, staring at his dark profile with a haunted sensation inside her. There was in the compression of his voice a raw note that was a reminder of a host of memories she had thought safely locked away in the deepest recesses of her mind. She did not want them released, could not bear it.

A high-pitched laugh pierced the night. Margaret was leaving the mint, clinging to her husband's arm. If the way she walked and the inane smile on her face were any indications, she had had too much to drink.

Riva sighed in relief at the sight. The man beside her let out his breath also in a soft sound that was an echo of her own.

10

Erin blew into the house like a clean breeze. She let the back door slam behind her, taking the stairs two at a time as she called out for her mother. She found Margaret with Riva where they were having breakfast on the upper gallery overlooking the pool at the rear of the house. She swooped down on them, giving them both an exuberant hug.

"Please, sweetie," Margaret said, lifting a hand to her temple, "my head."

Erin dropped into a chair and flung the thick, curling mane of her hair back behind her shoulders. She twitched aside the napkin covering the basket of croissants and took one, biting into it. "What's the matter? Sinus headache?"

"The champagne served at the benefit last night was undoubtedly cheap. It's given me the most terrible—"

"You're hung over!" Erin said in gleeful amazement.

"I am not!" Margaret gave the girl an outraged stare before closing her eyes in pain.

"You certainly look the worse for wear to me." Erin took another bite of her croissant, her eyes bright.

"Your mother isn't used to nightlife," Riva said.

Margaret opened her eyes to glare at her sister. "You needn't make it sound like I'm a countrified stay-at-home."

Riva's smile held sympathy as well as amusement. "I thought you might prefer it to sounding like a lush."

"I told you—"

"Oh, Mama, lighten up. Nobody thinks you got bombed on purpose!"

Margaret seemed to swell. "I did not get bombed. That's a fine way to talk to your mother, I must say! I don't suppose I have far to look to discover where you learned such disrespect. If I had known this was how it would be, I would never have allowed you to come down here to this wicked place for college. I don't know what was wrong with going to Tech. At least you would have been closer to home."

It was a familiar diatribe. Erin rolled her eyes heavenward but made no reply. Riva stepped into the breach. "Speaking of which, Erin love, why aren't you in class?"

Erin sent her a quick grin. "I skipped. It isn't every day my folks come to visit. I see you're playing hooky, too."

Riva smiled in agreement. She usually stayed away from work when Margaret visited. Her sister expected it. Besides, the thought of Constance and Margaret being forced to entertain each other in her absence had seemed a situation too problematical to risk. As it turned out, she need not have worried. Constance usually kept to her room until noon, then liked to stay up late, while Margaret rose early and retired to her room for a nap after lunch as a stirring prelude to an early night. The two women had hardly seen each other except to nod in passing.

"You got my message before you left, about the photographer?" Riva said to the younger woman. She had given Doug Gorsline's number to Erin's roommate when she called, since Erin had been out.

"Lord, yes. Isn't that weird, him going to so much trouble to get in touch? I gave him a call. He'll be over this afternoon."

It was said so blithely that it took Riva's breath for an instant. "You—you mean he's coming here?"

"Sure. Is there some reason he shouldn't?" Erin looked from Riva to Margaret, who sat with her hand shading her half-closed eyes, paying scant attention. "I mean, I know I probably should have asked, but my friends never seemed to bother you before, Aunt Riva."

Recovering, Riva waved a hand. "No, no problem."

"That's good, because I don't know this guy from Adam's off uncle, and I didn't want it to seem like a date."

"Very wise. Is . . . anyone else coming?"

"Who? Oh, you mean Josh?" Erin grinned. "You think you're going to have some kind of triangle on your hands?"

"The thought occurred to me."

Erin shook her head as she reached for the blackberry jam and a second croissant. "Josh has to man the phone at his dad's head-quarters. Actually, I was supposed to stuff envelopes after class, but Josh agreed being with everyone here was more important."

Margaret sniffed. "Kind of him."

"Yes, wasn't it. But it's just as well he isn't here. There's something I wanted to talk about to you both without him."

Margaret flung a quick glance of alarm at Riva before she spoke. "Something about Josh?"

"Yeah, sort of. There's a bunch from school planning a bicycle tour of the Colorado mountains during the break between the summer session and the fall semester, and Josh and I would like to go. We'd only be away a week, since that's about all Josh can take from the campaign. I thought we could all stay at your cabin, Aunt Riva, and take picnics and side trips, maybe an overnight bike ride or two. It would be so great! Most of the kids have never seen anything like your place up there, and it would save money, too."

"Well, I—" Riva began.

"Just a minute," Margaret interrupted, her voice strident. "You are asking me, young lady, to let you take off for a week to Colorado with Edison Gallant's son?"

"There'll be two or three other couples. The girls will probably sleep in one room and the guys in the other."

"Probably? *Probably?* What does that mean? If you think I'm going to give you my permission to go sleep with that boy or wallow all over each other in Riva's cabin with these other couples, having orgies and smoking pot and I don't know whatall, you've got another think coming! No, you can't go to Colorado!"

Erin threw down her croissant and sprang to her feet with tears forming in her eyes. "I knew it! I knew you'd turn it into something dirty. Well, the dirt's in your own mind, Mom. Josh isn't like that."

"They're all like that."

"How do you know, tell me that? Aunt Riva isn't like you, always seeing something filthy everywhere she looks and making me feel dirty about something as good and clean as sex."

Margaret leaned forward. "And just what do you know about sex, clean or otherwise, pray?"

"Not that much, but keep on and I may give it a try to find out what sets you off about it. Josh Gallant is fun to be with, and I like him. He'd be as good a man as any for starters, even if he is a year younger than I am."

Margaret lunged forward, as if she would strike Erin, then gave a strangled moan and clutched both her head and her heart at the same time. Erin flushed guiltily but swung toward Riva. "Tell her, Aunt Riva," she begged. "Make her see there's nothing wrong about this trip. You know Josh. He wouldn't do anything wrong."

Riva got to her feet, putting her hand on the girl's shoulder and clasping it in a soothing gesture. "Erin honey, I'd like to help, but I have to say your mother has a point. I mean, if you really aren't serious about Josh, don't you think this trip would be tempting fate?"

"If we wanted to tempt fate, as you put it, we could do it right here in New Orleans!"

"I see that, but—"

Erin's face twisted. "No, you don't see at all! You just expect people my age to hop into bed the first chance they get. It's enough to make a person wonder what you did when you were young or what you do now when you get the chance!"

"Erin!"

Margaret cried out at the same time, "That will be enough, my girl!"

"Yes, it will," Erin shouted, "more than enough. I'm of age, you know. If I want to go, if I want to sleep with Josh, or half the men in New Orleans for that matter, there's not a damn thing you can do, either of you, to stop me!"

Whirling away from them, she ran from the upper gallery. They heard her footsteps thudding down the carpeted stairs. Minutes later, her small car roared into life and screeched away down the drive.

Riva sat back down. She picked up her coffee cup and took a sip. The coffee was cold and bitter. She put it down again. Agitation thrummed along her veins until she felt as if she could not bear to stay in her own skin with it. Erin was so much like Beth, so much.

Margaret, still pressing her temple and her chest with her fists, turned her head to stare at Riva. "It's your fault. Erin never defied me before in her life, never said such things to me. You have ruined her with your liberal ideas, totally spoiled her by giving her everything she so much as hints that she wants. If she goes off with that boy and commits this horrible crime, it will be on your head. That's all I have to say. It will be on your head."

Riva looked at her sister, and her gaze was bleak. "There will be nothing new in that, Margaret. It's where it has always been."

"Yes. That's why you've got to do something, now, before it's too late."

"I'm trying."

"That isn't good enough. You know what Edison Gallant wants, he's made it plain enough. I saw it in his eyes last night when he thought I was you, and when he went over to speak to you. All you have to do is agree."

"Is that why you went off and left me with him, so I could?"

"You act as if it's the first time. What can be so terrible about it?"

"If you don't know, there's no way I can tell you." Riva clenched her teeth together to keep from saying more.

Margaret's face hardened. "It seems little enough to me, especially when your daughter's future is at stake."

Riva stared at the other woman. She could not believe Margaret had actually acknowledged that Erin was hers. Though she had made a game of trying to trick her into admitting it, there had also been times when Riva wanted to scream at her sister for her obstinate insistence, even in private, in claiming parentage. There had been days when Riva had whispered the words "my daughter" or "my little girl" just to assure herself that she had ever borne a child, so total had been Margaret's possession. It was almost frightening, now, to be permitted a claim to her.

She cleared her throat of the obstruction that had risen there. "Edison can't be relied upon to keep his end of the bargain. More than that, he may say he only wants this one thing, to get me into his bed, but it would be like him to demand more and more."

"Whatever he wants," Margaret said, reaching out and catching her wrist with hard fingers. "I still say that you have to give it to him. If you don't, I don't know how we're going to live with our-selves."

Before she finished speaking, Boots appeared in the doorway leading into the hall. He came toward them with a frown on his red-tinted face. "What's going on?" he asked. "What's the matter with Erin? She looked like she was crying when she passed me downstairs, and she didn't even say hello."

Margaret leaned back in her chair with a weary gesture. "Noth-ing. Nothing's wrong."

"That's not the truth, Margaret. I heard what you said to Riva, and I know it has something to do with Erin and with Edison's son. I want to know the problem."

There was something immovable about Boots. His mind might not be quick, but it was steady and sure, and once he settled on an idea he clung to it with bulldog tenacity. It seemed perfectly possible that he would stand there in that one spot in front of them forever in order to find out what he wanted to know.

"All right, then," his wife said, her lips tightening in exasper-ation. In a few clipped sentences, she told him exactly what had taken place up to the moment Erin left them.

Boots wagged his head back and forth when she was finished. "The thing to do is to tell Erin how she stands with Josh, that he's her half brother."

"Riva doesn't want her to know," Margaret said sharply.

"Erin's a big girl, she can take it." Her husband's words were dogged.

"Yes," Riva said with a wry smile, "but can I?"

"If it's your reputation that's bothering you—" Margaret began.

"Not mine, rather Staulet Corporation's," Riva said. "As Edison was so prompt to point out, it will affect a lot of people besides me if the story becomes public."

Margaret, her face grim, got to her feet. "There's only one thing to be done. Riva knows what it is; she's just too proud to do it. You'll have to excuse me now. I've got to take my medicine."

Boots showed no sign of following his wife. He stood in frowning thought until Riva spoke at last. "Would you care for coffee, Boots?"

"What? Yes, all right," he answered. As she poured it, he lowered himself into the chair Margaret had left. He spooned sugar into the cup and sat stirring it into the black brew, watching the swirling liquid, then pushed the cup back without tasting it. Finally he looked up at Riva.

"She don't mean it, you know."

Riva's mind had wandered to Erin and what she was doing, where she was going in such fury, and if she was too angry to drive carefully. "What?"

"Margaret, I mean. She don't really expect you to do anything you think's wrong. She's just upset. She says things she don't really mean when she gets in a stew like this. It's her way."

He really was a good man. Riva smiled with a shade of weariness. "I know. Don't worry about it."

The lines in his face eased, but he wasn't finished. "She's turning more and more religious nowadays. She reads her Bible a lot, and prays—why, she prays nearly an hour every night. That's the nights she don't drink more bourbon and Coke than's good for her or take a few extra Valiums. She's all mixed up in her mind. I think it's weighing on her, everything that happened all those years ago. This thing with Josh Gallant has brought it all back."

"Yes, for both of us."

"It's more than that, though. She—she's never quite got over not being able to have kids of her own. She should have had five or six to fuss over and look after and keep her busy. Instead, she just has the one. I think she's always been sort of jealous, resentful-like, that Erin was really yours. And I think, in a funny sort of way, she feels like it was a judgment on her, that if she hadn't taken your baby away from you she might have had one herself."

"She did what she thought was best at the time."

"But it was what she wanted, not what you needed or would have liked, and she's never forgot it. That's why when Erin came down here, she got afraid you were taking her back again, that Erin's head would be turned by all the stuff you could give her, all this fancy living, and that she wouldn't be happy with us anymore."

"I never intended anything like that," Riva said with a shake of her head. "I just wanted to give Erin some of the things I never had."

Boots nodded. "It's some of the things Margaret never had, too. She resents that down deep. She never says anything, but I know it bothers her that she never had all the fancy clothes and jewelry and cars you've had over the years since you married Staulet, never got to go to all the places you've been, see all the things you've seen. She feels it."

"I can't help that. I've offered to take her with me to Europe, and you know the two of you can use the places in Colorado or the islands any time."

"We know, but it's not just the places. It's the people you know and who know you, the things you can do, the whole way you live. I think sometimes she'd like to be you, at least for a little while."

"Oh, Boots, that can't be right. She has so much, you and Erin and so many years of decent family life among the same people she's known all her life. She has roots and real friends, instead of living on the surface, wondering what people are saying about her when her back is turned. She has you instead of—" She stopped abruptly. There were some things it was best not to put into words.

"Yes, and she's all right, most of the time, but there are days when it all eats at her."

Riva looked at the man across from her for a long moment. "You must love her very much to understand her so well."

"We've been married a long time," he answered, shifting uncomfortably in his chair.

"Yes, and it comes to me that you've spent a lot of that time taking care of my daughter, giving her a stable home, a good home. I've always been grateful, though I've never thanked you for it."

"Don't have to thank me now, either," he said, his voice gruff. "I feel like Erin's my own. Always have, always will."

Riva smiled as she met his straight gaze. After a moment, she said, "As for Margaret, I know she's a little snappy at times, but it doesn't matter. She has done so much for me that I have to forgive her."

"She knows that, too, and she depends on it. I'm just afraid she might depend on it once too often."

She searched his round, honest face, noting its deep color, the sheen of perspiration on his upper lip, the strain in his eyes. It had cost him a great deal to speak so openly about his wife. That he had made the effort was important. Slowly it came to her that his concern was for the possibility that Margaret would push her into doing something she had no wish to do, just as she had years before.

She gave a slow nod. "I'll remember," she said, "but don't fret. I won't do anything I don't want to."

"Maybe," he said. "But the trouble is why you might decide you want to do it."

To that Riva made no answer, for there was none.

Noel left Bonne Vie early. It was cowardice, he knew, but he didn't feel up to making small talk over the breakfast table, had no wish whatever to see Riva so soon after what had happened the night before.

He had lost it there for a moment.

She had looked so untouchable in her shimmering cream evening gown, had been so untouchable for him for so long, that seeing her in Edison Gallant's arms even for a second had been intolerable. It was as if she had been sullied in some way, and the fact that she didn't seem to realize it herself, might even have invited it, had been maddening.

More than that, he had wanted to make her as aware of him as she was of the other man. He might have succeeded too well. Riva had an acute sense about people.

God, but he hadn't felt such a sense of living on the edge since his first week as a military adviser in Vietnam. It had been what he needed then, when his father had kicked him out of the nest for the sake of the child bride they both wanted, and he had been so wrapped up in pain and disillusionment that it had scarcely mattered whether he lived or died. Or so he told himself. He had found out how much it mattered when he heard the first shell scream past overhead. Self-pity and the petty defiance that had made him join the marines instead of accepting his dismissal to the backwater of the Paris office had given way to a healthy rage. The rage had stayed with him. It helped to be mad as hell when people were trying to kill you. Half of the heroics for which they had pinned medals on him later had been because he refused to step aside anymore. He had done that once and left behind everything that mattered to him. He never intended to do it again.

Noel enjoyed driving himself, enjoyed the powerful purr of the twelve-cylinder engine under the hood of the BMW 750 IL, enjoyed leaning into the curves of the Great River Road that ran alongside the Mississippi. It was in his nature to be in control; whether that was an advantage or a fault he neither knew nor cared. A great many executives these days were concerned with security, hiring bodyguards and installing devices in their cars to foil kidnappers. Even George, whether Riva realized it or not, had had training in protecting his passenger, not to mention his hitch in the military with heavy-duty survival practice in Nam also. Noel, however, preferred to rely on the superior engine of his car, the licensed handgun in the BMW's glove compartment, and himself.

The feel of Riva in his arms came back to him in a wave of heat. It had been a long time since he had held a woman, an eon since the last time he had held Riva. He had known how it would be, and he had been right. Forbidden sweets. He had felt twenty-one years old again and still in the midst of a raging Oedipus tragedy. Or had it been a farce? It was difficult, at this distance in time, to tell.

Regardless, the taste and scent of her lingered in his mind. They were a part of him, as familiar as his own. He had conjured them up on a thousand sleepless nights, creating of them a warm and breathing image that crept into his bed beside him, all grace and tender caring, naked and endlessly accommodating. It had helped. Yet the reality had the power to make him doubt his sanity. Even now, thinking about it, he felt as if he were being consumed by fire from the inside. To keep the pain from showing required all his strength, all his energy.

"Take care of Riva."

He gripped the steering wheel in a stranglehold as those words filtered into his mind. His father had dared to say them to him as he lay dying. His father had held his arm with the last of his failing strength and looked at him with hope and despair and, yes, with love, and given him that command. Noel wished he knew what it had meant. Was it a sacred trust or, at long last, permission?

Noel didn't need permission, had never needed it. What he needed, then and now, was absolution.

He would take care of Riva.

Noel did not normally go to meetings of civic clubs. He had been approached about joining several on his return to New Orleans but had declined. He was not an organization person and had lost touch with the concept of civic betterment while in Europe. His call to a friend about the chamber of commerce luncheon he was going to attend today, then, had more to do with the guest speaker than his interest in the group's undoubted accomplishments. The speaker was Edison Gallant.

A few hours later, Noel sat watching and listening to the man, evaluating his appearance and his words with what he hoped was detached judgment. There was a façade of strength there, a good speaking voice, flashy good looks based on the tried-and-true Kennedy style—albeit with a Southern accent—and a doctrine of active leadership and spending cuts to bolster the state's economy. But there was no real substance. In addition, there was tension in the man's movements and in the lines of his face that suggested that he was not as confident as he appeared.

What Gallant had to say was well received, however, and when the luncheon was over, his well-wishers crowded around to tell him so. It was some time before Noel could speak to him. After a perfunctory compliment on his talk, Noel requested a few minutes of his time.

Wariness crept onto Edison's face. "Is it important?"

"It could be."

"What's that supposed to mean?"

"I have no way of knowing what you consider important. I was under the impression that campaign contributions were always of interest to candidates."

Edison pursed his lips. "I have an adequate campaign chest; I might even say more than adequate."

Noel inclined his head, though he was aware of some small surprise. "If you have more than enough, then I won't waste your time or mine."

"Hold on," Edison said. "What is it you want to talk about that involves money?"

"A matter of mutual interest, I believe the phrase goes."

Edison gave a snort of laughter. "I can always use a man of your influence in my corner. I'll be with you in a minute."

A half hour later, the two of them were sitting in the coffee shop of the hotel where the meeting had been held. They had it to themselves except for a crew of two in pink uniforms who were cleaning away the remains of the buffet and salad bar.

"You mentioned a contribution," Edison said when they had ordered coffee and the waitress had gone away to fetch it.

Noel sat back in his chair. The lack of finesse in the question was both annoying and gratifying, annoying because of the obvious attempt at pressure, gratifying because he had, after watching Edison, expected nothing else.

"I thought you had enough?"

"I've reconsidered. There's always room for more, especially if we're going to talk a deal."

"There is that possibility," Noel answered.

"How much?"

Noel met the politician's gaze squarely. "How much do you need?"

"Anything short of illegal," Edison said with a short laugh.

"Why stop there?"

The smile faded from Edison's face. He leaned across the table. "I'm in no mood for beating around the bush. What is it you want?"

Noel picked up the spoon he had unrolled from his napkin. He drew a circle on the table with its tip. He put it down again. Finally he said, "Information."

"About what?"

"Your association with Riva Staulet."

Edison grinned and sat back in his chair. "I should have known."

"Should you?" Noel sat without moving a muscle.

"You're out to get the bitch, too."

"I remind you that you are speaking of my dead father's wife, and I don't appreciate the term you just used. I take it as an insult to his name and to mine."

"God, I thought that shit went out with the Civil War."

"Your mistake."

"What the hell is this, then? You want to screw her out of your old man's fortune but without damaging her precious name?"

"I'm more interested in what you want with her."

"I want to screw her, period, if you must know."

"And what does she want?" Noel's voice was hard.

"God knows. I never did."

Noel studied him. "I don't think that's quite the truth."

"About as much as you've given me," Edison said with a tight laugh.

"Yes," Noel said softly, "but then you don't have anything I want."

"I thought I did. Information."

"Something I can always get elsewhere, though it may take longer."

Uneasiness crossed Edison's face as he met Noel's hard gray gaze. He waved a hand. "Never mind. You have a lot better chance to get back at the bitch than I do, and more power to you. How you go about it is no skin off my nose. What do you want to know?"

11

Riva watched from her chair in the shadows of the upper front gallery of Bonne Vie as Doug Gorsline arrived. It was midafternoon and Erin had returned perhaps a half hour before, in plenty of time for her appointment. One of the girl's many good qualities was that she remembered her obligations. She had avoided both Riva and Margaret, however, by taking over the entertainment of Noel's children from the nursemaid who had been found for them, one of George and Liz's granddaughters. Erin was out back in the pool with Coralie and Pietro, refereeing the water fights between the two and keeping the little imps more or less in the shady end to prevent sunstroke.

The photographer got out of his car and stood staring up at the house for long moments. Bonne Vie had that effect on some people, a combination of awe and nostalgia with a shading of envy. It gave Riva a better feeling toward him that he was susceptible to past grandeur, no matter how dedicated he might be to recording the present.

Doug Gorsline moved up the walk and disappeared under the gallery. A moment later, the doorbell rang. Riva waited a short time after she heard him being admitted, then rose and walked into the house and through the upstairs hallway to the back gallery.

She had never liked gambling, no matter how well calculated the risk. The palms of her hands were sweating and her stomach churned. Fanciful images ran through her mind, tilting her lips in a mirthless smile. She could not decide whether she was the spider who had invited the fly to enter or the grandmother with the wolf inside the door.

This was her daughter's life that she was attempting to manage. The idea made her feel guilty and manipulative. She had the best of intentions, but that did not really count. She had always felt it was wrong to interfere deliberately in other people's lives. There were times when it could not be helped, but it should never be on purpose, for a person's own gain. Her only gain in this case was peace of mind; still, the principle was the same.

She hoped, quite simply, that Doug Gorsline would be able to supplant Josh Gallant in Erin's affections. He was articulate, intelligent, and good-looking, and he had the kind of persistence that might appeal to a young woman. More than that, he was obviously smitten.

Or else he was an excellent actor, in which case his instincts as a newspaperman could be extremely dangerous.

From the upper back gallery it was possible to see beyond the pool, from the row of columns at the far end to the sweep of lawn set with ancient trees, which led down to the ornamental pond. The glare of the afternoon sun shone silver-white on the templelike folly in the middle of the reed-edged body of still water. Even from the gallery the huge, calm Buddha housed inside could be seen glinting in the interior dimness.

The folly had been a favorite place of Cosmo's. He and Riva had often had coffee there on summer mornings while they watched the sun rise. She had hardly been out there at all since his death. It was too much of a reminder of loss.

It felt strange, then, to see Doug Gorsline strolling in that direction, trespassing beyond what she felt were the acceptable precincts. It was all right for him to invade the pool area, but the place he was heading to was too private.

A moment later, Riva saw the reason. Erin and the two children had left the pool and were at the folly. They were having a picnic at the feet of the great Buddha.

"Who is that?"

Riva jumped, startled by Margaret's question. She had been so absorbed in the scene below that she hadn't heard her sister come out onto the gallery.

"That's Doug Gorsline," Riva answered, then waited for the explosion.

"Doug— But isn't that the name of the photographer who . . . What is he doing here?" Margaret's voice rose until it was a near shriek.

"Calm down. He wanted to see Erin."

"Are you crazy? You knew he was coming, didn't you? When you said something about a photographer this morning, I never dreamed you meant him! I thought it was something to do with the campaign or maybe with school."

"It has to do with an attractive young man being interested in Erin. Someone other than Josh."

"He's with a newspaper!" It was as if Margaret could not believe Riva understood the situation, as if yelling would make it plainer. Her eyes were wide with horror as she watched the young man reach the folly and, once inside, drop to one knee as if to join the picnic in progress.

Riva took her sister's arm and gave it a small shake. "Get ahold of yourself. Do you want everyone in the house to know what's happening?"

"They might as well. It will be no secret once that cretin gets his nose into the story."

"I don't think that's what he's after."

"You're a fool," her sister said.

"For heaven's sake, Margaret. He took a picture. That isn't a crime."

"It is if he comes sniffing around for more. I can't believe you let him come here, that you as good as invited him!"

Riva, however, was paying no attention to the diatribe. She made a quick gesture for silence as she stood in stiff concentration. There were voices coming from just below them. As they watched, a man emerged from under the gallery. He skirted the pool at a quick lope and headed toward the lake. As he left the shade of the live oaks, the sun caught his hair and was reflected in it by soft blond gleams.

It was Josh Gallant, apparently done with his duty at his father's headquarters. Erin saw him coming, for she called out, her voice floating joyful and welcoming across the lake. She got to her feet and ran down the path and over the bridge that led across the water to the templelike building. She flung herself into Josh's arms and lifted her mouth to be kissed. The two clung together for what seemed like endless moments before finally breaking apart and turning back toward the folly.

"Did you see that?" Margaret hissed. "Did you? It has to stop. You have to do something! If you won't do it, if you can't do it without making matters worse, then I will. Do you hear me, I will!"

Jerking away from her, Margaret stepped back, then turned toward the wide doorway into the house. Riva made no reply, for they were no longer alone. Noel's ex-wife stepped aside as Margaret passed her just inside the door, then Constance strolled out onto the gallery to stand with her hand shading her eyes while she stared at the folly. She smiled when she saw her children on the bridge behind Erin.

The two of them watched in silence as Erin, with Coralie and Pietro holding her hands and the two young men trailing behind, formed a group and moved in the direction of the house.

It was the first Riva had seen of Constance since the night before. The other woman had returned quite late and still was not dressed for the day. Her dark hair was tousled, she had no makeup on, and a robe in vivid sea-green cotton with matching slippers was wrapped around her. She was hardly more than thirty-five, and she was stunning.

To break what was becoming an uncomfortable silence, Riva said, "Did you sleep well?"

Constance gave her a smile that carried an edge of mockery. "Very. I quite like your friend, Dante. He's most sympathetic, an amusing man."

"Yes," she agreed politely. "You needn't worry about your children, as you can see. Erin has been entertaining them."

"How sweet of her. And I see that, like her aunt, she prefers her men in pairs."

"Excuse me?"

"Nothing, nothing," Constance said, retreating before the coolness of Riva's tone. "You just seem to have so many men friends. It occurred to me to wonder if you could spare Dante."

"He isn't mine to keep or to spare," Riva said evenly. "He makes his own friends."

"How magnanimous. Then you won't mind if I annex him?"

"For the length of your stay?"

"Or longer, if it happens that way." The woman's smile was predatory.

Riva turned to face Constance. "I'm not sure what you're getting at, but it makes no difference. As I said, Dante chooses his own friends."

"Strange."

"What is?"

The other woman shrugged. "You are serious. I find it odd that this is your reaction instead of jealousy."

"You have to be afraid in order to be jealous."

"And you aren't afraid of me. Such confidence."

"Does that bother you?" Riva asked. "Maybe it's because I know that Dante has other things on his mind at the moment."

"Oh, yes?"

The skepticism in the other woman's accented voice drove Riva on. "For instance, the sudden appearance last night of the drug XTC, otherwise known as Ecstasy, at his place on the lake. He's always managed to keep the premises clean of pushers and dope-heads before, but not now. And he doesn't want it to become known as another 'X' place, after this Ecstasy. He's worked too hard for it to come to that."

"You have spoken to Dante this morning? He came to see you?"

"He called."

"And he did not ask to speak to me?"

"Not that I know of."

Constance gave a pettish shrug. "I suppose he must have been concerned with this drug then, as you say. I'm not familiar with it."

The comment made it sound as if the XTC could not possibly be dangerous then. Riva said, "It's not exactly new, according to Dante, just rediscovered, but it's fast becoming a major problem.

It's made with amphetamine in combination with the mescaline of the Southwest Indians, but is more lethal than either. I understand it causes some extremely strange reactions, both physical and mental, though the great attraction at the moment is that it's supposed to be an aphrodisiac."

"Ah, I begin to see."

Riva doubted it. Her own worry was for the threat to Dante, rather than the effects of this latest designer drug. There were many, her sister Margaret among them, who felt that Dante knew more about drug dealing than he admitted, that he made such a big deal out of keeping his place on the lake clean so that he would look innocent. There had been whispers for years, since his days among the Italians around the French Market, connecting him with underworld figures and their unsavory ventures. She knew Dante had friends whose finances and activities would not bear close scrutiny, but the two of them, she and Dante, went back such a long way together that she could believe nothing really bad of him. He was a devout Catholic and the product of a conscientious upbringing by his Cajun mother. In all the years Riva had known him, through all manner of provocation, she had never seen him do a dishonest or dishonorable thing. That was good enough for her.

Now she said, "Yes, and can you also see that if your aim is a brief fling, you have the wrong man?"

"You think he won't be interested?" Constance stared at her with a challenging tilt to her chin.

"I couldn't say. I only know that Dante is . . . special."

"Oh, yes, a Cajun playboy."

"Not really."

"I hear otherwise."

"You hear wrong. Oh, he has his women, but only a certain type, never the kind who will be hurt."

"Are you saying that I—"

"By no means," Riva said hastily. "I'm only trying to let you know that Dante is the sort of man who, if he really decides to play, will play for keeps. It's possible he might be attracted to you, in which case I would warn you to take care. He could be easily hurt by the wrong person."

"I'm sure you ought to know."

Below them, Erin and the others were gathering around the pool. Riva felt a sudden urge to be with them, to join in their laughter, their uncomplicated banter. She swung away from the other woman. Over her shoulder she said, "Yes, I ought to know."

"I'm so ashamed," Rebecca had wailed to Dante on the evening when she had, for the first time, danced on top of a barroom table wearing nothing more than a pair of three-inch white heels with rhinestones bows and a piece of white nylon fringe held in place by a G-string.

It was the only job she could find. The position as dishwasher at the restaurant had been filled, during the time she was recovering from childbirth, by a mechanical monster that used water far hotter than human hands could stand and soap strong enough to eat gold-plating. She wasn't sophisticated enough or old enough to work as a restaurant hostess, and the only interview for a shop-girl position she could get was conducted by a buxom gray-haired woman with a mustache who had turned up her nose at Rebecca's shabby clothes and made her feel stupid because she only had a ninth-grade education. She had answered an ad for a maid, very nearly using her last nickel to ride the bus all the way out to Kenner, only to be told that a reliable middle-aged black woman was required.

She had been desperate. Margaret still insisted that she could not come home for her mother's sake and that Boots's salary just would not stretch to cover two households another week longer. Her sister had supported Rebecca for nearly two months after the baby was born and felt that was enough. Rebecca's rent was due, her electric bill was overdue, and the last can of cheap tuna was gone. For two nights in a row, Dante had shared his supper with her. When late one afternoon she had seen the Help Wanted sign on the barroom door, she had gathered her courage and walked inside.

The man who talked to her was so grossly overweight that his body bulged in odd places like a huge balloon filled with water. His head was bald, his eyebrows were like yellow caterpillars, and his expression was sour. Regardless, he didn't ask how old she was or how much education she had. He made her turn slowly around in front of him, then wanted to know if she knew how to dance. She said she did. It wasn't a lie since she and Beth and Margaret had learned the jitterbug, the waltz, and the rhumba, not to mention the twist. The man had then handed her the pair of white shoes with the shiny buckles and told her to try them on. They had fit. The man had jiggled his double chins in what could be taken for a nod and told her to come back that evening at six.

It was when she returned that he gave her the G-string. She understood what it was at once but didn't have the least idea how to put it on. One of the other girls showed her, a coffee-with-cream-colored black girl who called herself Trixie. She brushed out Rebecca's hair so that it reached to the middle of her back in a shining cascade and adjusted the fringe of the G-string so that it hung just so. The width of the little piece of fringe, she said, was carefully monitored by the police, so it had better cover what it was meant to cover. Talking up a storm about how much money the girls made in tips and the many ways the men tried to sneak a peek or a rub, Trixie had urged Rebecca to hurry before the boss man came to find out what was taking so long. He was a fat old bastard who expected his girls to waggle their tits and asses as if they meant it. And, by the way, if the police came around, Rebecca was to say she was eighteen and not a day less.

There was no mirror in the drafty closet of a room in back of the bar. Regardless, Rebecca could see enough of herself to know that she was as nearly naked as made no difference. She had walked past the door of the Bourbon Street bar with Edison once or twice, glancing in at the women waiting on the tables and sometimes dancing on them. She knew what was expected. Still, those women had never looked as naked as she felt.

"I can't do it," she said, and reached for her panties.

Trixie, wearing a piece of green fringe and green boots with turned-down cuffs like those of a Sherwood Forest archer, frowned and put her fists on her bare hipbones. "What is it?" she demanded. "You think you're better than the rest of us?"

"No, but I just can't."

"Maybe you got a sugar daddy to pay the bills? Maybe you're a rich bitch doing this for kicks?"

"I need the money or I wouldn't be here. But I'll just make a fool out of myself if I go out there!"

"You'll get used to it. All you have to do is not think about it."

"How? How can I do that with all those men looking?"

"Let 'em look! What does it hurt? Anyway, what've you got that's so special?" Trixie's gaze was cool and yet somehow blank, as if she had no memory of the feelings Rebecca was trying to explain, as if she had pushed them far back into some dark corner of her mind.

"Nothing, I only—"

"Listen, if you don't get out there, we're both going to find our asses in a crack. That fat bastard don't mess around. He put a girl in the hospital once for skimming off the drink money. If he has to go short-handed tonight, he could decide to take it out of your hide."

"He can't make me do it," Rebecca said, her lips tightening. She twisted around, searching for the fastening of the G-string.

"No, but he can make you wish you had. Anyway, if you leave he's liable to think I said something and come after me. You wouldn't want that." When she saw Rebecca hesitate, Trixie went on. "Besides, who's to know or care what you do, anyway?"

"I know."

"Yeah, but it's your body; you can use it to make money if you want. If there was anybody who cared about it, cared about you, then you wouldn't be here."

There was enough truth in that to hurt. Rebecca had discovered that she could deaden the pain by refusing to think of it, refusing to feel. She could sense that numbness stealing over her, taking away her anger and her righteousness, leaving only desolation. When Trixie took her arm, urging her toward the barroom, she did not resist.

It was like stepping into a nightmare, something terrible and scary and yet somehow unreal. The music was so loud it boomed in a solid echo off the walls. Men sat at tables so close together that the customers' shoulders touched, and Rebecca could not pass between them without bending this way and that over and around them, brushing against them while a few reached out to trail their fingers over her body. The smell of cheap whiskey and sour, acid wine hung with the gray blanket of cigarette smoke in the air, catching in the back of her throat and making breathing a chore. Within minutes, her body and her hair smelled just like it. The only good thing was the dim lighting. It not only made counting out bills for the drinks difficult—and leaving a good margin for tipping errors by befuddled patrons, according to Trixie—but gave a false illusion of modesty.

It may have been her freshness or her air of awkward embarrassment or possibly the long golden-brown swath of her hair and the sweet curves of her body with their fullness after her pregnancy that made her popular that evening. Whatever the cause, she was a favorite. Everywhere she looked, men stared at her, talked to her, beckoned to her. The first time she was helped onto the top of a table, Trixie was there. She leaned to whisper in Rebecca's ear, "Don't think, just do it. And make it sexy. Make it good."

Rebecca didn't know how. Instead she tried desperately to forget where she was and how she was dressed, or rather undressed, forget the man staring up at her from below with red-rimmed and avid eyes, the man who had bought this dance. She closed her own eyes and thought instead of Erin and her mother and the bills lying unpaid on her table. Then she let the music's hard, fast beat take her. It was a job, she told herself. It was just a job.

Dante was waiting when she finally came home in the early-morning hours. His face went pale, then red when she told him where she had been, what she had been doing.

"My God, why didn't you tell me? I'd have found something else for you, anything else!"

The feelings so carefully held back sprang forward with full force. Her face twisted. "There was nothing else. I looked, really I did!"

"They say the fat guy who runs that place is in with the mob, that he sets up the girls as dancers, then hires them out. He's a pimp, Rebecca."

"A pimp?"

"He sells women, sells their bodies to other men."

She stared at him as what he was saying penetrated. Her eyes filled with tears that spilled over her lashes and dripped down her face in warm tracks. "There's nothing else. What am I going to do, Dante? What am I going to do?"

He touched her shoulder in concern, then sighed and took her in his arms. "It's all right," he said into her hair. "It's all right. It's just that you are so far above it."

"I danced for one old man six times," she sobbed into his shoulder. "Six times. He never tried to touch me like the others, didn't try to put the money in my—my costume. He gave me twenty dollars every time, every time! When he gave it to me, he bowed and kissed my hand. I felt terrible."

"Forget it," he said, his voice low as he stroked her hair.

They stood in the middle of the living room of her apartment where he had been waiting for her when she got home. It was May, and the windows stood open to the balmy night air. The glow of the bare bulb hanging on its cord from the ceiling was yellow and not too obtrusively bright. His heart beat with a steady rhythm under her ear. His arms around her were warm and strong; there was comfort in them, and safety. She leaned against him. She was so tired, so very tired.

"*Chère*," he said, and his voice was compressed, thickened. She felt the firmness against her lower belly and realized what was happening.

"I'm sorry," she said softly, trying to pull away.

"Oh, *chère*." He whispered the words as he bent his head and brushed her lips with his own.

His kiss was gentle, almost diffident, as if he were afraid she would protest. It never occurred to her. He had been so good to her, and she owed him so much. More, she loved him with a quiet affection totally unlike the brief infatuation she had felt for Edison. And there was inside her a need to be wanted that was like an ache.

She led him into the bedroom. There in the darkness that was cut by an oblong shaft of light from the other room, they breathed each other's breaths and tasted each other's skin. He cupped her face in his hands and pressed his lips to her eyes, the hollows under them, the bridge of her nose, the points of her cheekbones and of her chin. He smoothed his palms over her shoulders and drew her arms around him, rocking her in soothing joy.

She clutched the firm muscles of his back and inhaled the scent of his body at the curve of his neck, tasting the salt secretion of it. With trembling fingers, she drew the T-shirt he wore from his jeans, sliding her hands upward to brush his chest with her thumbs.

Together they subsided onto the sagging mattress and creaking springs of the bed. He fumbled a little as he opened the buttons of her dress, then drew in his breath with an audible gasp as he rubbed the soft curves of her breasts with his closed eyelids and the planes of his face. She felt the hot, wet flick of his tongue on first one nipple and then the other. He spread his fingers over the flat, almost hollow surface of her abdomen, sliding downward until he touched the warm, gentle rise of her pubic mound.

He went still.

She felt him shudder. He caught her close, rocking her, burying his face in her neck. After a moment, she felt the hot seep of his tears.

"What is it?" she whispered in alarm. She moved her hands over him in distress, as if she could search out the injury that pained him.

"I can't. Oh, God, *chère*, I can't."

"But . . . why? Don't you want me?" Her voice was tight, almost choked. She ran her fingers quickly, lightly down his body, but the firmness was gone.

"More than life, more than life." He stopped for a moment, and she felt his teeth clench and his lips draw back in a grimace as he struggled with his grief.

Her voice rising in distress, she said, "What's wrong? Dante, please."

"Hush, hush," he said, his voice thick. "It's not your fault, it's mine."

"I don't understand!"

"It's how I see you. I—I see you as the Madonna with her child, a sacred lady, our little mother, too holy to be touched. I see you covered with blood and refusing to cry with the pain of birthing a baby. I see you as Mary, mother of God, who forgives the sins of men against her." His voice broke. "I see you so far above me."

"No, I'm not. I'm not like that!"

He swallowed with a convulsive movement of his throat. "You are to me."

"Mary was pure and she didn't make mistakes, not like me. She didn't desert her mother and her sister. She didn't give up her child. She didn't dance naked in front of . . . in front of men."

The tears welled up as if from a deep wound. She didn't know they were coming; they simply poured from her as if they would never end, tears of loss and guilt and sorrow. Mingled with them was despair that she and Dante could never have each other, be with each other. She had somehow expected they would be, always. She hadn't known how much she had wanted that, needed it, until she felt the hope fading away.

"Nor do you, in my mind. You . . . I don't know if I can explain. What I feel for you is so precious to me that it scares me. I worship you so that touching you seems wrong, like touching the Madonna. I don't think—I'm not sure I can ever love you."

"I don't want you to feel like that. I don't want to be like that to you!" Her body shook against his with her silent, gasping breaths.

"I can't help it. God knows I would if I could."

"I'm me," she cried in low tones. "I'm only me."

"Shh," he said, "I'm sorry, so sorry."

She tried to stop crying, scrubbing at her face as she sniffled. "It isn't your fault; it's mine."

"Don't say that. It's really nobody's fault, I guess." He wiped her face with the heel of his hand, then gathered her close with the breath of his sigh warm and moist in her hair. "It's just the way things are."

It was nearly dawn before he finally brushed his lips across her forehead and slid from the bed. She might have dozed a little lying in his arms, but she was not asleep. She watched him cross to the door, saw him pause there a long moment, staring back at her. There was such bleakness in his face that she wanted to cry again, but there were no tears left.

Finally he turned and went through the living room, letting himself out the door to the back stairs. It closed quietly behind him.

Rebecca didn't see Dante the next day. He didn't come to her rooms, nor did she seek him out. They needed some time before they met, at least a few hours. He would come, surely, before it was time for her to go to work. They were going to have to talk about her job at least, since he seemed to think he could find something else for her.

Then that afternoon a young stockboy came at a run from the grocery store down the street. There was a call, an emergency, or else the grocer would never have agreed to pass on the message.

It was Margaret who had called. Rebecca must come home. Her mother was dead, Margaret said, and it would look strange if she didn't attend the funeral.

Rebecca had been wrong, there were tears left. Still, she was grateful then to the old man who had given her so much money in tips. She used it for the bus fare and also for a decent dress to wear to the funeral.

She stayed with Margaret and Boots in the house where she had been born and grew up. She was there for one day before the funeral and three days afterward. Margaret hardly allowed her to hold little Erin at all during that time. It would not do for her to get too fond of the child, her sister said, not if she was going away again.

It was possible Margaret was right. The feel of the baby, the sweet scent and warm weight of her in her arms, made Rebecca want to cry again. Sometimes she sat stroking the fine hair on top of the small head as Erin slept while she thought wild thoughts. She pictured herself bundling the baby up and taking her away in the night, or driving with her into town and walking up and down the streets and in and out of the post office and grocery store saying, "This is my baby. She grew inside me. This is my baby."

She couldn't do it. She had nothing to give Erin except love, no way to take care of her. Who would keep her while Rebecca worked at night, and what kind of life would it be for her with a mother who danced topless on the tables in a Bourbon Street bar?

Besides, everyone thought the baby was her sister's child, born of Margaret's body. To tell them different now would not only brand Margaret a liar but would take away her very life. Margaret was crazy about Erin, dwelling minutely on every little thing she did, every smile and every sound. She fretted and scolded and warned Rebecca about the way she held the baby and the way she changed her, and all the while she watched Rebecca with anxious, frightened eyes.

Rebecca didn't tell Margaret where she was working or what she was doing. Margaret didn't ask, nor did she ask after Dante or if Rebecca had heard from Edison. It was as if she preferred not to hear about Rebecca's life in New Orleans, as if she were afraid to hear. And she spoke so often of Rebecca's returning that even Rebecca began to take it for granted that she would go back. It was only after she was on the bus heading south again that she realized there was no reason for her to go. Her mother was dead, the baby she had borne was safely registered as Margaret's child. What was there to make her go?

The truth was, she couldn't stay. It would be better for Erin if she grew up with Margaret for her mother and good old Boots for her father in a happy, normal family. Rebecca was not sure she could allow that, could watch it without interfering, if she lived in the same house. Besides, the house where she had been born had seemed tinier, the town shabbier, and the people there more narrow-minded since she went away. Margaret's voice had become more grating and Boots more stolid. She had grown away from them. She didn't belong anymore. Besides, she wanted to see Dante.

The last few yards to the apartment house on its back street were incredibly long. She walked faster and faster, then trotted across the courtyard behind the house, which was quiet and still in the warmth of the afternoon. She dropped her suitcase at the foot of her own outside stairs and ran the last few steps to Dante's front door.

The door was open, the screen unlatched. She snatched the wire-covered door open, calling out above the screech of its hinges as she stepped inside. "Dante! It's me. I'm back!"

They were on the couch, a man and a woman with bodies gleaming with sweat from their exertions, pale in their nakedness. Dante was on top, striving with piston blows, pressing in and out of the woman who had her head thrown back and her legs flung wide as she writhed and moaned. The muscles of his back and hips bunched with effort; his male member was turgid and engorged and slickly wet as he rammed it deep once, twice.

Then Dante turned his head. He cursed. The woman under him, her face caked with makeup and her nails painted bloodred, cursed also.

Rebecca whirled and ran. She didn't stop for her suitcase but heaved herself up the outside stairs as if the hounds of hell were after her. Her hands were shaking so that she could hardly get her key into the lock. Then it opened suddenly and she stumbled inside. Swinging around, she slammed and locked the door.

Dante came knocking at her door five minutes later. He called out to her when she didn't answer, but she was lying in bed huddled around a pillow and she didn't move or make a sound. He came back in an hour, and again an hour later.

"Let me in *chère*," he called, knocking softly with his knuckles. "Let me explain. It had nothing to do with you, what you saw; I promise it didn't. Let me in!"

She didn't open the door. She couldn't open the door. An hour after the last time, when he didn't come back again, she began to cry.

She went to work at the bar that evening and the next and the next. Dante was never anywhere in sight; she thought he must be leaving early for the restaurant. She was relieved that she didn't have to face him, though she was also sorry she had not let him in, that she had refused to talk to him. It was wrong of her to judge him; after all, he hadn't judged her that way about her dancing topless. The more time that passed before they spoke, the harder it was going to be. Once at work, however, there was no time to think about it.

The old man who had kissed her hand was there every night. He helped her up onto his table with a gallant air and sat very still, smiling faintly in appreciation, while he watched. There was such tolerance, such kindness, in his gray eyes. She could not help but be curious about him. He was not so old as she had thought, perhaps in his forties, though there was silver in his black hair. His clothes were different from those of the other customers, of better quality, more refined. In fact, he looked out of place as he rubbed elbows with oilfield workers and football players, frat men and furtive husbands, and the occasional embarrassed woman tourist. What he was doing there, she could not imagine. After she finished her dance each time, he was generous and never failed to thank her. Once he even said, "I'm glad you're back. I missed you and was worried about you."

It was a week after she had returned, and late in the night, toward the two o'clock closing time, when the fat owner of the bar sent for her. There was someone with him in his office, a dark, plump man with hair that shone with oil and an accent she thought was South American when he spoke in greeting, though she couldn't be sure.

The fat man tilted his head at her. "This the one?"

"That is her," the other man said in careful English.

"Come here," the fat man said to her with a smile that held relish but no amusement whatever.

Rebecca moved forward a step or two.

"Closer."

She bit the inside of her lip, but moved again until she was in front of his desk with the foreigner a foot away.

"Turn around and face the door," he said.

She looked from one man to the other. The music from the barroom, usually so loud, sounded faint with distance. The room was close, for it was a warm and humid night and there was only a small oscillating fan to stir the air. She could smell the oil the foreigner used on his hair. Suddenly, she felt more naked in her heels and G-string standing there in front of them than she had ever felt on top of a table.

She moistened her lips. "Why?"

"Do as I say," the fat man said, spacing the words with a hard deliberateness that made the hair rise on the back of her neck.

Slowly she turned.

"Bend over."

"But, no," the foreigner said, "is not necessary."

She felt his hand slide over the curve of her hip, his fingers slipping under the G-string. She gave a startled cry and swung around, backing away.

The foreigner laughed. He snapped his fingers as he turned back to the fat man. "Very nice," he said. "I will take her."

12

Edison Gallant was shaving when the knock came on the door. He cursed. Why the devil did somebody always have to come banging on the door when he was in the bathroom and there was nobody else to answer? A few minutes earlier and Anne could have got it. But, hell, no. It had to be now.

Grabbing a towel, he swabbed it across his face, then slung it over his shoulder. Wearing nothing except his pajamas bottoms, he stalked to the door and put his eye to the peephole.

There was a woman outside. She wasn't young and wasn't old, wasn't ugly but wasn't exactly a raving beauty. She was looking up and down the hall like a whore watching for the hotel detective while she patted her hair and rubbed her lips together to smooth her lipstick. The dress she had on was an expensive model, some kind of soft, flower-printed material, but it would have been better if it had been a size larger. The scarf she wore with it was cream silk, but she could not quite carry off the careless way she had it twisted around her plump shoulders.

He knew her. A second more and he had the name. A grim smile curved his mouth, then died away. He reached out and yanked the door open.

The woman gasped and put her hand to her chest. Her voice breathless, she said, "Hello."

Great. He liked them a little nervous. He scowled. "What do you want?"

"Don't—don't you know me?"

"Is there any reason I should?" He made the words cold, insulting, as he ran his gaze up and down her.

"I thought you might since I saw you just two nights ago."

She was actually pouting. God, what a ninny. "I don't have time for games. If you want something, spit it out."

She flushed. "I would like to talk to you. I—I'm Margaret, Riva's sister, your cousin Boots's wife?"

Of course he knew. However, it paid to keep people who wanted something on the defensive, and he'd bet his ass Margaret wanted something. That was all right. Could be he wanted something, too.

"You'd better come in," he said, and stepped back to let her cross in front of him before closing the door.

He watched her. He'd seen a lot of women step into hotel rooms, women of all kinds. This one wasn't used to it. She was nervous but getting a thrill out of it at the same time. She was looking around the suite as if she had never been in one, which, come to think of it, she probably hadn't. Old Boots had certainly never had the money to take his wife to anything so fancy, and she didn't look the type to find somebody else who could.

The thought drifted through his mind of his old bet with himself that he could have all three sisters. This was the last one. He felt a stirring in his groin at the idea. He was susceptible to hotel rooms.

Margaret turned to face him. "I won't stay long. I know you probably have appointments."

"I usually do."

"I just wanted to talk a minute, and I saw in the paper where your wife would be cutting the ribbon for a neonatal unit at some hospital this morning."

"Yeah." Old Boots's wife must have stood around downstairs until she saw Anne leave. He got a kick out of that, thinking of her sneaking around, watching the elevator. He'd lay odds she'd gotten the same kick, as if this was some big clandestine meeting.

There was a flush on her cheeks as she looked at him, then away again. "It's been a long time since the summer we all met."

"Has it?" He removed farther into the room, slowly wiping the water droplets on his chest with the end of his towel.

"More than twenty-five years. I used to think you might come back to town for holidays or family reunions, but you never did."

"That kind of thing doesn't appeal to me." Nothing about that town or the people who lived there appealed to him. He had made it a point never to go there again after that summer, not even on campaign, but there was no point in saying so.

She moved one shoulder in a quick gesture, her gaze on his chest and what he was doing with the towel. "I guess there's not much to bring you since your uncle and aunt died."

"There was never very much."

"No, not for someone like you."

He liked the appreciation in her voice. He'd had little enough of it lately from women. Regardless, he had a bankers' luncheon in a little over two hours, and he hadn't even looked at the speech his staff had written for it. Rubbing his towel over his neck, he said, "What's on your mind?"

Margaret moved to the couch and sat down, pulling her dress over her knees. Her face was flushed as she met his gaze. "I know you've been having some trouble with Riva. I thought I might be able to help."

He was still for a long moment as he stared at her. Finally he slung the towel back over his shoulder and ambled forward. He gave his silk pajamas legs a hitch and lowered himself to sit on the couch beside her. In dulcet tones, he said "Did you?"

"I don't know why I shouldn't." She gave him a defensive stare.

"Does Riva know you're here?"

"No, but what of it?"

"She didn't send you?"

"No, she didn't. I do something on my own every now and then."

Edison ignored the shading of resentment in the woman's tone. It seemed apparent that Margaret was meddling. On the other hand, it was always possible that it was merely supposed to look that way, that Riva had put her up to coming. "I doubt Riva will be pleased if she finds out."

"She certainly won't be." Margaret gave a small shudder as if the thought chilled her.

"You aren't afraid of her?"

"Of Riva? Don't be ridiculous! She has a sharp tongue at times, but she's my sister after all."

"She won't exactly thank you for interfering."

"Maybe not, but I think you'll agree that things can't go on as they are. Somebody has to do something, and I can't stand to just sit around and wait for Riva to make up her mind what it's to be."

"Is that what she's doing?" he asked thoughtfully.

"Yes, she is! She acts as if she's the only one who can decide Erin's life, as if I have no rights at all."

He shook his head as if in sympathy. "She has become rather high-handed in the past few years."

"She's downright bossy, if you want my opinion. She even tried to tell me to keep my nose out of this business. Keep my nose out, as if the woman Erin calls Mother, the one who raised her from a baby, has no say in this!"

"I thought it was a little weird myself."

"So it is. Riva may have given birth to her, but I'm her real mother."

Edison felt a surge of excitement, the same surge stumbling on somebody's dark secrets always gave him. "I'll be damned."

"Oh, God," Margaret whispered.

Edison stared at her, at her wide eyes, then his own narrowed to blue slits. "Tell me," he said in grating tones, "just how old is Erin?"

But Margaret was staring at him with her mouth open and the color receding from her face. "I forgot you didn't know," she whispered. "How could I forget?"

"Riva neglected to tell me something, it seems. Is Erin mine or is she somebody else's mistake, somebody before Riva caught old Staulet?"

Margaret made a whimpering sound as she jumped to her feet. "Riva will never forgive me."

Edison shot out his hand to catch her arm. "Hold on, we're not through."

Margaret tugged at his hold. "I have to go."

"Not just yet. There are a few things we need to clear up."

He gave a hard yank and she stumbled toward him, then

sprawled across his lap. She tried to push away, but he grabbed her shoulder, throwing her to her back on the cushions as he heaved himself up to crouch above her. "Now," he said, showing his teeth in a hard grin, "let's you and me have a talk."

"You're hurting me," Margaret cried. She tried to struggle, but his fingers were biting into her arms, and her movements brought her into contact with a rigid length at his crotch that made her freeze in shocked surprise.

"I'm Erin's father, aren't I?" he asked. "That's what this is all about. You and Riva are coming unglued because you think she's getting it on with my son, who just happens to be her brother."

"Half brother," Margaret choked out. "Now let me go!"

"Oh, no, I kind of like having you here. It's like old times. Remember the night out behind the house when you went to empty the scraps for the stray dogs? Huh? Remember how you let me kiss you? I kissed you before, at the store, but that time I'd have got more if Beth hadn't opened the door and hollered for you, wouldn't I? Now, wouldn't I?"

He rubbed against her as he talked, easing over until his crotch was at the juncture of her legs. Thinking about that time out behind the house in the dark, of how he had planned to take her down on the dew-wet ground, made him horny as all hell. The fact that she was actually afraid of him made it better. Her eyes were wide and staring, and she made a moaning noise in her throat.

He laughed deep in his throat. "Come on, baby, you really want it, don't you? How long's it been? Huh? How long's it been since old Boots really did it to you?"

He lowered his head, using his weight to press her into the couch as he kissed her. She turned her head from side to side, but he followed her mouth until he had it under his, until he had his tongue inside. He probed, shoving her tongue aside as she tried to keep him out, thrusting to give her an idea of what she was going to get. Her muffled protest filled his mouth, setting him on fire.

He lifted slightly to close his hand on her tit. He squeezed, enjoying the nice fullness of it, before he began to work at the buttons of her dress front. She heaved, trying to throw him off. He jerked her bodice open, grabbing at the edge of her bra and dragging it aside to expose a nipple. He opened his mouth and covered it, sucking, nipping hard while he squeezed tight.

"Be still and enjoy it," he said between bites, "and there won't be so many bruises to explain."

"Get off," she gasped. "Let me up or I'll scream so loud it'll burst your eardrums. I'll tell everybody, tell the police."

"Yeah, and then what are you going to say when they ask what you're doing here? I'll tell 'em you offered it to me, like a lot of women do. Besides, I have friends downtown. Nobody'll ever hear a word about it."

"I'll tell Boots. He'll—he'll come after you."

"Sure he will. I expect he knows you're here, too, just like Riva. He does, doesn't he? Huh? Huh?" He reached down to pull up her skirt, raking his fingers over the plump inner surfaces of her thighs. He felt the ridge of her panty elastic and pushed his fingers under it, seeking the moist crevice where her thighs joined. Her squirmings and desperate pleas urged him on. He got a mouthful of tit once more as he found what he was looking for and shoved his finger inside.

It wasn't enough, not by a long shot. He jerked down his pajamas and grabbed himself. She tried to clamp her legs together, but he kept them spread with his knees while he maneuvered himself to that hot, thatched, and quivering opening. Deliberately, he stuffed himself inside. He wrenched his hips, ramming deeper and deeper until he felt bottom and she gave a small scream.

An image of his first time with Riva crossed his mind as if from a dream. It had been something like this, almost the same. Had he done that on purpose?

"God," he groaned, then, holding the image, began the quick, hard pumping that would bring him to the height of pleasure.

The call came exactly ten minutes after Riva discovered Margaret was not in her room. Riva had thought her sister was sleeping in since there had been no sound, no sign of her. It was a little strange for Margaret, but not too much so. Bonne Vie had a relaxing effect on people. The house was so large, so quiet and comfortable, that guests often had a tendency to rise later than usual.

When the phone rang, Riva was actually reaching for the receiver to call George and ask if one of the extra cars had been taken out. She recognized Margaret's voice, but what she was saying was so garbled and shrill that it didn't make sense.

"Slow down," Riva said in soothing tones. "Tell me again. You're where?"

Margaret began speaking again. Her voice was jerky and her breath came in hiccups, but she was coherent enough.

"Stay where you are," Riva said when her sister had fallen silent. "I'll be right there."

"Don't bring Boots. Do you hear me? Don't bring him, don't tell him. Just come."

Riva repeated, "I'll be right there."

She heard the phone click and then the dial tone. She sat for an instant staring straight ahead, then she depressed the button for a clear line. Boots was not at Bonne Vie. He had gotten up early to take his car to the shop, something about a bad wheel bearing he had noticed on the drive down. That was probably one reason why Margaret had chosen this morning for her trip into New Orleans. Perhaps it was just as well. Margaret should know what she wanted. Riva shook her head, then, becoming aware of the buzz of the dial tone, she punched in the number that would connect her with the chauffeur.

"I thought you would never get here!" Margaret cried as she let Riva into the hotel room an hour and a half later.

"I came as soon as I could."

"You brought the things?"

Riva indicated the small suitcase she held. As Margaret took it from her, Riva looked around. The hotel room was far from clean. It looked, in fact, as if a bunch of college guys had had a beer party in it. There were stains on the walls, cigarette burns in the carpet, and a lingering smell of urine and disinfectant. The exterior of the place was nice enough, but it was too close to the dives on Bourbon Street for its own good.

"Why did you come here?" she asked. "Why not just come home?"

"I was too upset, afraid to drive. I tried, but I was shaking too bad, and I couldn't even remember how to get back out to the interstate. The car's still at the parking garage; I walked here. Do you know Edison wouldn't even let me take a shower in his room? He said his wife might notice."

Margaret's voice had stopped shaking, but her eyes were red and her voice husky from crying. There was a corrosive edge to her words that had not been there before.

Riva said abruptly, "Are you sure you don't want to go to the police?"

"And have them ask embarrassing questions and make me have an exam? You must be crazy!" The other woman's voice grew strident as she spoke. "Besides, everyone would find out, and I couldn't stand that."

"All right, I was just asking."

"I'd think you would want to keep it quiet, too. I'd have to give my reasons, wouldn't I, and everybody would know your secrets."

"That doesn't matter if you want to charge Edison." Riva meant it. Inside her there was a burning anger that scorned the consequences, at least for now.

"I don't. I can't!"

"What about calling a doctor? Maybe he could talk to you, check you over, give you something to calm you." It was odd how awkward she felt, Riva thought. She would like to put her arms around Margaret and hold her, but there was such tension in her sister's body, such stiff withdrawal, that Riva felt the gesture would be unwelcome. If Margaret didn't want sympathy or help, what else was there?

"I've already taken something my doctor at home prescribed for my nerves, thank you, I don't need anything else. Besides, he'd just want to poke and pry at my female parts, too, and I've had enough of that."

"Are you—are you sure you're all right? I mean, are you sure Edison didn't hurt you?"

"I'm sure." The words were short.

Riva pressed her lips together, but she could not prevent her concern from showing. "Well, you don't look all right!"

"How would you look if you had been thrown down on a couch

and used like a two-bit whore? As a matter of fact, it should have been you. If you had done what Edison wanted, I wouldn't have had to go see him and this wouldn't have happened!"

Riva stared at her sister for a long moment. "So it's all my fault? Again."

Margaret's lashes flickered, but she didn't look away. "If you had gone instead of me—"

"I have better sense than to go to a man's hotel room," Riva said with acid scorn, "particularly Edison Gallant's room. The truth is, it wouldn't have happened if you hadn't interfered in my business. Why did you?"

"You said I was welcome to try if I thought I could do better at persuading Edison!"

"And did you persuade him?"

"You know I didn't—you know—"

"You knew I didn't mean for you to do this, too. Why Margaret?"

"Erin's welfare is my business, too!"

"Only because I allow it, remember that."

"Erin's my daughter!" Margaret cried. "I'm the one who tended to her when she was little, who took her to the doctor when she was sick and kissed her hurt places when she fell down. I'm the one who bought her first prom dress and sat up until she came home from her first date."

"You're the one because you took her away."

"You didn't want her!"

"How do you know? Did you ever ask?"

Margaret stared at her as if she had never seen her before. Suddenly her face crumpled. "Oh, Riva, I told him."

A cold, hard weight settled in Riva's chest. She whispered, "You what?"

"I told Edison about Erin. I didn't mean to, really I didn't. Sometimes—sometimes lately I forget things. It just slipped my mind that he didn't know."

Riva breathed deeply once, twice. Her voice a tight ache in her throat, she said, "Do you have any idea what you have done?"

"Maybe it will be for the best. At least now he will understand why Erin and Josh must be kept apart."

"He'll use it against me."

"Maybe not. Why should he, after all?"

"Because that's the way he is. Can you doubt it? Especially now?"

Margaret looked at her with tears rising to her eyes. "You didn't have to remind me."

It was the same old familiar ploy, but it worked. The guilt Riva felt rush up inside her was just as familiar. She turned toward the telephone on a stand beside the bed. "Look, I'm going to call Boots. You need him with you. He'll know what to do to help you."

"No!" Margaret screamed. "I don't want him! You want to call him out of pure spite!"

"Spite?" Riva swung around. "What do you mean?"

"To get back at me because I told Edison."

"The thought never crossed my mind. Margaret, you're hysterical. What do you mean to do, keep it from your husband forever that you've been raped?"

"I have to, don't you see! He'll never look at me the same if I don't. It'll change everything." Margaret covered her mouth with her hands and above them her eyes were wide and staring and brimming with tears.

It was a moment before Riva answered, then her voice dragged. "Can't you see it doesn't matter? Everything's changed already."

"No, it isn't," Margaret said, her voice tight. "I'm going to take a bath now and put on clean clothes, then we're going to drive back to Bonne Vie. We'll tell everybody I decided to go shopping and had car trouble. Instead of just sending the limo for me, you came yourself so that we could look around the stores together. You can send some of your help after the other car, and that will be the end of it."

"You can't just ignore what happened to you, Margaret. It isn't healthy."

"I don't care. I'm not going to ruin my life because of Edison Gallant. That would be letting him win."

"It's not a game!"

But her sister was walking into the bathroom, paying no attention. "Anyway," she said over her shoulder, "I don't mean to ignore it. I'll pay him back someday."

"Don't be foolish," Riva called after her. "Children pay each other back."

Margaret slammed the door without answering.

There was one problem with Margaret's story: Boots didn't believe it. Not even the shopping bags filled with clothes, hastily collected at Margaret's insistence, served to impress him. He barely glanced at them as Margaret and Riva scattered them on the bed.

"You didn't tell me you were going shopping," he said, watching his wife with a look of dogged suspicion on his coppery-red features. "And you didn't ask for money."

"I have credit cards, don't I?" Margaret protested. "Besides, it was just a sudden urge to see what they had down at Maison Blanche, no big deal."

"Why'd you leave the car parked in the exit drive at the garage of the Royal Orleans? The man down there called and said you got in it to go when they brought it to you, but that you pulled up a piece, then just got out and left it setting while you walked off with the keys."

"I told you I had car trouble."

"It cranked just fine when they hot-wired it. That's why they called; they looked at the registration and decided to ask for permission. The man said you came from inside the hotel and you looked upset. What gives?"

"I didn't go inside. The idiot must have been thinking of somebody else. No, the car just quit."

"Why didn't you ask one of the guys at the garage for help?"

"I wasn't thinking."

"Why wasn't you thinking? Was it because something Edison Gallant said upset you? I know he's staying there, because I heard Erin mention it to you."

"He—he has nothing to do with it. I used the hotel garage because it was convenient, especially if I wanted to walk up and down the Quarter later. You know how hard it is to find a parking place."

It was just barely plausible. Another time, Margaret might have been able to carry it off. Now, she was too overwrought, her words too jerky. She couldn't quite meet her husband's eyes. Her hands, as she played with her hair and picked at her nails, were trembling.

"That ain't the truth, Margaret," Boots said. "You been up to something, I know. Now you tell me, or I'll have to call and ask Edison if you've been to see him and what it was the two of you had to talk about."

"You wouldn't!"

"You know I would."

It was apparent that Margaret did know. She broke into tears and in ragged sentences told her husband what had taken place. Toward the middle of it, Boots knelt on the floor beside the chair where she sat and pulled her into his arms. There was pain in his face as he listened, but there was also rage. It was so unusual to see such a look on Boots's face that Riva was frightened.

It was awkward, however, standing there while Margaret sobbed out her tale and her husband held her. When Margaret finally fell silent, Riva said, "She won't go to the doctor."

"I'm not hurt," Margaret said, defiance in the husky tone of her voice as she wiped her face.

"You've had a shock."

Boots released his wife and got slowly to his feet. "Best thing, maybe, will be if she goes to bed."

Margaret clenched her hands in her lap as she stared up at them both. "Don't talk about me as if I'm not here!"

"Be quiet now," Boots said. "You just get undressed and lie down."

"What are you going to do?" Margaret's brief anger disappeared as she stared at her husband.

"Never mind. Just do as I say now. Maybe somebody can bring you some soup or something for lunch, then you can try to rest."

"I couldn't eat a bite."

"You can try."

There was an undertone of iron in Boots's words. Margaret looked at Riva with bitterness etched in her face. "I told you it would change everything."

Riva exchanged a long glance with her sister but made no reply.

After a moment, she turned to leave the room. "I'll see about that lunch tray."

She didn't know Boots was following her out until Margaret called, "Where are you going?"

"I'll be right back," her husband said, then closed the bedroom door behind him as he stepped into the hall.

Riva paused to look back, then walked on as her brother-in-law joined her. It was a moment before either of them spoke, then she said abruptly, "I'm sorry."

He looked at her and frowned. "What for? It's not your fault."

"Oh, not exactly, but I suppose it wouldn't have happened if I hadn't started this whole thing."

"You couldn't sit back and do nothing."

"That's what I tell myself, but it might never have come to anything, anyway, this thing with Erin and Josh."

"Then again it might."

"I guess it's too late to worry about it now." When he made no answer, she went on. "You know, I can't understand why Edison did it. Not that Margaret isn't attractive, and going to his hotel wasn't the smartest thing in the world, but why? Why would he do it?"

"A lot of reasons, but mainly because he wanted to."

"You don't think it was to get back at me?"

"Oh, maybe a little, but it goes back further than that. I remember him saying once how you three Benson girls were the most gorgeous he'd ever seen, and he'd like to— Well, you know. But mainly, I expect, Margaret was there when the urge struck him. He never did have much control."

"Why would he take such a risk? It seems so stupid for a man in the public eye."

"People like that think they can get away with anything. They get the idea they're above everybody else, that nothing can touch them."

They had reached the stairwell at the back of the house. Riva stopped and faced Boots. "What are you going to do?"

"What makes you think I'm going to do anything?"

"I don't know. It's just a feeling."

"Edison is my kin. I thought I'd have a little talk with him, sort of in the family."

Riva looked down at Boots's fist which was clenched at his side, then up to his face again. "A friendly chat to explain the error of his ways?"

"Something like that."

"You'll be careful?"

"Don't worry about me."

Curiously enough, she wasn't worried. Another curious thing was that she had not the least inclination to try to stop him.

"I did think," he went on, "that I ought to warn you, in case you felt it would make a difference to what you mean to do about Erin and Josh."

"I don't know, I haven't thought about it," she said with a frown between her eyes, "but never mind. This is your business."

"So is Erin."

She met his steady gaze for a long moment. This man was more her daughter's father, had had more to do with making Erin the open, outgoing young woman she had become, than any of them. "I suppose she is, and it was foolish of me not to consider it. You should have said something."

"Oh, well. Margaret was making enough noise for the both of us."

It was unusual in the extreme for him to criticize his wife. It was an indication of his estrangement from her over what had happened. Riva said, "It's her nature to worry and try to manage people."

"I known. I also know you've been trying to do what's best for Erin without making a fuss. I hate that Margaret let the cat out of the bag about her. I mean to do what I can to make sure Edison don't use what he knows to hurt Erin."

"Such as tell her?"

He narrowed his eyes. "I think I can convince him that that wouldn't be smart. About the rest of it, I don't know."

By the last Boots meant he could not control how Edison might use the knowledge to hurt Riva. "Never mind about me. I'll take care of it."

"I thought you'd feel that way," he said. "But if there's anything I can do, any way I can help, just ask."

"I'll do that," Riva said.

Boots nodded, then turned and walked back toward the bed-room. Riva, watching him go, found she meant what she had said. There was more to Boots than she had ever known. As an ally, he might prove more dangerous than an enemy as he went blundering into this affair; still, it was good to have him on her side.

13

"He used me, Riva."

Margaret's voice came out of the dimness of the bedroom where she lay with the drapes closed. Riva sat in a chair beside the bed. Her sister had insisted she stay once she returned with the lunch tray. Margaret didn't want to be alone. Riva wanted nothing so much as to get away, away from her own guilt and compassion and anger at her sister, and away also from Margaret's self-pity. Didn't her sister know that she had been used, too?

Riva said, "Don't think about it."

"I have to, I need to, don't you understand? I'm so humiliated. I thought at first, when Edison let me into his room, that he was attracted to me. He smiled and acted so interested. But then he just—just pounced like an animal. It didn't mean a thing to him, not a thing. I didn't mean anything. He had something to prove and he used me to do it. He used me to get back at you!"

"I'm sorry. I never intended to involve you in this."

"I am involved. I've always been involved."

There was a spent sound in Margaret's voice. Riva thought the tranquilizers she had taken were finally beginning to work. She hoped so. Still Margaret was not finished.

"I used to think he was something special, so handsome and rich. So much more sophisticated than poor Boots."

"Edison?"

Margaret nodded in the dimness. "I envied you and Beth, I really did, because he wanted you, because he had you. Oh, I know it didn't turn out for either one of you with him, but that didn't matter. I used to think about him sometimes when I was washing dishes or in bed at night when Boots—Oh God!"

"Don't talk about it. You'll just upset yourself again."

Margaret ignored her. "I used to think that if I had been free, if I hadn't been half engaged to Edison's cousin, it might have been me he ran off with. I used to look at Erin sometimes and think what it would have been like if she had been my daughter by him. Isn't that silly? Isn't that the stupidest thing you ever heard?"

"Margaret—"

"If it wasn't for daydreams like that, I might not have gone to see him. Just think of all that wasted time, wasted feeling. And he wasn't worth it. He was never worth any of it. You might have told me."

"I did," Riva said quietly. "You just didn't hear me."

"He made a fool out of me, leading me on with a line coated with sugar. I'll never forgive him for that."

There seemed no answer to that. The silence stretched, broken only by the sound of the central air-conditioning kicking on and the whisper of the chill air through the vent into the room. After a time, Margaret turned her head fretfully on the pillow. In querulous tones she asked, "Where's Boots?"

Riva kept her voice neutral as she answered. "I don't know."

"He should be here. It's not like him not to be here."

"I'm sure he'll be back in a little while."

"Are you? But where did he go? He didn't—he wouldn't go after Edison, do you think?" Margaret raised herself on one elbow to stare at her sister in the dimness. "Oh, God, is that where he is? Tell me, Riva, is it?"

"Try to sleep."

"It is, I know it is. Why did you let him go?"

"I couldn't stop him."

"There's no telling what Edison will say to him, what lies he'll tell."

"I doubt he'll get the chance. Boots was . . . not in a mood to talk."

"Edison will call the police and have him arrested, I know he will."

"We can't do anything about it now. Just lie back and rest."

Margaret threw herself back down on the pillow with a moan. "I'm not tired and I'm not sick, I've been raped! Can't you understand that?"

Riva could. Her own first time with Edison had not been so different, from the sound of it. And there had been that other time, with the foreign man on Bourbon Street, almost. But she didn't say so. As her sister remained quiet, Riva leaned her head against the back of the chair and closed her eyes.

On that hot May night in the rear office of the bar on Bourbon Street she had backed away from the two men watching her. Their faces had shone in the overhead light, and the look in their eyes had been leering and confident. The foreigner had taken a wallet from the pocket of his suit coat and began to count out twenty-dollar bills. When the bar owner reached out a pudgy hand to take them, Rebecca turned, threw open the door, and ran.

Behind her she heard the scrape of a chair and a yell. Footsteps thudded. She glanced back over her shoulder to see the foreigner barging out of the office doorway with the bar owner behind him. Three-inch heels were not made for running; still, she sprinted down the dingy hallway toward the curtained opening that led into the bar.

The walls seemed to vibrate with the heavy footfalls behind her. The sound was like thunder, blending with the pounding of her heart in her ears. She felt horribly uncovered, without protection, totally vulnerable. In her mind was a hot core of terror and rage and determination.

The curtain over the opening into the barroom swayed in front of her. She batted it aside and stumbled into the crowded, noisy, rock music–filled room. She saw men sitting bleary-eyed at tables and watching nearly naked women sway and turn above them, saw the fog of gray cigarette smoke shafted by the spotlights on the tables. No one looked her way.

Her arm was caught from behind in a hard grasp. She slammed into the wall and she was swung around. Her breath left her in a gasp of pain that turned into a cry as the foreigner thrust himself against her and grabbed her throat. His hand was tight, digging into her soft flesh. His breath was foul. The smell of it, mingled with the greasy odor of the oil on his hair, was sickening. His teeth were bared in a grin of pleasure and anticipation.

"You won't get away from me that easy," he said, grinding his pelvis against her fringe-covered pubic bone. The bar owner, standing in the doorway, grunted.

Rebecca's hands were pressed against the foreigner's chest. She gave him a hard push so that he staggered back. A man loomed behind the foreigner. He grabbed his shoulder and spun him around, at the same time hooking a leg behind the foreigner's knee so that he went sprawling. The man on the floor took one look over his shoulder, then scrambled to his feet and dived out of the bar. Rebecca's rescuer turned toward the bar owner.

"Now, don't get mad, Mr. Staulet!" the fat man said, throwing up a hand and backing away. "How was I to know she wasn't willing? Everything's all right. Everything's cool. The gal can dance for you now, if that's what you want."

"The question is," the man called Staulet said, "what does she want?"

He turned to look at Rebecca. She stared back at him. He was the older man who asked her to dance for him so often, the one who tipped her with twenty-dollar bills. In his eyes was fading anger, infinite kindness, and odd bemusement, as if he were surprised at his own actions.

She took a deep, gulping breath. "I want out of here."

Staulet nodded. "Get your things."

There was nothing to get except her cheap cotton dress, her underclothes, and the grubby sandals she had worn to work. She changed out of the rhinestone heels and G-string in trembling haste, afraid that Mr. Staulet would leave without her. Kicking the excuse for a costume into the middle of the floor, she hurried out to join him.

He was still standing at the curtained doorway. The bar owner was nowhere in sight. Mr. Staulet took her elbow and escorted her from the bar, looking neither to the right nor to the left.

He stopped for a moment on the sidewalk out front. Bourbon

Street was littered with plastic cups, noisome with wet splashes where drunks had been sick, and nearly deserted. A few couples still straggled up and down in the multicolored light of the blinking neon signs, however, and a hot-dog vendor trundled his mustard-smelling cart along the gutter. Music with a hard beat played, though rising above it were the mellow and haunting notes of a blues trumpet, a sensual yet inconsolable sound.

There was such an abstracted look on the face of the man beside her, as if he were considering a matter of extreme importance, that Rebecca was quiet. A slight trembling ran through her whole body, but she tried to suppress it. Finally Mr. Staulet looked down at her, offered his arm, and smiled. He said, "My car is just along here."

"I can walk. It isn't far to where I live." She took his arm because it wasn't polite to let him stand there holding it out to her without some acknowledgment, and because she was afraid her knees might buckle if she didn't. His sleeve was silky under her fingers and the muscles of his arm were firm.

"Permit me to drive you," he said, and turned her gently in the direction he had indicated, where his car was parked on a side street.

It was a gray limousine. The driver, a young black man nearly as wide as he was tall, got out and held the door. If he thought it strange to see his employer escorting a young woman in cheap makeup and a cheaper dress, he gave no sign. Staulet spoke to him in a low voice. The chauffeur nodded, then shut the door. He got behind the wheel and they pulled away from the curb.

The limousine was like a cool, velvet-lined cocoon insulating them from the activity and noise of the close, narrow streets. It gave Rebecca a feeling of safety. At the same time, it was intimidating. She swallowed hard before she spoke and still her voice came out soft and uncertain.

"I should thank you for what you did for me."

"It was my pleasure, I assure you."

"I don't know what I would have done if you hadn't been there."

He smiled. "But then I'm always there to see you dance, or I was, as you must know."

"Really, Mr. Staulet—"

"Call me Cosmo, will you? I would like that. Do you realize this is the first time we've exchanged more than a few basic words such as hello and thank you?"

"Yes, I—"

"It must seem strange to you. It doesn't to me because I've talked to you quite a lot, in my head. I love you, you know."

She stared at him with her lips slightly open. She could not have heard him right. People like him just didn't say such things, not to people like her.

He laughed with the sound of burgeoning excitement in his voice. "That surprises you, doesn't it? You thought I was a dirty old man lusting after your luscious body. Well, I plead guilty, but it's more than that, more than you can know."

"You—you should not make fun of me."

"Is that what you think? I swear on my father's grave I'm doing nothing of the kind. And I don't take such an oath easily."

Rebecca looked away from the brightness in his dark gray eyes that was illuminated by the flash of street lamps as they glided past them. Still he was imprinted in her mind: the silver among the fine wings of hair at his temples, the strong line of his nose, the square set of his jaw, and the grace and strength of his hands. There was about him that indefinable something known as breeding and the self-assurance that comes with wealth. She was daunted by his monied sophistication, and she didn't like it.

She focused her wandering attention on the fence-enclosed area they were passing, one crowded with plastered white tombs and monument-like small houses above the ground that caused such cemeteries to be known as Cities of the Dead. She blinked. "This isn't the way to my apartment."

"No, I know. That's why I told you I love you so quickly. I wanted you to hear it before you discovered my treachery."

She moistened her lips. "What do you mean?"

"I mean that I'm not taking you home."

"Where—where are we going?"

"To my house, to Bonne Vie."

"I can't go with you!" The words were strained as she fought to stay calm.

"Why not?"

She slewed around on the seat to sit with her back against the door. "I don't know you. You don't know me."

"I know more than you think," he answered, and began in his calm, aristocratic voice to give the vital statistics of her life: her date of birth, birthplace, father's name, mother's name; the schools she had attended and her grade point averages; her favorite foods, favorite colors, favorite flowers; the date and approximate time she had left town with Edison; the date and approximate time Erin was born. Something in his voice told her he knew more but felt it better not to say it.

"How?" she asked on a startled gasp. "Why?"

"There are ways. As to why, I just wanted to know. Call it an obsession, and you won't be far from the truth. Men my age are allowed an obsession or two."

"I—I'm so embarrassed."

"For what reason? You have nothing to be embarrassed about. The shame is mine for spying on you, for taking away your privacy. For that I apologize."

"You know so much about me, and I know next to nothing about you," she said, her tone dazed.

"It's a long way to Bonne Vie. Permit me to tell you."

"But I can't go with you! Not like this, just—just driving off into the night." She had done that once and look how it had turned out.

"Why not?" he inquired. "What is there to keep you from it? Who is there, really, to care?"

The words should have been cruel. Instead, they were spoken with such quiet sympathy and caring that Rebecca shuddered, barely controlling the urge to cry that made the back of her nose ache. He was right, wasn't he? There was no one to care about her. No one at all.

"What do you want with me?" she asked, her manner wary yet with a shade less resistance.

"Just to take care of you and to love you, that's all. Mostly just to love you. I would start by giving you a late supper, since you are so thin. Afterward, I'll take you home. If, of course, that's still where you want to go."

"You're sure that's all?" She felt the weakness invading her muscles caused by receding fear and the calm of beginning trust.

"Positive, little one. It would mean a great deal to have you near me for a time, to have you see my home."

Somehow he made it seem so reasonable, so impossible to refuse. He had done so much for her that evening; how could she continue to be suspicious and disobliging?

Seeing the house at the end of the tree-lined drive, shining in the moonlight like the most fabled white-pillared mansion, she nearly demanded to turn back. But Cosmo was talking, telling some tale of how he had fallen from one of the famous old oaks of the alley in front of the house as a boy, and of how his mother had been more concerned with the limb he had broken from the tree than his own broken collarbone. Then the limousine was sweeping up to the front steps and Cosmo was helping her out. The house door was opened by a black man who answered to the name of Abraham, and Cosmo ushered her inside with her hand held in the crook of his arm as if she were an honored guest.

"Welcome to Bonne Vie," he said, and the pride and joy in his voice echoed down the long, darkened hall and came back to them in rich, deep reverence.

Then the tall, thick door to their left opened. A young man stepped into the hall from a library where mahogany bookcases with beveled-glass doors gleamed in the soft light. He held a textbook of some kind loosely clasped in his hand with his forefinger holding his place between the closed pages. He was thinner than Cosmo, and younger by many years. He wore his hair longer in the current style and was casually dressed in jeans and a cotton shirt. Still, the resemblance was unmistakable. A smile creasing his face, he said, "You're a little late, aren't you, Dad. Your little dancer must have been in rare—"

"Noel," Cosmo interrupted, turning so that Rebecca, hanging back on his opposite side, was drawn into the light, "here's someone I want you to meet. Miss Benson, may I present my son? Noel, this is the young lady I've been telling you about."

She saw the younger man's gaze flick over her from head to foot, saw the amazed contempt and embarrassment that stiffened his features. Heat flared into her face and her hand tightened on Cosmo's arm.

Cosmo glanced down at her, then at his son. The pleasure faded from his face. The eyes of the two men held in a brief, hard stare. Noel, as if in acquiescence to some silent command, looked back at Rebecca and inclined his head. "Miss Benson."

"H-hello," she said.

He met her gaze with his own clear gray one for what seemed an eternity. Rebecca had never been so examined and weighed in her life. That scrutiny was more devastating in its lack of approval than any she had ever endured on top of a table. She wanted to turn and run out of the house or else to slap Cosmo's arrogant son.

It was Cosmo who broke the tense silence between them. "Won't you join us in a late supper, Noel?"

"No thanks. I'm sure the two of you would rather be alone."

"As you say," Cosmo replied, outwardly unperturbed, though Rebecca could sense the taut rein he held on his temper. He moved with her down the hall and out onto the back gallery, where he led her to a table.

In a few short minutes, there appeared candles, wine, crusty loaves of French bread, and fluffy omelets stuffed with cheese and mushrooms and slivers of ham. Her appetite, at first small, enlarged dramatically under the gentle flow of small talk Cosmo made so that she was easily able to turn her attention to a dessert of bananas Foster. It was while she was eating the last of it that Cosmo asked her to marry him.

She stopped with her spoon suspended halfway to her mouth to stare at him. She could think of nothing to say.

He burst out laughing. "You think I'm crazy, don't you?"

"Insane," she echoed, her voice hollow and her eyes wide.

"Be crazy with me. Say yes."

She put her spoon down with care. "You can't do things like this."

He grinned at her with open amusement for his seriousness. "Can't I?"

"I'm a girl from Bourbon Street, a girl you've watched dance nearly naked."

"There's not much about what you look like that I don't know, then, you'll have to admit that."

"I'm young enough to—I'm younger than your son."

"Such tact. How charming."

She looked down at her dessert plate, only shaking her head.

"Do you find me too old?" There was as much apprehension as curiosity in his voice.

He wasn't too old at all. He was simply overwhelming. "No, but I may be too young."

"You'll age. What else?"

She picked up her spoon again, slowly dipping the tip of it into the melted ice cream. "You say you love me, but you haven't asked how I feel."

"How do you feel?"

"I don't know! I sometimes think I don't know what love is, what it's supposed to feel like. I wonder if I'll ever feel it."

"Do you feel nothing for me, then?"

"I feel—" She stopped, then, meeting his eyes with great courage, started again, "I feel safe with you. I feel comfortable, the way I used to feel when I would get up on cold winter mornings and there was no one awake except me and my dad, and he would wrap me in his robe to keep me warm while he waited for the coffee to drip in the pot."

She was not sure where the memory had come from. She hardly ever thought of her dad, who had died when she was ten. Still, what she said was true. Cosmo Staulet did give her that same sense of warm security and privilege.

He smiled gently. "I'm not your father, make no mistake about that. But it's a fair beginning."

There was in his very gentleness an implacability that frightened her. She put down her spoon again and blurted out, "You know I've had a child out of wedlock."

"A terrible crime—but one committed by the idiot who allowed it."

"You have no idea what kind of wife I might make!"

"A beautiful one. I don't need to know more."

"Your son doesn't like me." She looked away as she said it, the painful flush of shame returning to her cheekbones.

"You would not be marrying my son. Besides, he doesn't dislike you. If anything, it's probably me he despises because I saw you first and haven't the generosity to let you go."

"You're wrong."

"Marry me and we'll see, won't we?"

There was more—more arguments, more discussion, more persuasion. In time she got used to the idea that he meant what he said, that he really wanted her to be his wife. She had no idea why men were so attracted to her. She knew she was not bad-looking, but she didn't feel any different from a hundred other girls. It was gratifying to be desired, but also scary, because if she didn't know why they wanted her it was always possible there was no reason, and if there was no reason, they could stop wanting her as easily as they started. She had had enough of not being wanted.

Still, in the end, she became Mrs. Cosmo Staulet. That was after a shopping spree in New Orleans when Cosmo whirled her through the famous old department stores of Maison Blanche and Holmes, pointing at dainty underwear and daring gowns, elegant suits and dresses of casual style, handbags that smelled deliciously of leather and shoes that hugged her slim feet as if custom-made. To hold her finery for their honeymoon trip to Paris, he bought luggage of no particular style or value because, he said, they would replace it in London on their way back. He didn't care for Vuitton pieces, which he considered flashy and an open invitation to theft. The ones he used were from the same firm that supplied the queen. They were, he said, incredibly ugly and as heavy as iron, but just as indestructible.

There was a delay of some weeks as it was necessary for Rebecca to convert to Catholicism. During that time, she lived in an upstairs bedroom at Bonne Vie and slept alone. She tried once to see Dante, when she went to pick up her few belongings left at the apartment. She meant to tell him what she intended and invite him to the wedding. He wasn't at home. The girl Rebecca had seen him with on that memorable afternoon took her message, but Dante didn't call, didn't get in touch with her.

The wedding was small and private, with only a few of Cosmo's closest friends and his son in attendance. Rebecca wore a gown of delicate cream silk trimmed with peach ribbon and with its many layers of fragile material edged with handmade lace. It was Cosmo's choice, naturally. Just as naturally, he would not permit her to see the price tag. She stared at herself in her finery before she left for the church, also looking at her hair and makeup that had been done by a man who had come to Bonne Vie for that sole purpose. She was pretty, as ethereal as some fairy princess, though she took no credit for it. In truth, she didn't recognize herself, didn't feel like herself. It was as if she were slowly being transformed into someone she didn't know. It was both frightening and exciting.

Panic beat inside her and she forced it down. She had made a choice, hadn't she? She couldn't back out now, didn't really want to, if the truth were known. It would be too embarrassing for Cosmo, too hurtful. And she was too curious about what it would be like to live at Bonnie Vie, to belong there, and to be Mrs. Cosmo Staulet. It wasn't the money, it really wasn't. It was the position, the respect. And it was also the man. She was slowly becoming addicted to his gentle care, his protective cherishing.

The wedding reception was held at Bonne Vie, and it was not so small. Rebecca stood beside Cosmo to greet their guests in the hall. She was nervous, her mind spinning with names and faces. The smile she held in place had a tendency to tremble at the edges. She repeated the same phrases over and over until they seemed inane beyond belief, if not downright imbecilic. Everyone who came through the door seemed so sophisticated, so at ease. They knew everyone, were known by everyone, and moved from one group to another, certain of their welcome, certain they belonged. Their easiness with each other made Rebecca feel like an outsider. She was also aware of their whispers and glances and knew she was under discussion, knew she was being judged.

The one who made her feel most self-conscious, however, was Cosmo's son. Noel stood to one side, watching her through lash-shielded eyes as he sipped his champagne. He was undeniably handsome in his evening clothes, though he would have been more so if he had smiled. He did not. With sober thoroughness, he studied her every word and gesture as if intrigued by her performance.

It was a habit he had acquired, watching her, always watching. It made her intensely conscious of him also, as well as of herself. Though in the beginning he had been less than friendly, a nebulous truce had been established between them. They were not so far apart in age after all; it was not surprising that they should like the same music from rock to jazz or have the same offbeat sense of humor, humor that Cosmo often found incomprehensible, if not ridiculous.

On this evening, Rebecca had the feeling that Noel knew about the fluttery beating of her heart, could sense her terrible need to belong and understood perfectly the uncertainty that twisted inside her when she thought of the wedding night that lay ahead. She could see the empathy in the gray depths of his eyes as they rested on her. It was as if there were already an instinctive kinship between her and the young man, who after this evening, as incredible as it seemed, would be her stepson.

The pace of arriving guests dwindled to the point that Cosmo suggested they leave their posts at the door if no one else showed up in the next two minutes. It was then that Noel moved toward Rebecca. At the same moment, Cosmo turned away, distracted by a murmured consultation with his butler about the catering.

Noel took the hand Rebecca extended, but then, instead of kissing her cheek as so many others had done, he leaned to touch his lips to hers.

His mouth was smooth and warm and tasted of champagne. The contact was just as heady as the wedding wine, sending waves of vibrant pleasure along her nerves to coalesce in the lower part of her body. She drew back as if she had been burned. Her gaze met his and was held by the look of disturbed pain in his face.

"Congratulations," he said, his voice soft yet flavored with irony. "Dad was right after all; you'll do fine as the mistress of Bonne Vie."

Then releasing her, he turned abruptly and walked away.

Rebecca drew in her breath as if she had suddenly surfaced from underwater. Cosmo turned toward her and leaned to brush her forehead with his lips. "What is it, love?"

"Nothing," she said through dry lips. "Nothing at all."

He said no more, but there was a scowl between his brows as he looked beyond her and watched his son's back as Noel walked away.

Their official wedding night was delayed until they reached Paris. When the reception was over, Rebecca had been so exhausted, and with nerves so tightly strung from the strain of the past few days, that Cosmo had plied her with champagne, then bundled her into bed with brusque assurances that he was too tired himself to be romantic. He had held her until she slept.

Their flight for Europe left early the next morning from New Orleans International. They would be gone indefinitely. Their destination was Paris, and Cosmo wanted to return by way of London, but the rest of the itinerary was open, subject, Cosmo had said, to Rebecca's whim.

Paris was a fantasy come true. Their hotel suite overlooked an ancient square lined with limestone buildings. The bedroom walls were of pale green satin and the drapes edged with gold fringe, and there was a balcony with an ornate railing that reminded Rebecca of New Orleans. There was champagne waiting and a bowl of fruit. The two of them shared a pear and toasted the City of Lights while watching from their balcony as the day faded in a pink haze above the gray rooftops of Paris.

Afterward, Cosmo, with a solemnity belied by the soft gleam in his dark gray eyes, explained to Rebecca the use of the bidet in one of the bathrooms of the two-bedroom suite, then left her to luxuriate in the deep tub filled with mounds of scented bubbles while he went to make use of the other bathroom.

When she emerged at last, tying the belt of a silk housecoat around her, there was a gift lying wrapped and beribboned on the bed. Cosmo sat in a chair nearby wearing a soft navy cashmere dressing gown and holding a newspaper that he appeared to have forgotten the instant she appeared. As she gave him a tentative smile, he nodded toward the present.

"Open it," he said, his voice deep.

"What is it now? You've already given me too much."

The past weeks had seemed like Christmas, with hardly a day that went by without a gift of some kind, from bath salts and perfume to the enormous oval diamond on her left hand. It had become embarrassing, and even wearisome, to keep having to say thank you.

"This one is only partly for you. It's also for me."

Rebecca saw that her new husband was not quite as relaxed as he seemed. In fact, there was a flush under his skin and a shadow of doubt in his eyes. She could feel the heat of her own blush gathering across her cheekbones and the flutter of nerves in her stomach as she realized that the moment for intimacy had finally come. She had had a great deal of time to think about it, almost too long. She was half fearful and half intrigued, and all too aware of a sudden wild impulse to make a dash for the door.

"Please," he whispered, and, folding his paper, got to his feet and moved to stand beside her.

She turned away slightly as she reached for the gift. It was heavier than she expected and from inside came an odd subdued rattle. It was easier to pull away the ribbon and tear off the paper than to look at Cosmo. She uncovered a shell-shaped box of worn blue velvet. The catch gave her a moment of trouble, then she raised the lid.

Inside lay a double strand of pearls on a bed of shimmering white silk. The pearls moved slightly with the jarring of her heart as she held the box against her. So lustrous and iridescent were they that they seemed alive. They were the largest and most perfect she had ever seen, and though she had only a vague idea of how to appraise them, she knew instinctively that they were priceless.

"These are the Staulet pearls," Cosmo said as she stood staring down at them. "They were bought by one of my ancestors on a voyage to the Orient and given to his bride on their wedding day. My first wife, Noel's mother, never cared for them since she believed pearls to be a sign of tears. I hope you won't be as superstitious."

"No," she said, her voice low. "They are truly beautiful, but I don't know if I can ever wear them. I'd be afraid I might lose them."

"I doubt that. The catch is very secure. But you can begin by wearing them for me. They should go well with—with this."

He reached to catch the silk that lined the box and draw it out. It dangled from his fingers, attached to white silk cords that formed a shape that was familiar, all too familiar. It was a fringed white silk G-string, a G-string much like the one she had worn on Bourbon Street except for the finer material.

Rebecca lifted her gaze from the silk fringe to stare at her husband. He met her eyes, the look in his own beseeching. "Just this once," he said, his voice husky, shaking slightly. "Please?"

She had thought that she had put that part of her life behind her. She had thought she could forget the humiliation of it and start again. To discover that it wasn't so drove the color from her face and left her hands icy.

"Don't look like that," he begged in ragged tones. "I need you to do this because of what I am because I'm a vile old man. It has nothing to do with what you once were or what you are."

She heard his pain, felt it, and abruptly her own was gone. She forced her lips into a smile. "You aren't vile. You could never be vile, or old."

He made no answer but waited, scarcely breathing, as she put down the pearls, untied the robe she wore, and let it fall, then took the G-string from his hand. She stepped into it and pulled it up, settling it into place so that the fringe lay cool and silky over her pubic area. Then she turned to face him.

He did not look at her but reached for the pearls. He draped them around her neck and fastened them. Their weight settled between her breasts. He touched them, pressing them into her skin so that they became warm with her body heat and her flesh seemed to take the same soft, creamy-pink sheen.

He cupped her breasts in his hands, bent his head to kiss their tilted tips, then slowly he lowered himself to kneel at her feet. He let his hands trail down her body, following the curves, clasping, holding. Whispering her name, he pressed his face to the silken fringe she wore.

She could feel his warm breath, then the wet and heated flick of his tongue. She drew in her breath in protest and embarrassment, but he would not let her go. She closed her eyes. Her movements stilled. Her skin grew moist and heated. She gasped, a small sound in the back of her throat, quickly stifled. The blood throbbed in her veins. The lower part of her body felt heavy. She put her hands on his shoulders, squeezing them hard, holding on. The rapture started deep and rose in slow waves, engulfing her. It banished thought and fear, becoming a goal that beckoned. She wanted it, needed it, could not bear not to reach it.

Abruptly it burst over her. She gave a soft cry as she felt her knees giving way. Cosmo toppled her backward onto the bed, then struggled out of his dressing gown and dropped it to the floor. Stalwart in his nakedness, he put his knee on the mattress, then hesitated as if uncertain he was welcome. Rebecca opened her eyes and reached out to him.

14

They stayed in France for three months. Cosmo took great delight in showing Rebecca the monuments and museums, also in outfitting her at the great fashion meccas and escorting her to the places dedicated to the enhancement of feminine beauty. He enjoyed sitting at some sidewalk café while allowing her free rein in the shops along the Rue de la Paix and the Champs-Élysées. To his considerable amusement, she preferred the Galeries Lafayette for her shopping. He was not so amused, however, at her insistence on dragging him with her into the Metro to explore obscure corners of the city or for long walks that invariably took them past the book and flower stalls along the Seine or in and out of the antique shops of the Left Bank.

He took her to the Paris offices of Staulet Corporation, where he introduced her with every indication of pride and showed her the view of the Eiffel Tower from the top-floor windows. They had a long and leisurely luncheon with the president of the Paris branch, a man who treated Rebecca with a blend of flirtation and condescension that caused her to retreat into muteness. She didn't like the man, though when she told Cosmo so later she was unable to say precisely why.

"Shall I fire him then because you don't like him?" he asked with a quizzical smile.

"You mean you would do that?"

"I'm a great believer in a woman's intuition."

"I don't mean him any harm. I was just saying—"

"You must learn to take responsibility for what you say, my love."

"Can't I have an opinion without it meaning a man's job? Can't I say what I think to you without—without—"

"Without consequences? It hardly ever works that way. There are always consequences, no matter what we intend."

"In that case, it's a wonder people ever talk at all."

"Isn't it?" he said, and laughed.

They hired a car and drove into the countryside, crossing and recrossing the Seine that, once away from Paris, became as clear and as green as grass, and rambling through the wine country where the grapes were greener still.

Rebecca's birthday was celebrated somewhere near Marseilles, her seventeenth. Cosmo bought her a pair of diamond and aquamarine earrings and also a small purse-size pistol that he taught her to use. He would not always be around to protect her, he said. A knowledge of firearms would give her confidence at least to try to defend herself; sometimes just trying was enough.

They sunbathed topless on a beach near Nice, where they checked each other rather more often than was strictly necessary for sunburn and talked in a desultory way of buying a house in France, perhaps in the wonderful, unspoiled countryside they had come across near Menerbes. It was then Rebecca learned that Cosmo already owned houses in Colorado and on an island in the Bahamas. She could not for the life of her think what he needed with another one and told him so, which made him catch her and roll her in the sand and, lying with her clasped atop his long body, with their foreheads pressed together and her hair falling around their faces, tell her for the ten-thousandth time that he loved her. Because it made him happy, she told him she loved him, too, and was not certain it was not the truth.

The time they spent in France made a difference. Rebecca was not the same person when she stepped off the plane in New Orleans as she had been when she left. It was not just the fantastic cut and sheen of her hair or the delicate perfection of her makeup, nor was it the designer labels of the clothes she wore or the reflected luster of the pearls around her neck. It was the sense of having her own style, a casual and confident elegance that hinted at the aristocratic without straining after it. It was also the grace with which she moved, the tilt of her chin, and the clear, newly cultured tones that yet carried a rich hint of her undisputed background. Most of all, it was the warmth of her smile and the way she looked everyone she met squarely in the eye.

No one was more aware of the changes than Rebecca herself. She also knew it was due to Cosmo's subtle coaching, unstinting support, and impeccable example. She was grateful for all three, but especially for his subtlety, which had saved her from feeling awkward or in any way lacking in the qualities he expected in a wife. It had made her work harder to be what he wanted, what he obviously needed, even if he expressed no overt wish for it.

There was also the matter of her name. Cosmo had begun to call her Riva instead of Rebecca while they were in the South of France. She no longer looked like a Becky, he had said. Riva was another form of Rebecca, one with more style. Getting used to the change had taken a little while, but by the time they were ready to go home she had decided she rather liked it.

Noel met them at the airport with George and the limousine. The courtesy was unexpected. The last they had heard from him, he had moved out of Bonne Vie and was living on campus at Georgia Tech where he had transferred from LSU for the fall semester. The decision was sudden, but it was one Cosmo accepted with little surprise and no attempt to dissuade his son.

Riva was glad to see Noel and gave him a shy smile. He hardly spoke to her on the long drive home, however, concentrating instead on bringing his father up-to-date on the events that had taken place in their absence. Now and then he sent her a measuring glance but looked away the moment their eyes met.

He was uncomfortable with her, Riva realized. The question was why. She studied him covertly, trying to decide. It might be the change in the way she looked, of course, though somehow she didn't think so. She had learned on Bourbon Street to recognize appreciation in a man's eyes and she saw it now. At the same time, she thought he was covering something that went deeper, something very like a wariness close to fear. If that was so, something was going to have to be done. She did not intend to live with awkwardness or any kind of misunderstanding between Cosmo's son and herself.

Dinner was waiting when they arrived at Bonne Vie, a marvelous spread of all the Southern-style garden vegetables and spicy Creole and Cajun dishes they had missed so badly while away. Riva made a determined effort to join the conversation at the table and was rewarded by near normal give-and-take among the three of them and an appreciable easing in the atmosphere. They seemed almost a family, at least until the meal was over.

There were one or two business matters that Cosmo wanted to check on at once. Now that he was back in home territory, the corporation and its problems assumed a priority they had not had for months. He excused himself from the table and went away to the library to use the phone, leaving Riva and Noel alone. Riva, noticing the butler hovering as if ready to clear the table, rose from her chair. Out of politeness, Noel got to his feet also. As Riva moved out into the hall and turned in the direction of the back gallery, he walked beside her.

It was warm outside but not unpleasantly so since the humidity of summer was waning with the hot season. The darkness under the gallery overhang was soft and inviting. Riva moved to lean with one shoulder against one of the columns of the great house. Almost at random she said, "It's nice to breathe fresh air again."

"There was no fresh air in Europe?"

"Oh, sure. I just meant after all the planes and airports and air-conditioned cars."

"You enjoyed your trip, then?"

"Very much."

"It seems as if the honeymoon was a success."

She turned to face him, putting her back to the plastered bricks of the column that still held the slight warmth of the sun. "I suppose it was." When he made no comment, she went on. "Noel?"

He was watching her in the dimness, standing at ease with one hand in his pants pocket. The light from the hallway slanted across his shoulder and the side of his face but left his eyes in shadow.

"Yes?"

"I . . . want you to know that I'm no threat to you." The words were low-spoken but earnest.

"Aren't you?" The tone of his voice was politely dubious.

"Nothing's going to change, not really."

"No, because they've already changed."

"What I mean to say is, I don't want anything that belongs to you, will never take anything that is yours."

He stared at her for endless moments there in the semidarkness. There was in his face a tightness that seemed to hint at repressed anger and sadness and also a curious longing.

Finally he said, "You already have."

She stared at him in blank surprise. "What?"

He stepped closer. Reaching out, he picked up the strands of pearls that lay against her breasts. "By tradition, these are mine as the first-born son, to be given to my wife."

"You don't have a wife yet."

"And my father does. But when I do, when that time comes, will you give them up?"

"If that's the way it's supposed to be, yes." She meant it, though the words caused her a pang she did not want to consider.

"What self-sacrifice."

Stung by the derision in his tone, she said, "I didn't ask for them. Cosmo gave them to me!"

"I'm sure he did. The impulse must have been irresistible."

"You can have them back now, if that's what you want!" she cried, reaching up to unfasten the catch. "I don't want anything that's going to cause problems between us."

In a swift movement, he caught her hands to stop her fumbling at the clasp. "Don't be ridiculous! I don't want the pearls."

He was so near she could smell the aromatic wood and lime tang of his aftershave combined with a hint of starched linen and his own fresh maleness. The aura of his presence surrounded her, invading her senses. It was so intense, so peculiarly familiar, that she swayed toward him. In consternation, she recognized what was happening to her as the now familiar prelude to desire. It was so unlikely that she exerted every ounce of will she possessed to suppress it.

"I only—" she began, stopped, then started again. "I only want you to like me."

There was a moment of profound stillness before a sound left him that might have been a soft laugh or an exclamation of pain. He released her with deliberate slowness, then stepped back and thrust his hands in his pockets. "It's too late for that," he answered. "Much too late. I'd better go, since I have to be back at school in time for class Monday. I'll just say goodbye to Dad."

A mosquito buzzed around Riva's face and flitted away again. She didn't notice. "You aren't going tonight?"

"I think it's best," he said, his voice strained. "I really do."

He gave her no chance to answer but swung sharply and walked away, moving back into the house. After a long few minutes there came the sound of his car springing into life on the front drive. It was longer still before Riva moved to go back inside.

She and Cosmo settled into a routine. At first she stayed at home, but after so many months of being constantly with her husband, she found it dull. She embarked on a course of reading, starting in Cosmo's library and expanding to the public institutions in New Orleans. It was a program whose purpose was to repair the deficiencies of her interrupted education, one that was to continue for the rest of her life. For a few months that held her interest, but eventually it was not enough. There were clubs she could join, teas and luncheons she could attend, but she had no interest in them. It seemed Cosmo was reluctant to be away from her for so long also, for when he learned of her discontent, he cleared the office next to his own at the Staulet Building and installed her there.

For the first few days, he merely joined her for coffee twice a day and occasionally stayed with the door locked for a snatched half hour. Gradually, however, he began to discuss various problems with her, using her to blow off steam about the incompetence around him or to toss around new ideas.

She had no formal business training, and certainly no experience, but she had a quick and retentive mind and more than ample common sense, and she hated sitting twiddling her thumbs and doing nothing for hours on end. More than that, she was good with people, able to sense with some perception she could not explain the ones who were bright and genuine from those who expected to get by on fast talk and flash, those who were aboveboard from the ones who were underhanded. Within a month, she was doing small tasks for Cosmo, from making phone calls to compiling lists and composing memos.

There was a brief problem with his secretary of fifteen years who felt her position was being usurped, but once Riva admitted ruefully that she couldn't type or take dictation, had only the sketchiest idea of filing and didn't care to learn more, there was peace. The woman was soon typing the memos Riva dictated and taking messages for her as well as making her reservations and appointments for the hairdresser. At the end of six months, Riva was recognized as Cosmo's personal assistant, the person to see if anyone needed the boss's attention.

It was also widely known that in spite of being the young wife of an older husband, it was best not to come on too strong to her. She could freeze a suggestive comment with a single look, and a man was lucky if that was all that she froze. Any male so ill-advised as to lay a hand on her could be thankful if he got his fingers back.

When Cosmo's secretary first told her of what was being said about her coldness toward men, Riva was dismayed. She had not realized it was so obvious, though she had heard enough lascivious and degrading suggestions to last her a lifetime and had learned the hard way how to put them down. The more she thought about it, however, the less surprising it seemed. The truth was, she did not care for mindless, sexually shaded banter or even overt admiration from the men around her. Inside her there was something cool and hard toward them. It was there, sometimes, even for her husband.

It had not been that way in France. She had felt for a long time that she was a normal, healthy female with all the right responses. It had not lasted. It often seemed since their return that Cosmo made love to her by rote, as if it were something he had learned out of a book lately, a recipe he had to follow, so much of this and so much of that without regard for how she might be reacting. At other times it seemed that if she showed her pleasure in some caress or position, he immediately changed or shifted, as if her reaction was too exciting to him so that he came close to losing control, or else too stimulating to her so that she might reach her moment of greatest pleasure before he felt she should.

It seemed, in fact, as if he were thinking too much about what he was doing instead of feeling it, remaining too detached, watching her too closely to be certain she was fully satisfied. It made her do the same so that the pleasure seeped away or else the frustration of unfulfilled desire grew so painful that she could bear it no longer and simply turned it off. Either way, she was left empty and cold.

Talking about it did no good, for she tried. The subject seemed to embarrass Cosmo nearly as much as it did her; moreover, he seemed to take anything she said as a complaint. His reaction was withdrawal from making love or, worse, the inability to make love to her. Her only choice then was silence and pretending what she did not feel except on rare occasions. And increasingly she worried that it was something within herself that made it so difficult for her to find physical completion with a man.

It was Christmas before Noel was seen again at Bonne Vie. He claimed that he had been working on a project. His major was business administration, but his minor was in electronics, so it was just barely possible. Since his father did not question the excuse, Riva hardly felt she had the right, though she wondered.

The visit passed without real incident, if not without tension. On Christmas Eve the three of them, Riva and Cosmo and Noel, went to see the bonfires on the levee, those huge fires made of logs, scrap lumber, timbers, and cane bagasse, the last being the squeezed and dried stalks left after the extraction of the juice from the sugarcane. The bonfires, constructed in the rough shapes of pyramids and steamboats and even sometimes an antebellum mansion, were set on fire, so it was said, to help guide Père Noel in his flight along the river to deliver presents to the homes of Cajun boys and girls. Presumably to aid in this goal, there was also music and dancing on the levee by the light of the leaping flames, plus the liberal consumption of strong drink to keep out the damp, penetrating cold of December.

Cosmo was content to ride slowly up and down in the car viewing the scene or else, after they stopped, to sit visiting with friends who came up to speak while dispensing shots of bourbon from the limousine's backseat bar. He urged Riva and Noel on, however, encouraging them to get out and stroll among the others lining the levee, to have some of the jambalaya and hot cider being hawked by enterprising businessmen, and even to dance.

The music of fiddles and accordions and the sound of voices with lilting backcountry French accents raised in joy were infectious. Combined with the smell of spicy food and woodsmoke and the sight of the leaping flames reflecting yellow and orange in the dark waters of the wide and slow-moving river, they were like something out of another time. As a celebration it was fun; as a tradition it was joyous.

When Noel caught Riva's hand to draw her among the dancing couples, it seemed natural to go with him, to match her steps to his and follow the movements of others. The tune was a waltz, but one with a difference, with a stronger and faster beat. Noel moved with deft sureness in time to the music, as if he felt it pulsing in his veins. Together they circled and whirled, now spinning with dizzying speed, now breaking apart to sidestep and turn with one hand clasping each other's waists and the other placed behind their backs. Their eyes met and held in the light of the flames that leaped to the same rhythm. Riva stared at Noel's face that was slashed by a smile of breathtaking tenderness, of mind-shattering openness to her. The brightness that gleamed deep in the black irises of his eyes made her heart lurch with a painful quickening. A trembling began deep inside, growing with a terrible fear. She wanted to stop dancing, to break away and run back to the car, back to Cosmo where it was safe. At the same time, she knew there was no such thing as safety.

Later, they all went to midnight mass at an old and beautiful church at Gramercy nearby on the river road. The ceremony by candlelight was solemn and moving. Riva knelt on the kneeling bench with tightly closed eyes and clasped hands, but though she prayed she could find little comfort and less peace.

It was a relief when Noel returned to Georgia Tech. The turmoil of emotions he had aroused in Riva subsided. She went back to working with Cosmo, to learning to cope with the management of Bonne Vie, and to becoming gradually a part of the New Orleans social scene that was so frenetic from January to March as the usual winter charity-ball-and-culture season coincided with the carnival of Mardi Gras from Twelfth Night to Lent.

By the time summer came, Riva had decided that it would be best if she and Noel remained somewhat estranged. Friendship between them, she sensed, could be dangerous. And so she was cordial but cool for those months while Cosmo's son was at Bonne Vie and working at Staulet Corporation. She made certain she was never alone with him for any length of time and that any discussion between them was either extremely general in nature or else brief and to the point.

In this way a year passed. Then Noel graduated from college. He decided to use the house in the Bahamas to get away for a month or two, to relax before he took on the job of fitting himself into Staulet Corporation. Two weeks after Noel's departure, Cosmo announced that he wanted to talk to his son about his future. It would be best if it could be done well away from everything and everybody, and there was no better place for that than on the island. Besides, he and Riva hadn't been away for more than a day or two since their honeymoon. They both needed a vacation.

The island house, designed in the style of a Mediterranean villa, was plastered and painted white and edged with terraces that descended to the sea. It was not large since it had been built as a retreat rather than a place for entertaining large groups. There were only three bedrooms with adjoining baths, a kitchen and dining area, and a fairly large living room with sliding glass doors that overlooked the terraces and the beach. Surrounding the house was a wall with a wrought-iron gate. Inside the wall was a profusion of hibiscus and bougainvillea, croton and casuarina and sea grape, while overhead swayed the dark green fronds of majestic palms. The sea rolled in lazy green and turquoise splendor onto the stretch of pink and white sand that came right up to the steps of the lower terrace. There were no other houses in sight, no other people for at least a quarter of a mile.

The beauty of the island was insidious, a balm that seemed to smooth away difficulties and encourage the sybaritic enjoyment of the moment. Somehow the discussion that had brought Riva and

Cosmo was put off from one day to the next. The relationship among the three of them was so easy, the atmosphere so relaxed, that Riva began to think she had been imagining a problem.

Cosmo didn't swim. It wasn't that he couldn't, just that he didn't care for the feel of sand against his skin or the stickiness of chlorine or salt water in his hair. It was basically a messy, useless activity, he said, though he was ready to concede its benefit as exercise. His feeling about it was one of the reasons he hadn't been to the island house in recent years. It had been bought for the pleasure of his first wife, Noel's mother, as well as for Noel himself while he was growing up.

Riva loved swimming, loved the glide of the water against her, the feeling of near weightlessness as she floated on its surface. She particularly loved the sea with its changing colors, changing moods, and the song and motion of its endless waves. The idea of the beach had always appealed, and her introduction to the French Mediterranean had been grand, but she had not known how much she would love it until she came to the island.

One morning Noel got out the snorkeling gear. There was an area down the beach where it was possible, he said, to see fan and brain coral, plus vivid plue parrot fish and a dozen other odd varieties. Riva had never been snorkeling before but had discovered within herself an appetite for new things. She could hardly wait to try.

It was ridiculously easy. It was also fascinating to discover so many wonderful plants and animals beneath the surface of the water, easily visible through the translucent depths as they were penetrated by the hot tropical sun. No small part of it was the enthusiasm of the young man beside her, the camaraderie of swimming shoulder to shoulder and pointing out new finds to each other. Their shared pleasure in the day, with the infectiousness of close companionship, silly jokes, and horseplay in the water, made her feel young and carefree in a way she had not been in ages, not since before she had left home. She hadn't wanted to stop, hadn't wanted to go back to the beach house, not even when Noel told her the skin of her back was broiled to medium-rare and she would be sick if she wasn't careful.

She was not the only one sunburned. That he was red here and there, too, made this ending of their day comical instead of agonizing. Wincing at the rub of their suits on smarting flesh and their own foolishness, they trailed back down the beach toward the house as the sun leaned toward midafternoon.

Cosmo was taking a nap with the bedroom door closed. The house was still. The air-conditioning was chill on their heated flesh and wet suits. Since Riva could not get to her own bathroom without waking Cosmo, she showered quickly in the one of the extra guest room. She was also cut off from her clothes, and the thought of putting her suit, which was still embedded with grains of sand, back on was intolerable. Catching sight of a short cotton robe on the back of the bathroom door, she slipped it on.

Noel had been busy putting away the snorkeling gear. He barely glanced at her as he passed her in the hall, or so it seemed, but it was obvious he saw enough.

"There's a T-shirt and a pair of shorts in my room you can borrow, if you want," he said.

"Thanks, anyway, but I don't think I could stand anything that close fitting right this minute."

"Suit yourself. Let me wash off some of the sand, then maybe we can find something to eat. I'm starved."

He skimmed past, being careful not to touch her, then disappeared into his room. After a second or two, the bathroom door closed. It was some minutes before the water started to run.

Riva wandered out to the kitchen where she rummaged around in the refrigerator for a snack. The island couple who came in every morning to clean the house, take care of the flowering shrubs, and do the marketing and cooking were gone for the day. The wife had left baked chicken and salad for lunch, along with fresh pineapple slices and a plate of English tea cakes. Riva set these things on a tray with paper plates and glasses of iced tea, then carried it out to the shady end of the terrace.

The stillness of the waning afternoon had descended. The heat was oppressive. A lavender haze had appeared far out on the horizon over the water. Nothing moved except the waves lapping on the beach and now and then a palm frond stirred by a fitful breeze.

The glare off the sand was so bright that it was necessary to squint against it even behind sunglasses. The effort was tiring, especially along with the draining fatigue of sunburn. All Riva wanted to do was to have a long cool drink, eat something, then lie back in her lounge chair and sleep. She picked up a spear of pineapple and bit into it, then turned her head as Noel emerged from the house.

He wore only khaki shorts and his hair was tousled, as if he had done no more than run his fingers through it. His face was red across the bridge of his nose and the tops of his ears, and his shoulders were burned, but he was already brown from two weeks of island sun and would soon be browner.

He looked at her, however, and shook his head. "You look like a well-done lobster."

"Thank you, kind sir." she said with sugary sweetness. "Have some chicken."

"Don't mind if I do. Then we're going to have to do something about your skin, or you'll shrivel up and turn into a raisin right before my very eyes."

She tilted her head and pulled out the front of her robe so that she could look under it at her chest. "Is it that bad?"

"You're three shades redder than when we came in."

"Am I really?"

"Never mind, I have some cream. If we spread it on thick enough, there may be some vestiges of your former beauty left after you peel."

She looked at him in mock annoyance. "You're such a comfort."

"I'm glad you appreciate it."

As she met his gaze across the table, it was tinged with self-deprecating humor. Then the amusement faded, leaving it open and vulnerable and shadowed with something that could not be named. She felt a constriction in her throat and a burning behind her eyes. Blinking quickly, she looked down, pushing the plate of chicken toward him.

"Eat," she said.

"Yes, Stepmama," he answered in deep tones.

Once more they looked at each other, then quickly away again. Out on the horizon, where the sky met the sea, the haze had become dark purplish-gray and there came from it the dull percussion of distant thunder.

They were sitting in the same lounge chair, with Riva between Noel's spread knees and the robe draped open exposing her back to the waist, when Cosmo woke from his nap and walked out onto the terrace.

"What is this?" he said, the words hard-edged with anger and suspicion. The rising wind fluttered his hair. The sun had gone behind the cloud rising out of the sea so that his face was dark.

Riva raked the flying tangles of her drying hair out of her eyes. She automatically tightened her hold on the robe just above her breasts even as she attempted a smile. "I feel so dumb for staying in the sun so long. Noel had some special cream—"

"I'll just bet he did. Get in the house, both of you."

Riva could sense the blood draining from her face. At the same time, she felt Noel's hand leave off its smoothing action on her raw back, lifting away with guilty haste. An icy chill settled in the pit of her stomach. The contrast with the fever of her skin made her feel disoriented, ill.

"I mean now!"

It was an order. Noel could not move until she did. Riva tried to settle the robe around her, but the wind sweeping onto the terrace caught it, flapping it open to show a long length of naked thigh. She whipped it closed, then tightened the belt and pushed to her feet. As Cosmo stood aside, she moved in front of him through the sliding glass doors that led into the living room of the house. She did not turn, though she knew Noel was directly behind her.

"Put some clothes on," the older man said to her. "Then I want to see you back here."

She went into the bedroom and put on a strapless sundress without a bra. She brushed the tangles from her hair with hard, swift strokes and pulled it back on either side of her face with tortoiseshell clasps. She could hear the raised voices of the two men, but what they were saying was muffled by the closed door and drowned in the rumble of thunder. Still, the sound and what it meant made her so clumsy that it seemed to take twice as long as it should have to make herself presentable.

By the time she returned to the living room, it was much darker outside. Gray clouds were scudding over the heaving sea beyond the glass doors, and sand was blowing with a soft, sighing whisper against the house.

The two men turned to face her when she entered. Their faces were flushed and their fists clenched. They looked so much alike that she stopped in consternation, staring from one to the other.

Cosmo spoke at last, "I think we have agreed that it's best for Noel to work for the next year or two in the Paris office as he learns the business. That's what I intended to talk to him about when we came down here, and it seems doubly wise now."

"What do you mean 'now'?" Riva asked. Her anger had been slow in coming, but she could feel its rise inside her. "Didn't he tell you there was nothing going on between us out there?"

"You forget, I saw what was going on."

"You saw nothing!"

"I saw my son fondling my wife while she lay half naked in his lap. That isn't nothing!"

"If you say that, it's only because you have a dirty mind. He was putting cream on my back."

"I see you don't deny the nakedness." The words were said with trenchant scorn.

"I was less naked than the first time you ever saw me," she cried.

"And look where that got you!"

She drew back in shock, then her eyes narrowed. "What does that mean?"

Noel stepped forward. "Stop this! None of it matters. I'm not going to Paris."

"You'll do what I tell you," Cosmo said, swinging around to him.

"The hell I will!"

"If you don't, you won't work at Staulet Corporation!"

"Who needs Staulet Corporation?" his son instantly returned. Whipping around, Noel lunged across to the glass doors. He opened them with a hard shove and stepped through. In an instant, he was swallowed up by the growing storm.

"Noel, wait!" Riva called, moving after him.

230 •

Cosmo caught her at the door, swinging her around with hard fingers gripping her forearm. "Where do you think you're going? Come back here."

She stared up at him with the wind coming through the open door and fluttering her hair and her dress around her. "He's your son. You have to go after him."

"When he remembers he's my son and not my rival, he can come back. Until then, let him go."

"You can't do this," she pleaded, reaching to grip a handful of Cosmo's shirt in her clenched fingers. "It isn't right, not over me."

He stared down at her with fierce pain in his face. "There's no other way. I've tried to find one, but there is none."

"There has to be," she said, her voice taut as she gave him a hard shake that ended with a push. "There has to be!"

Dragging herself free of him, she flung herself out the door. She heard him yelling her name as he blundered after her. She knew when he stopped and cursed, then spun around and reentered the house, slamming the door behind him. She didn't look back. In an instant she had clattered down the levels of the terraces and was on the beach.

She narrowed her eyes as she looked up and down the long stretch of sand. The wind tore at her hair and dress and sand stung her face. As she grimaced against it, she could taste the salt of the blowing spray. There was nothing to be seen in either direction except the tossing waves and the fast-moving darkness of the storm. Then came the first raindrops, wet, warm splashes the size of silver dollars. They splattered around her, and she could hear them rattling on the sea's surface as if it were made of tin.

It was then she saw the footprints. They were no more than shallow depressions in the soft sand, which were fast disappearing with the smoothing action of the wind, but they made a line that had not been there before. They led away from the beach toward where the gardening shed stood beneath a cluster of rattling palm trees. Among the dark shapes of the tree trunks was the tall shape of a man.

Riva plunged among the palms just ahead of the rushing downpour. Half blinded by rain, she didn't see Noel coming to meet her until she crashed against his hard form and was gathered in his arms. She made a sound between a laugh and a sob, then his lips came down on hers. For long moments they stood locked together, mouth to mouth. When they drew apart, they stared into each other's eyes in fear and desire and the residue of anger, then as they felt the increasing wetness pouring down on them, they turned without words to seek the cover of the shed.

It was dim and dusty inside and it smelled of insecticide and potting soil, but the wind that entered with them swept the odors away. There was a canvas awning, a remnant of some long-forgotten party, rolled in one corner. Noel spread it on the sandy floor before the open door, then they sank down upon it, side by side, their arms about each other. The rain pounded on the metal roof and poured in splattering streams to the ground. The clatter and roar of it combined with the rushing wind and crash of the surf.

Riva shivered with reaction, though whether it was to the confrontation with Cosmo, the implications of Noel's kiss, or the wet weather she could not have said. Noel's arms about her, the feel of his body against hers were welcome. She huddled close, anxious and confused at the feelings that raged inside her. Still, she might have retained some sense of her obligation to Cosmo, some loyalty, if Noel had not cupped her face in his hands and kissed her once more.

His lips were warm and firm and sweet. He took hers as a right, tracing their sensitive line with his tongue, gently abrading the smooth inner lining. He smelled of sea air and sunburn cream and youth, and there was in his hold the hard muscles and sinews of a man still young enough to be daring and unsophisticated enough to be impetuous.

"I want you," he whispered into her hair. "In spite of everything, I want you. If I am to lose so much because of you, then there should be some reward."

In his words there was a timbre of despairing rage that seemed almost as if it were directed at her. "What?" she asked in confusion. "What did you say?"

232 •

"No, no forget that, I didn't mean it. It's just that I want you so desperately I'm ready to use any excuse."

She would have questioned him further, but his mouth covered hers. He drew down her strapless dress with his free hand and cupped her breast, brushing the nipple into stinging desire. Resistance held her taut for an instant, then it ebbed slowly. There was something right about his touch, about the feel of his body against hers and the taste of his lips; it was as if the two of them had been created for this moment, for each other. To deny it was impossible; to refuse, beyond her strength.

She pressed against him, accepting, offering, holding nothing back. Gently he lowered her to the canvas so that her weight was on her side instead of her sunburned back. His chest swelled with his pent-up breath of pleasure and disbelief, then as he let it out she felt its heat upon her breast following by the warm, wet tracery of his tongue.

She was melting inside. She had no strength. Her principles and her pride hovered somewhere beyond her ability to recall them. Excitement burgeoned, though within it was a strong vein of terror. What she was doing was forbidden, dangerous. She and the man who held her could be engulfed by the storm or, what seemed worse, discovered. It made no difference except to add intensity to the fire in her blood.

She was making love. For the first time—the only time—there was no sense of restraint as she accepted Noel's caresses and returned them with care and grace. She delighted in the sculpting of his body and the thick silk of his hair that grew low on his neck and gave herself to the gentleness of his hands. She was free and knew it. She made herself a gift, one that could not be taken and was not required, but could only be given by herself alone. And in return she received him.

He was eager, but the limits of his control were elastic, unending. He sensed her responses and tended them with care and as a joy. He was generous and as natural at his task, and as sweetly competent, as a young pagan. He was delicate but also inventive, blindly reveling in his own sensations but attuned to her every manifestation of delight.

And he was tireless in his superb strength, rhythmic and vigorous. He heard her moans of pleasure and, whispering his joy, increased them tenfold until, in rigid splendor, he joined them with his own.

The storm abated. They watched in silence as the clouds rolled away over the sea and the water turned once more from gray to blue. The waves on the sand still had an angry sound, however, and were dirty white on their crests. It was evening.

Riva waited for Noel to say something about their future. She had no idea what it would be, whether he would suggest telling his father that they were going away together or possibly ask her to discuss a divorce with Cosmo. The last thing she expected was for him to do nothing.

But that was what he did. He took her hand and pulled her to her feet, then walked with her in somber silence back to the house. He stood for a moment in the living room where Cosmo sat staring out at the sea. When his father said not a word, did not look at either of them, Noel released Riva and walked away, striding toward his room. He stayed there, not even coming out for dinner.

When morning came, he was gone.

At the breakfast table, Cosmo took Riva's hand and looked into her eyes. It was the first time he had acknowledged her presence since she had returned the evening before. He had spent the night in the guest bedroom, and she had heard him pacing in there until early morning.

Now his voice was gruff but calm. "I'm sorry you had to witness the break between me and my son. I'm especially sorry because I think you feel that I've been unjust in some way."

"Yes, maybe a little." Riva swallowed as she answered, unable to look at him. There was nothing in his voice to suggest that he suspected how she and Noel had spent their time while they sheltered from the rain, but she could not forget, would never forget.

"I was jealous when I saw you together, I will admit it," he went on. "But I soon realized no blame could be attached to you. It's my son's behavior that is the greatest pain to me. I never dreamed

234 •

. . . Well, it's always a shock when you learn someone you love is not what you thought."

She moistened her lips in dread. "What do you mean?"

"While you were getting dressed yesterday afternoon, Noel and I had words. I didn't want to tell you, but I think maybe it would be better for you to know what was said. He admitted to me that he had been making a play for you for the sole purpose of trying to come between us."

"You are saying that he—he wanted to break up our marriage?"

"That's it exactly, but it's not all. He told me you had been giving him the . . . I believe you might call it the 'come on.'"

"He what?" Dismay vibrated through her. She couldn't accept what she had heard.

"He said that you had been throwing yourself at him. I didn't believe it, and finally I got the truth. He had been leading you on, trying to get you into his bed just to make trouble."

"No," she whispered, blindly shaking her head.

"I'm sorry, my dear, I really am. I expect he was afraid he might have to share his inheritance with a half brother or half sister. Or else that you might become too indispensable to the corporation."

"I can't believe it." The words were dazed, edged with sick horror.

"I had thought to spare you the knowledge of just what kind of man my son Noel had become, but it didn't seem right for you to grieve over something not worth your tears."

She turned a wide stare on her husband. Had he guessed, after all? No, he could not have, not and still gaze at her with such loving understanding.

Noel. She felt as if something were being torn loose inside her. What of the closeness that had been between them, the sense that they had understood each other as few were privileged to do? Had it all been in her mind? In hers alone?

"It's horrible," she whispered, looking away again.

Cosmo gave a heavy sigh as he nodded his agreement. "We can only hope that a few months or years in the Paris operation will make a better man of him."

But Noel had not gone to Paris. He had joined the Marines and been trained as a member of their most elite fighting unit before being sent to Southeast Asia as a military adviser. His specialty had been electronics and his skill was much in demand. There had been long months, even the best part of years, when they had not heard from him, had no idea where he was or what he was doing. He had survived, however, and made a great many contacts among the French left in what they persisted in calling Indochina, as well as acquiring valuable Asian friendships. After the fall of Saigon, he had left the military. A short time later, he had shown up at the Paris offices of Staulet Corporation with some innovative ideas for making and marketing microprocessors. His father, informed of them, had given the ideas a green light at Riva's instigation.

Noel had sent the value of the staid Paris operation soaring like a rocket. He had discovered that the man in charge, the same one Riva had so disliked when she met him, had been skimming the corporate profits for years for the entertainment of a hot little number from Deauville. The man was out and Noel was put in charge. At the end of eighteen months, the operation was running as smoothly as oil on ice.

His marriage a year or two later to a Sicilian princess, the Lady Constance di Lampadusa, had been an event of the most *haute* society. Riva, by then making regular forays to Washington and Palm Beach, New York and Dallas, had heard rumors of its splendor. The bitchy types who had not been invited said that the "protective specialists"—otherwise known as bodyguards—of the Sicilian dons outnumbered the guests two to one. Riva was unable to confirm or deny the snide rumor; she and Cosmo had been invited but had not attended.

There had been a visit to the newlyweds in Paris eighteen months later on what Cosmo called an inspection trip of the revolutionized office. Riva felt certain the real purpose of the journey was to see his first grandchild, a little girl named for Noel's mother. By that time it had been many years since Cosmo had seen his son. Noel had changed, there could be no doubt of that. It wasn't surprising considering all that had happened to him in Vietnam; still, Riva was distressed to see him so withdrawn and uncompromising, so implacable in his judgments. The only subject he and his father seemed able to communicate about was business, and most of their time together was spent discussing one phase or another of Staulet Corporation's holdings. Riva, deeply involved in the management herself since she had instigated the diversification from sugar and cotton and oil leases into the insurance of shipped freight, was able to follow the details, for what good it did her. There was no satisfaction in communicating about such dull matters. Constance, who could follow none of it and had no interest in doing so, had had absolutely no reason for her obvious jealousy.

The divorce that followed the birth of Noel's second child was quiet, or at least it appeared so from the other side of the Atlantic. Noel had announced it almost as an afterthought at the end of an overseas call, one of those he had come to exchange every two or three weeks with his father. A few months later, he had flown to Louisiana for a special executive meeting. It had been at that time that Noel had taken Riva aside and asked her how long it had been since his father had had a medical checkup.

It had been some time. Cosmo was hardly ever ill. He ate moderately, got a reasonable amount of exercise from walking, did not smoke or drink to excess. If he had a bad habit, it was his dedication to work.

He should have lived to be a hundred; instead he had barely made it to seventy.

When he had received the final prognosis, heard the terrible word, the big C feared by so many, he had sent for Noel. Blood had triumphed. It was obvious to Riva that Cosmo meant to deliver the company he had worked so hard to maintain and increase to his son. It had seemed only right. She had been shocked when she was told that she would be listed as a co-owner, equal in authority and in power.

That was not the only shock of those days. Late one night, when the room where Cosmo lay was still and dim, lighted only by the lamp beside his bed and the miniature reading lamp attached to the book Riva read as she sat beside him, her husband had called to her.

"Yes, Cosmo," she said, putting her book down and getting to her feet at once to move to his side. "I'm here. Are you hurting?"

He shook his head. "Not yet. No, there is something—"

"Do you want a drink of water? Or the urinal?"

A shadow of annoyance crossed his face and was gone. As he spoke, his words were shortened by pain and the fluid slowly gathering in his lungs. "I have to tell you. I lied. That day on the island, I lied."

Something shifted inside Riva, but she kept it from showing on her face. Or thought she did. "What do you mean? You lied about what?"

"Noel never said what I told you. He never tried to come between us. If he made love to you, he did it for himself."

The words were like knives slicing deep. The greatest surprise was not the knowledge they contained, however, but how much they could still hurt. Still.

"But why did you say it? What made you do such a thing?"

He looked at her with perspiration dampening his thin, almost white hair and with pleading in his faded eyes. "I was afraid. God help me, but I was afraid you would love him. I was afraid of my own son, so I sent him away. I sent my son away."

Tears formed in the corners of his eyes and ran into the hollows beneath. She watched them with anguish rising inside her, for herself, yes, but also for him. And for Noel. She reached for a tissue, and blotted the moisture away with gentle care, then took his hand to hold it between her own.

"Never mind," she said. "It doesn't matter. He's back again now."

"I lied to him, too. I told him that you were trying to seduce him and that you meant to put the blame on him so that I would disown him."

"Dear God," she whispered before she could stop herself.

"I hurt you, I know. I'm so sorry. So sorry."

She breathed softly in and out, once, twice, three times to control the terrible, exploding agony under her breastbone. Finally she said softly, "No harm done. It—it doesn't matter, not really."

"Oh, it matters. Only I think I hurt myself more than you. I've never known what you would have done. If you would have loved me just the same."

"Of course I would." She put her cheek against the back of his hand to hide the seeping tears.

"Of course you would," he repeated on a sigh, but he did not sound as if he believed it.

An hour later, with his hand still in hers, he gave another long sigh, then his breathing stopped.

Riva, sitting in the darkened room at her sister's bedside, rubbed her temples with the fingertips of both hands. So much love, so much pain, and so many years. She still could not believe Cosmo had been so ruthless, so manipulative, in separating her from his son. She sometimes wondered if Noel knew, if Cosmo had brought him home especially to tell him. If so, there had been nothing in the six months since to show it.

But then what did she expect? She and Noel were no longer young and thoughtless and prone to impulse. There was too much resentment, too much suspicion between them.

Yet he had kissed her in the darkened limousine. Why had he done that? Why? Had it been the sheer male need to dominate physically where he could not do so on a business level? Had it been to make a point about his father's memory? Or did it mean that he still felt something for her, if only desire?

What did she feel? She wished she knew. There had been a time when he first went away that his absence had felt like a death. His image had haunted her, rushing in upon her at unexpected moments. There had been songs popular that summer that she could not bear to hear because she and Noel had heard them on the island together, and it had been a long time before she stopped finding excuses not to go back there. Nevertheless, she had forgotten. The songs had lost their power to hurt, and she had filled the island house with people and noise and gaiety. Cosmo had surrounded her with love and trust, and she had been happy. She really had been happy.

That she had responded to Noel's kiss with astonishing fervor need not mean anything. It had been a long time since a man had held her, since well before Cosmo's final illness. It could have been no more than a purely physical response; it didn't have to be love.

She wasn't sure she was even capable of the kind of love she read about in books, the all-consuming passion for which no sacrifice was too great. She was basically self-contained. She was grateful for the love and affection that came her way, yes, but still sufficient inside herself without it. She sometimes wondered if in her efforts toward self-control, toward never letting anyone suspect she was Erin's mother, and in forgetting what had happened during that island storm, she had somehow lost the ability to love.

It would, perhaps, be a fitting penalty.

15

Anne Gallant picked up the cream-colored silk scarf that lay on the hotel's bedroom dresser. She looked at it for a moment with raised brows, then shook it out. It was large and fine, beautifully hemmed and marked with a designer's insignia, but it was not hers. She never wore that color.

She had just come in from the luncheon that had followed the ribbon-cutting ceremony. The scarf had been lying there, carefully folded. She could not imagine where it had come from. At least, she didn't want to imagine it. That it was lying there in plain view and so carefully placed made her think it might have been put on the dresser by the maid; other things gathered up during the twice-daily inspection of the room had found their way there: a belt that had slipped to the floor behind the dresser while Anne changed in haste, one of Edison's ties slung over the bathroom towel rack.

With the scarf in her hand, she walked to the phone, picked up the receiver, and called Housekeeping. A few minutes later, the floor maid was knocking on the door.

"I found the scarf behind the sofa, Mrs. Gallant," the young brown-skinned girl said in her soft voice. "I didn't tear it or anything, I promise."

"No, no, I know you didn't," Anne said. "The only problem is, it isn't mine. It must have been left by a previous guest."

The girl frowned. "I don't see how. We vacuum behind the sofas after every checkout. Maybe the lady visitor left it."

"The lady visitor?"

A cautious look came over the maid's face as she met Anne's

narrowed gaze. "'Course I might have just missed seeing it. I can take it to Lost and Found."

Anne's worst suspicions were confirmed. She forced a smile. "Oh, I know. It must belong to the reporter. A woman was supposed to interview my husband this morning."

"That'll be it," the girl said with a wide smile of relief. "I was working the other side of this floor and saw her get off the elevator. I remember she had the scarf around her neck. She must have pulled it off and forgot it."

"Yes, I'll see she gets it back. I'm sorry to have bothered you."

"That's all right, Mrs. Gallant."

The maid left the room, but she gave Anne a quick backward glance just before the door closed behind her.

There was no reporter. Anne knew it, and the maid knew it. Hotel personnel always knew when there was something sneaky going on. There had been a woman with Edison here in their hotel suite after Anne had left. The question was: Who was she? And what, exactly, had she been doing there with Edison?

Edison arrived back at the hotel from his own luncheon a half hour later. Anne was lying down. She swung her feet off the bed when she heard his key in the door. The silk scarf was lying spread out over one of the chairs in the living room. She picked it up as she entered the room and, holding it tented between two fingers, went to meet him.

"Your guest left this," she said, and gave him a chill smile. "Don't you think entertaining women in your hotel room is ill-advised under the circumstances?"

Edison made no attempt to take the scarf. Anne let it drop, and it fluttered gently downward to lie over the polished toes of his shoes. He looked down at it, then at his wife.

"It isn't what you think."

"Isn't it? You will remember that I'm a fair detective since you made me that way. There are damp spots on the sofa. So what is it, Edison? What is it this time?" Her voice rose as she spoke. She could hear the strident accusation in it, but she couldn't help it. There had been too many other times, too many other women.

"The woman who was here was Riva Staulet's sister, Margaret. She came to tell me that Riva's out to get me."

Anne stared at him. The excuse was so unexpected, so unlike anything he had ever tried, that it was long seconds before she could assimilate what he had said. "Riva Staulet? Why in the world would she do that?"

"I knew her once, a long time ago."

"So?" Dante had suggested as much. She should have known he was right.

Edison stepped around her, shrugging out of his coat. He loosened his tie and slipped it free, throwing it over a chair arm on his way to the credenza where the tray of bottles sat. Anne watched as he mixed himself a stiff drink. She knew he was stalling, giving himself time to think. She held on to her patience with an effort.

"I may as well tell you," he said as he turned. "Years ago we . . . had a thing going for a while, Riva and I. She got pregnant. I just found out today that I have a daughter. Erin."

"Erin? You mean Erin in your office, the girl Josh . . ." Her voice sounded stupefied. That was because she was.

"Exactly. Riva Staulet wants them separated. She sent her sister to give me an ultimatum."

"Did she, now? Of what kind?"

"I must get Josh out of New Orleans, send him to one of the north Louisiana campaign offices, or she'll make the whole thing public."

"For pity's sake, send him then!"

"And let her think she can push me around? Not on your life!" His words were rough with anger. He drained his drink in a few swallows and turned to pour another.

"But we can't let Josh go on with Erin. It wouldn't be right."

"Screw right. It's boy-girl stuff between them, nothing to worry about."

"You don't know that!" As he only shrugged by way of an answer, Anne went on, thinking out loud. "Anyway, what else can you do? You don't want a scandal."

"Neither does she," he said as he turned once more. "It's all a bluff, nothing to worry about. Darling Riva has just as much to lose as I do, maybe more."

There was something in his words that didn't ring true. Hard experience told Anne it was best to look deeper. A memory stirred, surfaced in her mind. "I don't think today is the first time you've heard of this. It's what Riva Staulet wanted to talk to you about at the rally, isn't it?"

He didn't deny it, though he looked down into his glass as he spoke. "Then it was a suggestion. Now it's a threat."

"A threat. Through her sister."

"She's a devious bitch."

"If that's true, what makes you think she won't find a way to cause trouble without harming herself?"

"There are other ways I can handle it if she wants to get ugly."

"What are you talking about?"

"Erin thinks Riva's her aunt. Riva must want it to stay that way."

"And you could suggest that you might enlighten Erin. What if it doesn't work?"

"Let's just say I have friends in high places."

"The media?"

"Don't worry about it. It won't happen."

His answer was an evasion, but she knew it would do no good to pursue it. Anyway, she had other things on her mind. "So it was a threat? That doesn't explain the damp spots."

"Actually, I think it was Margaret's idea to come. She always did have a yen for me, and I needed her on my side."

Anne had seen Margaret only once or twice during the years of her marriage, but she knew well enough that she was the wife of one of Edison's cousins. She had noticed her at the ball at the old mint, a woman past her first youth, almost matronly. The thought of her with Edison did nothing for her own self esteem. "So you made love to her."

"That's what she came for."

"You bastard!" Anne said through clenched teeth.

He set his drink down with a crash. "What's the matter with you? You asked me and I told you!"

244 •

"How can you stand there and say something like that to me? I'm your wife! Don't you know I have feelings?"

"If you have so much feeling, why did you keep on about it? I think you like hearing it. I think it gives you a charge. I bet if I took you to bed right now, you'd be hot and ready."

"You're revolting."

"So you say, but you keep hanging around."

"I may surprise you one day!" Anne flung the words at him in bitterness that was directed as much at herself as at him.

"Oh, sure," he sneered. "I've heard that before, too."

"One day you'll push me too far."

He snorted. "You like being a famous man's wife too much."

She shook her head. Her voice trembling, she said, "That's not it, you know. What I like is the feeling of honoring my obligations. But I might decide to try another man just to see if I like how that feels."

He was upon her in an instant, shoving her against the wall with his hands clenched with bruising force on her arms. "Try it, and you won't like what I do about it."

Her back was burning and her arms ached, but she stared into his eyes without flinching. "Oh, I don't doubt it," she said in compressed tones. "But I'm not like you. I wouldn't want you to know, so I'd be certain you never found out."

"Have you ever?" he asked, his voice rasping as he pressed her harder against the wall. "Have you?"

"No, never," she whispered. "I've never had any man but you. Yet."

His face twisted. "I'm warning you, I don't have time for this shit. I've got meetings all day tomorrow, then I have to be in Shreveport the day after and over the weekend to clinch the *Times* endorsement. I'm taking Josh up there with me, but I don't need you. You can stay here and take care of this end because we'll be back, both of us. The reason we'll be back is, I don't take well to threats from women—not Riva, not Margaret, and not you. You give me any trouble, do anything to hurt me in this campaign, and you'll be one sorry bitch, nearly as sorry as darling Riva!"

He let her go with a wrench that flung her halfway across the room. Anne rubbed her arms as she looked at him but made no answer. Somehow she had lost all need to cry.

The following morning, Edison had a breakfast meeting scheduled with a congressman. Anne dressed in a leisurely fashion while he was getting ready, but the instant he left the hotel, she went to the phone. She dialed a number she had dug out of her handbag, one she had never thought she would use. Her heart was beating so hard the collar of her dress fluttered as she waited for the phone on the other end to ring.

Dante's voice was sleep-husky but rich and warm as he answered. In the background she could hear the squawking and whistling of his parrot. Her throat closed so that she could not make a sound.

"Hello?" he said again.

Anne swallowed hard. "This—this is Anne Gallant."

"Anne, how are you?"

She could hear the surprise in his voice. She couldn't blame him; she herself couldn't believe that she was calling him. "I'm fine. I just . . . I wondered if I could see you. There's something I'd like to discuss."

"Sure. What did you have in mind? Lunch?"

"I have some shopping to do. I thought I might go to Canal Place or else the Riverwalk. Maybe we could have a cup of coffee or a drink somewhere nearby?"

"There are several places at the Riverwalk. I'll meet you at the fountain in the plaza, say, around eleven? Is that all right?"

"Fine." she said, then repeated quietly to herself after she had hung up, "Fine."

She had not told a lie. She did need to shop for a dress for a special garden wedding. She found nothing at Canal Place, however, not even at Saks. Everything was either too short or too long, too fancy or too plain, too bright or too pale, too chic and dramatic or too young and utterly romantic. It was possible the fault lay with herself. She couldn't keep her mind on what she was doing, didn't really feel like looking at clothes. She wandered here and there, up and down, in and out over the shopping center, in the process declining the help of innumerable saleswomen. It was a tiring way to wait for eleven o'clock.

She was early at the Riverwalk. She passed under the gold lettering of the great entrance sign set in its white ironwork that proclaimed the shopping area built where the World's Fair of '84 had been held. Making her way across the plaza with its geometric mosaic floor of cream and rust and gray, she found a place on a bench with a view of the wide Mississippi River. She watched the towering jets of water in the great round basin of the fountain and the tourists who grouped themselves in front of it to have their pictures taken. The white of the excursion steamers that sat waiting to depart from this point was blinding in the sun, while the gray smoke of their engines smudged the blue of the sky. That the smoke came from diesel engines instead of the wood-burning furnaces that once graced the steamboats that landed here made little difference; it was still a spectacle.

"You look comfortable."

She turned her head to squint up at Dante, and unconsciously her mouth curved in a smile of welcome. "It's an illusion, I'm melting."

"I should have told you I'd meet you inside," he said with a rueful grin.

"Not to worry. I was enjoying the view."

"Next to Jackson Square, this is my favorite spot, but it's a lot easier to appreciate in the spring and fall. Shall we?" He indicated the glass-fronted entrance into the Riverwalk shopping area. She rose and walked beside him toward the doors with their steamboat motif picked out in gold.

He held the heavy glass panel for her to enter. The action was not one of superiority or even a meaningless courtesy, but rather a gesture of protective concern. Anne sent him a covert look. There emanated from this man such a sense of caring that she had to wonder if it was just for her or for everyone. She was also forced to consider that the feeling might only be in her mind, a form of wishful thinking.

He was casually dressed in khaki pants and Top-Siders deck shoes with a green polo shirt. Her own camp shirt and khaki skirt were a close match for this outing, unlike the time before. The discovery gave her a nice feeling, as if they were a couple, though the feeling was quickly followed by a grimace. It had been a long time since she had been juvenile enough for such things to matter.

The mall was crowded, though most of the people seemed to be tourists or teenagers. "Did you say you come here often?" Anne asked as they navigated around the flowing streams of people.

"Now and again. There are some quality shops. Did you find what you were looking for this morning?"

"Not really." She went on to explain the problem.

"Did you try Yvonne la Fleur's?"

"What's that?"

"Not what but who. This way," he said, and guided her into the shop they were just passing.

It was like stepping into a Victorian hatbox. It smelled deliciously of violet perfume and was strewn with that signature flower, while summery creations of antique lace, muted watercolor florals, bridal white, and soft half-tone solids were draped here and there, along with a few elegantly feminine and richly colored suits. Then there were the hats, every one elegantly creative and wildly becoming to the female face, and yet, with their wide brims and softly alluring trim, reminiscent of a royal garden party. No two items were alike, and each was proudly labeled as an Yvonne la Fleur original.

Anne was drawn at once to a dress of pale lavender lawn embroidered with delicate sprays of lilac and a matching hat of dyed straw with silk lilacs curling around the crown. The ensemble was totally unlike anything she had ever owned or thought of owning; still, she liked it.

"Try it on," Dante urged. "I'm a great believer in first impressions."

The dress softened her features, making her look younger. The fit was perfect, the workmanship exquisite. The hat added an undeniable something extra. The price on the tag was fairly high but not unreasonable for an original design. She could see in the dressing-room mirror, however, that it was a ensemble with a definite feeling of romance, and she was suddenly shy of herself in it.

"Come out and let us see!" Dante called, and the saleswoman echoed his request.

Anne realized with a sense of wonder that she had never been shopping with a man who was interested in how she looked. Edison's sole concern was usually for how long he was kept standing around. He was embarrassed by women's shops and thought she looked all right so long as she never wore anything that might call attention to herself. If she asked for an opinion, she usually got a shrug or a brutally frank comment on her shape or her taste.

"You look wonderful," Dante said.

She smiled at him over her shoulder as she slowly turned for his inspection. "You think it would be all right for a garden wedding?"

"Perfect. The only danger, *chère*, is that you may outshine the bride."

"Sheer flattery, but I love it," she answered, and was able to keep her tone light because she recognized the real admiration in his eyes.

Dante carried the dress on its hanger from the shop while Anne swung the hatbox from its cord. She caught sight of the two of them reflected in the glass of the display window. They looked so happy. And so intimate.

A chill moved through her. What an imbecile she was. This was how people got caught in their infidelities, by allowing the pleasure of the moment to overcome prudence. She hadn't quite realized how public the Riverwalk was, how central to the city, but once she knew, she should have insisted on going somewhere else. She should do just that right now.

But how could she make such a request without having it seem as if this meeting were some clandestine rendezvous? The last thing she wanted was for Dante Romoli to get the idea that she expected more from him than fashion advice and friendship. Wasn't it?

"About that coffee?" She said.

"We could have lunch. It's beginning to be that time now."

He meant after the delay caused by her shopping. "All right."

Something in her manner must have alerted him to her discomfort. "I don't think some dim corner in a place with a bar would be a good idea. What do you say to simple but good seafood and a table overlooking the river?"

Her answer was a smile edged with relief.

They went to Mike Anderson's on the Bon Fête level. It was fast food with a long line and plastic bowls, but the servings were generous and the smell delicious. They took their trays outside on the deck. There was a magnificent view of the river, an overhang for shade, and a cool breeze off the water, but, best of all, the tables were scattered and undiscovered by most of the crowd. They dug into their crawfish gumbo and étouffée, crumbled their crackers to feed the red-legged pigeons that fluttered about, and watched the slow glide of river traffic: the tugboats, ferries, and freighters.

At last Anne sat back in her chair. With her gaze on the cup of lemonade she held in her hand, she said, "You must be wondering what the urgency was this morning. I don't mean to be mysterious; it's just that I don't really know how to start."

Dante used his napkin, then crumpled it and tossed it into his empty bowl. "Let me help you. It's something about Riva."

"How did you know?" She searched his face with quick concern.

"It seems logical. I know she has a problem, and I'm fairly sure it concerns your husband. I was there, you will remember, that day at the rally when they went off together, besides which I've known Riva for a long time. I can guess at what's going on, but that isn't like knowing. If you can shed some light on the subject, I'll be grateful."

"I had thought you might help me understand," she said with some asperity.

"Could be we can help each other."

Was there something more behind his words? Anne could not tell from the expression in his dark eyes. They seemed to harbor sympathy and concern, but it could have been no more than a refraction of the bright light. Pushing her cup away from her with a gesture of finality, she began to tell him what Edison had said about Riva Staulet, his child, Erin, and the threat Riva had made.

He was frowning when she finished. "I don't see it. There has to be something more."

"What do you mean?"

"It's too weak."

"How? It can hardly help Edison to have it known he fathered an illegitimate child."

He agreed thoughtfully, then went on. "Of course, there was the trick marriage."

"The what?"

They stared at each other across the table for long seconds. At last Dante said, "I'm sorry, *chère*. I thought you knew since your husband told you so much else."

She shook her head with slow emphasis. "He only mentioned an affair. Are you saying that Edison went through some kind of fake ceremony with Riva?"

"Not fake to her, but he was already married to you, so there was nothing to it. It was invalid."

"And Erin was born from this bogus marriage?"

"That's right."

"But how—" she began, then stopped, her gaze moving past him to rest in blind concentration on the river. Long seconds ticked past. When she spoke again, her voice was tight with strain. "I can see how that would be damaging, if there was proof."

"I don't know if there is any. But just the rumor of such an underhanded game, even if it happened long ago, could be ugly."

"Yes, I agree." Anne sat forward. "I think you should know that Edison will do everything in his power to see that this is never made public. Mrs. Staulet doesn't realize what she's doing, what she's asking."

"All your husband has to do, the way I see it, is to separate Josh and Erin."

"He'll never do it, not now."

"For God's sake, why?"

She lifted her hand in a helpless gesture. "Arrogance, ego, stubbornness—call it what you will. He simply won't give in to an ultimatum. On top of that, he's almost incapable of bringing himself to believe he can't control the situation. But once he realizes it, he can be extremely dangerous, totally unscrupulous. I think that he's beginning to suspect that Riva Staulet is the one person, the one woman, he may not be able to control."

Dante's voice was hard as he said, "What makes you say that?"

There was a troubling sense of disloyalty inside Anne. She had been married too long for her to be comfortable speaking of her husband and their relationship with anyone else. Still, she had to do something. Josh was her son, too.

"He intends to counter Riva's threats by threatening to tell Erin that she is his daughter. I don't know whether this will be sufficient to return matters to the status quo or not, but I don't think he will stop there. He wants revenge for being made to sweat this thing. He'll take it any way he can."

"If he tells Erin he is her father, then that will automatically achieve what Riva wants, an end to her daughter's romance with Josh."

"Yes, but Riva must not want Erin to know or she would have told her herself."

"No," Dante agreed, then let his breath out in a sigh. "No."

"So Edison will be holding the trump card. The question is: What will Riva do about it?"

"If she carried through with her threat to expose the past, then Erin would have to know. Knowing Riva, I expect she'll call his bluff, counter with a promise to carry out her threat by going public."

"Edison will stop her."

"How?"

"I'm not sure. He spoke of highly placed friends. The way he said it wasn't . . . nice."

"Then I am more grateful than I can say that you came to me. He isn't the only one with friends."

Did he mean that he himself would stand as Riva's friend or that he had friends as highly placed as any Edison could claim? Anne didn't know, nor did she care to ask. It was enough that she had delivered her warning.

"I'm glad," she said simply.

His dark eyes rested on her as if in speculation. He tilted his head. "It's none of my business, and I've said it before, but if you have so little respect for Gallant, if you are so doubtful of what he might do, why, in the name of all that's wonderful, do you stay with him?"

"He's my husband," she protested.

"There is such a thing as divorce."

The words were quietly spoken, but they carried a faint note of censure. She responded to it with a defensive smile. "It's an easy word to say. But I have so much invested in my marriage, and I see so many difficulties in tearing it apart that it almost seems being widowed would be easier."

"It's not something that's likely to happen for your convenience."

"I know," she agreed, and felt her smile slip.

He reached to touch her hand where she had begun once more to play with her cup. "I didn't mean to hurt you. I just—"

"I know. The problem is mine and I'll solve it as best I can, when I can."

She was afraid he might have taken offense at her choice of words. She looked at him quickly, but his attention was on her arm below the short sleeve of the cotton sweater she wore. Glancing down, she saw that he was staring at the new bruises left by Edison's fingers. She reached self-consciously to pull the sweater sleeve down.

"He got rough again, that's why you're here," he said abruptly.

"If you think it's just to get back at him in some—some domestic quarrel, I promise you—"

"I never said that," he interrupted, "or thought it."

She met his gaze for the space of a heartbeat before her irritation subsided. "No, I can see you didn't.

"Thank you for that."

She only shook her head.

"So polite, so calm, and yet tonight you will go back and sleep with a man who threatens and abuses women, and would rather see his son commit incest than bow to any will other than his own. How can you do it?"

"Habit?" She tried for flippancy, but didn't quite make it.

"No, I'm curious to know. What is it about him that makes you stay or that once made someone like Riva go away with him? Is he so charming in private moments? Is he so wonderful a lover?"

She laughed. She couldn't help it. It came bubbling up out of her with a derision so bitter she thought it would burn her throat.

"No?"

"No."

There was a pause. In the midst of it, she raised her lashes to look at him and could feel the naked anguish she had kept hidden inside for so long laid bare. He did not look away but reached to clasp her hand in his, holding it with warm strength.

"You are a beautiful woman. There's no need for you to live without love. As I said before, if there's ever any way I can be of service, I hope you will let me know."

In his voice was an undercurrent of meaning that had not been there when he had first made that offer in the courtyard of his house. The sound of it made the breath catch in Anne's throat. There was no time to answer, however, for they were interrupted by shrill and childish cries coming from a few yards down the deck.

"Mr. Dante! 'Ello, Mr. Dante!"

A pair of children had just emerged from inside the building. As they called out, they broke into a run. Their mother, burdened by a tray of Cokes and hamburgers, followed more slowly.

"Pietro," Dante said, his features dissolving into a wide grin as he got to his feet. "And Coralie. What are you doing here, you little scamps?"

"Erin said to us that we should see the Riverwalk while we were here," Coralie answered, though her gaze strayed to Anne.

"So you should," Dante said, adding as the children's mother came closer, "And I see you're trying our American cuisine."

There were enthusiastic assents. Afterward came the inevitable introductions. Anne could feel her face flaming as Constance Staulet surveyed her with irony in her large dark eyes. Anne kept her polite smile, however, and was glad of the training that allowed her to extend a greeting that was both cool and cordial.

"You can have my place at the table," she went on, looking around for her packages. "I have to be getting back to the hotel."

"I'll come help you find a taxi," Dante said.

"Don't bother, I'm sure I can manage," Anne said. "You've done enough just giving me lunch."

"No bother," he said with polite insistence as he reached to take the dress on its hanger once more.

Constance, busy setting out food, said pleasantly, "It was nice to have met you, Mrs. Gallant. Dante, you must return to join us for another cold drink. I'm sure the children would enjoy it if you would give us your company."

Amid the cries of joy and excitement, Anne saw Constance and Dante exchange a long unsmiling glance. It was moments before she could recognize the emotion that look aroused in her, and then she was horrified. It was jealousy.

16

Riva found Dante at the house with Constance and the children when she returned from the office that evening. It was a cozy scene. Constance and Dante were having a drink on the back gallery while the children sprawled on the cool brick floor nearby busily peeling stickers and applying them to the special albums bought to hold the collection they had started that day. Riva greeted them all, then looked to where Boots was sitting by himself at the other end of the gallery with a drink in one hand and his feet propped on the railing. She walked over to her brother-in-law.

"How are you doing, Boots?"

He saluted her with his drink. "'S' fine."

She had never seen him quite so close to being drunk. His eyes were red-rimmed and his face flushed. His body lay in the chair in such a loose fashion it was a wonder he didn't fall out of it.

"You don't look just fine," she said frankly.

"How'm I s'pposed to look when my wife been out givin' it away?"

"What are you talking about?"

"There I went, tearin' off to beat the hell outa my cousin, and you know what? He laughed at me. Laughed! Said I was a fool. Said it wasn't even good *putain*, which was prob'ly why she was offerin' it around."

Riva looked hastily behind her to see if Constance or her children had heard. That Boots could use such language in front of her was

256 •

a distressing sign of how loaded he was. His language was usually squeaky-clean, at least in female company.

No one was paying them any attention. She turned back. "If you're a fool, it's for believing Edison."

"Yeah? You don't know. I been hearin' how wonderful he is for years. Years and years. I guess maybe Margaret did give 'im some."

There was no point in arguing with him in his state. "Where is Margaret now?"

"Upstairs, resting."

"Is she all right?"

He shrugged. "Says she's got a headache, but she felt up to goin' to town today. I think she just don't want to have nothin' to do with me."

"I'll check on her after I change."

Riva moved back into the house. It had been a hot day, and though she had been in her air-conditioned office and her suit had the built-in comfort of natural linen, she felt stale and stifled. Anyway, she could never relax and put aside the business aspect of her life until she had taken off her business clothes and put on some kind of loungewear.

She heard Dante's chair scrape back after she had passed where he was sitting. He caught up with her on the stairs.

"Could I talk to you for a minute?"

His voice was flat. Riva gave him a searching look. She did not like the look of the anger she saw simmering in his eyes. With a short nod, she led the way to the sitting area in the upstairs hallway. It was not particularly private, but the two of them could not be overheard if they kept their voices low. Anything that might encourage Dante to keep his voice down seemed appropriate.

When they were seated, he leaned forward with his hands clasped between his knees. "You really haven't trusted me, have you, since you found me in bed with that other girl twenty-some-odd years ago?"

Riva had considered a great many things that he might want to say to her but somehow never this. "Don't be ridiculous," she said on a surprised laugh. "Of course I trust you; there's no one I trust more."

"I don't think so. As a matter of fact, I think that you would never have seen me again, never have spoken another word to me if I hadn't come barging back into your life before you could forget me."

She shook her head with a smile at the memory. "You barged in with a fistful of moss roses stolen from the garden of the Ursuline convent after you scaled the wall. It's a wonder you weren't arrested. Or excommunicated. How could I forget someone who would do that?"

"I was trying to apologize, and I didn't have the money to buy flowers."

Dante had come back into her life not long after Noel had left, at a time when she had needed a confidant with just Dante's blend of care and concern. He had apologized for not coming to her wedding. He never received the invitation, he had said, never heard of it until the girl who was living with him had flung the news in his face before she walked out on him. By degrees, then, they had grown close again, bound by mutual pain. Cosmo had liked him, trusted him also. Unlike his son, he had never seen a rival in Dante.

Now she said, "It worked, didn't it? We've been friends."

"I thought so, but apparently not."

"I don't know what you mean."

"From that time to this, you've allowed me to hover around the edges of your life, but never really to know what you think, what you feel. And the important times, the important things, you keep to yourself."

"That isn't so!" she protested.

"Then why, in God's name, did I have to learn from someone else that you are trying to blackmail Edison Gallant?"

"I'm not," she said, her brows snapping together in a frown.

"I don't know what else you'd call it. Oh, I'll grant that your reasons are pure enough, but I don't know why you couldn't have told me what you meant to do and let me help you."

"What could you have done? Edison is not a man who accepts advice." Her voice was taut with irony.

"I have connections, friends who owe me favors. Believe me, I could have persuaded him."

"Connections," she echoed, staring at him. She had never asked him about his mafia friends; there had never been any need. Now a chill moved through her.

He threw up his hands. "I don't mean I could have had some-body—what's the phrase? Lean on him? Though come to think of it, it's not a bad idea. I mean I know people who have what Edison wants, which is political influence. He would have sent his son to Timbuktu for it, but that was before he figured out that Erin is his daughter."

Was Dante telling the truth? Something about the way he spoke made her uneasy in spite of his assurances. Then again, it might only be in her mind. She felt off balance, caught between past and present, truth and falsehood, wrong and right. She had felt that way really since this whole thing began.

Abruptly, the exact words he had used penetrated. She sprang to her feet to stand over him. "Who told you that he knows, any-way?"

"Anne Gallant," he said, and rose slowly to face Riva. "She was . . . concerned."

"I'll bet!"

"I don't mean she's vindictive; there was never any suggestion of that. But she is Josh's mother."

His words were quiet and even. Riva realized that it was she herself who was making the most noise during this encounter, when she had thought she would have to see that he kept quiet. It was sobering. She swung away from him, wrapping her arms around her upper body.

"What does she intend to do?" she asked.

"Anne? Nothing that I know of."

The answer brought no relief. "She told you so, I suppose. I didn't know you two were such friends."

"We aren't. For some strange reason she thought that I might know what you intend to do now."

She ignored his sarcasm. "I don't know what to do. We seem to be more or less at a standstill, Edison and I. But I do know that it isn't your fight."

"Even if I want it to be?"

"Even so."

"You see? You always hold me at arm's length."

"There were reasons for that," she said, turning to face him.

"I know," he answered, his dark gaze steady, "but now he's dead."

"There were others. You remember—"

"I remember," he said, his voice harsh as he cut across her words. "Twenty-four years is a long time, but it's one failure I'm unlikely to forget."

She was handling this badly, but she couldn't seem to help it. "Oh, Dante, why bring it up after all this time? We were all right as we were."

"Things change, people change. Do you want my help or not?"

"Does it carry a price?"

He stared at her long seconds while the skin around his mouth whitened. "I guess that means no."

Her face twisted as she felt his pain somewhere deep inside. She cried, "I want your support, but I don't need your help!"

"Then you don't need me," he said.

He swung away from her and walked down the hall.

Riva watched him go, and it was as if one of the columns of the house had given way. The roof itself might hold, but there was a serious weakness in the structure.

What had she done to make him go? What could she have said to make him stay? She knew, of course, but could not think why it was suddenly so important to him that their relationship become something different.

He had as good as said that she had used him, giving nothing in return. Was it true? Had she been that selfish? If she had, it was because she had thought he was happy as they were, good friends with the added warmth of an old attraction.

She could not believe he would not return. Still, he had never been so distant before or seemed so determined.

It crossed her mind to wonder if there was someone else. Constance made no bones about the fact that she considered him a delectable man. The two of them had been comfortable together on the gallery when she came in. Nevertheless, she didn't think Dante had stopped just now to say good-bye to Noel's ex-wife. The sound of his car driving off had come too soon for that.

Frowning in thought, Riva moved down the hall and into her bedroom where she pulled off her suit jacket and threw it on the bed. With a tired sigh, she reached up to unfasten the back neck button of her silk charmeuse blouse.

She supposed she could have let Dante help her. Depending only on herself, however, meant she need not be troubled by anyone else's opinion of her conduct. If she didn't ask for their help, they had no right to try to tell her what to do. She had grown to like it that way. What she didn't like was needing someone. More often than not, the ones she needed had deserted her, by death and otherwise. It was less painful to depend on herself alone.

There was also the fact that by being independent, she need not impose on anyone else. She hated to think that she might take advantage of whatever feeling Dante had for her. She thought sometimes that he wished she would. She could not; it wouldn't be fair. The only trouble was that Dante seemed to think it was unfair of her to do without him.

She took off her blouse and slipped out of her skirt, then moved to the closet to hang them up. She stepped out of her shoes and bent to place them over the shoe trees on the rack. Annoyance crossed her face. There was a pair of her shoes lying on their sides on the floor and on top of them was a dress. Margaret had been in her closet again. There was black grease on the dress. It had come, she saw, from the soles of the shoes.

Riva hated that kind of sloppiness. She might not always put her own things away, though she tried, but at least she draped them over a chair to prevent creases. Sometimes she wondered if her sister deliberately mistreated the clothes she borrowed. It was as if she needed to express how little she was impressed by their cost, though at other times Riva suspected it might be to get back at her for daring to own them in the first place. It was not possible to speak to Margaret about it now, anyway. Her sister was upset enough already. Still, she should go and talk to her, find out how she felt this evening, if her heart was giving her problems.

Riva found her sister sitting alone in the dimness of the front parlor. She was drawn up in the corner of the sofa with her arms wrapped around her knees. She gave Riva a wan smile as she greeted her.

Riva sat down beside Margaret. "What are you doing holed up in here by yourself?"

"I'm not fit company for anything else."

Fit how? Riva wondered at the choice of words but saw no point in adding to whatever species of depression it was that had Margaret in its grip by dwelling on it. "You should be out there with the others, anyway. Moping isn't going to help."

"Much you know about it," Margaret answered, tight-lipped, then covered her face with her hands. "Oh, Riva, what will I do if Boots leaves me? He's all I've got. I'll die, I just know I will."

"You'll go on, just as the rest of us do when we lose someone important to us. It isn't so easy to die of grief."

Margaret looked at her sharply, as if caught by the lack of expression in Riva's voice, a lack that hinted at denied pain. But the moment of arousal from her self-absorption was brief.

"But I love Boots," she cried.

Riva wondered if her sister thought she herself had never loved her child, her husband. There were other losses Margaret knew nothing about, but she was not interested in learning about them. For Riva, the sense of isolation in her own past griefs was still profound.

"Have you told him you love him?" she asked.

"I couldn't. That is, we don't—"

"Then don't expect him to know it or for it to make a difference."

"It's all Edison's fault. The man's an animal, a rabid beast who ruined my life. He didn't care a thing about me, only about what he wanted, what he needed. To him, I was just a body, another conquest to puff up his male ego!"

The familiar litany of blame was suddenly one excuse too many. Riva could feel the pressure of anger growing inside her. She tried to control it but could not.

"Edison behaved like an animal, yes. But he didn't come to you, Margaret; you went to him. What happened was, in part, your own fault. But it isn't the end of the world. We all make mistakes. Admit it and forget it. It's all right. It's allowed, so long as we learn something from it."

"How philosophical. I hope you can remember all that when it's your turn with Edison. You're the one he's really after."

"I've had my turn," Riva said.

"You'll have another one if he isn't stopped."

"That's what you wanted not so long ago, for me to have another turn, for me to give Edison whatever he wanted. Have you decided it isn't so easy to do that, after all?"

"I've decided you should do something about him. You're Riva Staulet. That should be worth something!"

"What are you suggesting?"

Margaret made a helpless gesture. "I don't know, that's your department. You know all sorts of people, have all sorts of powerful friends. Call somebody. Don't sit around waiting for what Edison will do next; you do something instead."

There came the sound of a car outside. Riva turned to look through the lace curtain that covered the windows under the old silk drapes. Her voice laconic, she said, "It appears to be a bit late to get ahead of Edison."

"What do you mean?" Alarm edged Margaret's voice.

"He's coming up the drive."

Her sister's face grew white and her grip on her knees tightened. "What does he want? I can't see him, I just can't! Where can I hide?"

"Don't be foolish," Riva said sharply, then went on more soothingly. "There's no need to hide, certainly no reason for you to see him or he, you. Stay where you are. Abraham will find out why he's here."

Margaret did not look convinced, but she sat still in her seat. The two of them listened while the butler moved with an unhurried tread to answer the pealing doorbell. They heard the elderly man ask Edison to step into the library. A few seconds later, there came a tap on the parlor door and Abraham put his head inside.

"There's a gentleman to see you, Miss Riva," he said, stressing the word *gentleman* in the way older servants in the South do when a man's status is in doubt.

"Thank you, Abraham," she said. She glanced at Margaret, but her sister was huddled in her chair as if she could hide in its depths. Straightening her shoulders, Riva got to her feet and moved toward the door.

The old man cocked his head. "Shall I tell Mr. Noel to come? He got home just a while ago."

"That's all right, thanks. I'll take care of it."

Abraham looked doubtful but stepped back to let her pass, then moved to open the library door for her. As she went inside, he closed it carefully behind her.

Edison was standing with a book in his hand, Cosmo's first edition of *The Sun Also Rises*. He shoved the book back on its shelf as he spoke. "Very nice. My taste in investments runs more toward racehorses and risk stocks, but each to his own."

Riva stood there hearing the disparaging tone of Edison's voice, watching the careless way he handled a valuable book that had given Cosmo much joy to own, watching his assumption of ease in the room that was most central to all that Bonne Vie stood for, and she was consumed with rage. She wanted, quite literally, to kill him. If she had had a weapon in her hand, he would have been dead. It was frightening, and exhilarating.

"What are you doing here?" she demanded. "How can you show your face after what you did to Margaret?"

"To Margaret? I didn't do anything she didn't want."

His smile was so self-satisfied she wanted to wipe it off his face. Permanently. "That's a lie."

"Is it? I don't see her screaming for the police."

"Is that your criteria for judging whether a woman wants sex with you, if she does or doesn't scream for the police when you lay hands on her?"

"You always did have a nasty tongue in your head," he answered, his smile a shade dimmer.

"And you always had an incredible ego. I'm surprised you aren't afraid you might meet Boots."

"Old Boots? Now why should I be afraid of him? He's about half convinced himself that his wife was asking for it."

"You mean you convinced him of it."

"What if I did?"

"Did making Boots think the worst of Margaret help you feel better about yourself?" she demanded. "Never mind. Whatever your answer, I'm sure it will be self-serving. What do you want here?"

He put his hands on his hips as a flush stained his face. "All right. If that's the way it's going to be, why should I be civil? I'm here to tell you one thing. Bring your ass to my bed like your sister or I tell Erin who her mother really is."

She had known it was coming; it could be no other way, given the way Edison thought. "Tell Erin? An excellent idea, really, one I've been giving some thought myself."

"Don't give me that. If you were going to take that way out, you'd have done it long ago."

"Possibly. Then again, possibly not." She moved across to the window, turning to place her back to it. The light of the semi-tropical summer dusk gleamed beyond the lace curtains, casting its glow into the room. In that clear light, she studied Edison's face. It looked bloated, lined with dissipation, not at all handsome. His hair was thinning visibly. It made him look weak. Finally she said, "I wonder if you realize what you are losing by refusing me the small favor I ask. Someone I know was talking about influential friends and men with money this evening. Maybe I should remind you that just as I can help you if you cooperate, I can also harm you if you don't."

He laughed. "That's the weakest threat I've ever heard!"

"Don't mistake the words for the deed."

"Neither one scares me. I'm on my way, lady, and there's nothing you can do about it. I don't need your money and I don't need your friends because I have plenty of both. What I do need, though, is you under me. I want it and I'm going to get it because you're going to give it to me. You're going to give it to me for the same reason that you aren't going to go around blabbing about what happened years ago or trying to ruin my chances with the money men, and that's because you're afraid. You're afraid you'll lose what you've got. You like being Aunt Riva and Mrs. Staulet of Bonne Vie and Staulet Corporation. I've got you by the short hairs, lady, and the sooner you admit it, the happier we'll both be."

There was enough truth in his words to turn her rage into cold defiance. Quietly she said, "I'd rather die first."

"That can be arranged, too."

The threat was there. She heard it, felt it invade her body through the very pores of her skin. She didn't think, however, that he had meant to say it, for she saw his narrowed eyes suddenly widen, as if he recognized a mistake.

So intent was she on the man in front of her that she didn't hear the door to the hallway open.

"I seem to have a habit," Noel said, "of arriving in the middle of your quarrels."

Her relief and disquiet at having him appear were so mixed and so intense that it was a moment before she could summon words. Finally she said, "There's no quarrel. Edison and I were straightening out a small difference. Since we have just come to an understanding, he was on the point of leaving."

Noel looked at the other man. "Were you?"

The words were smooth, but they carried all the quiet challenge of generations of Southern gentlemen intent on protecting their property and those who lived within its boundaries. That Edison recognized it was obvious from the murderous look he gave Noel. He squared up to him with his feet spread wide and his fists on his hips. "I'll leave when I get good and damn ready!"

Noel moved with the sudden and powerful release of coiled-steel muscles. He caught Edison's wrist and spun him around, twisting his hand up and pressing it into the middle of his back. At the same time, he clamped a tight grip on Edison's neck that pushed it back at a strained angle. The candidate for governor was shoved, gasping curses and with his eyes glazing, out of the room and into the hall.

Abraham, who hovered there, moved smartly forward to open the door. Noel ejected Edison from the house and sent him staggering across the gallery to the steps. The butler closed the door with a sharp slam and dusted his hands. Whistling tunelessly, the elderly man nodded in satisfaction to Noel, winked at Riva where she stood in the doorway of the study, then moved away down the hall.

From outside came the sound of Edison's car as it started with a muted rumble, then was slammed into gear and driven away. Noel swung to look at Riva and began to move toward her. Riva, disturbed by the grim light in his face, stepped back into the study, turning toward the far side of the room.

Over her shoulder, she said, almost at random, "I suppose Abraham brought you."

"He seemed to think I might be interested."

"Did he?" How much had Noel heard? How much had he understood? It was impossible for her to tell from the hard impassivity of his voice.

Noel didn't answer as he stared at her. The last pink light of the evening falling through the windows made a rose-colored nimbus around her as she stood outlined against the lace of the curtains. In her cream caftan and with her hair brushed out across her shoulders, she appeared ethereal, not quite flesh and blood. He had heard Edison threaten her and had come through the door looking for an excuse to lay hands on the other man. The urge to compound the error by taking hold of Riva and demanding answers was near irresistible.

He glanced down, making a pretense of adjusting his shirtsleeves, as he fought for self-control. At last he said abruptly, "If I embarrassed you by resorting to he-man tactics, I'm sorry. I didn't much care for Gallant's tone of voice, and this is my home."

"So it is. I was forgetting."

"I doubt that, but I only meant that I'm responsible for what happens under its roof. No matter how much or how little I may be involved in what's going on between you and Gallant, he will not insult you here and get away with it. I won't allow it."

"I suppose I should thank you for that."

"Don't bother; I didn't do it for you alone. I also did it for myself and, in a strange sort of way, for my father."

The stiffness of anger was gone from his voice. She turned slowly to face him as she answered, "Regardless, I benefited—and I do appreciate it."

"In that case, you're welcome."

It was an impasse. Riva rested her considering gaze on the taut angles and planes of his face, wondering if he had created it on purpose, and if so, whether it was to prevent further gratitude or just further stilted and painfully unproductive communication between them. In either case, it worked. They stood for long moments looking at each other until, mercifully, Abraham came to announce dinner.

Anne lay still with her face turned away and her eyes tightly closed as Edison grunted and labored above her. When he had finished and rolled off her and out of the bed to pad into the bathroom, she still did not move, did not close her legs or pull her nightgown back down. She lay in the early-morning darkness with her muscles stiff with anger and the engorgement of unsatisfied need, and she thought of adultery.

What would it be like to make love, instead of just be used because a man wanted to get rid of his tensions or ensure against needing a piece too badly before he got back from a political jaunt? What would it be like for a man to touch her in tenderness and genuine concern for her needs? She had tried in the few minutes just past to pretend that it was Dante Romoli who was making love to her. It had helped to make it easier but not appreciably more fulfilling.

She could have refused. She had actually thought of doing it, of shoving her husband away and demanding to be left alone. It had not seemed worth the certain bruises. Something had happened the evening before at Bonne Vie to put him in a rage, that much she had understood from his cursing. He had a violent need at the moment to dominate someone, and since it could not be Riva Staulet, it had been her. She could retaliate, however. The method was old and secret and most suitable.

It was not a new thought. For years it had occurred to her at intervals, sauce for the goose and so on. The idea had always seemed sordid and demeaning to everything she felt about love and the sacred nature of her wedding vows. That was before she had met Dante. Now it was just a question of courage. Did she have enough?

Anne had packed Edison's suitcase the night before. It was only a suit bag, since he would be gone for no more than three days, four at the most. Regardless, Edison called a bellman to come up for it. Heaven forbid that such an important man, a gubernatorial candidate, be seen doing anything so menial as carrying his own luggage, even if it was five o'clock in the morning. Edison would have to carry it himself from the airport terminal out to the Beechcraft Bonanza he flew for these quick trips, but that was different since there would be no one to see him.

Anne pretended to be asleep as Edison paced impatiently up and down the room while he waited for the bellman to appear. When the man arrived, her husband left without a word. She was relieved. She did not want to have to say good-bye, either.

After a few minutes, she pushed herself up in bed and reached to turn on the lamp. She picked up the book she had begun the night before and tried to read. After a time she grew sleepy and turned out the light again. She stretched, enjoying the roominess of the bed with only herself to take up the space. When she woke again, it was nearly ten in the morning. She reached for the phone book and found Dante's number. Taking a deep breath, she picked up the phone and punched the button for an outside line.

It was the middle of the morning, and Riva was deep in a discussion with a Staulet vice-president concerning an insurance claim on several thousand tons of bananas that could not be unloaded at an African port when her telephone rang. She was momentarily annoyed, though with herself; she had forgotten to tell her secretary to hold her calls.

It was Dante on the other end.

"Am I interrupting anything important?" he asked. "I can call back later."

"No, no," she said, lightening her tone with an effort. "Look, about yesterday afternoon—"

"That's why I wanted to talk to you. I acted like a horse's behind, walking out that way, and I'm sorry."

"Never mind," she said with a covert glance at the executive sitting across her desk. "I suppose I should have told you what was going on. Why don't we have dinner and—"

"You don't have to tell me anything. It's really not my business, is it? I can only plead overwork, and worry about this mess with the Ecstasy out at the place on the lake."

"Still no word on who's peddling the drug?"

"None. It's almost as if there's more than one, as if my place has been targeted. I have some feelers out about it, but everybody's keeping a tight lip. As a matter of fact, I was thinking about getting away from the whole thing for a day or two to get a new perspective on it, maybe going to the mountains or something. I don't suppose you'd like to come keep me company?"

"I wish I could," Riva said, and meant every word. "But I just can't leave with the house full of guests and this thing with Edison. But I tell you what. Why don't you go up to the house in Colorado? It's just sitting there. Somebody ought to get some use out of it."

"That would be grand, if you don't mind."

The last was mere politeness. "You know I don't," Riva said. "I've been telling you for years you could have it anytime."

"You're sure I can't persuade you to come?"

"It's tempting, but I'm afraid not."

Riva promised to have her secretary call the young couple who kept the mountain place ready for visitors, former flower children who made and sold herb tea on the side. After another pleasantry or two, she hung up. She was smiling, conscious of a great feeling of relief. She hated to be at odds with anyone, but especially with Dante.

Smiling still, she returned to business. Her last thought before plunging back into contractual obligations was that she just might be able to get away after all, at least for Saturday night and Sunday. If she called Erin and arranged to take her with her, there might be a chance to deflect her from this Colorado biking tour with Josh. Margaret wouldn't mind then if Erin left for a short trip. At any rate, it was worth a try. Dante was such a reasonable man and a faithful friend. He deserved a surprise.

17

There was a storm brewing in the gulf. Anne had gotten a report on it from her taxi driver on the way to the airport. It made the air muggy, so thick with the tropical warmth and humidity boiling up from the Caribbean that it was almost like breathing hot bathwater. Walking beside Dante on the concrete apron, Anne could feel the wet heat rising around her ankles, see it shimmering in waves between her and the planes taking off on the far runways. It made the Cessna 310 that Dante had chartered for their flight to Colorado seem to be doing a shimmy on its rubber wheels. It also made Anne feel sick.

It wasn't the damp heat alone, of course. It was sheer nerves, paroxysms of terror that attacked her stomach and made the palms of her hands clammy with sweat. She had never done anything like this before. How banal, but how true. She had never met a man secretly at an airport, never deliberately set out to disguise her appearance with dark glasses and a hastily bought blond wig. She had never bought fancy lingerie that she might wear only once, then destroy; never entrusted her body and good name to a man she hardly knew. It was no wonder she was terrified. It was a good thing she was equally determined or she would have cut and run.

Dante, walking beside her, looked grim. She thought he was no happier about the need for subterfuge than she was, maybe even less so. Oh, he smiled when he looked at her and told her how well she looked and how much fun they were going to have, but she

didn't think it was the most exciting day of his life. That was another reason for her anxiety. She felt as if she had forced him into
this weekend since it was she who had suggested it, putting him
in a position where he could not refuse to honor the commitment
to be of service he had made so lightly. It might all be in her own
mind, of course. She was of a generation of women used to waiting
for the man to do the asking. To step out of her assigned role made
her uncomfortable even as she enjoyed the freedom it gave her.

And she did feel free. Despite the terror and the sickness, there
was rising inside her, like yeast in a warm kitchen, a swell of ex-
hilaration. It was going to be all right when they were in the air.
Everything would be better when they were finally out of New
Orleans.

It was a jolting, jouncing ride. The tropical storm gathering
somewhere northeast of the Yucatan peninsula had disturbed the
normal weather patterns over both Texas and Louisiana. There
were tornado watches in effect for southeast Texas that were expected to spread northward, becoming more severe as the storm
moved closer to the mainland. It was going to be a wet and unsettled
weekend along the gulf coast, a good one to leave behind.

The pilot of the Cessna was a Texan, young and tall and friendly,
but with a professional air about him. Anne thought he had given
Dante and herself a curious glance or two as they boarded, but for
the most part he ignored them while he got on with his job. The
plane was roomy. She and Dante sat on opposite sides of the narrow
aisle so that they could talk across it. However, comments worth
shouting above the roar of the engines were not easy to find. Once
Dante leaned to point out a landmark below that was visible through
her window. Her bare arm brushed his shoulder, and for an instant
she could feel the musculature of his shoulder and the warmth of
his skin through his shirt sleeve. The shock of pleasure it gave her
was disturbing. A moment later, as he drew back, his fingers
touched her crossed knee. So tightly strung was she that her leg
muscles twitched, and her knee jerked in reflex as if it had been
struck by a doctor's precision hammer. She gave a light laugh but
could feel the flush that mantled her face, and she was unable to

meet his eyes in her embarrassment. It was some moments before she thought of anything to say to gloss over the incident.

Finally Anne took refuge from both her nerves and the strain of talking by opening a magazine. In time, the droning of the engines and intermittent swing and bounce of the aircraft, combined with her broken rest the night before, made her drowsy. She closed her eyes.

It was just as hot in Denver as it had been in New Orleans, but at least the air was dry and the serrated purple line of mountains that lay on the western horizon held the hope of change. Dante turned on the air-conditioning the minute the doors were closed on the four-wheel-drive Jeep Cherokee they picked up at the rental agency. With it going full blast, they hit Interstate 25 and headed out of town.

The change, when they left the superhighway and began to climb into the mountains, was almost miraculous. They turned off the air conditioner and rolled down the windows, letting the cool, fresh, oxygen-rich air filter through their fingers and swirl into the Jeep. They exclaimed over the awe-inspiring views that appeared around the curves, views doubly amazing because they were so scarce in low-lying Louisiana. The colors of the wildflowers, the blue lupine and brilliant red-orange Indian paintbrush, were so much more vivid than the wildflowers they knew, and the rugged rock formations, tumbled and jumbled and lying on a slant in every direction, were also a novelty. Anne pulled off her wig and tossed it in the back, loosening her hair with her fingers and letting the wind blow through it. Her spirits rose, and she and Dante looked at each other with sudden laughing pleasure laced with anticipation.

The mountain cabin was perched on a slope covered with pine and spruce and overlooked a winding, rippling stream edged with a tender green band of willows. Solidly embedded in the rock, with a huge boulder jutting up through the deck on one corner, the cabin had a view down the stream's valley toward a far range of blue mountains veined with the silver of unmelted snow.

The house was a cabin in name only. Actually it was a sprawling architect's dream of cedar and glass, of angles and light surfaces and carefully planned vistas. There was a great room with a fireplace faced with gray stone to which lichen still clung. Indian rugs were scattered on the hardwood floors and hung as tapestries on the walls, and there was a wall of windows at one end reaching as high as the cathedral ceiling two floors above. Stairs made of polished mountain pine led up to the balcony, which surrounded the upper level of the great room and gave access to the bedrooms.

The focal point of the great room, and therefore of the house, was a bronze fastened to the tall stone face of the fireplace. Imposing in its size, it was a figure that was half Indian and half eagle caught in a moment of an attempt at soaring flight. Its wings were spread and straining, but flight was impossible, for the feet were embedded in rock. On the bronze Indian's face was a look of superhuman effort combined with torment for the indignity of his earth-bound state.

Staring at the bronze, Anne felt the pain and the joy of the artist. It mingled with her own, becoming a consuming ache inside her. Then Dante, moving close behind her, wrapped his arms around her and held her close. Forgetting the bronze, forgetting everything, she turned to him.

What Anne liked best was that Dante did not talk. She could not have borne the humiliation of it if, like Edison, he had mouthed vulgar, degrading words and lascivious suggestions as he made love because it excited him and made her focus on him. Dante was quiet and skillful and lovingly concerned. He touched her with the same knowing gentleness with which she touched herself, but with a firm persistence that made her feel as if she were made of fine crystal, strong and clear and resonant. Ecstasy, she found, was no less powerful for being silent.

Curled together, with their legs entwined and his chest against her back, they slept and breathed the cool, intoxicating, evergreen-scented mountain air that poured in the open window. They woke refreshed and made love again, then, driven by starvation, padded naked through the quiet house in search of food. It was then they found the note left by the young caretaker and his wife, the first time either had thought of where that couple might be. They had gone to the Springs, the note said, meaning to Colorado Springs, and would not be back until Sunday evening.

Dante and Anne took the food back to the bed, where they consumed the barbecue and beans, the sourdough bread and fruit and wine with gusto. Then putting aside the leftovers, they turned their attention to getting to know each other.

Made bold and even generous by her joy, Anne explored a man's body for the first time. Thinking to bring pleasure, she found it. And when she began to cry, Dante held her and soothed her, and gave her peace in equal measure.

"You must be the last of the gentlemen, the last of the gentle men."

Anne was sitting propped on three down pillows piled against the headboard of the king-size bed. She had a view through open, uncurtained second-floor windows, a view framed by the gray-blue of tall spruce trees growing around the house and of the distant mountains that veiled the morning in drifting white swaths of clouds. Her view also included the long stretch of Dante's uncovered body. His head was in her lap, and she was feeding him grapes one by one in a playful parody of a thousand such scenes enacted between illicit lovers. It was the very corniness of it that appealed to her. She felt mushy and stupidly infatuated, all those things she had so carefully avoided in her life. Before she had thought them tasteless. Now, for this moment, she wanted nothing more.

Dante, crunching seedless red grapes between his square white teeth, swallowed before he answered. "I don't know what you're talking about. I'm no gentleman, I'm a restaurateur."

"It's a great waste of talent. You could make millions as a paid lover, maybe billions."

"I don't think I have the stamina for it," he said sadly. "Now maybe when I was younger—"

"When you were younger, you probably didn't have the . . . shall we say, training?"

He opened his eyes wide. "That's the answer! You're a genius, *chère*. You've discovered why gigolos went out of style. Young men today don't have the patience, and by the time they learn, they're too old."

"Young men lack self-control."

"A woman after my own heart—and gray hairs."

"Of course," she said pensively, "some older men aren't much better."

"Only the stupid ones."

"And the ones too engrossed in getting off themselves to learn. There are a lot of those. As I said, you are the last of the gentlemen."

He ignored the grape she held for him, his gaze steady upon hers. "That bad, huh?"

She moved her shoulders in a gesture of resignation. The motion jiggled her breasts. She was a little self-conscious about sitting there naked in the morning sun, but not too much and then mostly because she thought her breasts had seen too much of the effects of gravity. She kept her mind on that, deliberately blocking out thoughts of Edison.

"Then as I've said before—"

"I know, I know." She absentmindedly ate the grape she held herself, at the same time transferring her attention to the mountain view and unconsciously inhaling deep breaths of the pure air flowing through the windows. "I've been thinking, since our lunch at the Riverwalk, in fact, that if I was on my own I could go back to school. I used to be good at languages. I could take some education courses, brush up on my French and maybe be a French teacher. Or I might use my contacts as a political wife to start a decorating business specializing in historic preservation; I think I would enjoy that."

"Good for you, *chère!*" he said, his eyes widening in surprise.

"Money would be a problem; I'd have to change my style of living, though I do have a small income from my father's estate. There's the difficulty of abandoning a life I've spent more than twenty years building, of leaving my friends, my clubs and committees, my whole carefully constructed social world. I don't kid myself about these things, because I know they would change. Making Josh understand and accept it would be another big step. But worst of all would be facing Edison and all the threats he will probably use to try to stop me from going."

"If he becomes too abusive you can always go to the police—or to me."

Her smile conveyed her gratitude for his last suggestion; still, she shook her head. "I just don't know. It's such an enormous change, and once it's started, there's no going back. The truth is, I'm a coward. I've always been a coward."

"I don't believe that," he said. "It takes courage to stay as well as to go."

She gave him a wry smile. "Let's talk about something else, shall we. It took courage to come here, too, but I wouldn't have missed it for the world."

"Nor would I," he answered, his voice firm as he followed her lead for a change of subject.

"So gallant."

"I don't know why you say that." There was a hint of irritation in the words.

"Because it's true. Because I know that your heart isn't really in this."

"And just where is my heart?" he demanded, pushing himself up and turning to face her with his upper body braced on one elbow.

"Back in New Orleans, I think," she said quietly, "with Riva Staulet."

He blinked, and a flush of color rose under his olive skin. "We're friends, that's all."

"Oh, I don't mind, really I don't. I never thought you were dying of love for me." She reached out to brush the dark and fine hair back over his ear where it had curled forward. "It's just something in the way you mention her that makes me think you've been hung up on Riva for a long time. Just as Edison is, though in a different way."

He turned his gaze to the view lying so conveniently before them. "If I'm hung up on her, as you say, maybe it's because I want it that way. It almost seems that as long as she wasn't free, then there was no risk for me. I had someone to love, someone to be with now and then. At the same time, I could go my own way, could concentrate on my business. What do you think of that?"

He really wanted to know how she viewed his situation. It was a compliment. "I don't know," she said. "I suppose it depends on how you feel now that she's a widow."

"I'm not sure. Sometimes I think that if she was ever going to be with me, she would have left Cosmo Staulet long ago, that he would never have been an obstacle. And I think that I don't want to go my way alone anymore. I think about maybe having a family, children. It's not too late, you know."

"Heavens, no. Men in their fifties and sixties—"

He made a quick gesture with one hand. "I know all that, but the thing is, it could be too late for a real marriage, one of those married love affairs where even growing old and gray together sounds pretty good."

She smiled. "As I said, the last of the gentlemen, and a romantic to boot."

"If I'm such a perfect guy, why are you renouncing me?"

"I'm not, not really," Anne protested.

"It sounds that way to me," he said as he met her gaze.

"But you want a young woman who can have those children you mentioned."

The corners of his mouth turned down. "Oh, well, if the urge to father little Romolis had been all that strong, I expect I'd have done it long ago instead of generating restaurants. It could well be I'd make a better grandfather, since you can always send the offspring home with their parents."

"To be a grandfather, you have to be a father first," she pointed out.

"Or marry somebody who already has a child, such as a son old enough to be a father."

Anne hovered between wry humor and gratification. "You can't be serious."

"There you go again! Listen to me carefully: You're a gorgeous, desirable woman, and the hours we have spent together these past few days have been wonderful. They have meant more than I can say. Love is a word I've pretty much avoided, one I've been saving, but I know that I could love you, easily, with the tiniest bit of encouragement."

She forced a laugh, at the same time screening her eyes with her lashes. "I'm the one who invited myself for a weekend with you, remember?"

"Only because I didn't dare invite you, didn't dare think you might consider it."

For the first time since they had left New Orleans, Anne was certain she had Dante's complete attention. Her laugh was more than a little breathless. "How good you are for my ego, among other things."

"That wasn't my intention."

"Wasn't it?"

"My intention was to find out if you could bring yourself to want more than a weekend with a middle-aged Cajun-Italian with graying hair and too-ample love handles."

"What gray hair? There's only a little salt among the pepper yet. As for love handles, you look like a well-proportioned Greek statue, and it's my opinion you know it very well."

Anne looked at him then, waiting with her heart in her throat for what he would say. It was too soon, this talk of love, or at least it was too soon for her to believe in it. She wanted to, though, she wanted it more than she had anything in a long time.

He met her soft hazel gaze, seeing the apprehension there and the warmth, and a smile rose in his dark eyes. With consummate tact, he followed her lead. He insinuated his hand under the sheet that covered her from the waist down with smooth ease and began to stroke the sensitive inner surface of her thigh.

"All right, have it your own way," he said on a mock sigh. "I'm an Adonis, a prince, a paragon among men. I'm also so mad for your body that if you give me up with such saintliness again, I refuse to be responsible. Isn't there anything at all about me you would like to have your own way with?"

"Well, now that you mention it . . ."

"Yes?" he inquired, the picture of restrained hope.

"Well . . ."

"Only tell me what you want."

There were times, Anne discovered, when ecstasy could be vocal and still lovely.

There was a light mist falling when Riva left the Staulet Building on Friday afternoon. Earlier there had been a thunderstorm that had washed the streets, flushing the usual trash and debris into the gutters. The many pumping stations of the low-lying city had drained away the excess water; still, the streets steamed gently, as if the city surrounded by its bowl of levees was a giant, simmering cauldron.

George met Riva at the door with an umbrella and put her carefully into the car. She thanked him, though she would just as soon have felt the rain on her face. She could have used that moment of freshness.

It had been a long day. She felt guilty about being away from Bonne Vie for so long. She had intended to be at the office only the few minutes it would take to sign some papers that couldn't wait, but she had gotten involved in a hundred other details. She should have known it would be that way. It always was.

She had stopped for a moment at Noel's office on her way out. He had still been working. When she told him it was time to quit, he had looked at her as if she were crazy. She wasn't sure whether his expression meant he could not believe she was actually ready to leave or just that he had not realized the time. She supposed the latter, since he was as much of a workaholic these days as she was. At any rate, he had glanced at his watch, laughed, and begun to shuffle papers together, putting them away. She had waved and walked on.

The traffic heading out of town was dense; it seemed everyone wanted to get away for the weekend. Driving conditions were not the best. The earlier rainstorm had dumped enough water to stir up the viscous mixture of oil and dirt and auto exhaust on the roads, but not enough to wash it away. The mist still drifting down was just right to keep the road surface slick. In addition, the overcast sky made for an early dusk. Some drivers had turned on their head-lights for safety, but there were more than a few who hadn't both-ered.

They were delayed for ten minutes while the police straightened out a lane-blocking collision between a shrimp truck and a thirty-year-old, fin-tailed Cadillac. As they idled in one place, George turned the radio on and tuned in a weather station, listening to the report of the tropical storm in the gulf. Riva tuned in her own radio and turned up the volume. Any gulf storm could turn into a hur-ricane this time of year, and any hurricane in the gulf could swing at a moment's notice and make for New Orleans. It was best to keep up on conditions.

The storm had not quite reached hurricane strength, though it was close. It was veering toward the coast of Mexico just below the Texas border, an area where its rains would be welcome. In the meantime, there were flash-flood warnings out as an indication of high-water conditions expected from spin-off storms and heavy rains in their area, and small-craft-warning flags were flying on the bays and bayous, lakes and rivers.

Finally they were moving again, turning off the interstate and whipping along the highway known as Airline. As their speed in-creased, Riva settled back and took out a sheaf of reports she had brought with her to study. Soothed by the tapping of the rain on the windshield, the regular clacking of the wipers, and the occa-sional clicking of the turn indicator as George sent the big car weav-ing in and out of traffic, she began to read.

The next thing she knew, the limousine swerved with a squeal of tires. She was thrown forward off the seat, landing in a sprawl of books and papers on the floor. George, fighting the wheel and cursing under his breath, yelled over his shoulder, "Stay down, Miss Riva, stay down!"

They were on the river road; she could tell from the nearness of the trees to the roadway. They must have turned without her noticing. It was not a wide thoroughfare by any means. The shoulders, where they were kept in repair at all, were of gravel. As Riva fought her way into a crouch, she could feel the car picking up speed and swinging wildly back and forth across the narrow lane from one shoulder to the other, could hear fine rocks clattering in the fender wells as they were thrown up by the wheels of the car.

But there was a more ominous sound. It was the whining and screeching tires of another car in pursuit, careening along just behind them. From George's actions at the wheel, she thought he was trying to keep it from passing them.

"What is it?" she cried.

"That car back there came off a side road out of nowhere! Tried to block the highway. Man in the front right has an Uzi!"

It was unbelievable. Her mind refused to accept it. She eased upward until she could peer over the back of the seat.

There were two men in a green sedan. They were wearing dark suits and mirrored sunglasses, and one was hanging out the window with a snub-nosed submachine gun in his hands.

This kind of thing happened in Italy and Argentina, not in Louisiana. It happened to international executives, billionaires, diplomats, and political figures, the kind of people who traveled with hordes of bodyguards. It couldn't happen to her, not in Louisiana on a designated scenic highway like the Great River Road. It didn't seem possible it could take place on an ordinary blacktop highway full of potholes and crooks and turns, one lined with little towns and crisscrossed a hundred times a day by dogs and chickens and old men trailing cane fishing poles.

The back window shattered under a burst of shots. Glass filled the air like a sleet storm and holes ripped across the inside roof of the car. At the same time, George shouted a warning. Riva had already begun to duck, but she threw up her arms to protect her face and dropped to a crouch with her head down and elbows braced against the seat until the glass shower ended.

"Use the phone!" Riva cried. "Call 911!"

"In a minute!" George yelled. He needed both hands on the wheel because of oncoming traffic.

He held the car steady. A pickup whizzed past in the opposite direction. The driver's eyes were wide and staring, but there were two teenagers in the back who leaned out and called: "Hey, mister, is it a movie?"

It was not. It was deadly real. The limousine careened around a curve on two wheels. Wind rushed in through the back window with a boiling mist of rain and the smells of gas fumes and hot metal. The noise of the car screeching out of the curve behind them was loud. The sedan drew out to pass again, pulling up within yards of the limousine's back bumper.

They held their places as they sped through a small community. A man on a riding lawn mower watched open-mouthed as they flew past. Three men at a gas station with their heads under the hood of a truck snapped erect, one of them bumping his head on the raised hood. George reached for the telephone, then had to drop it as he swerved to avoid an old woman with a load of empty aluminum cans on a cart who scampered across ahead of them. The old woman turned to shake her fist. Then they were out in open country again.

The sedan began to inch forward. It drew nearer and nearer. Riva could see the gunman. He looked as if he were pointing the Uzi at the chauffeur. George was slouched far down in the seat, with only the top of his head showing. She thought he was reaching toward the dangling phone or maybe the glove compartment. He grunted and cursed as he strained against his seat belt. The limousine swerved onto the shoulder, throwing up dirt and green bits of torn clover. The back wheels skidded, and they sideswiped a mailbox as George wrenched the long vehicle back on the road again. Then he flung himself upright. In his hand was a Smith & Wesson pistol.

He caught the wheel with his gun hand as he reached for the control of the power windows. The glass glided down. He leaned out to fire backward once, twice.

The sound of the shots exploded inside the car along with the nose-burning smell of gunpowder. The sedan behind checked for only a moment. The shots had gone wide. George could not drive at their present speed and aim back over his shoulder at the same time. The sedan began to ease forward once more. Its driver swung his wheel.

The two cars slammed together with a solid thud and the grinding shriek of metal on metal. The limousine slewed off the road. Riva's head thudded into the armrest as she was slung against it, then she surged back to her knees again as George regained control. In dazed amazement, she realized that the men in the other car wanted to force them off the road so that they would be easier targets. Or she would be an easier target.

At the same instant, an image of Edison's face the night before flashed through her mind. If she had wanted to kill him as she faced him in the library, it now appeared he had felt even more vindictive. The threat he had made had been real.

Slowly the dark sedan gained. The emblem on its hood eased closer and closer. When it reached the door post just behind George's seat, the passenger window would be even with where Riva knelt. She would be a perfect target, with no place to run, nowhere to hide.

The emblem was at the back bumper. At the back wheels.

A curve. George got off a shot as they rounded it. There came the tinkling sound of breaking glass as a headlight of the following car was smashed. The sedan dropped back six feet but came on again.

If she was a target for the gunman, then he would also be a target for her. Riva threw herself onto the backward-facing seat, leaning toward George. "Give me the gun," she cried.

"You can't shoot!"

"Yes, I can! Give me the gun!"

"All right. You got four shots left. Make 'em count!"

Closer the sedan came. The emblem drew even with the door post. She could see the barrel of the Uzi and the gunman's hand on the grip, could see his face. It was the right angle. But if she could see him, he could also see her there on the forward seat. Hard on that realization, she threw herself across the space between it and the rear-facing seat. At the same moment, the Uzi spurted fire.

Holes with jagged edges appeared in the side window and bloomed like pale, stuffing-colored flowers across the forward seat where she had been sitting. George yelled out, then cursed.

There was no time to see how badly her driver was hit. At least he was still upright. She twisted around, rose to one knee, and steadied her arm on the seat back, then put two shots into the windshield of the sedan.

It was a pleasure to watch the other car's windshield turn into a glass spiderweb, then blow inward. She saw the two men hunker down, saw blood appear on one's face, but the sedan swerved before she could tell how badly she had hurt them. It must have been no more than cuts from flying glass. The other car dropped back a few feet, then began to surge onward again. The man on the passenger side leaned out once more with the Uzi. Riva flung herself down out of sight.

The shots pinged and thudded into the car's body. Hard on them, metal crunched on metal as the sedan slammed into them. George, ducking out of the line of fire, lost the wheel but grabbed it in time to keep them from going into a ditch filled with scum-covered water. As the limousine straightened out again, he strained his neck upward to look in the rearview mirror.

"Hot damn!" The words were exultant.

"What? What?"

She craned to see. She had to know what he was looking at. It might be the state police if they had passed an observation point; the troopers sometimes patrolled this road. Or it might be the parish deputies if some of the people they had seen had called the sheriff's office.

It was neither. It was Noel.

He had left New Orleans behind them. Now he was closing in, a look of intense concentration on his face. His powerful BMW trailed a blowing plume of mist with the acceleration of his speed. The heavy vehicle looked as if nothing could check it.

The men in the sedan had spotted Noel. They craned their necks backward to watch him barreling down upon them. Their vehicle's pace slackened so that it fell back almost a car length. Then the sedan swung forward once more, the man on the passenger side firing another burst of shots. Only one struck, ricocheting harmlessly off the window chrome.

Still Noel came on. The man with the Uzi spun around again

to fire a wild burst in the direction of the BMW. Noel swerved in evasion but never slowed. The BMW was untouched. It seemed to pick up velocity. Its dark and glossy blue paint gleamed with rain. The tires sang as they sprayed water.

Deliberately Noel lowered his electric window. He put his arm out. In his hand was a black, snub-nosed pistol.

The men in the sedan saw their danger and tried to step up their speed. It was useless. They wove back and forth. It did no good. The heavy BMW bore down on them. Closer it came, then closer.

Noel fired. The shot struck the sedan somewhere in the trunk section. He fired again and a wheel cover spun away like a self-propelled silver discus. Inside the sedan, the face of the man with the Uzi twisted in vindictive menace. He faced forward. He pointed his weapon at the limousine through the sedan's blown-out windshield and clamped down on the trigger.

Bullets sprayed with the staccato explosions, thumping into metal, shattering glass. Riva dived to hug the floor. Her heart was thudding in her chest with sickening strokes. She had been shocked, enraged, vengeful; had acted on instincts of self-preservation she had not known she possessed. Still, she had not been terrified until that moment. In the last instant of sight before she hit the limousine's plush carpet, she saw the BMW leap forward and knew with stunning clarity what Noel meant to do.

The BMW struck the green sedan with the sound of a battering ram. Metal shrieked and the air was filled with the stench of burning rubber. The spattering shots abruptly stopped.

Riva leaped up in time to see the sedan, with a crumpled left rear fender, slow down, then brake in a sudden, grinding halt. In his BMW Noel whipped around the other vehicle on the right. The sedan reversed with screaming tires, swinging about in a tight circle. It bounced and jolted down into the ditch, then spun out again in a shower of mud and gravel. It zoomed away with the left rear wheel smoking and squealing, heading toward New Orleans.

The BMW gained on the limousine, drew even. Noel, the planes of his face taut and his eyes gray-black with strain, turned his head to look at Riva. She stared back at him as slowly she regained her seat. Noel gave a nod, then looked at George. The chauffeur sent him a high sign. The BMW pulled ahead in the position of escort.

George didn't even slow down, nor did Noel. They didn't stop until they reached Bonne Vie.

18

Noel got out of his BMW and slammed the door as the limousine pulled up behind him. He walked to the rear door of the other vehicle before George had time to do more than turn off the engine. He pulled the door open, then reached to help Riva out.

Her face was pale, and there were two or three smears of blood on one cheek and temple from small cuts. Her hand in his was cut also, and icy. Her suit was torn and blood-spotted, and she had lost a shoe. However, it was the sparkle of glass in her hair, like shattered diamonds, that made him pull her into his arms and hold her close against him.

He could feel the fine tremors that ran over her in waves. At the same time, her curves against him were firm and real, and the way she clung to him for support was heart-stopping. He closed his eyes for the space of a single deep breath, then opened them again.

George, climbing out, said, "Pair of amateurs, that's what they were. Must've seen too many movies. If they'd been professionals, they'd have tried to shoot out the tires first thing, the way you did. They should've known it ain't that easy to stop a car, even with one of those Israeli tommy guns."

Noel released Riva and stepped back. He smiled at the driver and shook his head. "They didn't expect you to give them so much trouble."

"Huh, I learned to drive before them two was wet behind the ears. And the Cong in Nam would have had 'em for breakfast if they couldn't shoot any better than that. You're the one gave 'em trouble, though. It's been a while since I saw better driving."

"Yes, but look at your car," Riva said to Noel.

Noel and George turned to look at the dented fender and bent bumper on the left front of the BMW. Noel quipped, "You should see the other guy."

"I did that." George shook his head. "But I must be losing my grip, letting those two yo-yos sneak up on me that way."

"Somehow it's the last thing you expect," Riva said.

"I don't know, Noel here told me just a couple of days ago to start carrying that pistol. I should have been on my guard."

Noel could sense Riva's gaze as she turned her head to look at him. He kept his attention on George. "Is that blood on your sleeve? Why, in God's name, didn't you say you were hit? Come on in the house so we can look at it and see if we need to get you to the hospital."

"I've had worse than this in my eye," George said in disparagement as they turned toward the house. "My old lady can patch me up."

"Maybe so, but we still have to report this business—unless you called on the car phone."

"That I did," George said, "on the way in. I hope the police get those bastards—pardon the language, Miss Riva."

Noel frowned as he walked. "It goes against the grain to let them get away."

"Yeah, but it don't pay to argue with an Uzi, even if they was amateurs," George answered.

The front door was standing open. Abraham must have heard their approach and alerted the house. As they neared, Liz came running out, still wearing her apron. Constance, Margaret, and Boots were right behind her and a pair of housemaids were on their heels. Hands reached out to them, drawing them inside. Exclamations and questions rose in a babble. Pietro's voice was a shrill treble as he ran here and there among the adults. "Was it the terrorists?" he shouted in excitement. "Did they bomb my papa's car?" Constance quieted him, murmuring in Italian. Then came the distant keening of a siren, approaching fast.

The sheriff's car sat on the drive at Bonne Vie with its red lights flashing and its radio emitting static and occasional garbled calls for the best part of an hour. The parish sheriff, Cajun born, with a body like a beer keg and a mind used to convoluted thinking from figuring out his degree of kinship to nearly everyone in a fifty-mile radius, took statements while at the same time laughing and talking, sipping coffee and eating one of Liz's fried apple pies.

Noel wasn't fooled. The man was shrewd and he was less than satisfied with the possible reason they gave for the attack. The careless-sounding questions thrown out about this detail and that were designed to uncover the secret the sheriff sensed behind the façade of their good-mannered cooperation.

It was, of course, a game that could be played by more than one. There were few masks so effective as that of gracious courtesy. Noel watched Riva with appreciation as she smiled and answered questions, poured coffee and suggested second helpings of the pies. There was little to show that less than an hour before she had been in fear for her life. She had washed the blood from her face and hands and applied a Band-Aid or two, changed into a loose robe of cream-colored silk, and brushed her hair. She was a little pale, and there were a few livid scratches on one temple and cheek made by flying safety glass, but otherwise she might have been presiding over a ladies' social. Even George was doing his best imitation of militarily correct respect. For himself, Noel, like the others, was being as obstructive as he could manage though with the best manners possible.

"None of you ever saw these two guys before?" the sheriff asked.

"Never." Riva did not even look up from her coffee cup as she drank.

"Not me," George said.

"No." Noel did not elaborate.

"And you're satisfied it was your common, everyday kidnapping attempt, with the big idea being ransom?"

Noel met the sheriff's gaze without evasion. "It must have been."

"You have to admit," the lawman said with a shade of asperity, "that it didn't seem to make too much difference how banged up their victim might be, I mean, that limo's like a sieve."

Noel narrowed his eyes slightly as he considered the sheriff. "I can only suppose they lost their heads when they met with resistance—unless you have another idea?"

The lawman wasn't ready to meet a direct challenge. "Beats me. I'm just saying it's funny. Now, let's see. You say there just happened to be a pistol in the limo?" the sheriff asked the chauffeur.

"That's right, sir," George said.

The chauffeur was lying to protect him, Noel thought. The reason was probably because George knew there was no real explanation for why the gun was in the car except a hunch, and sheriffs weren't any happier with weapons concealed for no reason than they were about unexplained murder attempts. No doubt George thought it would call for less explanation if it could be made to sound as if the weapon had been there for some time. However, he could not be allowed to get into trouble over it.

"As a matter of fact," Noel said, "I asked him to carry it."

"Noel asked him to carry the gun," Riva said, "but actually it was my idea. There were a few weeks just after Cosmo's death when I felt nervous about the long drive back and forth to work every day. You understand, I'm sure. I'm told widows often go through spells like that. Really, I had forgotten the thing was there. I think we had all forgotten it."

Noel, interrupted in his aim, sat back and watched the ploy going forward with silent admiration. It was plain that Riva was shamelessly using Cosmo's name and her widowhood for their sympathy value in glossing over the presence of the weapon. That the sheriff recognized the tactic could be seen in the skeptical look on his face, but it was also obvious that the man had no intention of risking the embarrassment of trying to prove it. Nor was he ready to charge so prominent a person as the widowed Madame Staulet with the misdemeanor when she had just escaped an attempt on her life.

It was, perhaps, unfair of them to expect action and protection from the authorities under the circumstances, Noel thought. However, under ordinary circumstances, they were upstanding citizens, respectable and law-abiding members of the community, full supporters of law and order. It was just that there were some matters that were private, some the law did not have to know about fully in order to do its job.

It might have been instructive, Noel felt, if he could have joined with the sheriff in ferreting out the reason behind this attempt; he was actually no closer to understanding it than the other man. Another time, he might have been tempted to use this opportunity to force Riva's confidence. But not now, not after she had come so close to being killed.

Erin arrived in the midst of the interrogation. She was not alone. With her was Doug Gorsline. Noel had nothing against the young man, but he could have wished him at the devil then. This was no place for a photographer with newshound instincts.

Doug was right in the middle of it, however, trailing along behind Erin, who pushed into the dining room where they were all sitting around the table. It was the signal for Margaret and the others to crowd in also, breaking up what had been a fairly private discussion until that moment.

Erin's opinions on the supposed kidnap attempt were partisan and vocal. That anybody could attempt to injure her Aunt Riva was shocking. The two men should be hunted down like animals. She couldn't figure out what the sheriff was doing wasting his time at Bonne Vie when he should be out chasing the criminals. She wanted to jump in her car that very minute and go hieing down the road to find them herself. It was Doug who persuaded her that it would be useless. He was more intent on hearing the details of the event under discussion.

He wasn't the only one. Margaret exclaimed and shuddered and wondered aloud why the sheriff didn't do something at once. Boots went on and on about the damage to the two cars, the probable repair bill for one and the replacement bill for the other, and his doleful satisfaction that some insurance company would have to pay. Constance made a few comparisons to events in Italy and Sicily, seeming to take pleasure in the fact that such things could happen in America, land of the cowboy law officers with their white hats.

There was so much pressure put on the poor sheriff that the man finally called his office. What he had to report was not popular.

Though he had been called less than two minutes after the attack was broken off, no trace had been found of the two men in the sedan. They seemed to have vanished.

The kidnapping attempt, then, if that's what it was, gave every sign of being a carefully timed operation, with contingency plans in case of mishaps. No doubt the sedan would show up abandoned on a New Orleans back street or shopping-mall parking lot in a day or two, or else would disappear into some junkyard to be torn down and sold piece by piece into Mexico and Central America.

It was while those gathered were coming to this conclusion that Noel noticed Riva's cup rattle in its saucer as she put it down. She immediately stilled it, but her grip on the fine china was white. He straightened from where he stood leaning against the wall after giving up his chair to Margaret. "This should be about enough, don't you think, Sheriff? It doesn't seem likely there's much else to be gained by discussion."

"It does seem that way," the lawman agreed in dry tones.

"Then I believe it's time Riva, and George as well, were allowed a little peace and quiet. I'm sure they're ready for it."

"All I ask," the sheriff said in an attempt to regain some semblance of control, "is that all of you remain nearby, in case something comes up on this deal."

"I thought it was the bad guys who were told not to leave town," George said.

"Speaking of which," Riva said with a trace of amusement, "does this mean I shouldn't go to Colorado for the weekend?"

The sheriff ignored George as he got to his feet. "Not exactly, ma'am, just that I sure wish you wouldn't."

"You could always reach me at our cabin there. I had already made plans—"

"I doubt you're going to feel much like it in the morning. Unless I miss my guess, ma'am, you're more shook up than you know. Whoever it is you're supposed to meet will understand."

"It might be best if you kept close to the house, period," Noel told her with a shade of irritation. "Or at least that you don't go anywhere alone for a few days. It's possible whoever was after you could try again."

"I appreciate your concern," she answered lightly, "but I wasn't alone this time; George was there."

Noel shook his head. "I think you know what I mean."

"He's right, too," the sheriff said. "No use asking for trouble. It would be a pure shame if you wound up in a ditch somewhere."

Riva said no more. There was a sudden rush of concern for her and George, as if they were invalids. Margaret escorted Riva out of the room, murmuring something about seeing she got right in the bed. Liz took George away, though he was saying something about a stiff drink to go with his stiff arm. The others dispersed. Noel saw the sheriff out to his car, then stood on the drive until the red glow of the official vehicle's taillights had disappeared and the sound of the engine had died away.

He looked up at the sky. The misting rain had stopped and an uneasy wind had taken its place. From far off somewhere in the night there came the dull boom of thunder. Lightning blinked on the tree-crowded horizon. Behind the house, down near the ornamental pond, a bullfrog croaked and peeper frogs warned of more rain.

Noel stood for a moment looking up at the sky, then his gaze fell on the limousine and his own car still sitting in the drive. They needed to be put away, especially the limo with its back glass out. He felt in his pocket for the keys to the BMW. They were there. The keys to the other vehicle were in the ignition since George had intended to return to it later.

Noel attended to the cars, then closed the garage doors. The frogs were still calling down by the lake. Thrusting his hands into his pockets, he strolled in that direction. He wasn't ready to go inside. There were bound to be more questions, more discussion. He'd had enough of that.

The small temple of the folly was a pale gleam in the darkness of the pond. It served as a destination since he had no other. When he reached it, he moved inside and leaned against the Buddha. The bronze was as warm as living flesh, still holding the heat of the day. It made the ancient statue seem like a friendly presence there in the dark. He put his own hand on the hand of the Buddha where it rested on the bronze knee, then stood looking at the house, staring at the lighted upstairs windows that were rectangles of glowing yellow above the darkened lower floor.

He knew which room was Riva's, the room she had moved to when his father became so ill and the nurses began to stay with him around the clock. The drapes were drawn in that room. As he watched, the lights went off. He thought about her taking off her robe, sliding into bed, spreading her hair over the pillow.

He swore.

Noel deliberately switched his thoughts to his son, to Pietro's loud demands to know if the terrorists had bombed his papa's car. It was ironic that such a thing should happen while Constance and the children were here since he had always maintained that his part of the world was safe from such terrorist-type threats. Both Pietro and Coralie, to his eyes, were much better now than when they had come; they had lost much of their European city pallor, and their manners were freer and more natural. Just yesterday, Coralie had been rolling out pie crusts in the kitchen with Liz without caring about the flour on her nose or scattered down the front of her dress.

What a shame it was that Constance could not have kept both children in the house and away from the bullet-riddled car. For that matter, what a crazy world it was where a six-year-old boy knew about bullets and bombs and terrorists. He would have to talk to Pietro about it, make him understand how rarely attacks such as this happened, and that he, the boy himself, was safe. Or was he? Had the world gone mad?

No, there was a reason for the attack on Riva. He would swear it had something to do with the business with Gallant, could guess at the reasons, though there was something in the violence of it that left him puzzled and afraid for her. He wished she would trust him, confide in him, but he supposed that was asking too much. He was left with the role of watching and waiting. It was not one he enjoyed.

A figure appeared on the upper gallery of the house. It was pale and luminous, ghostlike, as it drifted up and down. Noel stood still, his gaze intent. After a moment, the wavering shape disappeared. Within a few seconds, however, it materialized on the lower gallery and emerged under the live oak trees and palms around the swimming pool. Insubstantial yet purposeful, it moved toward the lake.

It was Riva. She still had on her robe of cream silk. The material was light enough to flutter in the gusts of damp wind. As she neared, she called, "I'm sorry if I'm disturbing you, but people who want solitude should not wear white shirts in the dark."

"How did you know I wasn't Boots?"

"I know where Boots is; he's drinking again on the upper gallery."

"But not wearing off-white. I saw you up there. You looked like a ghost."

"Probably the source of half the ghost stories in the world, some woman running around in her nightclothes and afraid to admit to anything so embarrassing."

"Could be," he agreed. "Anyway, I wasn't after solitude so much as quiet."

"I won't make much noise then, or at least not for long. It's just that I saw you down here and realized that I never even said thank you for what you did this afternoon."

"I'd rather you didn't."

"Oh, I know that. I won't dwell on it, but I am grateful. I'm rather fond of living, and I might have been killed "

"Since I feel that that would have caused a definite decrease in the quality of life here, you're very welcome."

"Good, I'm glad we got that settled," she said.

He waited for her to go on, hoping she would say something about the reasons for the attack, hoping against hope that she would trust him with her fears about it, her thoughts and suspicions. When she did not, anger stirred. He shifted his position. "Don't you think I deserve to know why?"

Her voice was low when she at last answered. "What makes you think I know?"

"I understand about secrets. I've kept enough of them."

He thought she sent him a flashing glance in the dimness. There was an intrigued note in her voice as she said, "Have you?"

It was a moment before he answered. "I used to come out here when I was little. The Buddha was my friend. I told him everything. My mother thought it was cute. My father thought it un-manly, that I had my head too far in the clouds. I was maybe eight, nine, not much older than Pietro."

"I don't suppose the Buddha had much to say."

"No, but he didn't tell anybody anything, either. He was never shocked, and he never scolded."

"People aren't often like that."

"No, which is why I still come to see him."

"He's very old. I suppose he's heard a lot, seen a lot, in his time."

She spoke almost at random, as if her mind were on something else. He could sympathize. The wind brought her scent to him, one compounded of fresh-laundered cotton, delicate perfume, and her own sense-quickening female fragrance. He answered, "I suppose."

"There's something I could tell him."

"Is there?" It was what he had wanted. Regardless, gaining her confidence did not seem so important when she was so near.

"Actually, it isn't my secret, but one Cosmo told me."

Noel's brows drew together. He wished he could see her face, but even in the darkness her head was turned away from him. "What is it?"

"Cosmo told me he lied to you, told you I was encouraging you years ago on the island, coming on to you in order to make trouble between you and him; that I wanted to separate you so that I could have the Staulet fortune for myself."

"He did tell me that, yes."

"Did you know that he also told me you were stringing me along in order to make trouble between me and him, to get rid of me?"

"My father was an intelligent man, sometimes too intelligent. He was also afraid of losing you."

"It wasn't true, none of it was true."

"I know."

"He confessed what he had done to you, too, then, before he died."

"He didn't have to tell me; I always knew. It took time to accept his reasons for saying it, but I always knew."

"Then you went away for nothing."

"No," he said, his voice deep. "It wasn't for nothing."

She swung toward him, and a flash of lightning, coming closer, showed her face blue-white and filled with pain. "I didn't want to take your place with your father, I only wanted to share it. I didn't want to steal your position at Staulet Corporation or take over here at Bonne Vie. Everything came to me by default because you were gone."

"If I had stayed," he said, "would everything now be the same?"

There was silence for the space of a heartbeat. In it were a thousand unspoken things.

Finally she said, "I don't know, but everything wouldn't have been so wrong all these years."

"No, it might have been worse. What happened between us that afternoon in the gardener's shed might have happened again. And if it had, if my father had been forced to stand and let it happen, it would have killed him. He worshiped you. You were his shy young bride who had brought him youth and hope, plus something more I never quite understood but was like a secret sin. He was entranced with you. I wasn't sure he could live without you."

"But you could?"

He opened his mouth to speak, but nothing came to him. He could not say it, could not make that simple agreement that would cut them free of each other.

Instead he said in slow reflection, "Do you remember the gardener's shed and the way it rained? It was almost like this evening with the thunder and lightning and the wind."

"It wasn't at all like this." Her voice was taut as she moved away from him. "For one thing, it wasn't evening, it was afternoon. For another, we could see the sea waves instead of just little wavelets slapping in a pond."

"But you'll have to admit there was water and a bare shelter like this."

"It was a shed with bamboo walls and a tin roof, not a temple of stone, and it smelled of insecticide and gasoline engines."

"If we listen, we can hear the palm trees around the pool like those around the shed." He stopped at her shoulder. The wind flapped the hem of her light robe, fluttering it against his legs with a soft movement that seemed to both cling and repel.

"Those around the shed were taller," she said, "and closer."

"There was the storm."

"It nearly drowned us, blew us away, instead of holding off.'"

"We had been quarreling."

"We haven't been quarreling now."

"Haven't we? I thought we had been at odds for more than twenty years, always silently quarreling."

"I was married then." She made the reminder in a quiet voice.

"And now you're not. That much I'll admit is different."

She looked up at him. "The only thing that's close to the same is the two of us, and even we're different, older and more experienced, less driven by feelings we don't understand and so can't control."

"That may be, but you can't deny that you remember."

"No. I'd never do that." Her voice was shaky but forthright.

"In that case, are you sure we're so different?" he whispered, and leaned to touch his lips to hers.

She didn't resist him; there was a bittersweet poignancy in that fact. Her lips were sweet, so sweet. As he lifted his hand to her face, her skin was soft and resilient over the fragility of her bones. She moved against him, lifting her hands to clasp them behind his neck.

Her compliance might have been from gratitude or even pity, but he didn't care. He caught his breath and held it deep in his chest as he tasted the moist and tender inner surfaces of her mouth and held her warm, yielding body to him. He saw the play of lightning against his closed eyelids and felt the dull percussion of thunder in his blood. The wind swirled her hair so that it touched his face with a silken caress, and the delicately enticing scent of Paradise that was so much a part of her mounted to his brain. He felt dazed with the wild beat of his heart and the too sudden appeasement of strained longing.

He wanted her, God, how he wanted her. But not on the gritty floor again, not in a wet and hasty tumble where anyone could chance upon them. He wanted her in the privacy of his room and the comfort of his bed, and with undisturbed eons to learn the thousands of tiny details he craved to know about her body and its pleasures, about her feelings and the intricate processes of her mind. He would have liked the security of trust, but failing that, he would settle for no less than locked doors and thick walls and a long night.

Bending, he caught her up with one arm under her knees and the other across her back. He strode from the folly with its serene Buddha back across the bridge and over the lawn toward the house. Lightning flickered with silver fire and thunder rumbled closer as he mounted the steps to the lower gallery. Crossing it, he pushed through the double doors that Riva had left ajar.

The downstairs bedroom Noel used opened immediately to the right inside the hall. It had been redecorated since Cosmo's death and all of the paraphernalia of the sickroom banished. The massive mahogany bed and armoire that Cosmo had preferred had been consigned to a guest room, exchanged for a rosewood set by the old New Orleans furniture-maker Seignouret, which had belonged to Noel's mother. The colors of royal blue and gray, with touches of red, that had been paired with the antiques gave the room an updated, masculine look without making it seem too modern.

The single lamp glowing on a marble-topped table beside the bed cast no more than a mellow glow in the vastness of the room. Still, as Noel placed Riva on the high mattress of the bed, she turned and stretched out her hand to turn it off. Regardless of how dim the light, it was too bright. It was not modesty that prompted her; rather, it seemed that the tie that bound her to this man, the desire that stretched between them, was too tenuous to withstand the glare. In the dark they could be more the way they had once been and less the way they had become.

The bed shifted as Noel lowered himself to lie beside her. He reached out to touch the tender curve of her cheek, his fingers warm and caressing. With his thumb, he brushed the smooth surface of her lips so that the sensitive edges tingled. He trailed the back of his knuckles along the line of her jaw and down the curve of her neck, pausing to test the steady throbbing of her pulse at the hollow of her throat. Then he bent his head to press his warm lips to that gently frantic beat, at the same time brushing his hand lower, gliding across her breast and down the sloping indentation of her waist.

On a ragged indrawn breath, he caught her to him, holding her close with his face against her neck as he rocked her slowly in his arms. "I've dreamed of this," he said in a rough whisper, "so many times. So many times."

Riva could feel the swift pace of the blood in her veins and the sweeping wave of a flush moving over her so that she felt heated, incandescent with longing. The feel of his body against hers, hard and powerful and protective, made her feel reckless, uncaring of the consequences these moments might bring. In the tension that shivered through his muscles, she could feel his restraint, the rigid control he held on himself, and she was aware of a fierce and perverse yearning to make him discard it.

She slid the palm of one hand over his shoulder, kneading the long ropes of muscles under the fine cotton sleeve of his shirt and turned her face to meet his mouth as she pushed her fingers through the crisp hair at the back of his neck. With her tongue, she traced the chiseled formation of his lips, then gently, delicately explored the line where they came together, the polished edges of his teeth, the sweet and tender interior surfaces.

Pleasure burgeoned inside her, settling heavy and urgent in the lower part of her body. She moved closer, kicking off one slipper and sliding her cool, bare foot over his ankle and hooking around it to hold herself more firmly against him. She was lost and she knew it, awash in sensations and old memories. It was the same between them, beautifully, wonderfully the same. Yet there was a difference, too, and the difference was that they had the maturity to approach this moment with care and to appreciate its rarity.

Noel did not lose control but rather relinquished it with grace and without regret. At the same time, he unleashed a tender assault upon the defenses with which Riva armored herself, tearing them away one by one as he stripped away the clothes that covered them.

"I want you, God, how I want you," he said, his voice rich and low, vibrating deep in his throat as he loosened the belt of her robe and pushed one sleeve down her arm. He cupped the round globe of her breast that he had uncovered, tasting the rose-peach nipple, abrading it with his tongue in sinuous play before he went on. "Say you want me."

"I want you," she whispered, and to prove it arched toward him.

"I've missed you," he said, his breath warm and moist on the flat plane of her abdomen as he smoothed the silken skin there with his lips through the silk of her robe before he slid it down in order to reach bare flesh. "Say you missed me."

"I've missed you so much." The words were a soft cry, aching with truth. With trembling fingers, she reached to fumble with the buttons of his shirt, releasing them from their holes.

"No one has ever made me feel as you do," he whispered, his voice husky with an echo of amazement for that admission.

Without prompting, Riva replied in the same tone, "It's the same for me."

He bunched the robe in his hand, pulling it away from her thighs and calves and from under her before tossing it aside. There came the rustle of cloth as he stripped off his shirt, then unzipped his pants and skimmed out of them. Easing close once more, supporting his weight on one elbow, he put his hand on the softly curling mat at the apex of her thighs and held her with his warm strength for vital seconds, before slowly and with infinite care he sought for the moist and heated center of her being.

Thunder boomed outside, rumbling closer, and beyond the windows that opened onto the gallery and the terrace the wind sighed and sang in the live oak trees. It seemed to Riva that the growing storm was in her blood, a vital part of her, and when it broke she might be swept away. She was wary of the violence she sensed in it, but at the same time she strained toward it.

"We loved each other once," Noel said in tones so compressed they seemed a part of the wind, "but I never heard you say it. Will you? Now?"

"I . . ." she began, then stopped as her voice caught in her throat.

"Say it," he urged in the darkness, "even if it isn't so."

She whispered the words in soft compliance and reached out to him, touching the firm, resilient length of him, seeking to return the tremulous pleasure that bloomed inside her. He drew in his breath with a hissing sound and, feeling her joy, let the silence surround them until, with a soft cry, she flung herself against him.

Lightning flashed against the windows as he rose above her. It tinted his hair with blue fire and outlined his shoulders in gold. And then as he sank into her, Riva closed her eyes tightly against the jolting excess of ecstacy. Clutching his arms, she lifted her hips to meet him, engulfing him, striving toward a promised completion.

Strong, he was so strong, endlessly enduring, and he moved with such flawless rhythm to the surging beat of the blood inside her. Their breaths rasped and caught; their limbs grew slippery with perspiration; the beating of their hearts canceled out the thunder. Time stretched backward, drawing them closer, pulling the moment closer around them. Tighter and tighter.

The perfect instant took them unaware, splintering, multiplying, exploding in a chain reaction that seemed to fill the dark night with its magic. They collapsed upon each other, rocking each other and murmuring soft, incoherent words as they sought for breath, pressing their mouths together in mindless mutual gratitude for the liberation of overwrought senses. And in the impending quiet they heard the rush and flow of the rain.

The seconds ticked past. Their breathing quieted. The wind died down and the rain became a muted, steady drumming. Still they lay with arms and legs entwined and eyelids tightly closed. Noel brushed the hair back from Riva's damp face and pressed his lips to her brow. He shifted slightly to keep his weight from her, but made no move to leave her. He drew a deep breath, holding it a moment as if he intended to say something that meant much to him.

Abruptly the bedroom door was thrust open to slam against the wall. There came a soft click and the chandelier overhead sprang into stunning brightness. Riva sprang up to see Constance with her hand on the switch she had just flipped on. Her face was mottled with the red of her fury, and in her voice as she spoke was malicious triumph. "I knew when you two disappeared at the same time I'd find you here," she said. "There are places, you know, where what you have been doing is considered incest."

Noel was already reaching for the overhanging edge of the bedspread on which they lay. He swept it up to cover them. Rage, no less virulent for its quietness, rasped in his voice as he spoke. "Get out."

His ex-wife cocked an eyebrow as she countered in brittle irony, "You don't believe me? See Leviticus: 'The nakedness of thy father's wife shalt thou not uncover.' It is certainly stepmothers who are meant, for actual blood mothers are covered, or uncovered as the case may be, under a separate verse."

Noel could have strangled Constance where she stood; the urge to do it roared in his blood with the ebb of passion. Her casual besmirching of what was between him and the woman in his arms was intolerable. Beside him, he felt Riva stir and met her imploring gaze. It was in answer to what he saw there that he grasped at the remnants of his temper and reason.

Turning on Constance again, he said, "I hardly thought the Bible your choice of reading matter."

"It is when it suits me," she answered

"Then you should realize that my father is dead; therefore, Riva is no longer his wife."

"True, but people have long memories, and some things are a matter of instinct rather than logic or law. They know what you are doing is wrong without knowing how they know, and they can be cruel."

"I don't know it."

"Then you're a fool!"

Noel held her gaze with level concentration. "Not so big a one that I fail to see what you're doing. It won't change anything."

"Won't it? I defy you to take your stepmother in your arms again without being aware that you're taking your father's place. Of course, that may be what you want, what you've always wanted."

Riva spoke then, her voice vibrant with fury. "That's a disgusting thing to say!"

"And disgusting to contemplate!" Constance flashed in reply as she turned her malevolence on the other woman.

"Only in your mind. There is no tie of blood between us, no legal bar."

"I never said there was. Only the prohibition is an old one, and there are reasons for it."

"None that apply now that Cosmo is no longer alive."

"No, your husband is dead, and aren't you glad!"

Riva stared at Constance with the color draining from her face. Before she could answer, Noel intervened, his grip white-knuckled on the bedspread across his legs, as if he meant to lunge off the bed. His concern was not for himself—there was little his former wife could say that had the power to hurt him—but Riva lacked his defenses. "You have no idea what you're doing, Constance. Stay out of it, do you hear me? And now get out of here before I throw you out!"

"How charming," Constance said, "but then some women seem to bring out the protective instinct in men. However, Riva may have lost one of her knights. She should be careful about Colorado. I don't think our dearest Dante is alone in the mountains. The children and I saw him lunching with a woman before he left. She was introduced as Anne Gallant."

Noel felt Riva stiffen as she absorbed the implications of the other woman's words; however, he did not look at her. Instead, he flung the bedspread back from his legs. Constance's face changed, and she backed quickly from the room, slamming the door behind her.

There was a moment of stillness. Then Riva stirred, reaching for her robe, and slid from the bed. Noel kicked the bedspread aside and reached for his own clothes.

"You don't have to come with me," Riva said, her voice strained.

"Yes, I do."

There was such finality in the words that she said no more. They dressed in silence. Riva pushed her fingers through her hair but made no other effort toward repairing her appearance. When she turned toward the door, Noel, ready himself, reached to open and hold it for her.

The rain seemed to have abated, for they could hear it dripping from the roof outside in the stillness of the big old house. They mounted the stairs with slow steps and moved along the hall to the door of Riva's bedroom. He turned the knob and pushed the panel open, but made no move to go inside.

"I'm sorry," he said simply.

She breathed slowly in and out. "So am I. It wasn't the way Constance tried to make it sound, I know that. We just—just needed each other. Sometimes people need someone to hold."

If he had never loved her before, he would have then as she stood with dark shadows under her eyes and glass cuts on her face trying to make him feel better about wanting her, his father's wife. He lifted his hands to cup her face, brushing her cheeks with gentle thumbs, caressing one corner of her mouth. "I know," he said in soft accord. "Storms have that effect on me. They have for a long time."

Her smile as she searched his face trembled slightly at the edges. He could feel that faint movement under his hands. Before he could follow his urge to make the trembling go away, he brushed her mouth with his own warm lips, then stepped back.

She braced her shoulders as she gazed at him in the dimly lighted hall. "Goodnight," she said softly.

"Goodnight," he answered.

She closed the door with slow care. It was a long time before she heard his footsteps retreating down the hall.

Her mind was curiously blank, as if in self-protection, to keep her from the pain of examining the things she and Cosmo's son had just said and done and what it might mean.

Her bedroom suddenly seemed like a refuge. She moved deeper inside. Somewhere the central air came on, and she shivered a little in the sudden draft of cool air from the vents.

There was no light on in the room, but she wanted none, needed none. Beyond the window the lightning flickered, then flared up again as if the storm was not quite done after all. As she stood there in the dark, she could hear the sweeping clatter of the wave of returning rain. Wrapping her arms around her and rubbing her forearms with her hands, she moved to the window to stare out.

This storm came from a different direction from the first and was more violent. It swept over Bonne Vie, waving the heavy arms of the oaks, speckling the water of the swimming pool, drenching the lawns. There was no reason to think she heard the sound of the sea and the clatter of the palms in its fury, no need to make of it a reminder of desire past and present.

Tonight she and Noel had met as lovers tempered by time and circumstances, two people able to accept the moment and make it theirs without expecting it to be more than it was, more than it could possibly be. That was it; that was all there was to it.

She had told him she loved him, but he had not spoken words of love in return.

He had never said he loved her that day on the island, either. He had made love to her, then he had gone away and stayed away for years.

Desire, that was what lay between them. Noel had never made a secret of the fact that he wanted her. In the same way, she had always been drawn to him. Mutual desire, that was the attraction, the binding force between them. It had been there when they were young and had been revived now.

It was a powerful thing, desire. If combined with love, it could be used to create something of lasting worth; without love, it could become a weapon of destruction.

Why had Noel turned to her at the folly? Why had he taken her into his arms? Why?

Why had she responded, if it came to that? Oh, she could tell herself that it had been reaction to her brush with death and Noel's rescue or insist that desire was excuse enough in itself. Still the question remained.

This wouldn't do. She required a distraction, a calm voice far removed from the storm outside and the turmoil that had been unleashed inside her. She needed to forget the charge Constance had made. Incest was such an ugly word. It hardly applied to her and Noel, not really, and yet the idea of it disturbed her pro-foundly. The reason was not hard to find. It was the same word she had been hearing over and over in her mind as she thought of Erin with Josh Gallant.

She had told him she loved him.

She couldn't think about it anymore, couldn't bear it. There must be something else, someone else who could divert her thoughts and help her regain her equilibrium.

In Colorado it was an hour earlier, not at all late. She moved to the table beside her bed and picked up the phone. In the light from the receiver, she pressed the buttons. The phone began to ring.

"Hello," Dante said.

Before Riva could speak, a background noise came, like the sliding of a glass door, followed by a woman's voice. "Darling, come out and see. It's the most spectacular afterglow from the sunset on the— Oh, excuse me."

Riva recognized that voice. She was not sure she would have if Constance had not mentioned meeting Dante and Anne Gallant. She had not, after all, heard Edison's wife speak often or at length.

She reached in haste to depress the button that would break the connection. For long moments afterward, she stood holding the receiver, staring at nothing.

19

The Beechcraft Bonanza was a good plane, Edison assured himself as it pitched and swung in the gray soup of clouds, but it wasn't built for flying through a hurricane. Maybe he should have paid more attention to the weather reports. But, hell, he'd had it up to here with waiting around, listening to the newspaper people hem and haw, being put off about this damned endorsement. The bastards didn't know diddley about politics, couldn't find their own asses in the dark with both hands, if the truth were known. Why the hell he had to depend on such sanctimonious dimwits to get elected he'd never understand. So there had been an irregularity here and there; anybody with an ounce of savvy knew politicians had to make accommodations. That was how the game was played. The trick was to get the most while giving the least.

Bringing Josh with him had been a master stroke. It paid to have a clean-cut college kid on his side, one who could stand flat-footed and boil with outrage at the innuendos about his father and, what's more, mean every word. They had made brownie points there, he thought; he should probably thank Riva for putting the idea in his head. Though thanking her wasn't exactly what he had in mind. It had been more than two whole days and nights since he'd had a piece. He didn't like going without that long.

He'd thought about fixing Josh and himself up the night before, making a call to a woman he knew who could supply clean girls. It hadn't seemed too smart on second thought. Josh took after his mother, had weird ideas about fidelity and all that crap, and that fine outrage of his son's might not have been so ready next time.

Anyway, the kid was done in, sound asleep back there, from a Saturday-night dinner with the guys from headquarters that had included a couple of glasses of wine, then a few beers at the joints on the Bossier Strip. It was all he could do to drag the boy out of bed this morning for the flight home. What would he have been like if he'd gone a round or two with a woman on top of it?

This was like flying into a wall of water, with small rivers streaming past on the side windows while lightning crackled in all directions. He was a damn good pilot, but conditions like this made him nervous. Instrument landings made him nervous, too; he hated letting any damned machine take over. Still, he'd be lucky if he got a glimpse of runway lights before touching down in this mess. He reached out to pick up the mike. He'd better let somebody know what he had in mind.

The downward glide of the approach was rough. The slope felt steep, but with the bouncing around it was hard to tell. Anyway, it always felt that way to him. Regardless, he had to fight an impulse to take over, to pull the nose up. The clouds whipped past, gray, white, and gray again. Wheels down. Where the hell was the runway?

Lower and lower. The dull roar of the engine rose and fell as it struggled. His ears rang with its high-pitched whine. There was a jolt that felt as if it loosened every tooth in his head. He was gritting his teeth, he discovered, and consciously relaxed his jaw. A few minutes more. Just a few minutes. He strained his eyes, reached to wipe at the windshield with the backs of his fingers as if he could remove the cottony haze. It didn't help. Any second now, any second.

Breakthrough!

Holy shit! Too low, too low! The runway was three goddamned miles away. Coming in short. Too short!

He slapped the automatic pilot off, grabbed the wheel. The engine roared, straining, straining. Static on the radio, telling him something he damned well already knew. Josh awake, yelling. Treetops, every leaf plain and wet. Swampland zipping underneath. Airport fence ahead, low enough. He was going to make it.

He didn't see the cypress looming up on the right, taller than the rest. The wing tip scraped the treetop, caught, released. Tipping. Losing it. Runway lights like a pinwheel. Spinning over the fence. A wing scraping. The spar going, rending, snapping with a booming thud. Metal sheathing crackling like foil on a gum wrapper. Electrical sparks. God! Struts shrieking along the concrete, grinding, dragging, slowing. The crumpled plane slewed sideways, spun around. Stopped.

Edison sat for long second with his hands clenched on the wheel. His seat was cocked up so that all he could see was the gray sky. He tasted blood, knew he had bitten through his lip. But he was alive. Alive. Somewhere he heard the hiss of escaping air and settling metal. He smelled fuel and fluids of different kinds. He was dizzy and his head ached. But he was alive, by damn. And he hadn't shit in his pants, either, not quite. His luck still held, the famous Gallant luck.

Josh.

He tore at his seat belt, yanked it free, fell out of his seat. He had to stand on the side wall to climb back toward the passenger seats. The fuselage was caved in. Josh was lying half under the broken spar, head to the side, unconscious. Running at an angle along the bulkhead was a red trail of blood.

It was a nighmare of flashing lights and shouted orders, of smothering chemical foam and hands dragging at him, pulling at him while he screamed and cursed and begged for somebody to get his son out of there. They raced up with a truck carrying acetylene-cutting torches. Finally Josh came out on a stretcher. The spar had caught his arm, half severing it. The bleeding had been checked, but he was in shock. It would be touch and go. Edison clamped his fingers on his son's cold hand, holding it until the last minute, until they shut the ambulance doors.

A policeman asked for his name and he stared at the man as if he were crazy. Why the hell should he give him his name?

God, it would be in all of the papers by dark. He would look like an incompetent idiot. He could hear the punsters now. If Candidate Gallant couldn't keep his plane in the air, how could he expect to make a state fly? How, if he was so inept a pilot? He wasn't! Something had gone wrong in that plane. Something had gone too damn wrong.

Right now, however, it paid to be Congressman Gallant. There would be a police escort to the hospital and a place for him in the front seat beside the driver. Before the patrol car door closed on him, he turned to an airport official. "Call my wife," he said. "Royal Orleans Hotel. Tell her to meet us at the hospital."

Five hours later, Josh was out of surgery and in intensive care. He was stable, barely. The team of doctors at Oshner's Hospital thought they had been able to save the arm, but it would be forty-eight hours at least, maybe longer, before they could be sure. There was nothing the congressman could do to help matters. He might as well go home, get some rest; he looked as if he could use it.

Edison didn't want to rest. He wanted to know where the hell Anne was, why she hadn't answered at the hotel. He wanted to know what had happened to his plane and who was responsible. He didn't want any damned pills for his nerves. He wanted answers. And answers were what he was going to get.

The hotel room was empty. Anne's clothes hung in the closet, but there were one or two things, a pair of slacks and a favorite sweater, that were missing. Also missing was her small overnight case.

He called their house in Alexandria on the chance that she had gone home. It was not the first time he had tried; after she failed to show up at the hospital and he was told she could not be reached at the Royal Orleans, he had called once or twice with no answer. Still no answer. It was late Sunday afternoon. The house was empty since the maid didn't come in on the weekends.

Edison slammed down the receiver on the tenth ring. He thought of calling some of Anne's family but decided against it. He didn't want to start a furor if she had simply gone to visit friends. More than that, he had no stomach for repeating the whole rigmarole of the plane crash with Josh's grandmother or aunts or being forced to listen to their exclamations and intimations that it was all his fault. Let Anne talk to them. As for where his wife was, there must be some simple explanation. There had damned sure better be one.

He needed a drink. He moved to the credenza and poured a stiff jolt of Jack Daniel's and swallowed half of it. Holding the glass, he returned to the phone. He positioned a hotel notepad where he could read the numbers written there and punch them out at the same time. When the phone at the airport was answered, he asked for a man he knew in the maintenance department. Edison had called him earlier also. Now he got the report he had asked for before. The automatic pilot of the Beechcraft Bonanza had been out of kilter, just as he thought. Someone had tampered with it.

Someone had tried to kill him. Few pilots walked away from the kind of crash he had survived. The plane usually went in on its nose, taking out the pilot first. That he was alive and virtually unscathed was a sign of his luck, his incredible, phenomenal luck. He had always been lucky, while Josh, dammit, had nearly bought it. Josh, his only son. When he found out who had done this thing, he would see to it that they would be glad to die.

There came the sound of a key in the lock. He set his glass down. By the time the door swung open, he was beside it, slamming it shut behind his wife. She whirled to face him, her eyes wide but wary.

"Where the hell have you been?" he demanded. He put his hands on his hips as he waited for an answer.

"What is it? Is something wrong?"

"Oh, no, nothing much. Only your husband's plane crash-landed and your son had to be rushed to the hospital, and you weren't here."

"Josh? What happened to him? Is he— How is he?"

"I asked you a question first," he said in grim satisfaction for the panicky concern he saw in her face.

"What? You mean—"

"Where the hell were you?"

"I—oh, I went home." She grabbed his arm. "Damn you, Edison, tell me!"

He shook her off. "Sure you went home. I called and you weren't there. Besides, if you went home, why didn't you take that piece of bronze junk you bought for the garden room?"

"If you called, you must have just missed me; I left early, had lunch on the way. I didn't think there was any reason to rush. As for the cherub, I meant to take it but forgot. Now, Edison, please!"

"Your son nearly had his shoulder sliced off. He's in intensive care, condition guarded. He may lose his arm."

The color left her face. She sat down suddenly on the nearest chair, dropping her purse and her overnight bag beside it. Her eyes never leaving his, she said, "You bastard. You knew that, and yet you kept it from me long enough to pry information out of me."

"What the hell? I found out what I wanted to know, and it doesn't make any difference to Josh."

She surged to her feet. "It makes a difference to me!"

"Why? You were off having yourself a good time when he was hurt, weren't there for him when he needed you. What does a few minutes here and there matter?"

"Who is with him now?"

"Nobody. He's there alone because his mother—"

"He has a father, too! Why aren't you there? What are you doing here getting drunk?"

"I'm having a drink because I needed one. I'm here because I wanted to know where the hell you were."

"What does that matter? Josh needs someone there!"

"Yeah, you. You're his mother."

"I should have known you'd twist it around for your convenience. You never understand any point of view except your own. You're never interested in anybody's wants and needs except your own."

"Well, pardon me! I was almost killed this afternoon. It makes a man touchy."

"You're always touchy, or worse, but I'll never forgive you for what you just did."

He snorted and moved to pick up his drink, taking a swallow. "There's nothing wrong with a man finding out what his wife's been up to."

Anne stared at him for long moments. Abruptly she made a sound that might have been an echo of his contemptuous laugh through his nose. "The fact is, you haven't found out anything. I wasn't at home. I was in Colorado."

She swung away from him, heading toward the door. He caught up with her in three long strides, grabbing her forearm. "What do you mean, Colorado? What in hell were you doing there?"

"If you must know, I was in bed with my lover. Now let me go! I have to see my son."

"Let you go? I'll beat the shit out of you, you bitch! What the hell kind of thing is that to say?"

"The truth. But then I never expected you to recognize it, having so little acquaintance with it."

"You mean you—I don't believe it!"

"Why?" She gave him a hard stare at close range. "Because it threatens your ego? You thought you were the only one allowed to stray into other beds?"

"Because you're a frigid cunt!"

"Oh, no. If I've been frigid, it's because you're a rotten lover. I learned that much this weekend."

He felt as if he had been kicked in the solar plexus. "You can't—you don't—" he began in confusion.

"I can and I do. I can and I did several times. Now get out of my way." Anne tugged her arm free.

He flung his glass away so that it thudded on the carpet and rolled into the bedroom. Then he was upon her, spinning her around, hitting her with his fist so hard that she slammed into the door facing and careened off it again to slide along the wall. He followed her, grabbing her hair to haul her upright. "Who was it?" he asked in grating tones. "Who is your lover boy?"

There was anguish in her eyes and a place on her jaw that was red with a blue shadow. Still her lips trembled into a smile. "Go to hell."

"I'll find out, and when I do, he'll be one more sorry bastard."

"I'd be careful if I were you. Could be you're the one who will be sorry."

His grasp eased as his features tightened. "He has that kind of influence, does he?"

"Let's say he isn't without friends."

"The kind of friends who might not give a shit if they killed your son while they were trying to get to me?"

316 •

He watched the horror invade her eyes, enlarging the pupils, watched her lick her lips before she said, "You don't mean—"

"The crash was no accident."

"He wouldn't," she whispered. "He couldn't, not Dante."

Edison grunted in surprise, then laughed aloud as he pushed her away from him. "He probably wouldn't, not for you. But he might for Riva Staulet."

"What are you talking about?" The words were brave, but the look in her eyes was bleak.

"I think you can guess, but never mind. You go see Josh, then I want your ass back here. We're not through by a long shot."

She straightened, smoothed her hair. Looking around, she found her purse beside the chair and retrieved it, slinging the strap over her shoulder. She turned toward the door, then, with her hand on the knob, turned back. "Is that loverlike request supposed to make me want to stay with you and continue with this marriage?"

"It's supposed to let you know where you stand, which is right beside me all the way."

"Strange, I didn't hear it like that. Do you know, people like me seldom say what we mean, what we really think. Everything is said pleasantly to hide the ugliness. Or else it's smoothed over to avoid trouble, to make living easier, nicer. But it's always there under the surface. I'm tired of living with what's under the surface, Edison."

"You're my wife, and that's that."

"Even with my halo so tarnished?" The words were mocking.

"We'll go into that later."

"I am to repent then? Sorry but I'm not in the mood. This marriage, if you can call it that, is over."

"You won't leave me and the prospect of being the governor's lady, not for some dago who owns a drug-ridden eating-and-drinking joint."

"Maybe, maybe not. But I won't stay for a shallow, egoistical man who can't control his temper, his desires, or even his own orgasms."

"You'll be back," he said, knotting his fist and raising it toward her. She didn't answer. She went out, quietly closing the door behind her.

Edison seethed with the sense of ill-usage inside him. Someone had tried to kill him, his son was lying half dead in the hospital, and his cold cunt of a wife had suddenly found somebody to heat her up. His career was in jeopardy because of this plane crash and the way the public was going to react to his competence at the controls. And if that weren't enough, his wife was threatening to make a laughingstock of him, plus finish him off at the polls by leaving him.

He glanced at his watch, then threw himself down on the couch and reached for the remote control fastened to the nearest end table. The news was on. There was a political story from Washington, then his own face leaped off the screen at him. Plane crash—bad weather—approach to the runway too low. There was a shot of the wreckage that sent a shiver running along Edison's spine as he wondered how anyone could have gotten out alive, much less two people. Then there he was hurrying into the hospital as the stretcher carrying Josh was wheeled inside. God, but he looked wild, shaky as all hell. He couldn't even remember the cameras being there. If he had realized, he'd have played it cooler. The female commentator oozed sympathy, but that changed as she began to talk about the possibility of an investigation into the crash.

An investigation! He had to think. Somebody was going to find out about the automatic pilot. What then? Could the fact that it had been tampered with be turned to his advantage, used to create voter sympathy? Or would the search for a reason lead to questions he didn't want, questions that might just open up the barrel of snakes he had been trying to keep a lid on for so long?

As the picture on the screen switched to scenes of the damage from a tornado in east Texas, he snapped off the TV. God, he was sweating. He didn't like it. He rubbed his hands together to get rid of the moisture on his palms. He clenched a fist, then opened it, looked at it.

He shouldn't have hit Anne. Not that she didn't deserve it; it just hadn't been smart. He needed her, needed the façade she presented. Everything had to look nice and normal. But who would have dreamed she would find another man? How could she do that to him? And threatening to leave him now, in the middle of the campaign. He couldn't believe it. And the man she chose, that dago Dante, Riva's friend. His wife had stolen Riva's man. What a laugh!

Or was it? Suppose it was Dante who had made the move on Anne? Suppose Riva had put him up to it? That had to be it. Anne never would have stepped out of place otherwise. And it would be just like Riva, the conniving bitch. She was the cause of his troubles, all of them. If it wasn't for her, he'd have been home free all those years ago. But no, she had to be there. She was always there, getting in his way, seeing what she ought not see, messing up his mind, threatening him.

He had thought he had that settled. It was one reason he went out of town, so as to be far from the scene. He had waited all weekend, but there had been nothing on the tube about an accident involving Riva, not a damn thing. Just went to show you couldn't trust anybody.

But wait. What if Riva had found out? What if she had not only put a stop to what he had arranged for her but had turned it against him? God, that was scary. She had nearly killed him. Who would have thought she had those kinds of connections, that kind of guts? She was a deep one; there had always been more there than he could figure, even when she was a kid.

Edison settled back on the sofa. He had to think about this thing. He had to think about just what he was going to do. He couldn't just leave it alone. Not now. Besides, he still wanted her ass. God, how he wanted her ass.

"Why didn't you tell me?"

It was a cry of pain. Erin was on her feet in an instant with shimmering tears rising in her eyes. Doug Gorsline, who had been sitting across from her as they played a quiet game of gin rummy, stood also. His thin young face was dark with concern as his gaze rested on Erin.

"I would have if I had known," Riva said quietly. "The crash happened earlier, but Liz only just heard it on the news in the kitchen and came to tell me."

That was not the whole truth. Edison had called, but he had sounded so strung-out and been so abusive that Abraham had told him Riva was not at home. Since he had shouted something about a plane crash, the butler had gone to the kitchen to turn on the small TV Liz used to keep up with her favorite programs while she cooked. It was Liz who had hurried at once to tell Riva what had taken place, leaving Abraham still dithering about whether to disturb her or not over the call.

"Josh, what about Josh?" Erin asked.

"He's at Oshner's. They gave his condition as guarded, whatever that may mean."

"I've got to go to him, see him. Do you think they'll let me in?" Erin's gaze as she looked at Riva was trusting, expectant, as if she thought the woman she knew as her aunt must have all the answers.

"I don't know. I imagine it depends on—on how bad he is. But there's really nothing you can do."

"I have to try, anyway."

"Are you sure? Even if you can see him, it will be for a few seconds at the most. From the sound of it, I doubt he'll be able to talk to you. We can call and find out his condition, if that's what you want."

Riva didn't care for the idea of Erin being around Edison just now. He was sure to be at the hospital, and if he was as wild as Abraham had indicated that he sounded on the phone, then there was no way to guess what he might do, what he might say. Moreover, if, as she suspected, it was he who had tried to have her kidnapped or killed, once he learned the attempt had failed he might try to strike at her again through Erin.

"No, I want to go," the girl insisted, her voice rising. "I want to be there."

"I really don't think you should drive since you're this upset, and the limousine is in no shape for use." Riva had no right to forbid her daughter to go, though she wished she did. More than likely, it would have done no good; Erin was too old for such tactics, and too independent, like her mother.

"I'll drive her," Doug said.

"Oh, would you?" Erin said, turning to him and putting out her hand to take his in a blind gesture of thanks. "That's great. Are you sure you don't mind?"

"Ready when you are," he answered.

If there was any jealousy for her concern about another man in Doug's mind, he was good at keeping it from his face, Riva thought. "I'm sure you have the best of intentions, Doug, but I doubt Josh's parents will be happy at the arrival of a newspaper photographer."

"Then I won't go as one. I'll lock my camera in the car, scout's honor."

"I can't see how it will matter what he is," Erin protested. "I'm sure the Gallants won't mind so long as he's with me."

Riva made no further objections but came to an instant decision. If Erin had to go, then she herself would be there to protect her. Noel had said she should not leave the house alone just now, but she would not be alone if she was following Erin and Doug, nor would she be unprotected herself; she would see to that. "I'll go, too."

"You don't have to," Erin said.

"No, but I may as well be there as sitting here worrying. Besides, if I drive my car, I can bring you back here afterward. That way, Doug won't have to make the trip again." It was an excuse, of course, but one she hoped Erin would not recognize.

"I don't mind," Doug said.

She gave the photographer a faint smile. "I know, but I do. It wouldn't be fair to impose on you."

"Please do."

Her smile grew warmer. "Maybe another time."

It was well after dark by the time they reached the hospital. They made their way to the intensive care unit where the normal rules of visiting hours were permanently suspended. The waiting room attached to it was a place with grubby chairs and lounges, crumpled newspapers and dog-eared magazines, and wastebaskets that overflowed at this time of night with Styrofoam coffee cups and cold drink cans. There was no longer anyone manning the phone there at that hour, but friends and relatives could call the nurses in ICU for a report of their patient's condition.

Anne Gallant was sitting alone, turning the pages of a magazine. She tossed it aside and got to her feet when she saw them enter. Erin went to her at once and enfolded her in a quick hug. "How is he?"

"Still holding his own," Anne said, her smile dim as she drew back.

Riva met the eyes of Josh's mother over her own daughter's shoulder. The look Anne Gallant gave her was intent and questioning, yet held a hint of embarrassment. A moment later, her attention was claimed once more by Erin.

"Do you think they'll let me see him?" the young woman was asking.

Anne glanced at her watch. "They aren't letting anyone in, though you can see him through a glass partition during the ICU visiting periods every four hours. It's nearly time now."

"That would be something at least."

"Just be prepared. He's . . . different, pale, even waxy, and with bandages practically to his eyebrows. He hasn't opened his eyes or made a sound since—since the surgery." Anne's voice caught. Tears welled up in her eyes, and she wiped them away distractedly.

"Will you come with me?" Erin said.

"They only allow one at a time and then just for a few seconds. You go first, and when you come back, I'll go. You can wait at the door at the end of the hall if you like. It shouldn't be long."

Doug went with Erin to keep her company during the wait. Riva was left alone with Anne. They sat down, trying to relax in chairs that had conformed to the shapes of too many bodies through too many long nights. Silence crept in upon them, broken only by the muted ring of a bell tone followed by an announcement in the corridor outside the room.

Anne spoke. "Josh and Erin really are alike, aren't they, extremely alike."

It was a declaration of sorts, a means of conveying a message without actually saying it. To Riva, it was a relief. There was no longer a need to guess where she stood.

"Yes, they are," Riva answered. "They could almost be true brother and sister, couldn't they? I'm sorry about your son, and the accident."

Anne looked up at her with so much pain in her eyes that she seemed ten years older. "Do you know anything about it?"

"Well, no, not really. I only heard about it a short time ago."

"You're sure?"

"Is there some reason I should?" Riva's tone was perplexed, her gaze steady on that of the other woman.

"You know, I believe you."

A shudder ran through Anne and she looked down at her hands, aimlessly clasping and unclasping them. At that angle of her head, Riva could see the shadow of a recent bruise, only partially concealed by makeup, on her jaw. "I think," she said slowly, "that you're going to have to explain that."

"I suppose. Edison—Edison has this theory that you might have arranged the plane crash."

"What? No!"

"There is some question of foul play." The words were hollow, almost toneless.

Riva's mind raced, selecting and rejecting possibilities. "I see. And am I supposed to have done this in retaliation?"

Anne looked up with a frown between her eyes. "I don't know what you mean. I presumed it to have been more in revenge."

They were obviously talking at cross purposes. Edison's wife did not seem to know about the attack on Riva and her driver. Quickly Riva outlined what had taken place. In return, Anne told her the little she had been able to gather about how and why the plane had gone down short of the runway.

Riva gave a slow, disbelieving shake of her head. "Just how am I supposed to have managed this? Did I track down a mechanic with expertise in electronics, or did I just call my local hitman?"

"Neither. The idea is that most likely you called Dante Romoli."

"Dante?"

Riva stared at the other woman. Anne Gallant did not avoid her gaze but returned it steadily. At last Riva said, "And if Dante was so obliging as to consent, who did he do it for? Me or you?"

A spasm crossed Anne's face, as if she had clenched her jaw together. Hot color rose under her skin. "I see you know about us. And I thought I was being so careful. It seems I'm not cut out for this hole-in-the-corner business. But the question really isn't important, is it? What's important is: Would he do it at all?"

"You don't know?"

It was ignoble of her, Riva thought, to make that small dig, but she couldn't help it. She had no right to be jealous of Dante, and, in fact, had never resented the long line of females who occupied his bed for a night or a weekend. But the others had not been a threat to his loyalty to her and she had known it. Anne Gallant might be different.

"I honestly don't think he would," Anne said in painful concentration, "but then it's true that I told him I would rather be a widow than go through a messy divorce. Beyond that is his relationship with you. I understand that it's . . . special since he won't discuss it, but I don't know how deep it goes or how far he will go for it."

"I would hate to think it depended on that alone."

"You've known him for years while I . . . Well, it's only been a matter of days for me. Surely you can tell me?"

"I wish I could. I can see how you would think that I could. But there are some parts of Dante's life he doesn't share, parts where I don't intrude. This is one."

Anne shook her head. "I'm so confused. He seemed someone to trust, so sympathetic, so compassionate. And now my son is lying there . . ."

"Don't think about it."

"How can I not? What if Dante did do this thing? Something will have to be done to prevent him from doing it again. We—you and I—can't just do nothing."

"I don't intend to do nothing. I'll talk to him, though I'm not sure what it will gain. If he's innocent, it's not likely he can prove it, and if not, he won't be foolish enough to confess it, even to me."

Riva had hardly finished speaking when a man's tall form appeared in the doorway. Catching a glimpse of that arrival from the corners of her eyes, she looked around. It was Edison. Annoyance and uneasiness washed over her. She had begun to think she might get through this visit without having to see him.

He checked an instant when he recognized her, then came on at a deliberately slow walk. "Well, well. What's this, a hen party?"

There was no point in answering as far as Riva was concerned, nor did Edison's wife seem inclined to reply. Riva stood up, her gaze on Anne. "It must be almost time for the two of you to see Josh. If you'll excuse me, I'll go find myself a cup of coffee."

"There's a snack room with a coffee machine down the hall and around the corner," the other woman offered. "What you get isn't great, but it's hot."

Riva neither avoided Edison's stare nor held it as she moved around him. Still, she breathed easier when she was out in the corridor. The situation was an odd one, and she wasn't sure how to handle it. What did you say to a man you are sure has tried to have you killed, one who thinks you may have hired someone to kill him? Ordinary politeness didn't quite seem to cover it, but if there was not enough evidence to make accusations, what was the alternative?

She hoped Erin's need to see Josh was satisfied and they could go home soon. Confrontations of this kind, no matter how civil, were hard on the nerves.

Anne was right, the coffee was hot. Riva sat down with her full Styrofoam cup at one of the Formica-topped tables. The chair was plastic and cold to the touch. Hospitals were always cold, even in the summer with their superefficient air-conditioning and especially at night. She stirred powdered creamer into her coffee, then lifted a hand to the back of her neck, massaging the taut muscles there, moving her head back and forth to ease the tension.

There was an older woman standing at one of the cold-drink machines. She wore her hair in a bun and had on a polyester pants suit that drooped on her thin frame like washing hanging on a limp line. The woman inserted her money and made her choice, and the can came tumbling down. With the diet drink in her hand, the woman flashed Riva the sympathy-tinged smile usually exchanged by hospital visitors. Turning, she shuffled from the room.

"How very nice of her to leave us alone," Edison said with savage politeness from behind Riva. "I was hoping we could have a moment to talk."

Riva almost knocked her coffee over as she swung around, but caught it just before it tipped. She used a napkin from the holder on the table to clean up the spill. Busy at the job, she said, "I would have thought you'd want to see your son."

"It won't help him." The words were serious, almost as if he expected her to be impressed by his excuse.

"Suppose he doesn't make it? Suppose—"

"Oh, Josh is going to make it; you don't have to worry about that. Your worry is whether you'll make it. Or whether I'll make you."

"Crude. But I never expected anything else from you."

"What you expect and what you get are definitely two different things. Anne says you had a little run-in with two men and an Uzi. I'll bet you never expected that."

How sure of himself he was. He had hardly lowered his voice. Certainly he thought he could handle anything she threw at him. It made her want to look for the biggest rock she could find.

She said, "It was a surprise, yes. It was nearly as much of one as you finding your runway too close for comfort."

"So it's a standoff, right?"

"It might be, except for one detail."

"Which is?"

"I had nothing to do with your problem at the airport. You'll have to think who else would like to see you dead."

"Besides you."

"Oh, yes, I'm in there among their number. From where I sit, though, it's quite a crowd."

He gave her a loose-lipped grin. "There are a lot of people who appreciate me, too."

"Women, I suppose you mean? I can't say much for their taste."

"There was a time when you liked me well enough."

"You're kidding yourself. I was overwhelmed by grief and my own sexual urges. It had nothing to do with you."

"Maybe, if that's what you want to think. But there was certainly Beth."

"Who died because of you, not a great recommendation. I wonder how many others have wound up sorry they ever had anything to do with you."

"There were more who were sorry they didn't."

"Like Margaret, who paid later for getting away years ago?"

"Yeah, and one or two others, like that bitch of a civil rights worker. She laughed at me, laughed out loud when I made a pass. She didn't laugh long, I saw to that. And I saw to it that you kept your mouth shut, too."

Something clicked in Riva's mind, but she could not stop long enough to grasp it in the midst of their verbal exchange. "That only proves my point. This may come as a shock, Edison, but you aren't universally loved. Odd, isn't it, for a man who wants to be governor?"

"God, what a smart mouth. I'd like to—"

"Excuse me, Candidate," she said abruptly as she rose to her feet and picked up her purse to tuck it under her arm, leaving her coffee. "I think I've heard this part of your speech before."

"No, you don't! Not this time." He shot out a hand to grab her wrist, yanking her back toward him.

She was ready. She gave her wrist a quick twist, breaking his grasp. In a second, she was in the corridor. Safe. Or was she? Behind her, she heard the quick scrape of his footfalls.

The long, highly polished hallway was empty, the only thing in sight a cart of cleaning supplies far down the way. She could scream, but her mind could not accept that she was in real danger in the middle of an enormous medical complex filled with doctors, nurses, technicians, aides, patients, and visitors.

Then it was too late. He tackled her from behind with a hard arm at her waist, then shoved her toward a door marked SUPPLY CLOSET. The door swung open and an automatic light came on. She was thrown inside. She had a glimpse of shelves stacked with bundles of paper towels, bed liners, toilet tissue rolls, and neat rows of bottles and spray cans of disinfectant and deodorizer. Then the light was cut off as the door slammed shut, and she was freefalling into darkness.

She lost her purse as she hit the shelves, and red bursts of pain exploded behind her eyelids. She cried out, stunned that Edison would risk so much. Hard hands brushed her in the blackness, closing on handfuls of her dress bodice and twisting in the silk to haul her against him.

She gasped as he closed a hand on her breast. To bring her knee up between his legs was an instantaneous reflex. He shifted away, cursing as he squeezed the tender globe of her breast. Sickness moved inside her. She hit out at him with her fist. She wanted to scream, but there was no time, no breath. She needed it to fight.

He pulled at her, forcing her against him. She clawed for his eyes. He whipped his head away, striking out. The blow caught her across the temple. For a moment there was a blurring, fading sensation. She clutched at the shelves, rattling bottles and cans and sweeping them onto the floor so that they thudded and clanged. Her fingers closed around the cool metal of a spray can.

The top was on it. She needed two hands to twist it off. Bracing her back against the shelf for support, she struck at Edison's head with it, hammering once, twice. He was cursing in a low and steady monotone, threatening, ridiculing her efforts as he reached for the can. She evaded his grasping fingers, holding the can far over her head.

With a sudden jerk, he pulled her feet from under her. Her hip burned as she scraped along the shelf, then he was upon her on the floor. The can bounded from her hand and went rolling as she struck the floor. She dragged herself after it on her elbows, while Edison plunged onto his knees behind her, wrenching her skirts upward.

For a moment, just a moment, she let him dig his fingers into her flesh as he rubbed the hard lump of himself against her. She scrambled after the spinning, skittering can as he tore at her panty hose. She heard the sheer nylon shredding, felt the give as the hose was peeled away. She caught the can in both hands.

The can top broke free. Instantly, she whipped around, pointed the can where she thought his face would be, and pressed the button. Edison gave a hoarse cry and fell backward. She shoved him, wrenching her legs from under him.

Too slow. He sprang back, grabbing for her hair, sinking his fingers into it and clenching them until it felt as if the strands were being torn from the roots. Then under her she felt her purse.

She fumbled for it, pulled it open, pushed her hand inside. She closed her fingers around the small pistol, which she had tucked inside before she left the house, the one Cosmo had given her. She pulled the pistol out, rammed it into Edison's belly.

"Stop right there!" she cried.

It was in that instant that the closet door opened. The light came on. Anne was highlighted in the doorway. She seemed to take in the situation at a glance: Riva sprawled with her skirts above her waist, her underclothing torn, and the gun in her hand. Edison crouching over her with his eyes red and tearing and a murderous grimace on his face. In one smooth forward motion, without apparent thought or effort, she stepped into the closet, picked up a metal-handled broom, and swung it in a hard, level blow at her husband's head.

There was a dull crack. The twisted fury on Edison's face vanished as his features went blank. He wavered for an instant, then toppled forward like a sack of potatoes.

"Quick, before somebody comes," Anne said.

Riva was already pushing herself upright and getting to her feet. She shoved the pistol back into the depths of her purse and straightened her clothes, checking for damage. There was comparatively little. She put her hand on Anne's arm. Her voice husky, she said, "Thanks."

"You're welcome. In fact, it was my pleasure. Now, could you help me get him out into the hall?"

"Yes, all right. But what are we going to—"

"I think he had a dizzy spell, probably from the effects of the plane crash only just now showing up, don't you think? He hit his head as he fell."

"I . . . yes," Riva said. "Yes, I see."

They dragged him out into the open. They had not quite got him into position near the wall when a man in a lab coat rounded the far corner, coming from the direction of the ICU. Immediately, Anne dropped to her knees, patting Edison's face, the blows a little harder than necessary.

"Oh, Doctor," she called. "Help me, please! My husband has passed out!"

21

She owed Margaret an apology, Riva thought as she watched the dark highway roll toward her on the drive back to Bonne Vie. She had been sure her sister had refused to go to the police with the story of her assault by Edison out of a need to deny it had happened, so that she could deny her own part in causing it, and also because of fear of what people would say if the tale was made public. It had never occurred to her that Margaret might have been merely protecting her sense of personal privacy. Riva still didn't know the exact reason why Margaret had refrained. But she knew that she herself would not have called in the authorities if Edison had succeeded in his attack. The last thing she wanted was to have to deal with the police.

Edison's behavior defied understanding. What made him think he had the right to harass a woman and attempt to force his attentions on her? When had he become so sure of himself that he thought he could get away with it? It was women like Margaret and herself, she supposed, who failed to charge him with his crimes of assault and therefore permitted him to indulge in his egomania, but there had to be some basic fault in his thinking in the first place.

She was not detached enough to follow his mental processes or even to be curious about them for long. She loathed him for the pain and apprehension and weakness he had made her feel. She did not like acknowledging these things. To know that she must face them left her with a disturbing sense of vulnerability.

That he had not succeeded in his attempt was a victory of sorts.

She was fiercely glad of it, and grateful to Anne for the part she had played. At the same time, Riva had a terrible need to wipe out those few minutes in the closet, to forget they had ever happened. It was important to her sense of self to do so. She would like to wipe out the past, too, to change it so that she had never known Edison, never fallen prey to him. She couldn't do that. Even if time itself had not made it impossible, she would not efface those few weeks simply because Erin had resulted from them. She might not be able to acknowledge her as her daughter; still, Erin made what she had gone through worthwhile.

She was bruised, and not just in body. There was an essential part of herself that had been damaged. Even more than the attempt on the river road, this personal attack had undermined her defenses. She wondered if the only way to make it right again wasn't some form of retaliation, even revenge. There were some who would call it justice if she destroyed him. Was it wrong to take personal vengeance in the name of public good?

Did it really matter?

Edison was right. She could not ruin him without ruining herself. He would bring her down with him. It was fine to bluff and bluster and make threats. The truth was, she was not sure she could carry them out. Once she might have been able to do it, once, before Noel had kissed her. Now she could almost glimpse a faint hope of happiness. It seemed that somehow she and Cosmo's son might work out their differences, might overcome past misconceptions and build toward something fine and good in the future. But not if Noel knew what she had been, what she had done. He had accepted so much; he could not be expected to swallow that as well. It wasn't the disgrace of it that she feared so much as the deceit all these years. He was not a man who could easily forgive such a large lie. To have it exposed would, perforce, call into question everything she had ever said, everything ever said about her. That would be insupportable.

Erin, on the front seat beside Riva, did not have much to say. The younger woman was withdrawn, staring out the side window, as if seeing Josh had subdued her normally ebullient spirits. Death was still an abstract at twenty-four; seeing how close it could come was always a shock.

Riva had said nothing to Erin about the incident in the closet. she had repaired her appearance in the restroom before joining the others: brushed her hair, checked that her bruises were covered by her clothing, pulled off her torn panty hose, and thrown them in the trash. There were no outward signs of her inward disquiet. That being so, there was no point in burdening Erin with an account of Edison's perfidy. Her daughter had enough to upset her. Besides, if the police were not to be called in, there was no reason to mention it at all. The fewer who knew, the better it would be.

"You don't like Josh, do you?"

Riva swung her head sharply at Erin's question. In the light from the dashboard, the younger woman's eyes held accusation, but also a species of suspended judgment.

"Why do you say that?" Riva asked. It was a bid for time, nothing more.

"You didn't go in to see him. Anyway, it's what Josh thinks. He told me before he left on this trip with his dad."

"It wouldn't have helped Josh for me to see him, since he wouldn't even have known I was there. Anyway, I like him well enough."

"Just not well enough to think I should go to Colorado with him."

"I really don't see what difference it makes whether I like him or not. It isn't me he's coming to Bonne Vie to see."

"Maybe not, but he admires you, thinks it's great the way you handle things, business and social situations and all that. He can't figure out what you have against him, and it bothers him. He wishes you liked him."

It had never occurred to Riva that Josh was astute enough to pick up on her misgivings about him. How easy it was to hurt people without knowing it or meaning it. She didn't dislike him, of course; she was just uncomfortable having him around her daughter and reluctant to encourage his visits. But how was she to explain that without getting into things that could never be spoken of?

Choosing her words with care, she said, "Josh is a nice enough young man. It's just that I would rather you didn't get too serious about anyone just now."

"You seemed pretty welcoming to Doug Gorsline." There was a shadow of resentment in Erin's tone. It didn't make Doug Gorsline's chances sound good.

"Was I? Well, he's a nice young man, too. Don't you like him?" The trouble with asking intimate questions was that it gave others the right to ask them in return. It was just as well that Erin discovered that fact early.

"What's not to like?" the young woman answered with a quick shrug. "He may not be knock'em-dead handsome, but he's smart and funny and he listens to what you have to say."

"But you like Josh better?"

"I didn't say that. It's a different kind of thing, really. With Josh, it's as if I've known him all my life."

Greatly daring, Riva suggested, "Like a brother."

"Sort of," Erin agreed, "but not quite."

Riva did not have the nerve just now to go into what that meant. She allowed it to pass.

They were on the river road. They had left the traffic behind for the most part. It was late; the Sunday night church crowd had long gone home to bed, as had everyone who was honest and neither dating nor partying. The air conditioner in the car hummed, an undertone to the muted rumble of the engine. The night was overcast, though the rain had stopped as the storm from the gulf moved farther inland away from them. In the still-damp night beyond the car windows could be heard snatches of sound: the whir of insects, the croak of a frog from some canal, the call of a nocturnal bird. It was peaceful, and there had been so many uneasy nights of late, that Riva began to feel sleepy.

There was a flash of light as the headlamps of a car fast approaching from behind caught her car's side mirror. The speed of the vehicle, the way it was overtaking them, sent a tremor of alarm through Riva. It was too much of a reminder of what had happened on this stretch of road only two days ago. There was nothing to be afraid of, she tried to tell herself; it was probably just some Romeo heading home after a hectic weekend, anxious to get in a little sack time before the grind began again on Monday morning. Regardless, it seemed Noel was right: she should not have gone out without George, at least, for protection.

The car dimmed its headlights as it drew nearer. Closer it came, and closer still, as if getting ready to pass. Riva held her speed.

Abruptly, the headlights of the car flashed on bright for long seconds. They dimmed again. The car began to slacken speed, dropping back. At a reasonable following distance, it held its place, keeping pace.

Riva increased her speed. The car accelerated also. She slowed. It slowed. At a straight stretch she both slowed and moved as far as possible to the right in an invitation to pass. The following car failed to take advantage of the opportunity.

Coincidence. That was it. Maybe Romeo happened to feel like traveling at the same speed she did or else lived not too far ahead so that passing wasn't worth the effort. Riva stared into her mirrors, both side and rearview, but could not identify the car as that of one of her neighbors. In fact, the car was so obscured by the glare of its headlights that she could not see it well enough to recognize it. Regardless, it held its position and the miles slid away behind them both.

At last the drive for Bonne Vie appeared. Riva flicked on her turn indicator and slowed. The car behind slowed also. She turned into the drive. The car made the turn behind her.

Riva pressed down on the gas, racing up the drive. Erin clutched the door, turning toward her in amazement. "Aunt Riva, what—"

"Listen to me," Riva interrupted. "When I stop in front of the door, I want you to jump out and run into the house. Don't look back. Don't stop. Just run."

"Why? Is it those men again?"

"I don't know. Just do as I say."

Erin searched her face in the green dashlight. "What about you?"

"I'll be right behind you."

Riva swung the wheel in the turn before the house with a spray of shell and gravel. She jammed on the brakes. Erin threw open the door and ran. By the time Riva had released her seat belt and got out, the younger woman was up the steps and across the gallery.

Abraham was waiting up for them, with the front door swung open. Erin plunged inside, then looked back. She stopped and started laughing.

Riva turned her head. In the light from the fixture hanging under the gallery, she saw a bright red Alfa Romeo.

She slammed her car door and stalked back to where Dante was getting out of his sports car. "Damn you," she cried. "You scared me half to death!"

"Sorry," he said, smiling, though his eyes were dark. "At least it made you speak to me. I was afraid you wouldn't."

"Because you abused my hospitality by taking Anne Gallant to the cabin? That's entirely your own affair."

He grimaced. "I thought that might be you on the phone. Not many people have that number, and no one else knew I was there."

"Very clever."

"Not clever enough. I got caught. Will you let me come in and explain—and defend myself against this idiotic idea that I might have tried to kill Edison?"

"Is it so idiotic?"

He was silent for a moment and there was pain in the depths of his eyes. "I can understand Anne; she doesn't really know me and she's upset over her son. But I can't understand you, Riva, never you."

Riva looked away from him with a sigh. "I suppose she called you, told you about our talk?"

"Yes. Could I come in?"

She had promised to find out what she could from him about the airplane crash. It might as well be now. She gave her assent and led the way into the house.

Abraham was still on guard. Dante shook his head at the butler's offer of coffee and cake, and Riva also refused before dismissing the elderly man. Erin had apparently gone up to bed, for she was nowhere in sight. There was a light in the library, a sign that Noel might still be up. Otherwise the house was dark and quiet.

Riva led the way into the parlor on the opposite side of the hall and shut the door. Dante did not wait for her to face him. To her

336 •

back, he said, "I didn't do it. I know my saying it doesn't mean much, but I have to tell you I didn't do it."

She released the doorknob and turned to look at him. "I want to believe you, really I do. The only problem is, someone did it, and you had the best opportunity—plus an excellent motive."

"Anne being the motive, and my supposed mafia connections the opportunity?"

"Can you deny either?"

"Not on the face of it, no. What bothers me is that I should have to deny it to you."

"Anne seemed to think that was another reason, that you might have done it for me."

"I might have, if you had asked me."

"Don't!" she said sharply.

"Why not? It's the truth."

"It doesn't make it any easier for me to believe you!"

"I can't help that."

"But it turns me into something I'm not, don't you see?" she cried. "You set me up as a madonna, a woman somehow pure and impossibly good, someone worth that kind of sacrifice of your principles. I'm not like that! I'm just me. I don't want to be worshiped. I want to be loved with all my faults, in full knowledge of them. I just want to be loved!"

His face appeared as if carved in stone. "I've always known that what I felt wasn't enough. That doesn't mean I would kill for you in the hope of making it more."

"If you didn't make the attempt, either for Anne or for me, then who did?"

The door that led into the dining room creaked as it opened. "Excuse me for eavesdropping," Constance said as she sauntered into the room, "but I have been wandering around in total boredom all night, looking for something to do, and I find this conversation too fascinating to miss. Besides, I have a thing or two to add to it."

Surprise held Riva silent. She watched the other woman as she moved toward Dante with the amber silk of the robe she wore outlining her curves with lascivious fidelity. Constance spread her arms in a gesture that was wholly Italian, one that encompassed and, at the same time, asked that she be viewed as totally candid.

"I have interfered in your life, Dante Romoli," Noel's former wife said, "I admit it. My reasons were—well, I will tell them to you sometime, if you are interested. Never mind that now. It was I who suggested to Riva that you had taken Anne Gallant with you to the mountains."

Dante's brows met over his dark eyes in a frown as he stared at her. "You did what?"

The woman walked right up to Dante, so close it almost seemed she would fling her arms around him. She stopped short of that, but the look she gave him from under her lashes was bold. "It was an impulse; I'm very impulsive when I'm angry. But to repair the damage in some small way, and to satisfy my own suspicions, I made a few inquiries among family connections here in New Orleans—Sicilian family, you understand? I am ready to swear that you are not the person who arranged to have the plane of Edison Gallant—shall we say?—fixed."

There was absolute silence for the space of ten full seconds. Dante studied the Sicilian princess as if he had never seen her before. Constance returned his gaze with an embarrassing lack of reserve.

At last Riva said to the other woman, "Do you know who did do it?"

"That isn't the kind of information one is freely given," Constance answered without taking her gaze from Dante's.

"But they gave you the other?"

"Yes."

"Did they, by chance, tell you who hired the men to attack me and my driver?"

Constance turned to give Riva a mocking stare. "That was Edison; the fact was mentioned to me in passing, as a matter of curiosity. Edison has been . . . acquainted with these connections for some time, at least to the point of taking their money. They have been reassessing their support of him in the last few days, however. He's been getting greedy, asking for too much. He attempted to talk them into undermining Staulet Corporation, buying up stock for a hostile takeover bid, but too much was held by you and Noel for it to succeed."

Attempting to attack the company was, Riva thought, just another avenue explored with the design of bringing her to her knees. It might well have worked.

Constance turned back to Dante. "It seems Gallant also asked his 'friends' to concentrate on your place on the lake for distribution of the drug Ecstasy. This was done out of spite. You were a friend of Riva's, therefore he wanted to make trouble for you. There now! You see how I trouble myself for you? Aren't you grateful?"

"Immeasurably," Dante said, his voice without expression. "And do your informants intend to go on trying to ruin me?"

"I think not," Constance said, pursing her full lips. "I told them it was stupid, but they knew it already. With all of Gallant's demands, plus the request for men to attack Riva, it begins to appear to them that their candidate is unstable. They talk of abandoning him. I would imagine the recent accident, with its whiff of incompetence and personal enemies, will make it certain."

Riva frowned in concentration as she spoke. "I still don't see why, if you found out so much, you can't find out who caused the crash."

Constance gave a shake of her head, which ruffled her dark hair. "I heard a lot of excuses, but I think it may be that it wasn't done through the families. In other words, they don't know."

"This business of the restaurant on the lake," Riva said to Dante. "Surely some of your so-called friends could have told you Edison was behind it?"

Dante shrugged. "My friends are just that, friends I made when I was a teenager working around the French Market and the restaurants; they are not in any way business contacts. If one of them heard a rumor, discovered something concerning me, they might tell me. But their influence does not extend throughout the entire New Orleans mafia."

"Then why the secrecy all these years?"

"People don't understand. Anyway, it's not something you discuss, or those involved don't remain friends, and some of them I've known as long as I've known you, or even longer."

"To Italian men, such friendships are a bond to match that of brothers." Constance reached to put her hand on Dante's arm, smoothing it slowly up and down.

Constance's patronizing tone set Riva's teeth on edge. Dante appeared not to hear it. Riva could only suppose, given her actions, that Constance was being so helpful toward him because she was attracted to him. If that was so, Dante must take his chances. He seemed to be adept at juggling his women.

"Anyway," she said to him, "I still think you might have asked and saved Constance the trouble."

Still Dante did not look at Riva. "I might have, except I was afraid of the answer."

"What do you mean?" Riva's voice held impatience.

Dante glanced at her then. "I knew I had been set up. Everything pointed to it: the overnight appearance of the drug, the great quantities available at the club but not at other places nearby, the new people who had appeared, people with bad reputations and plenty of money to spend."

"You never said a word."

"I didn't want to accuse someone who might be innocent."

"Such as?"

Dante's face hardened, and he reached to clamp his hand on Constance's hand, which she was sliding up his arm to his neck. "Such as your houseguest here."

Dull color surged into the woman's face. She jerked her hand free and stood massaging her wrist. "What are you saying?"

At the same time, there came the sound of sharp, steady clapping behind them. They swung around to see Noel leaning in the doorway, applauding. How long he had been there was impossible to say, but it was obviously long enough for him to have a good idea of what was taking place. His hair was ruffled, as if he had been running his fingers through it while he worked, and under his arm he carried a sheaf of profit-and-loss statements. He inclined his head toward Dante as he said with quiet emphasis, "Congratulations. It's not often men see through the lady so quickly."

Constance gave her ex-husband a fulminating look, clenching her hands into fists, before she turned back to Dante. "Explain what you meant. Explain at once!"

"By all means, Romoli, let's hear it," Noel agreed.

Dante cleared his throat. "Well, it was like this. I'm not exactly Prince Charming, so I was a little surprised at first at getting a play from the princess. When it kept up, I became downright suspicious, especially when I realized that our conversation always came around to you, Riva. I began to realize just how much Constance disliked you."

"Me?" Riva asked, frowning. "But why?"

"You need not try to look so innocent," Constance exclaimed. "You destroyed my marriage."

"That's crazy," Riva protested.

"Hah!"

Riva glanced at Noel, but his face gave away nothing of his thoughts. He was looking at Dante. "You were saying, Romoli?"

"I was saying that Constance seemed so set on collecting my scalp, and so big on vendettas in general, that I was forced to wonder if she wasn't using me to score off Riva. On top of that, she was more interested in the club than it deserved for someone who makes a habit of going to places such as Maxim's. The old Sicilians were just like what she was saying about Edison; they used to carry their acts of revenge against an enemy even to the close friends of that enemy. I couldn't be sure Constance had New Orleans connections, but it made sense that she might. I had to suspect, then, that she was setting me up. It seemed that if I didn't succumb to her charms, thereby hurting Riva, she might blow the whistle on the drug situation she had created at the club."

"Such a thing never crossed my mind!" Constance cried.

"For which we must be thankful?" Noel said.

His ex-wife faced him. "Truly, I would not have carried a vendetta so far. And if I had thought to do so, I would have had the sense not to be so obvious about it!"

The lean planes of Noel's face did not relax. "I think I believe you, on both counts."

"Oh, you're impossible!" Constance swung away from him.

Riva stirred. "Where does that leave us?"

Constance, her arms crossed over her chest, spoke at once, as if to divert attention from herself. "It could be this is a question for you, Riva. There is still the matter of this man Gallant. From what I can discover, you are the one who would most like to see him dead. Perhaps you arranged it but accuse others to cover your own guilt."

"No," Dante said, his voice sharp. "She would not."

"No?" Constance accepted the reproof with no more than a toss of her head. "Well, then, there is Noel. Gallant was a threat of some kind to Riva, therefore to Staulet Corporation. Protecting the company his father built would be all-important to him."

"No!" Riva said. "Anyway, he had no idea of Edison's trip."

"Didn't he, indeed?" Constance smiled with a sly glance at her husband. "He went to visit him only a short time before, you know."

Riva's eyes widened. Her voice stifled with disbelief, she said, "He what?"

"Odd, isn't it? But I know he went, for I heard him making the calls to find out where this Gallant would be. You did go, didn't you, darling?"

"I saw him," Noel agreed.

"But why?" Riva asked.

Constance answered for him. "He was concerned. About the corporation, of course."

"I was concerned for everything and everybody who might be affected by Gallant's actions. It was important to discover what those actions might be."

Constance gave him a scathing look. "How very reasonable."

"I am that, above all else." Noel returned his ex-wife's gaze with such steady force that the woman looked away.

"And reasonable men," Riva pointed out, "don't usually try to kill, even when others are unreasonable."

She met Noel's gray gaze for only a moment before looking at Dante. There was such sympathy in her old friend's face that she turned away at once. There were times when the ties of friendship could be too close.

"Someone did it," Constance pointed out impatiently.

"Edison must have other enemies." This observation came from Noel.

"That may be," his ex-wife said. "But none have attacked him before this time, and it is here at Bonne Vie that he has caused the most recent disturbance."

Riva could only agree as she thought of Boots and Margaret, and also of Dante and Anne, though they could not really be said to be of Bonne Vie.

Dante gave a tired sigh and rubbed his hand over the back of his head. "This is getting us nowhere. I think I had better go. Anne is alone at the hospital, and someone should sit with her." He looked at Riva. "Will you see me out?"

She followed him from the parlor and into the hall. At the door he turned, taking her hand. "I'm sorry if all this has upset you; I didn't mean to start it. I just couldn't rest knowing you thought I might be to blame for what happened to Josh."

She managed a smile. "If I did, it was only for a moment."

"Thanks for that much." He leaned to press his lips to her forehead in a quick salute. "Good night."

There was a curious tentative quality to the words. She thought that something had changed between them this evening. Whether it was caused by her lack of trust or Constance's belief, her questions put to him or her failure to question Noel's motives, it was as if Dante had withdrawn ever so slightly from her.

Or was the withdrawal within herself? She could not be sure.

When the door had closed upon him, she turned to find Constance directly behind her.

"You warned me not to hurt him," Noel's ex-wife said, "but you have hurt him more than I ever could."

She was right, Riva knew. The ones we care about were the ones who could hurt us the most. Still, it wasn't necessary to admit it to the other woman. Riva said, "Why the concern now?"

"He's a man of strength, and smarter than I expected. Coralie and Pietro like him."

"That isn't a reason."

"I like him very much."

"If you are warning me again, you needn't bother."

One corner of Constance's mouth turned downward. "I can see that, though it's only courteous. I am not, perhaps, so reasonable as Noel, but I am courteous."

Riva, at a loss, said, "Thank you."

"Not at all," Constance said. Turning, she walked with slow grace back toward the stairs at the end of the hall.

Noel had moved to stand in the parlor doorway with one shoulder resting against the frame. He rolled the papers he still held into a tube that he pushed back and forth in his hands. As Constance's footsteps receded on the stairs, the house settled into silence around them.

He said, "I didn't have a chance to ask before: How is Gallant's son?"

"The same," Riva answered, "which is apparently considered good news."

"And Erin?"

"She's all right. She wants to go back to the hospital tomorrow."

"If you expect to go with her again, I hope you'll tell me or at least take George. And you might try to get some rest. You look as if you could use it."

A brief smile curved her lips for his unusual lack of tact, but it did not quite reach her eyes. "I expect so," she answered.

There was an awkward pause. Neither quite met the other's eyes. It was the first time they had been alone since the night before. The tension between them stretched. Riva's pulse began to throb in her head.

Abruptly, Noel pushed away from the door and turned in the direction of his bedroom at the end of the hall. "Well, good night."

Her voice was strained as she called after him. "Noel?"

"Yes?" He swung around to walk back toward her.

For an instant, she forgot what she wanted to ask him. Even when she remembered, she still could not put the question of his guilt to him as bluntly as she had to Dante. She clenched her hands and looked down at them as she searched for words.

"What is it?" he asked.

Finally she looked up. "Did you know that Edison would be leaving for Shreveport, flying his plane?"

The seconds ticked past as he searched her face. "What if I did?"

"I'm just trying to get what happened straight in my mind." But that was not all. Another possibility was slowly creeping in upon her. It was so devastating that she felt the blood drain from her face. She moistened her lips. "What else did he tell you?"

He studied her through narrowed eyes. "A great deal, though none of it very important. Why?"

She could breathe again. He would certainly think her past important since it must, inevitably, reflect on his father and the Staulet Corporation. "There was nothing said—nothing that would cause you to think Edison might be better dead?"

A short laugh escaped from him. "I thought you were satisfied on that point. For the record, I've never made a habit of trying to kill the people who might cause me trouble."

She lifted a hand to her face and was not surprised to find it trembling. "No, no, I know that. I just . . . Somebody did try, and Josh may die. I can't get away from that. Normal people don't do such things, but it's not always easy to tell who is normal."

Quietly he said, "You won't find out by asking."

"No, I suppose not." She herself had said as much to Anne, then forgotten it. She gave him a tight smile, relieved that he wasn't angry, though she did not know why he wasn't; she had fully expected his anger.

The cause was, perhaps, his own abstraction, for he made an aborted gesture, as if he would reach out to touch her. Before it was completed, he drew back as from a fire. He curled his fingers around the tube of papers in his other hand, and the crackling sound was loud as they were crushed.

"What is it?" he asked. "Something's wrong, something more than worry over Josh Gallant, threats against Edison, or even against you. Has someone hurt you?"

That he could read her so well, could see her disturbance when others had not, was disturbing. "Not really."

"But they tried, is that it? Who was it? Gallant's wife?"

She shook her head in a quick negative. "It doesn't matter."

"It does. It can't have been Erin or Doug Gorsline. Gallant then. He must have been at the hospital."

She had seen this relentless quality before in his business dealings, but this was the first time she had experienced it. "It was nothing much—a difference of opinion."

"Over what? Whether you would or would not let him make love to you? I thought so. How far did he go?"

Irritation at his persistence flared through her. "If you want to know if he succeeded, the answer is no!"

"But he tried, tried hard?" When she did not reply, his face hardened. "Why are you protecting him? Why is everyone protecting him? What is it about him that makes you and Margaret and even his wife do it?"

"It could be we're protecting ourselves," she said, her gaze level as she willed him to understand.

"Is that it, or are you all in love with him?"

"Of course not!" she said scornfully.

"You might as well be. The effect's the same, immunity for him for whatever he does."

"It can't be helped."

"Yes, it can, and should be. Men who never have to face the consequences of what they do come to think they are privileged and so do things the average man wouldn't dream of doing."

"Are you saying it's my own fault Edison attacked me?"

"No, but there is an old saying: If an enemy attacks you one time, it's his mistake. The second time, it's yours."

"I don't want revenge, only peace."

"Sometimes they are one and the same, if it puts an end to the danger."

She searched the clear gray depths of his eyes. "I suppose so."

There had always been this hardness somewhere inside him. It had made it possible, all those years ago, for her to believe that he would use her attraction to him to seduce her, then be rid of her. It had been a long time before she could acknowledge that he was as just as he was implacable.

They stood looking at each other for a long moment. He glanced down at the crumpled papers in his hands, then back up to the delicate planes of her face. His gaze lingered on the hollows under her eyes. "Are you all right?"

Did he mean physically or mentally? Was he inquiring, with that general question, if Edison had hurt her or if she was in distress over what had occurred between them the night before? Or did he just want to know if she was going to be able to cope with the fast-moving events? In any case, the answer was the same.

"I'm fine," she said.

He reached to flip the mangled profit-and-loss statements he held onto a silver holding tray on the hall sideboard, then put his arm around her shoulders. "Come on then," he said, "time to go to bed."

For one wild second, she thought he meant with him, hoped he meant with him. It would be an affirmation that the love they had made together meant something. More than that, the thought of lying in his arms was like the prospect of reaching a haven. She wanted nothing more than to lose herself in a man's arms—this man's arms—to forget everything that had happened this week and in the past.

But he released her as they neared the end of the hall where the stairs rose on one side and his bedroom door opened on the other. "Good night," he said again.

"Good night," she answered, and moved away up the stairs, alone. She had reached the upstairs hall before she heard his door close softly behind him.

Riva didn't sleep. She took a bath and put on her gown. She turned out the light, climbed into her bed, and closed her eyes. She fluffed her pillow just so and pulled the sheet to the exact position she liked. It didn't help.

She lay staring into the darkness until her eyes burned. She refused to think of Noel. What was the point? Thinking would not help. She thought instead, deliberately, of Edison.

The words he had said to her, the things he had done, played over and over in her mind. There was something important in them, she knew, something she could not quite capture. She thought until her mind turned in circles, forced herself to review every word, every nuance of meaning in them, until the cells of her brain ached like a muscle suffering from overexertion.

She could come to only one conclusion. It was vague at best. Still, the decision drawn from it was plain enough.

Edison, with his egoism and selfish demands and careless tinkering with human lives, had turned one of the people around him into a murderer. She, in her fear and pride, had helped him. There was only one thing to be done.

22

"This is Riva Staulet. May I please speak to Doug Gorsline?"

"One moment, please."

Riva could feel her palm sweating where she held the receiver as she waited for whoever had answered the phone in the newspaper newsroom to find Doug. She prayed that he was there. She was not sure she could force herself to call again. The actual deed she planned held no real terror. The preliminaries were what she found unnerving.

"Hello?"

She gave herself no time to think. At the sound of Doug's voice, she said at once, "This is Riva Staulet and I need your help. I want to set up a press conference. Can you tell me how to go about it?"

The pause as comprehension sank in was infinitesimal. He did not ask why or even what for. All he wanted to know was when and where. When she suggested the following morning at Bonne Vie, he said, "I've got it, Mrs. Staulet. Consider it done."

"Thank you, Doug, I'm very grateful."

She was, too, and not just for what he was doing but for his making it so easy.

If it had to be done, it was just as well that it was easy. It had taken twenty-odd years to build her life at Bonne Vie. There would now be twenty-odd hours to wait until it was over. Then it would take twenty minutes, maybe less, to tear it apart.

It had been a mistake to schedule the press conference for the next day; she should have made it for this afternoon. She would have, if she had thought it could be arranged that quickly, but she wanted to be sure everyone could find the time to come. Now the waiting began. She could already tell that it was going to be worse than the preliminaries.

There would be time, however, to say good-bye. She did not doubt that it would be necessary. Noel would not want her at Bonne Vie once he knew, and the house was his. There would be no public opinion, no disapproving friends of his father to prevent him from throwing her out. No doubt he would be generous with other assets, since he was a fair man, but he would want the stain on his father's memory—and perhaps on his own—removed. And who could blame him?

Riva left her room to walk out onto the upper gallery overlooking the drive. She listened to her footsteps echoing on the wooden floor as she slowly paced its length. Reaching out, she ran her hand along the railing. She knew every nick and dent in its long length, was familiar with every loose baluster. The outside walls of the house would need repainting soon. She would have to remember to leave a note for Noel with the exact name and number of the peach-pink-colored paint, and the same for the antique white of the columns and railings and the dark green of the shutters. There was a special place where replacement hardware for the shutters could be bought; he should know that, too. And he would have to be reminded to keep an eye on the ferns growing on their stands beside the doors with their fronds moving gracefully in the warm breeze. If someone wasn't told to water them, to turn, repot, and fertilize them, it would never get done. They would be dead within two weeks after she left.

She paused in the middle of the gallery to look down the long, dark green tunnel of the oak trees lining the drive. They were beautiful with the morning sunlight falling through their branches, making shifting shadow patterns on the ground below. So ancient were they that they seemed hardly to have changed since she came to the house. Oh, there had been a limb or two lost in high winds or a crisis caused by insects, but for the most part they seemed to go on and on in perfect symmetry, weathering all storms. They would be there long after she was gone. How many people they must have seen come and go, how many more they would see.

She had been so young when she first came to Bonne Vie, so full of awkwardness and wonder. She had married Cosmo out of gratitude and affection. She had meant to make him a good wife, to be what he wanted, and had succeeded in the end almost against her will. She had not expected to fall in love with his son, had not wanted to tumble headlong into an affair.

She had been in love with Noel, the first, the only time she was really in love. How deep her feelings had gone was something she had not known herself until he had left Bonne Vie. She had never stopped loving him, not really. Seeing him at intervals over the years had been a painful pleasure. The news of his marriage had been like a sword to her heart, one drawn out only with the news of his divorce. She could not have said which hurt more, however; the fact that he was no longer free or, later, that he was free again and she was not.

And yet she had enjoyed her years as chatelaine of the big old house; Cosmo had seen to that. He had given her everything a woman could desire and more, had surrounded her with unceasing, unquestioning love and attention. She had reveled in the responsibility of being an active partner in the corporation with him, had learned to love his home and take pride in being his hostess there. She had grown confident within herself so that she took pleasure in entertaining and lost her self-consciousness at being entertained. However, she never quite lost her awe of the public figures she met: the presidents and other statesmen, the famous writers and actors and others in the arts; the well-known sports figures; and those whose claim to public recognition came from inherited wealth. Still, she moved among them with ease, and if she was never quite as assured as she looked, no one ever knew it.

She had never wished for Cosmo's death. When it came, it was a loss of immense magnitude, one made more poignant instead of less so by the knowledge of what he had done to separate her from his son. It proved that he had known how she felt and had moved to keep her. In doing so, he had sacrificed his son's love. He had chosen her over his own flesh and blood, and been forced to live with the bargain while knowing it could, and probably should, have been otherwise. It was a burden for Riva to be the cause of that choice, a burden to be so terribly loved.

Time was strange. Sometimes, as she thought back on the hours she had spent with Noel in the gardener's shed, it seemed like yesterday. Other times, it was as if it had happened to another person in another life or else to lovers in a dream. Sometimes she could remember every word Noel had said, every look, every touch. And sometimes she could not be certain the memories were not something she had made up in her mind, purest fantasies.

She loved him still. If she had ever doubted it, in those days after the funeral when they were so far apart while living under the same roof and working in the same building, she would have known it after the night of the storm. Why should she not love him? He had risked his life to save hers, then had held her against her terrors, keeping her safe. His arms had been a haven, a home. There had been such a sense of belonging, of perfect accommodation, of completion.

She had not been alone in her feelings, she knew. For a short time it had been as it was on the island. He had wanted her, needed her for a few brief moments. She had meant something to him beyond an unfortunate mistake of his father's, and of his.

Constance had spoiled it. For whatever reason, Noel's ex-wife had spoken the words that brought back the guilt and the old pain and once more turned what she and Noel felt into something sordid and ugly.

But it could never be erased, not as long as she drew breath. It would live inside her as one more forbidden memory, joining the others she had held for more than two decades.

Riva went through the house, touching an antique vase of fragile china or the smooth, cool side of a silver bowl, pausing to finger the cut work of a tablecloth or memorize the colors of a portrait. She visited the kitchen, then took a turn outside, stopping here and there to sniff a gardenia or a rose or to pull a weed from a bed of begonias.

She saved the folly for last. Inside its shelter, she stood for a long time with her eyes closed and her back resting against the knee of the great, serene bronze Buddha. In her mind, it was raining, though the sun rose higher and higher in the sky, shining down hot and without mercy.

Finally Riva sighed and started back toward the house. There were other things still to be done.

Margaret cried out, "You're going to what? But you can't!"

She was lying like an invalid propped up on pillows on a chaise longue she had had moved into her room. The remains of her breakfast tray sat to one side, and a stack of magazines spilled over the surface of a small table beside the chaise, colliding with a bottle of nail polish and a pharmacist's bottle of tranquilizers. It had been nearly three days now since she had been out of her room. Her face was blotched and bloated from crying, and she had not combed her hair or changed her clothes since she had shut herself away. It was Boots who regularly brought the pills to his wife. He had sobered enough to perform that service, but he did not linger in Margaret's room. When he was not needed, he escaped to the garage with George, where the two sat talking about Vietnam and football and duck hunting.

Riva looked at her sister with mingled concern and exasperation. "I would have thought you'd be glad to know that Edison isn't going to get off scot-free for what he did to you."

"You're about to brand me a liar to everyone I know, a woman who has claimed her sister's child as her own all these years! You're going to do this to me, and you expect me to be glad?"

"Why not? It was a generous thing."

"But I've always been so against people who keep things hidden, unwed mothers and all that sort of thing. What will people say? What will Erin think?"

Riva sighed with weary patience. "There's nothing I can do about your hypocrisy, Margaret."

"You're so cruel, too cruel, Riva. You don't understand. My heart, oh, my heart."

Riva gave her a long look. "Isn't it odd that your heart never troubled you through Edison's rough handling? I would have thought it would have been an appalling strain."

"Are you suggesting I'm faking it?" Margaret sat up on the chaise, her listlessness giving way to wrath.

"I have no idea. Are you?"

Her sister fell back on her pillows again and turned her gaze to the ceiling. "I'll die with a heart attack because no one will believe me. That, and the fact that no one understands what I went through, how I feel, is enough to drive me crazy."

"I'm sorry, but if you go on hiding in this room and brooding as you've been doing, it won't be surprising."

Margaret's mouth opened, then shut. Finally she said, "You've grown hard, Riva. This isn't like you at all. You would never have thought of saying such a thing to me a few months back."

"I suppose I wouldn't, but that's all to the good. I have to be hard now."

"You're going through with it, then?"

"Yes, I am." The words sounded more firm than Riva felt at the moment, but they had to be said.

"You—you aren't going to tell how I was raped?"

"There's no reason why I should do that, and anyway, it's your business."

Margaret closed her eyes. "Thank God for that much." After a moment, her eyelids flew upward again. "But what if Edison takes it into his head to make it public, telling all about it in that nasty, mocking way he has? I'll never be able to hold my head up again. Never!"

Riva controlled her voice with an effort. "He has to be stopped, don't you see? He can't be allowed to go on doing the things he's done."

"If I can forget it after what he did to me, I don't see why you can't do the same thing."

"I did forget it, years ago, or tried to. As a direct result, he tried to have me killed. Doesn't that mean anything to you, Margaret? What if he does the same to someone else, someone less protected?"

"He wouldn't—he couldn't—be so stupid."

"The truth is," Riva said slowly, "he could. He killed a woman before. Why shouldn't he do it again?"

"What, in heaven's name, are you talking about?"

Riva turned away, moving to the bed where she sat on the end. "It was something he said last night, something about that woman civil-rights worker who was killed that summer years ago. Do you remember? She was driving a truck and was shot by a boy behind the wheel of a carload of redneck rowdies out joyriding. I saw that car later, Margaret, saw it going down behind the house toward the pond."

Her sister sat up straight, a frown between her eyes. "What are you saying?"

"I think Edison was driving that car. I think he killed that woman. He as good as told me so last night. What's more, I think that's why he brought me to New Orleans so that anything I said against him would sound like petty vengefulness for the way he had tricked me."

"What about now? What's it going to sound like if you drag up such ancient history?"

"Who cares what it sounds like? He killed a woman, Margaret! And think of what he did to Beth. On top of that, he not only tried to have me killed, but I told you how he attacked me again last night. He might even have murdered me with his own hands when he had finished with me. I have the means to stop him. If I don't do it, I will be responsible for whatever he may do from now on. I couldn't live with that."

"Can you live without friends? Can you live with disgrace? Think, Riva!"

"I'll have to do the best I can. But I'm not asking your advice, Margaret. I'm telling you what I intend to do so you can decide how you are going to handle the consequences."

"What about Erin?"

"I'll tell her, too. It wouldn't be fair to let her learn by hearing it blurted out in front of a television camera."

"Oh, Riva, why not leave it at that, just telling Erin? You'll have what you wanted when you started. Erin will know Josh is her half brother, and that will put an end to anything between them. She'll know I'm not her mother, but the whole world won't have to know." Margaret fumbled for a tissue, using it to dab at her eyes.

Riva gave a slow shake of her head. "It isn't enough. Think what it would be like to have a man like Edison in power. There's no telling what he might do, who he might hurt."

"I thought he was in the hospital. Won't it seem a little malicious to bring public charges against a man lying in the hospital and whose son is at death's door?"

"I checked this morning when I called about Josh. They only kept Edison overnight. I agree the timing is bad, since Josh's condition is still uncertain, but what can I do?"

"There must be something!" Margaret declared, her voice shrill. "There must be!"

"If there was, I would do it, I promise. There is nothing."

Her sister stared at her with eyes of stone. She wiped her face once more, then, letting her hand holding the crumpled tissue fall to her side, she turned her head away.

Riva did not speak to Erin immediately. She had already left the house for the hospital. Riva thought of getting dressed and going herself, but that would be asking for trouble. There was no point in going to work; she could not concentrate enough to be of any use. Anyway, Noel had gone. He would take care of whatever came up; that was one thing she did not have to worry about.

She still dreaded the talk with Erin and wished she could get it over with, but in an odd sort of way, she felt good. There was in the back of her mind the growing euphoria of impending relief. She had kept her past hidden for so many years, lived with the constant fear of discovery for so long, that she hadn't realized what a weight it had become.

She was tired of secrets. They were dangerous things. They festered like a thorn under the skin, poisoning the blood. The body might absorb the thorn's infection, might grow a tough core around it, but you never knew when it would flare up again. The only thing to be done was to cut it out and be rid of it. The operation might be painful, might even leave a scar, but it would be for the best.

The morning was long, but finally it was lunchtime. Then the afternoon gathered a momentum of its own, spinning by so quickly that Riva could not think where it went. It was dusk when Erin returned. She was not alone; Doug Gorsline was with her. The two of them came out to where Riva sat on the back gallery. Josh was the same, Erin said, though Anne Gallant was hopeful he would be all right. But what was this about a press conference? Doug had told her there was to be one but was being mysterious about the purpose of it. What in the world was going on?

Riva had thought she was ready. She had made tentative plans for the gradual way she would lead up to the subject of Erin's birth. Now they flew to the four winds, and she could think of nothing to say. She wasn't ready at all.

"Aunt Riva? What's the matter? Is something wrong?"

She smiled with a tremulous movement of her lips. "Only everything," she said.

Somehow she told it, about the summer of '63 and how she had come to marry, or think she had married, Edison, and of how he had left her in New Orleans. She told of her days in the restaurant kitchen with Dante and the birth of her child and how Margaret had claimed her; of her rescue from the Bourbon Street bar by Cosmo and the nature of her marriage to him, including a carefully censored version of her affair with Noel. Cosmo's death, Erin remembered, as well as the day at the rally. And she was intelligent, Riva's own daughter; therefore, she began to guess at what was left unsaid, to leap ahead with questions and answers, though her face was white and stunned and her voice a whisper in her throat.

At last Erin said, "How can it be? How can Josh's father be the monster you claim when Josh is so—so kind, so sweet?"

"I can't explain it, except to say that heredity is a strange thing, and he is also his mother's son."

"And my brother, my half brother. I can't believe it." Erin stared down at her fingers, which were twisted together in her lap as she sat in a wrought-iron chair. Doug, standing behind her, put his hand on her shoulder and pressed it firmly.

"Nor can I believe it, sometimes," Riva answered.

The younger woman gave a soft laugh. "I used to wish that you were my mother. I felt guilty about it, but I did. Part of it was the money; I thought you would buy me anything I wanted and I would never have to hear that you couldn't afford it. But another part was that I wanted to be like you, always poised and gorgeous, always knowing the right thing to do, the right thing to say, always your own woman. Now I'm not so sure."

Riva felt a tightness close around her heart. "Why is that?"

"I'm not sure I would ever want to do something like this business with the press conference to somebody."

"I'm not doing it out of revenge," Riva protested.

"Aren't you? If what Edison Gallant has done is so bad, why not go to the police?"

"There's no real proof, nothing except my word."

"Then how can you be sure?"

"I know."

"Do you? Are you certain it's not because of what he did to you all those years ago?"

"Erin, please! I'm not a vicious woman. I wouldn't do it without just cause."

"So you say, but do you really know why you're doing it? Is there no alternative except to hold Josh's father up to public scorn? What if you're wrong? It can never be undone. You will have ruined a brilliant political career all because of a mistake made years ago."

Riva shook her head. "It may have been made years ago, but it was compounded in this past week. Don't you understand? I know you feel you should be loyal to Edison, and I'm well aware of how persuasive and personable he can be when he chooses, but don't let it blind you to what he is. This man you persist in looking up to as some kind of political genius forced himself on your aunt and tried to force himself on me. I can't prove he killed that woman years ago or that he tried to have me killed, but the first two things cannot be denied."

"It can't be denied that someone tried to kill him, too. Maybe it was the same person who tried to have you killed. Have you thought of that? Maybe you're both victims!"

"It won't work, I tell you—"

Erin jumped to her feet. Her nose was red and there were tears standing in her eyes. "No, don't tell me. I don't want to hear it. I can't stand to hear any more."

Riva rose also. "I know it's a lot to take in, and I'm sorry I had to unload it on you all at once. Let's have something to drink and just talk quietly—"

"I've had enough talk for one day." Erin turned to the young man behind her. "Doug, could you take me somewhere, anywhere?"

"Wait," Riva said, putting her hand on her daughter's arm. "Don't go off like this while you're upset. I won't say another word."

But Erin only pulled free and half walked, half ran from the gallery. Doug, with a quick glance that might have been of apology or censure or both, went after her. In a few minutes there came the sound of his car as it roared into life and rumbled away down the drive.

Riva went to her room and stayed there. Abraham brought her a tray at dinnertime, but she could not eat. A while later, there came a quiet knock and Noel called to her. She didn't answer, couldn't answer. She sat in a chair in the dark, staring at nothing.

What was she doing? Was it the right thing or was she committing a crime more brutal than anything Edison had ever thought of doing? Was she destroying a man for her own ends or balancing an uneven scale of justice? And even if it was the last, who was she to play God?

But this was the way it was done these days, wasn't it? This was the equivalent of the public pillory, this trumpeting of a man's sins in the public press. It had to be this way or else the private sins of the great and near great would never be known. It was too easy for such people to manipulate facts and laws and to turn all that pertained to them from sins of black and white to shades of gray. Therefore, this public disgrace was necessary to make the glare of light too bright for them to hide.

But was it right? Was it fair? Did the rules apply when the deeds done went past mere indiscretions, illustrated more than character flaws?

Justice or revenge? Which was she after? Did she really know herself? Where did one end and the other begin?

Maybe Margaret was right, maybe she had done enough by telling Erin and ending the possibility of a relationship between her daughter and Josh. Maybe she should play it safe and hope that Edison would do the same. Surely he would not dare to go farther with his threats now that so many knew what he was and what he had done?

Safety. Was there ever such a thing?

Morning came with a flush of light beyond the lace curtains. Riva rose from her chair and took off the clothes she had worn the day before. She showered and changed into a dress of soft turquoise silk, then did her makeup and put on her pearls, the Staulet pearls that made her look classically elegant, indisputably well dressed. Her appearance gave her confidence. She needed it.

She was having coffee—all she could stand for breakfast—when she heard the first car on the drive. She knew this thing she had set in motion had really begun when she looked through the windows to see men in shorts and T-shirts dragging out the cameras and sound equipment, saw the men and women in tailored clothes standing before the house and beginning to speak into microphones.

By nine-thirty, a half hour before the conference was to start, the driveway was full of cars and the lawn under the trees was a mass of wires and black boxes and silver camera cases. The noise was incredible. To maintain some kind of order, Abraham was serving coffee and hot biscuits on the gallery. Erin had gone out to help with the coffee, passing out napkins and bringing fresh cups from the kitchen. Margaret was still keeping to her room, almost in hiding, while Constance was secluded with her children to prevent their exposure to the press. Boots and George were directing traffic and shouting themselves hoarse to keep people away from the flower beds and out of the precious branches of the famous trees. Noel, it appeared, was stationed in the hall to keep everyone out of the house until the time came. He would let them in a few at a time at nine-forty-five, but not a second before. He didn't want them overrunning the place, poking in where they did not belong.

Riva was ready, or hoped she was. Her stomach cramped with nerves, and her throat was so dry she was sure she could not speak. Words jostled in her head as she tried without success to think of exactly what she was going to say. The opening line would not come. If she could only think of how she was to begin, then the rest would be easy, she would know how to go on. As it was, she wasn't sure. She still wasn't sure.

Abraham left the front gallery long enough to bring her more coffee and try to press a biscuit on her. Some of the press, he said, had got hold of a rumor, come somehow through the mafia families, that she had some dirt on the gubernatorial candidate Gallant. They wanted to know if it was true. What was he to tell them?

"Tell them nothing," she said, and he nodded wisely and went away to do just that.

At twenty minutes before the hour, Riva left her room and walked down the hall. Her face was composed and her breathing even. She walked with slow, steady steps and tried not to think about what she was doing or why.

She had reached the bottom step of the stairs when the back door opened and a man stepped through into the hall. He looked up in time to see her standing with her hand on the newel post. He smiled without humor.

"Surprise," he said, his voice low but savage with satisfaction.

It was Edison.

23

Riva stood absolutely still. Her voice was compressed as she said, "What are you doing here?"

"What, isn't it a party?" he mocked. "Don't tell me I'm not invited? Here I was thinking I was the guest of honor."

"How did you—" she began, then stopped as he interrupted.

"Connections, baby. What would a politician be without connections?"

"Mafia," she said in scorn.

"Let's just say friends in interesting places, if not high ones."

At the other end of the long hall, the front door opened at that moment. Noel stepped inside, then checked when he saw Riva with Edison. The pause was fractional, then he closed the door behind him and started toward where they stood. He moved with swift and sure purpose.

"Enough chitchat," Edison said, speaking fast and low as he watched Noel's approach. "We have to talk, Riva, you and I. There's a thing or two you don't know."

"I have nothing to say to you."

"That may be, but I have a hell of a lot to say to you. If you're smart, and if you give a damn about our dear little Erin, you'll listen."

"What about Erin? Where is my daughter?"

There was fear, sudden and sharp, in Riva's voice. Edison was not acting like a man who had come to witness his own destruction. He obviously thought he had something he could use to stop her. What else could it be except Erin?

362 •

He gave her a tight grin. "Oh, don't get in a sweat; our daughter's outside. But I think we should go somewhere and talk about her—and about her future. Now!"

Noel was upon them. His features were grim as he spoke. "Is there something I can do for you, Gallant?"

"I don't think so, Staulet. Riva here is going to do it. Aren't you, darling?"

She clenched her teeth at the sound of the endearment. To be forced to agree with it ringing in her ears was galling almost beyond endurance. "Give us a few minutes. Please, Noel."

The look he turned on her held equal parts of derision and disbelief. He jerked a thumb over his shoulder. "You don't have long before that horde out there breaks the door down."

"Yes, I know. Please?"

There was stiff reluctance in his movements when he turned. His last words were not for her but for Edison. "Five minutes," he said. "No more."

Riva moved around the staircase and led the way into the dining room. The morning sun streamed through the windows, gleaming on the long, polished table, shimmering in the antique Baccarat crystal chandelier overhead. She stepped into a pool of light that brought out the muted tints of the old Brussels carpet on the floor before she turned and faced Edison.

"What is it?"

He wasted no more time than she. "Do this, and I'll drag you down with me."

A soft sound left her that was not far from a laugh. "I never thought otherwise."

"Oh, I don't mean a little gossip, a little tarnish on your image as the lady of the manor. I mean I will put you back out in the street, dancing naked on tables and maybe trying to sell a piece now and then to pay the rent. You're a bit old for it, but you'll get by."

"You have to be insulting as well as melodramatic, don't you? I warn you, I'm not impressed."

His voice lowered to a sound of pure menace. "Don't warn me, Riva, I don't like it. And I don't like threats like this half-assed press conference. Now, you're going to walk out there and tell all the damned media you made a mistake, or I'll have your ass for breakfast."

"I don't like threats, either, Edison. Unless you tell me in the next five seconds what you meant by bringing Erin into this, I'm going on exactly as planned."

"Open your mouth about me, you bitch, and I'll tell the world you're not Riva Staulet and never were. You're Rebecca Benson Gallant. You're my wife! How do you like that?"

In the abrupt quiet, the clamor outside the house seemed suddenly louder. Riva swallowed hard. "What?"

"That's right. My wife! That means anything you say out there is going to sound like a messy domestic squabble. It'll hurt me, sure, but it will put you back where you started twenty-five years ago."

"No." The word was a whisper. It was the only sound she could make. She felt as if she were falling, whirling backward. She put her hands up to her temples, as though that would stop it.

"Oh, yes, baby! You thought we weren't married, you stupid little bitch. Believed every word I said, didn't you? I just wanted out, and I needed to put an end to everything that happened that summer. I couldn't have you coming around, draining me for money, saying things that might make my trustees ask questions. So I told you I was already married. Hell, you didn't even ask who my wife was, where she had been all that time, where my damned wedding ring was. You didn't care. You didn't care one damned bit."

Slowly, Riva's mind stopped spinning, began to function again. "You never got a divorce?"

"How the hell was I going to do that without people asking questions? Besides, the marriage was filed in Arkansas. Nobody ever checks marriage records across state lines."

"But if I'm still married to you, then Anne—"

"That's a laugh, isn't it? Anne, poor straitlaced, uptight Anne, has been living in sin for years."

She frowned in concentration. "If Erin is legitimate, then, your son is . . . not."

"Never mind." The smile disappeared from his face. "What's important here is that you were never Mrs. Cosmo Staulet. The marriage—here's the joke—was invalid. That means you never had any right to be here, not a damn bit of right. Cross me, and you'll be out on your ear. Cosmo Staulet's son out there will see to it personally."

"You are willing to keep quiet about this if I cooperate, is that it?"

"That's it." His smile was snide.

"And I can, of course," she said with delicate irony, "depend on you never to use it against me."

"You'll have me by the short hairs, too, won't you? Who knows, you might get to like the grip." He chuckled at his own ribald suggestion.

He was so confident, and so obnoxious with it. Was it all a show? Or did he really think that she could walk out there and get rid of the press, smooth things over without intolerable repercussions?

Could she? Could she possibly make up a tale of some kind, maybe of a big charitable donation, to account for bringing on the media carnival outside? Did she want to do that?

It would please Margaret and Erin. Some of the truth had been exposed, but no one need know the whole story. The furor would die down eventually and things could go on more or less as they were. She could keep all she held dear, stay at Bonne Vie. And possibly, after a time, the change in the relationship between Noel and herself that had taken place in the past few days might continue instead of turning to contempt and rejection. She could encourage that, nurture it, because she knew that she was not now, nor had she ever been, his stepmother.

Noel didn't know it. What was worse was that she could never tell him if she placed herself in Edison's power by doing as he suggested.

More than that, the man had to be stopped. He had hurt so many, done so much damage with so little regret. His regard for what was moral and right was so meager that for most of his life he had lived in a marriage that was a lie, thereby robbing his own son of his birthright. He was not quite sane. His lack of conscience and pandering to his own ego, his own twisted desires showed it beyond doubting. A man of his kind should not be allowed to move freely among normal people, much less to govern them.

"Is that all?" she asked.

A scowl of annoyance crossed Edison's face at the calm that had crept back into her voice. "Yes, that's all."

"Then I have an appointment to keep."

She turned away from him, but he reached out to grab her arm. "What are you going to say?"

"What do you think?"

His grasp tightened. "I'm asking you."

"I'm going to tell them the story of my life," she said evenly, her green gaze steady on his, "in complete detail."

He muttered an oath and lunged, reaching for her throat with his free hand. Riva blocked his arm by bringing up her own in a quick reflex action. He caught her arm, and they grappled, staggering back and forth.

"Stop it, stop it, stop it!"

The cry came from Margaret as she stumbled through the door that led from the butler's pantry. Her eyes were huge in her pale and bloated face, her hair was a frizzed tangle, and her housecoat was rumpled and stained. Clutched in her hands, wavering up and down, was Riva's small pistol.

At the same moment that Margaret cried out, the door into the hall crashed open to slam against the wall. Noel plunged into the room, then came up short as he took in the situation.

Riva wrenched herself free of Edison's hold and stepped away from him. She started toward her sister. "Give me the gun, Margaret."

Margaret backed away a hasty step. The pistol shook with the violent tremors running through her body but remained trained on Edison. "No, Riva. I called Edison, got him here so I can stop this thing, and that's what I'm going to do. I'm going to stop him for good. You said there was nothing else to be done, but I told you there was. I told you."

"This isn't going to help. It will just make things worse."

"How? How can they be worse? I tried to get rid of him and

make it look like an accident. I went to see Jimmy, Beth's husband, you know? He still keeps in touch. He's a mechanic out at the airport, works with electronics; he's been there since he came out of the air force. He said he could make Edison's plane crash, no problem, and he wouldn't take a cent for it because he had an old score to settle. But he didn't know Josh would be on board. Neither did I. I'm sorry, real sorry, about Josh."

Her sister's voice had a droning quality, as if the usual rise and fall had been smoothed out by the tranquilizers she had taken, Riva thought.

"Margaret, please," she said, "let me—"

"No! I'm more sorry the crash didn't work. But I can fix it. I thought about it after you told me how you got away from Edison in that hospital closet. You should have shot him then, but no. Well, I found your gun; I knew just where to look for your purse. Now I can do it. If I shoot Edison here and now, it'll be the same thing. There won't be any reason to tell everybody everything. That way, people won't be talking about me. That's right, isn't it? Isn't that right?"

Edison twitched, stuttering into speech. "F-for God's sake—"

"Shut up!" Margaret ordered, pointing the pistol at his chest. "Shut your lying mouth. Lies, that's all you ever did was tell lies. I thought you were something wonderful, but it was all a lie. You can kill people with lies. They die inside real slow."

"She's crazy!" Edison exclaimed in disgust. "Don't listen to a word she says."

"You're the crazy one," Margaret cried, "treating people as if they were dirt under your fine shoes! But I know all about you. You tried to kill Riva. But you did kill Beth, yes, you did, with your lies, using her for your whore as if she didn't matter. And you shot that other girl, too, didn't you? I saw your car that night just like Riva did. I woke up after she got out of bed."

"Margaret," Riva whispered, but her sister's attention was riveted on Edison.

"You thought you were safe," she told him, "but I saw you driving like a bat out of hell down behind the pond. I never told anyone. I never told, and I raised your daughter and loved her as if she had been my child, mine and yours. Wasn't that silly of me? But Boots swore it was an accident, you shooting that girl. He swore you didn't mean to do it, and I believed him. But you did mean it, didn't you? You meant it because she laughed at you. Boots told me that, too. He tells me everything."

Riva listened, transfixed. Margaret had sat listening to her tell of seeing Edison herself and never said a word. Why? Then suddenly she understood, saw why Margaret had protected Edison, why she had insisted on taking Erin and even pretended the child was her own. The reason was love, a twisted kind of love, but still love.

"You can't prove a thing!" Edison shouted. "Anyway, the bitch deserved it."

"Maybe I can't prove it, but I can tell what I know, and so can Boots. He will now, too. He hates you. Don't you, Boots?"

Her husband had entered the room behind Noel. He stood frozen in place, a big, awkward man, uncertain of what to do. Still, there was remorse in his eyes as he looked at his wife, and sorrow.

Since Margaret had not shot Edison at once, it seemed likely that the greatest danger was that she might do so by accident. Riva moved deliberately between her sister and Edison. She heard Noel's soft imprecation, heard the whisper of his footstep on the Brussels carpet as he eased closer. She refused to look at him in her concentration on her sister.

Her voice soothing, Riva said, "Think, Margaret, only think. You can't do this, not this way. Everybody will know who killed Edison. The front lawn is full of newspeople who will broadcast the story far and wide. They will want to know your name, where you live, why you pulled the trigger, plus a thousand other details. It will all come out."

Margaret looked at Riva with confusion clouding her eyes. The muzzle of the pistol lowered a fraction, wobbled to the left. "I forgot about them. Do you think that's what will happen?"

"I know it. Just let me have the pistol and I'll put it away again before everybody sees it and starts asking questions."

Another moment, and it would have been all right. Another moment, and Riva would have had the pistol in her hand. Then

Edison lurched forward. He grabbed Riva from behind, dragging her against him as a shield. Margaret screamed and fired. The shot hissed past Riva's head, thudding into the wall behind her. Noel leaped for Margaret, sweeping her gun hand upward as he wrested the pistol from her clawing fingers.

Margaret cried out, then dissolved onto the floor in a sobbing heap. Boots went down on his knees beside her, lifting her up, murmuring softly as if to a child. Margaret leaned her head on his knee and cried with the racking sobs of limitless regret.

Noel, the pistol in his hand, swung toward Riva and Edison. Black rage burned in his eyes as he looked from one to the other, and there was a white line about his mouth.

A nervous laugh broke from Edison. He let Riva go and stepped back, his hands held wide apart and palms out. "Take it easy, Staulet," he said. "You don't want to do anything rash."

Noel made a soft sound of contempt. "You don't have to worry."

Edison relaxed visibly. He even managed a grin. "Yeah, I always did say one woman was just like the next."

"You're a fool." The words had the slicing edge of a razor. Noel swung toward Riva. "And you're doubly the fool for protecting him. Again."

Riva felt the lash of his scorn and stiffened in disbelief. There was a pounding noise in her head, though she couldn't be sure whether it came from somewhere outside or was only the throb of her heartbeat in her ears. Her voice thick, she began, "But I wasn't—"

There was no time for more. Suddenly the room was full of uniforms. The five of them were surrounded, jostled, held under the cover of a half-dozen pointed guns while questions were shouted and answers demanded.

Noel spoke, his voice hard and succinct. The weapons were put away. The stances of the policemen eased and they stepped back, some of them almost to the wall. The officer in charge gave a short, almost embarrassed laugh. "Sorry, Mr. Staulet. We were called for riot duty, I know, but when we heard shooting, we got a little carried away."

"Stick around," Noel said, his voice grim, "the fun has just started. In the meantime, you can keep an eye on that man."

The policeman looked startled. "You mean the candidate here?"

"That's the one." Noel turned to Riva. "Madame Staulet, I believe you called a press conference?"

Had he stressed the courtesy title, giving it the sound of irony, or was it her imagination? Had he overheard? Did he know? She could not tell from the closed-in expression on his features. His touch on her arm was impersonal as he guided her from the room. He walked beside her down the long length of the hall with all the stern silence of a guard leading the condemned to the place of execution. It almost seemed that if she faltered, if she tried to turn back, he might force her on. And why should he not? When she had had her say, he would be free of her, done with the woman who had been an embarrassment as his father's much younger wife. He would be rid of a reminder of an episode he would surely like to forget, and a burden for whom his care had been entreated on his father's deathbed. Without her, he could run Staulet Corporation as he wanted, put his own imprint on it. Without her, the wealth accumulated by his father, though with her help, would be his to use as he saw fit. Without her, Bonne Vie would be his to enjoy alone. Why should he not help her to destroy herself?

They paused in the hall near the front door. There was not enough room for all of the media people who had gathered to be accommodated in the parlor. Noel suggested that, instead of letting them into the house, she join them on the front gallery. It would be less formal, plus it might save the furniture.

She agreed. It made no difference to her where she spoke to them. All she wanted was for it to be over.

Noel stepped to the door. With his hand on the knob, he paused. "Ready?" he asked, his voice low.

Riva clasped her hands together. She moistened her lips. She wondered in a vague sort of way if her hair had been disarranged by the scuffle in the dining room and if her dress was straight. She didn't really care. She lifted her gaze to Noel. Her expression anguished, vulnerable with her doubts, she asked in stifled tones, "Am I doing the right thing?"

His eyes were dark gray and unflinching as he answered, "I think you are. It seems appropriate that the truth should be known at last."

He did know. Whether he had overheard or discovered it in some other way, he knew, and he despised her. There was nothing left to fear, no pain that could be greater.

Cold to the lips, she said, "I'm ready."

24

The news crews jostled forward, holding out microphones and minirecorders, waving pads and pens, shouting questions. There was the flash and whir of still cameras. A battery of lights bloomed hot and blindingly bright as television cameramen converged from every direction. Riva had been in front of cameras before, but never at the center of this kind of concentrated tumult. It was unnerving. She swallowed, trying to clear her throat, waiting for silence. The longer she waited, the more clamorous the gathering became:

"Was that a shot we heard?"

"Who fired the gun?"

"Was anyone hit?"

"Who were the police after?"

"Anyone been arrested?"

"What's the purpose of this conference?"

"Any connection with the shot?"

Riva took a deep breath and lifted her chin. Raising her voice, she said, "I have a statement to make."

The noise increased.

"If you will let me talk—"

The questions came louder and more insistent.

Noel, standing with his back to the front door, stepped forward. "Quiet!"

The word was neither harsh nor particularly loud, but it carried the sound of command. The volume of the hubbub suddenly muted, then began to die away.

"Thank you," Riva said, "and a special thank you to all of you for coming today. If you will bear with me, I believe I can answer everything you have been asking. The story is a long one, however, so I ask for your patience."

It wasn't easy. She had never realized, until she began to try to find the words to tell her tale, how private a person she was, how private she had become. To strip away years of self-protection and subterfuge in a few sentences was like undressing in public. There was honesty in it, but it was impossible not to shrink from the exposure.

It was a warm day beyond the shade of the gallery. That warmth, combined with the heat of the lights and press of bodies around her, brought perspiration to her forehead and across her upper lip. She became aware, as the moments passed, that Noel was still at her side, standing shoulder to shoulder with her. Whether it was a gesture of protection for one who still represented the Staulet name or simply a sign of the line he would not permit the media to step across, she did not know. Still, having him near gave her strength. It showed in her voice, making it steadier, and with its normal melodious timbre, as she spoke of the deaths of her sister and the civil rights worker; her seduction by Edison and their marriage; his desertion of her in New Orleans; the birth of her child and how her sister had taken it to raise it as her own. As she told of her despair, however, tears rose in her eyes, brought by the rise of memories long suppressed, never quite accepted, memories of the sweetness and delicate perfection of the baby she had borne and given away for the promise of a better life than she could give her.

The crowd before her was no more than a mass of red-faced and sweat-damp bodies. It was almost by instinct that she found the place where Erin stood. She managed a shaky smile as she met her daughter's eyes. And through a film of moisture, she saw Erin give a slow nod before she detached herself from her place beside Doug where he stood with his camera slack and unused in his hands at the back of the crowd. Erin slipped around men hefting minicams, stepped over cables, murmured apologies as she pushed forward in front of people. Then she was at Riva's side, hugging her close.

"I'm sorry," Erin whispered, "I'm sorry."

As Riva went on, after a brief moment, she had her daughter's arm around her.

Somewhere in the long recital, perhaps as she spoke very briefly of Cosmo and his falling-out with his son, Noel reached to clasp her waist from the other side. It was a hold of silent support, steady, firm, asking nothing. Once more, tears threatened to choke Riva. She tried to swallow them, but they spilled over, sliding down her face, dripping in small wet spots onto the silk of her dress. By fierce concentration, she conquered them and was able to continue.

She omitted little, though she glossed over her sister's precise reason for her involvement, as promised. She did indicate something of what had just taken place in the house, however, including Edison's self-incrimination in the death of the civil rights worker all those years ago and his glancing reference to his connections to the mafia.

At last the story was over. There was perfect silence for the space of a breath as she stopped speaking. Then came pandemonium. The crowd surged forward, shouting, yelling questions, waving recorders and microphones as each one tried for a special quote.

Noel looked over his shoulder and nodded. The squad of riot police, most of them sheriff's deputies, moved in, surrounding Riva.

For a heart-stopping instant, she thought she was under arrest, that somehow she was to be implicated in the crimes of which she had spoken, possibly at Noel's instigation.

Then Noel, with his arm still around her, urged her backward within the shielding circle of uniforms. The front door swung open behind them. Riva stepped inside with Noel, Erin, and the police. Abraham, with immense hauteur, slammed the door shut again, closing out the noise and bright TV lights.

Outside, there was an immediate rush for cars and vans. Cameras were thrown into their padded bags and cables whipped in the air as they were coiled. Doors slammed and engines roared into life, then shifted as wheels spun away down the drive. In less than five minutes, the members of the press were gone. All that remained to show they had been there was the trampled grass of the front lawn and a litter of foam coffee cups, cigarette butts, and crumpled bits of paper.

It was only when the last van and car had disappeared that the sheriff's car carrying Edison drove away. No one was sure what the charges against him would be, whether murder or manslaughter, rape or assault or attempted assault, or even bigamy. There was no lack of possibilities to choose from, but the composition of the final indictment would be decided by the lawyers. In the meantime, the New Orleans chief of police wanted to have a personal talk with him about the drug situation in the city and surrounding suburbs.

Boots left with Margaret shortly thereafter. Margaret could not stop crying, would not stop talking. Her husband had called a specialist in nervous disorders arising from assault and also arranged for a consultation with a second man whose area of expertise was addiction to prescription drugs. The two were waiting at Oshner's to see them. There was a special program there for cases like Margaret's, one that included a stay of weeks or months at a minimum-security rehabilitation center. Her husband was going to check her into it if the doctors thought it would help. She would be there if the police wanted to talk to her. And so would Boots.

Riva had stopped short of exposing her sister's guilt in causing the crash of Edison's plane. It was possible Edison would accuse her himself, but it was also possible he would not since it would mean admitting a great many uncomfortable truths about Margaret's motives in trying to kill him. What would happen with her, then, and with the airport mechanic who had been Beth's husband, only time could tell.

The housekeeper Liz, conscious of the requirements of hospitality, conjured up a buffet luncheon of vegetable soup, sandwiches, and plates of hors d'oeuvres along with coffee, wine, and fruit-juice spritzers. She knew none of them were hungry, she said, but it would give them something to do while they wound down from the excitement of the last hour.

It was too hot to eat on the gallery. The food was laid out in the dining room. It gave Riva a queasy feeling to go back in there, especially when she glanced at the hole in the plaster where the shot Margaret had fired had struck. However, the discomfort lasted no more than a moment. It wasn't rooms that caused pain, only people.

Constance was standing alone in the room as Riva entered. The other woman turned and her gaze was narrow with appraisal as it rested on Riva, as if she were searching for flaws. She said sharply, "Where is Noel?"

"I'm not sure," Riva answered. "He was busy with the sheriff and his men until they left with Edison just now. I heard him say something about checking on Coralie and Pietro, in case they were disturbed by all the excitement."

"I must have just missed him, then," the other woman said, "not that he need have bothered about the children. They have seen cameras and the paparazzi before; they are quite able to ignore such people, so long as no one is chasing them to take their pictures. Actually, they have been watching television, which they adore, and all the commercials have made them ravenous. I came down to see what was available for them to eat."

It seemed an unlikely excuse since Constance was not shy about ringing a bell or cornering a maid to get what she wanted. It had to be curiosity that had brought her downstairs. Riva waved toward the buffet. "As you can see, lunch is ready."

The other woman picked up a plate. "How calm you are for someone who, if I have it right from Abraham, has just been shot at in this very room."

"There's not much to be gained by hysterics except attention, and I've had enough of that to last a lifetime."

"Even Noel's attention?"

Riva stiffened at the sarcasm shading the woman's voice. "Noel has nothing to do with it one way or the other."

"I think otherwise." The Sicilian woman's manner was grudging as she went on. "Oh, yes, when I first came I had plans to make him jealous and to win him back. It was a matter of pride. I could not understand why he had left me, you see. Noel refused to explain, but I knew you were a part of it, so I hated you and wanted to hurt you. But I listened from the gallery upstairs just now, and

I put what you said with what I know. I see now why you claim Noel's mind above other women."

"Hardly that," Riva said, uncomfortable at such plain speaking.

"Of course that! He is a romantic man—aren't they all? He made for you the beau geste and pretends now that all the years in exile don't matter, but it's a lie. Do you intend to reward him?"

"I don't know what you mean."

Constance flung up her free hand in a gesture of disgust. "Americans! Why do they not admit what they feel? Have it your own way! Keep everything to yourself as Noel does; you will make a fine pair!"

Riva was prevented from answering by the approach of footsteps. It was Dante who appeared in the doorway, and he was not alone. With him was Anne Gallant.

No one spoke for long seconds until Riva, from years of habit at playing hostess, greeted them. "I didn't hear you come in. How long have you been here?"

It was Dante who answered, his voice grim. "We just got here. We saw the start of the news conference on the waiting-room monitor and came as quickly as we could, but it seems we missed the party."

"I'm afraid so." Riva looked from one to the other, noting their pale faces, as if they had not slept during the night, and also the solidarity of the front they presented as they stood shoulder to shoulder.

"Indeed, yes," Constance said, her gaze sharp on the couple also. "The police have already taken the lady's husband away. Aren't you lucky?"

"He isn't my husband, and never was," Anne said with a lift of her chin.

Riva said, "You . . . heard what I had to say, then?"

"We listened on the car radio as we drove here," Anne replied, "but I figured out that Edison and I weren't married days ago, as soon as Dante told me of the ceremony Edison went through with you. My son was born nine months after my so-called marriage, you see, and I knew that Erin was older by almost a year, which meant that the marriage to you had to have come first. Mine, then, was invalid. It was . . . quite a shock."

"A convenient one," Constance suggested. "You could have your Colorado fling without guilt, could you not?"

Anne exchanged a brief private glance with Dante, then looked away again with color high on her cheekbones. "Not entirely without guilt," she said, "but certainly without regret."

Constance made a small, dismissive gesture with one shoulder. Turning toward Dante, she gave him a sultry, carefully calculated smile. "Coralie and Pietro have missed you. I was just going upstairs to take them some food. Wouldn't you like to come and visit a while?"

"Sorry, I can't just now," he said with firm impenitence. "Tell them I said hello."

The smile faded and Constance turned abruptly toward the buffet. "I doubt I will have the time. I must begin packing."

"You aren't leaving?" Riva asked. "Noel has hardly had a chance to see the children."

"That isn't my fault, but I suppose they can stay. Noel can bring them to Paris at the end of the summer."

"That's . . . very generous of you." Riva watched the other woman as she began to pile the plate she held with food in a swift, haphazard fashion.

"Not at all," came the prompt reply. "I have had an invitation to join a lengthy cruise to the islands of Micronesia. I had not been certain I wanted to go. Now I am. Isn't it marvelous?" Constance, the plates filled, swung to face them. She gave them a long, cool stare, then left the room without a word.

Dante hardly waited for the woman to get out of hearing before he reverted to the subject at the forefront of his mind. "About Edison, Riva, do you have any idea where they were taking him?"

"Not really. To the courthouse, I suppose."

He frowned, rubbing a hand over the back of his neck. "I don't suppose there's much we could do, even if we showed up there."

"I've been thinking about that, too," Anne said. "I don't like leaving Josh for too long, and I doubt Edison will expect me to come and hold his hand. I believe the best thing to do would be to notify his lawyer about what has happened, then go back to the hospital."

"Whatever you think's best," Dante agreed.

Anne turned to Riva. "May I use your phone?"

She told her to use the one in the library and tried to insist that Anne come back and eat something, or at least have a cup of coffee, when she was done. Anne nodded with a vague smile, then went away.

"You might have called me," Dante said to Riva when they were alone.

"There was nothing you could have done."

"I could have been with you."

She gave him a tired smile. "I suppose I should have let you know what was happening. You could have warned Anne."

"Touché."

"I didn't mean it that way. You have a right to be with whomever you please."

He shook his head. "I guess I would have been here, would have known, anyway, except that I was embarrassed. I ruined everything, didn't I?"

"No, not really. I never had the right to question where you were or with whom."

"You could have had it any time, if you had wanted it. I wanted you to have it. It could even be why I took Anne to the mountains, to make you question it. It didn't work, did it?" He turned back to her, his eyes dark.

"I was jealous, if that's what you wanted, I suppose because she wasn't your usual bit of fluff, brainless and just over the age of consent. She was someone who could take my place."

"You may have been hurt, but not jealous. It was friendship you thought you were losing instead of love. The truth is, as hard as we tried, we never quite made it."

She met his gaze for a long moment, her own somber. "No, I guess we never did."

"But we'll always be friends, you know, no matter what happens," he went on, reaching to take her hand in his warm grasp. "We go back too far to change now."

Friends. It was the traditional vow of a lover on the point of departing. The best thing she could do would be to let him go. After all, she had never meant to hold him. She smiled, looking up through the veil of warm tears that came so easily these last few days. She wiped them with a quick gesture. "Yes, we will."

"Thank God for that."

"Thank you," she said, and leaned to kiss his cheek.

A few minutes later, Anne returned, then she and Dante left the house. Riva saw them out, standing on the gallery to watch them drive away. Finally she turned back into the house.

She met Erin in the hall. Anne had not only called Edison's lawyer, she had also checked in at the hospital and Erin had been on hand to hear the report. Josh was awake and coherent. The doctors still weren't sure he would keep his arm, but the chances looked good; the patient was grumbling and demanding something to eat beside the bouillon and crackers he had been offered. And he was demanding to see Erin.

Erin was ready to go to the hospital. Some time in the next day or two, maybe even tonight, she and Anne together would choose the time to tell Josh he had a half sister. Doug had offered to drive Erin, if her mother didn't need her. Was it all right?

Riva watched Erin go off down the walk with the young photographer. Her mother, she had said. Erin thought of her already as her mother. She was Erin's mother.

Riva smiled, then shook her head as she heard Doug and her daughter arguing as they left the house over whether they were or were not going to stop for a pizza on the way to the hospital, who was going to pay for it, and whether they would take a piece to Josh.

The resilience of youth was wonderful. It had taken Erin a little while to accept Josh as a half brother, but it seemed the process was nearly complete. There had been a sly suggestion from her daughter that there might be a threesome going backpacking in Colorado the next summer, Erin, Doug, and Josh. Riva had given her daughter a fierce hug and sent her on her way. There would be time enough to worry about Colorado later.

Right now, at this moment, she must pretend to eat the snack

Liz had prepared, then find some way of making her final farewells to Bonne Vie, to Abraham and George and Liz and the others, and, yes, to Noel. She hoped she could manage it with dignity and a minimum of tears.

She didn't belong. She never had.

It was funny, but she still felt as if she belonged.

She and Noel arrived at the buffet table at the same time. They were alone. Everyone had scattered. She and Noel picked up plates and silverware. They both headed for a dish of mushrooms broiled in bacon strips at the same time, then he stepped back, letting her go ahead.

It was her first opportunity to speak to Noel alone. Until this moment, he had been so busy with the authorities, with fielding calls from the Staulet office and from local dignitaries who had heard rumors, that there had been no time. Quickly, before she could lose her courage, she said, "May I talk to you in a few minutes?"

He gave her a direct, unsmiling look. "Of course, any time you like."

"Maybe in the library? There are a few problems we have to work out privately."

"Arc you sure you feel up to it?"

"I'm sure; the sooner the better."

"What's wrong with now, then, while we eat?"

"Not a thing," she said, her voice hollow as she spooned mushrooms onto her plate.

They carried their food into the library. It was the most private room in the house, insulated not only by the empty hall, the outside gallery, and the master bedroom that surrounded it, but also by the heavy bookcases of mahogany and glass that lined the walls. The silence was profound, as Riva and Noel ate their small sandwiches of ham and fresh tomatoes, their chicken and andouille sausage gumbo, cold boiled shrimp, crabmeat au gratin, and broiled mushrooms. The only sound was the clink of silverware against china.

Eating a meal with the man you love was supposed to be a sensual experience, one approached with immense appetite. The idea was wryly amusing. Riva had never found anything sexy about it, and certainly didn't now. Her throat was so tight she could hardly swallow, and the food, spicy and seasoned to perfection, had no more taste in her mouth than a vending-machine snack. She finally gave up all pretense and sat back, sipping a glass of orange juice and seltzer.

She was searching her mind for a way to begin what she had to say when Noel threw down his napkin, drank the last of his wine, then spoke.

"Will you marry me?"

She stared at him blankly. She understood the words, but her mind refused to accept them or to respond. She recalled a fleeting memory of another proposal made while she ate. Proposals at meal times, and surprise tactics, seemed to run in the family.

"I mean, after you are free of Gallant, of course," he went on. "I heard what he said in the dining room."

The words Noel had just spoken, their meaning, and the reason behind them in association with the information he had just given her, coalesced in her brain.

"No!" she answered him with astringency.

"What do you mean? I did hear him say you were still his wife."

She sat forward, putting her glass on her tray. "I mean, no, I won't marry you. Oh, it's very noble of you to ask, but it's impossible."

"I see nothing impossible about it." His voice took on a tinge of anger and his fingers on his wineglass stem were so white-knuckled that it seemed a miracle the crystal did not break.

"I won't be married out of charity or because you think I somehow deserve it after all these years."

"What do you intend to do, just walk away from everything you've worked for, everything you built with my father? Oh, yes, I admit it was your doing in large part. My father was an intelligent man, but he was too conservative, too satisfied with small pleasures and small gains to have brought Staulet Corporation this far alone. By the same token, it's unlikely you could have done it without his backing, his support. You built something together that is strong and enduring. You can't leave it now."

"I have to," she cried. "I have no right to it."

"You have every right, just not the legal title. I can give you that, then everything will be as it was. Why, in God's name, won't you let me?"

She rose to her feet and walked away to the window. Over her shoulder, she said, "What right do I have here? It's all been a lie, all these long years."

"You thought you were married. Cosmo thought you were married, had every intention that you should be his wife. The ceremony the two of you went through was, I think, the only religious rite you ever celebrated. You were, in his eyes and those of the church, his wife."

"Legally I was no more than a kept woman—well kept, I will admit, but still a kept woman."

"I can change that."

"I robbed you of your birthright once without knowing it. I won't do it again knowingly." He put down his glass and got to his feet.

"You never robbed me of anything."

"Oh, please," she said, turning to face him. "We both know that's not true."

"What happened was nothing you could have helped. I've always known that."

She searched the angles and planes of his face that made up his strong features. The need for reassurance was not something that she could help. "Did you really?"

"I felt instinctively that my father lied, and knew it for certain the minute I saw you again after all those years away."

"I could never quite believe what he said about you, either, except . . . Why else did you go, if not because he put you out for trying to destroy his marriage?"

"Because I guessed what he would tell you and knew that if I stayed, he would be right."

"You hated it so much?"

He gave a slow shake of his head. "I loved you so much."

A trenchant smile twisted her lips. "You're determined to take this to the bitter end, aren't you? You didn't have to say that."

"I know I didn't," he answered with asperity. "I said it because I mean it."

"Suddenly? After all this time? You have a very convenient heart, then. If you love me so much, why did you lead me out to face the press like a revolutionary leading Marie Antoinette to the guillotine?"

"Because the whole sorry tale had to come out, every shadow had to be removed, before there could ever be a chance for us. There was too much guilt, too much suspicion, for it to be otherwise."

She closed her eyes, then opened them again, and her expression was bleak. "You have an answer for everything, don't you?"

He breathed a soft curse, then swung away from her. Moving to the desk that stood at one end of the room, he took a key from his pocket and opened the desk drawer. He drew out a sheaf of papers and then, straightening, brought them to her and thrust them into her hands.

"What is this?" The words were taut with suspicion.

"Read it."

The papers were curling slightly around the edges and turning cream-colored with age. They were fastened by a small metal clamp that had rusted on one corner, leaving a stain. On the top page was her full name, including her maiden name, and a date. The date was mid June of 1964. Beneath it was a single typed word: *Report*.

Riva looked up at Noel in sudden doubt. She was not sure she wanted to see what the papers contained.

"Read it," he repeated, his voice hard.

She lifted the top page and scanned the others. It was a detailed file on one Rebecca Benson Gallant. There were her parents' names, their birthdates, and their marriage date. Her sisters' names and dates were given, including Beth's date of death and official, though not the true, cause. There were Riva's school records complete with the time in the third grade when she had been absent for three weeks with what the doctors had called a mild case of polio. There were also her clinical records for colds and a cut or two, as well as her dental records and her immunization record from the local public health unit. There was more information gathered in one place, in fact, than she had known existed on her early years. There was also the record of her Arkansas marriage. After it were two damning lines: *No record of divorce in Arkansas, Louisiana, or surrounding states. Marriage presumed to be intact.*

Riva stared at the last words in frowning concentration, then turned back to the front of the report and looked at the date once more.

Finally she said, "This is the report Cosmo had done while I was working at the bar, before we were married. He mentioned it once."

"Exactly. It's been locked away here in this desk drawer for more than twenty-four years."

She swallowed, asking without looking at him, "You knew it was there?"

"I put it there when I found it where my father had thrown it on the floor."

It was an admission she was not ready to face. Instead she said, "But why didn't Cosmo say something? Why did he go through with the wedding if he knew I was still married?"

"Who can say? Maybe he thought the report was wrong and the Arkansas marriage was really invalid as you said. Maybe he expected you to leave him in a few months or years, and this way you would have no hold on the estate. Maybe he was afraid to mention it for fear you would contact Edison and go back to him. We can't ask him, not now."

"Suppose—suppose I had had a child?"

"It's probable there would have been a quickly arranged divorce and another ceremony. I can't see my father doing it any other way."

"Unless he was protecting you," she suggested.

"My inheritance, you mean? I doubt that would have weighed against the rights of any child you and he might have had together."

"What about you? Why did you keep the secret, at least after— after the funeral? It would have been to your advantage to make it public."

"Make it public? I did everything in my power to suppress the information contained there, even going to Edison and sounding him out on a campaign contribution to keep him from telling you, from using it to manipulate you."

"You did that?" she said, lifting her gaze to his in slow wonder.

"Oh, yes, though I should have known Edison would honor the agreement we made just so long as it suited him, so long as he didn't need the information to save his skin."

She gave a small shake of her head. "I still don't understand."

"Don't you? I wanted you here. I wanted to be sure that nothing would cause you to leave, ever. Isn't that clear enough?"

"But at the price of half of everything that was rightfully yours?"

He took the report from her and flung it on the desk. "That wasn't important years ago, and it isn't important now. My father was happy with you, and you made the house come alive. I was afraid that if you knew you were free, you would leave—especially lately. That was the last thing I wanted."

"But years ago, when Cosmo told you I had tricked you, when he turned against you because of me?"

"You were always more important than any house, no matter how old and historic, more important than a raftload of corporate stock."

"So you made your beau geste—"

"God, no! It wasn't like that!"

She smiled at his vehemence. "Constance's description, not mine. But anyway, you went away and left it all behind, left it to me."

"It was what my father wanted."

That was true, though she knew, as surely as she knew the sun would rise tomorrow, that it was not the full reason. She shook her head, her gaze bemused and softly green as she looked at him. "I can't believe you did it."

A muscle flexed in his jaw. "What will it take to convince you? What can I say? What can I do to make you understand that I want to be with you, to have you beside me in my bed for all time, to stand beside you in all things, here and at Staulet?"

"To take your father's place?"

His eyes were defiant as he answered, "To take mine that I let him have years ago."

"Out of love?"

"Out of love," he agreed, "and also out of respect and compassion, and because he had earned your love and I had not."

"I thought you despised me because I shielded Edison. Why the change?"

"I listened to what you said out there in front of the cameras later, and I knew I had been wrong. It had to be Margaret you were protecting, trying to keep her from ruining her life. That made sense once I knew the sacrifice you had made for Erin."

Daring, finally, to ask the question whose answer threatened the most pain, she said, "You don't mind about Erin? That I have a daughter?"

"How can I mind, when I have both a daughter and a son? Besides, Erin is special to me because she reminds me so much of you."

Her heart swelled inside her, causing such pressure that tears rose, aching, behind her eyes. "So magnanimous," she said with difficulty. "I suppose you think I owe you something in return."

"No." His voice was suddenly tired and the look in his gray eyes defenseless. "I want no charity, no more sacrifice, any more than you."

She stepped toward him then, opening her arms, taking his and clasping them around her. "Would you accept a gift?" she asked with quiet certainty. "A gift of love that has always been yours?"

He caught her close, yet his hold was tentative, as if he could not believe she would not break away. He whispered against her hair, "Always?"

"Always, I promise," she said with rich joy.

He lifted his head to look at her, and in his face was love so deep and boundless it verged on pain. He echoed the vow she had made in a whisper.

"Always."

AUTHOR'S NOTE

The antebellum mansion and its setting in *Love and Smoke* is an amalgam of several famous Louisiana houses and sites. The exterior front with its majestic avenue of oaks is based on a house known in its heyday as Bon Séjour, though it has become more familiar in modern times, and no doubt instantly recognizable, as Oak Alley. The interior was taken from the floor plan of a house called Uncle Sam, which was destroyed in 1940 by the United States Army Corps of Engineers in order to strengthen the Mississippi River levee system. The idea for the folly in the center of the ornamental pond came from the gazebo holding a bronze Buddha that is located on Avery Island, on the grounds of the home of the McIlhenny family of Tabasco sauce fame. It was a great pleasure to re-create these places in fictional form.

I am indebted to a number of people for specialized information included in the story: Jimmy C. Teat, attorney, Jonesboro, Louisiana, for explaining the laws of Louisiana as applied to bigamy; Steven Watts, narcotics officer with the Jackson Parish Sheriff's Department, for prompt assistance with information about the drug XTC and also Parish police procedure; Jerome Faucheux for information concerning "X" places and car preferences in New Orleans; Scott Woodward, pilot with the United States Customs Agency for recommendations on types of private aircraft and their inherent crash possibilities; Samuel Lampkin with the Jackson Parish Sheriff's Department and Ted and Kay Colvin of the Jackson *Independent*, Jonesboro, Louisiana, for help and advice concerning the effective use of an Uzi submachine gun; and especially my husband Jerry Maxwell for advice on corporate business matters, for valuable editorial suggestions, and for loving support. My gratitude to them all is as unending as my questions.

Jennifer Blake
Sweet Brier
Quitman, Louisiana
October 1988

ABOUT THE AUTHOR

JENNIFER BLAKE was born near Goldonna, Louisiana, in her grand-parents' 120-year-old hand-built cottage. It was her grandmother, a local midwife, who delivered her. She grew up on an eighty-acre farm in the rolling hills of north Louisiana and got married at the age of fifteen. Five years and three children later, she had become a voracious reader, consuming seven or eight books a week. Dis-illusioned with the books she was reading, she set out to write one of her own. It was a Gothic—*Secret of Mirror House*—and Fawcett was the publisher. Since that time she has written thirty-two books, with more than nine million copies in print, and has become one of the bestselling romance authors of our time. Her recent Fawcett books are *Surrender in Moonlight, Midnight Waltz, Fierce Eden, Royal Passion, Prisoner of Desire, Southern Rapture, Louisiana Dawn,* and *Perfume of Paradise*. Jennifer and her husband live in their house near Quitman, Louisiana, styled after old Southern Planters' cottages.